A Rossler Fo

Genetic Bullets

A Thriller

By JC Ryan

This is the third book in the Rossler Foundation Mystery Series.

Want to hear about special offers and new releases?

Sign up for my confidential mailing list www.jcryanbooks.com

ISBN-13:978-1500596347

ISBN-10:1500596345

Your Free Gift

As a way of saying thanks for your purchase, I'm offering you a free eBook which you can download from my website at www.jcryanbooks.com

MYSTERIES FROM THE ANCIENTS

10 THOUGHT PROVOKING UNSOLVED ARCHAEOLOGICAL MYSTERIES

This book is exclusive to my readers. You will not find this book anywhere else.

We spend a lot of time researching and documenting our past, yet there are still many questions left unanswered. Our ancestors left a lot of traces for us, and it seems that not all of them were ever meant to be understood. Despite our best efforts, they remain mysteries to this day.

You will find some fascinating and thought-provoking facts about archaeological discoveries which still has no clear explanation.

The Great Pyramid at Giza, The Piri Reis Map, Doomsday, Giant Geoglyphs, The Great Flood, Ancient Science and Mathematics, Human Flight, Pyramids, Fertility Stones and the Tower of Babel, Mysterious Tunnels and The Mystery of The Anasazi

Don't miss this opportunity to get this free eBook now.

Click Here to download it now.

Table of Contents

Prologue

Jaasiel walked in the gardens surrounding the hospital where his beloved had lain ill for seven turns. So many had fallen to this illness, but the doctors counseled hope, for there was nothing else to be done. Others railed against the isolation, though that was what brought them here in the first place. This was a beautiful place of peace and tranquility; a place to withdraw from the hurly-burly of business and crowds. Here there was no hunger, no violence, no striving; only peace and beauty.

But now this quiet, peace, beauty and isolation threatened their very existence. Someone had come here ill, and exposed another. That one exposed two or three others. Soon everyone whose forebears came from the lush valley of the land to the north of the sea and between the impassible mountain ranges were ill, and many had died.

Adnah would die soon, too, God willing. How she suffered! Jaasiel could see no hope for her recovery. Her body burned; she cried out for relief from the pain. It would have been an act of kindness to press her pillow to her face and let it end. He could not do it, though, and the inability was bitter. He loved her too much to be without her, and not enough to set aside his selfish wish to keep her alive by any means possible, so that, in the event of a miracle, she might be restored to him.

This agony of indecision and grief made him careless, or perhaps it was because Jaaseil himself was ill, though the symptoms had not yet made themselves known. In any case, his decision was taken from him in that moment, as his foot slipped off the path and he stumbled, then fell. Instantly, before he even had time to register the pain of being burned alive, he was swallowed by the fumarole that steamed beside the path. There should have been a barrier, but Jaaseil didn't have time to register that thought.

Not even a scream passed his lips, though an exhalation of surprise disturbed the algae on the surface. His last thought, cut off almost before it formed, was that his beloved would soon be with him in eternity.

Chapter 1 – We have to go back

Professor Charles Summers was unaccountably nervous. It annoyed him, because he knew he had widespread support for what he was to present to the Board of the Rossler Foundation today. In fact, partial funding had already allowed him to begin the planning, and everything was set to go except for final funding for the expedition itself. Today's presentation was just a formality.

There was little that could go wrong, except that the expedition director, JR Rossler, was a bit of a wild card. Sometimes he didn't filter his observations, and Summers had reason to understand that he could be volatile. Nevertheless, he'd proved himself both courageous and resourceful on the last trip, and when he requested the position, Summers was happy to take him on this time. Especially since JR's older brother, Daniel Rossler, was the CEO and Chairman of the Board of the Rossler Foundation, under whose auspices the expedition would take place.

Firmly setting aside his nerves, Summers straightened his tie for the last time and stepped out of his office to head for the Board room. As he passed the next office, the door opened, and Dr. Rebecca Mendenhall joined him.

"Showtime, Dr. Summers."

"Indeed, Dr. Mendenhall. Thanks for your support."

"Charles, there's no need to thank me. I'm as eager to get back there as you are. I keep dreaming of a tropical paradise surrounded by Antarctic ice, and the secrets you might find under all those vines." She gave a light laugh. It was true, against all odds. The place she dreamed of was as real as the building the two stood in, although a place of mystery, certainly.

It was also the place where she had come to value JR Rossler as more than a troubled family friend. The dangers they had faced together had served to give JR back his self-respect, stolen by events beyond his control in Afghanistan. Her admiration had become love. Now the thought of being with him in that place again, after all that had happened since then, was like going back for a do-over to perfect an event that had gone wrong, erasing the ugliness of being attacked and having to kill or be killed.

Besides, it would help JR overcome his demons. His Afghanistan-induced PTSD had worsened in a way, though he had learned to control the self-destructive behavior. He no longer drank himself senseless, or chased anything in a skirt. Rebecca was responsible for that. More than anything, he wanted to keep her respect. He still had moments, though, when he despaired of being a normal person with nothing bothering him but the petty concerns of daily life. That occasional depression was driven by his nightmares of killing the men who had attacked them. Only going back to the place and facing the demons rationally would set him free, Rebecca was convinced. As a medical doctor with significant experience in treating PTSD patients, she had reason to believe she was right.

Summers and Rebecca arrived together just as Daniel was calling the meeting to order. They hurried to their seats. Across the table, JR winked at Rebecca, who acknowledged him with a smile. Daniel finished his opening remarks and turned the podium over to Summers.

He cleared his throat. Now that the time was at hand, his nerves were steady. He was prepared; it only remained to begin.

"Ladies and gentlemen, thank you for allowing me to speak in behalf of the Rossler Foundation's latest project. I hope you will agree with me that it is vitally important that we complete it as soon as possible. Briefly, we are seeking funding to return to Antarctica, this time to locate and excavate ruins in the hidden valley that we found during last season's ill-fated expedition. We believe that the only way to honor those who lost their lives earlier this year is to finish the job we went to do at that time.

"For those of you who have joined this august body since those events, let me briefly recount what occurred. As you all know, the body of knowledge that we refer to as the 10th Cycle Library contains accounts of a civilization that flourished thousands of years ago and was superior in many ways to our own. Their records contain statements that even earlier civilizations existed.

"Based on the momentous changes the discovery of the 10th Cycle Library has brought us, we would like to believe that you are with us in our desire to uncover the truth of any site that may contain information about those earlier civilizations. The 10th Cycle Library led us to go looking for a site mentioned in the annals, a site purported to be of 9th Cycle origin. We have reason to believe, both from those records and from inscriptions we found in the cave system that led to a wondrous hidden valley, that 10th Cyclers were quite familiar with this valley.

"The very fact that the valley exists challenges all modern day evidence that Antarctica has been covered in ice for millions of years. We owe it to the world today, as well as to the 10th Cyclers who went to so much trouble to let us know of their existence, to reveal it at last. In fact, this could be one of the most important and exciting scientific expeditions ever undertaken.

"We now know where the ruins we sought are located, although we didn't find the location in time to begin exploration last season. As you know, we were attacked by mercenaries sent by the Orion Society, and barely escaped with our lives.

"Now we are seeking funds to return to finish the job we started. Most of the surviving members of the first expedition are on board and eager to get there as soon as the weather breaks. In front of you are detailed plans for a three-stage expedition, which we hope you will have taken the opportunity to study before now. I will now accept questions."

"Why three stages?" asked the member from Australia.

"We anticipate needing a large crew of excavation workers," Summers replied. "In order to preserve any and all historically important details in the valley, we propose to house them for the most part in the canyon where we found the cave entrance that leads to the internal valley. That will require that a semi-permanent base camp be constructed for that purpose. As you can see, the first phase is construction. We are using pre-fab buildings flown in by helicopter, as well as heavy equipment that will prepare the site for the buildings. It shouldn't take longer than a month, including accounting for bad weather at the beginning of the summer season."

The member from Chile objected. "Last year you encountered heavy winds as you crossed the Ross Ice Shelf. For nearly a month, as I recall. How can you expect construction to occur in those conditions?"

"You're correct, we did," Summers conceded. "However, last year we were crossing on the ground, in Sno-Cats with trailers attached, which meant that the wind conditions were a bigger problem than they will be if we encounter them this year. The Sikorsky choppers we've chartered were built for heavy loads in heavy weather, and of course flying means they won't be exposed for as long as we were. We anticipate no problems in getting them in and out of the canyon on days when the wind is more subdued. Inside the canyon itself, the canyon floor is somewhat protected from the winds, which generally blow from a direction across, not into, the mouth of the canyon. Are there any more questions?"

"Yes," said Australia. "You've explained one phase. What about the other two?"

Someone hadn't done his homework, reflected Summers. He gathered his patience to answer.

"The second phase will be just the core group of scientists, including myself and several others, to locate where excavations should take place and begin experiments on the flora and any fauna or human remains that we might find while excavation takes place. Once we find the ruins we expect to find within the valley, we'll bring in the third phase, the excavation crews and support crew. There is no need to house and feed over fifty extra men for the week or two it will take to map the valley on our own. Does that answer your question? Are there any more?"

"Yes," came the answer from a different, and unexpected quarter.

"JR? What's your question?"

"What are we going to do about the Orion Society?"

Chapter 2 - A healthy and hale young man of only sixty-eight

Three months earlier

JR and most of the rest of the surviving members of the expedition were feted and interviewed almost mercilessly after their return. It was to be expected. They had been presumed dead, their survival a miracle in itself. Expected or not, though, some fared better than others. Cyndi Self, the IT specialist and electrical engineer, with her bubbly personality, happily gave interviews whenever asked. Angela Brown, the cartographer, was more retiring, and hated to give on-camera interviews, although she was willing to talk to print journalists.

Robert Cartwright, the geologist, had flown home from Christchurch while the others returned to Boulder. Maxhulin, aka Roosky, had left Antarctica before the others, having left soon after the avalanche that trapped the other in the valley. Summers was used to giving interviews, but reluctant to talk about the end of the expedition because he feared he hadn't acquitted himself well, while Rebecca flatly refused, citing her schedule and the disruption for her patients as the reason. However, her real reason was different. JR was in near-seclusion, his family protecting him from requests for interviews for reasons of their own.

Because everyone expected a new expedition to be mounted at the earliest opportunity, Charles Summers interviewed the survivors to determine their interest in returning to Antarctica despite the fact that they had almost died there. Not surprisingly, everyone wanted closure, and everyone eagerly signed up. That Rebecca and JR had been the first to do so surprised everyone, though.

JR was a special case. He hadn't volunteered for the first expedition originally, but his reasons for going were inarguable. That his brother felt crushing guilt over the near tragedy was beside the point. Because JR had played a pivotal role in the survival of the five remaining members, his legal troubles stemming from a disorderly conduct charge prior to leaving on the first expedition were now behind him. But his PTSD had been triggered again. Unlike before, when his nightmares were of atrocities he'd witnessed but had not participated in, this time he suffered from nightmares of killing the Orion Society squad that had been sent to kill them.

Rebecca had witnessed some of his actions, and fully understood his angst. From a psychological perspective, she was intrigued by this manifestation of the specialty she was interested in pursuing. As a woman, her heart hurt for him, the man she had come to admire and love. As a friend of the family, she took every opportunity she had to observe his progress and to be near him. Perhaps it was inevitable that the handsome and psychologically damaged young man and the beautiful and intelligent young woman who loved him would reveal their feelings to each other. Within a month of returning, Rebecca had invited JR to move in with her, welcoming him into her arms as well as her home.

Once she had him under her influence daily, Rebecca used every tool in her considerable arsenal of medical and psychological arts as well as her generous love and affection to heal him. Her goal was to help JR understand that his actions had been in defense of her and the others, even though the fact that he was outnumbered forced him to use stealth. His sense of honor had been damaged, but Rebecca constantly reminded him that they had been both outnumbered and without weapons adequate to defend themselves. Her mission was to restore his confidence and his self-respect. The return to Paradise Valley, as they had named it, would help to accomplish that.

Meanwhile, Charles Summers, the lead scientist in both the original expedition and the planned one, wasted no time in beginning to plan for the next one, aided by an interim grant from the Rossler Foundation. They'd brought back sufficient evidence in the form of photos on their cell phones to convince Daniel and the small committee that approved small grants that another expedition was required.

After convincing Daniel that the different circumstances would mitigate the danger that had taken lives in the first expedition, and showing him the list of volunteers that wanted to return, Summers obtained Daniel's cautious support. He almost lost it again when JR applied for the position of expedition director. Daniel objected; he had almost lost his brother to the Antarctic and didn't want to risk him again. However, a talk with Sarah and Rebecca had changed Daniel's mind, and once Daniel agreed, it was settled.

It was almost the last straw, though, when Sinclair O'Reilly, the Foundation's linguist and a dear friend of the Rosslers, decided he wanted to go as well. O'Reilly had to be approaching seventy. There was no way that Charles was going to agree to risking his life in the harsh conditions of Antarctica outside the hidden valley. He had to admit, though, that Sinclair had an underhanded way of getting his way, even when it wasn't in his own best interest. He appealed to the patriarch of the Rossler clan, Nicholas, Daniel's grandfather. And Nicholas didn't see any reason why a healthy and hale young man of only sixty-eight shouldn't go to Antarctica if he wanted to. After all, they now had pleasure tours there, and plenty of septuagenarians went on them. In fact, Nicholas was thinking of taking Bess, his wife, on one, and they were both in their eighties. Charles was outgunned, but at least he'd be able to limit Sinclair's presence to phase three of his plan.

Chapter 3 – They MUST go before we go

Summers hastily left the boardroom after JR dropped his bombshell, all too aware that he had failed in his leadership capacity on the previous expedition, in no small part thanks to the damned OS. It wasn't a particularly graceful departure, as he'd hurriedly deferred to Daniel to answer the question, and stated that he had work to do and nothing to add to the discussion at hand. Daniel and Rebecca stared at his retreating back and then turned their attention back to JR, who hadn't uttered another word yet.

"JR, please clarify your question," Daniel said in a calm and quiet tone, though his thoughts were anything but calm. Rebecca had cautioned the family to keep conversations as low-key as possible to avoid a trigger reaction when speaking of stressful subjects with JR, and the last place that needed to happen was here in front of the Board.

"It's pretty clear isn't it? Those bastards have dogged you from the minute you started investigating the mysteries of the Great Pyramid, and they almost killed our entire expedition. There must be something in that valley that they want, or think they want. We've seen time and again that they will stop at nothing to get what they want or keep others from getting what they don't want people to have. There's no sense in putting on another expedition until we've wiped them out. I've been thinking about it."

Daniel was stunned at the vehemence in JR's voice, as well as at having been blindsided by this now, in front of the full board of directors. "And you're just now bringing it to my attention?" he asked, more frost than he intended in his voice. A quick glance at Rebecca revealed that she was shaking her head slightly, while staring at him with evident intent. Okay, he needed to tone it down.

"Sorry, JR, you just caught me by surprise. Please, give us your thoughts."

"Okay," JR said, standing and sauntering to the mic beside his brother. He reached over and pulled it toward him and six inches higher, effectively making Daniel relinquish it. Rebecca glowed with pride as her man cut an impressive figure at the head of the room. He was doing fine, no sign of agitation.

"Is there anyone here who is not aware that my sister-in-law was kidnapped and other members of my brother's circle of investigators killed or threatened by a secret society known as the Orion Society?" He paused, looking around the extensive conference table, almost twenty-four feet long. Seeing no one raise a hand, he continued. "Let me remind you, then, just how dangerous these people are. They first revealed their interest in the Pyramid Code by killing my sister-in-law's former professor, Mark Simms. They then held our grandparents hostage, killed Sarah's boss, Professor Barry, and kidnapped Sarah herself. When my brother rescued her, they killed their own operatives to keep them from talking to the police, and finally made a desperate attempt to kill Daniel and all of his colleagues as they fled for protection. Finally, they killed a CIA informant who had been one of them, along with his protectors. In all, a minimum of ten people dead, and who knows how many others of their own? They are heartless and without mercy. You may not have heard the details of how they concealed their crimes, decapitating and mutilating their victims by removing their fingers so that they couldn't be identified.

"You also know by now that our expedition was ambushed

16

inside the valley we found by operatives from the same group. They were aided and abetted by a member of our expedition who was there as a spy and subsequently killed herself while in custody. Another spy in our group was killed by the squad that attacked us, but not before she may have been instrumental in the death of our expedition director, Paul LeClerc. I believe, though I can't prove it, that the avalanche that trapped us inside the cave was not a natural event. At least four members of our expedition were murdered by them, maybe more. If we hadn't stopped them, you could add five more to that. The only other members of our expedition who survived but whose whereabouts at the time were unaccounted for was Mikhail Maxhulin, the explosives expert, who is now missing, and Bart, our expedition cook, who has never been found.""

Everyone around the table understood what he had not said; that he had single-handedly taken out the squad sent to murder them, thereby saving what was left of the expedition. A gasp went up from some quarters of the table, including the member from Russia and Daniel, who looked questioningly at JR.

"Roosky was outside, tasked with getting us out in the event of a rock fall or anything else. What better person to instead bring the mountain down on us and trap us inside?" JR answered Daniel's unspoken question.

A speculative expression stole over Daniel's face. He had invited Maxhulin to the memorial service, all expenses paid, but the man had declined. Was this the reason? He turned his attention back to the table as the member from Russia pounded a fist on the table and stood.

"Do you accuse my country of sabotage and attempted murder?"

"No, sir," was JR's calm reply. "I accuse a *citizen* of your country of being an Orion Society tool. Can you assure me that no citizen of your country is or has ever been an employee of the OS? If so, it will be the only country we know of that has been free of the vermin. Based on just the interaction of these criminals with my family and our expedition, how can we believe they haven't done similar damage to other research projects over the years? What murders might they have committed, what thefts of priceless knowledge or artifacts? I have it on the authority of our head of security, my sister-in-law's uncle, Luke Clarke, that they've put a price on our heads, all the survivors of the expedition. And the highest of all is on my head. I propose to return the favor." A predatory grin accompanied his last statement.

Shocked silence greeted that challenge, but JR noted that Rebecca's eyes were shining. He smiled faintly at her.

"This is not the time for infighting, ladies and gentlemen. We have seen first-hand how extensive the criminal enterprises of this organization are, how they have tried time and time again to steal or prevent wide dissemination of information that does not fit with their plans for total domination of world finances. We've seen that they are violent, morally bankrupt and utterly ruthless. All I'm suggesting is that the absolute necessity of clearing them out take place before we go back to Antarctica. After that we can again attempt to discover whatever it is that they didn't want us to know. We can't safely go on this expedition until they are completely and utterly destroyed. If we do, we're just inviting trouble and death along with us again. So I say, *they must* go before we go."

A smattering of applause began, soon swelling to a sound tribute, with most members getting to their feet in a standing ovation. JR glanced at his brother, still standing beside him, and then at Rebecca, the only people in the room whose opinions mattered one whit to him. Both were applauding enthusiastically, and his Becca's eyes were moist.

After that, the vote on the funding of the expedition was an overwhelming yea, as the Board almost casually dispatched that agenda item and turned to an added one. Then and there, they drafted a resolution to be presented to the governments of their various countries calling for a rapid and concerted effort to eradicate the Orion Society for good. Unaware of the widespread tentacles of power that the OS had in financial institutions, multi-national corporations, big oil and big pharma conclaves, not to mention national security and military organizations worldwide, they demanded that each government place their secret services and military might under the orders of the CIA for the effort. It was a noble gesture, though one that was ill-conceived because no one really understood the OS, what it stood for, or how powerful it was. But, they would learn soon enough.

Chapter 4 – We demand

Daniel, true to his reputation as the eternal diplomat and persuader, considered carefully to whom he should present his copy of the resolution first. It was worded rather strongly, the influence of the more bombastic of the Board members. If he presented it directly to President Harper, it could be bad for their friendship. On the other hand, if he gave it to anyone else, he'd better be prepared to explain why to Harper when he did learn of it. Then the answer came to him, but before he implemented his plan, he should talk to Sarah about it. He picked up the phone.

"Sweetheart, it's me," he said when she answered.

"I thought it might be. How'd the Board meeting go?"

"It went great until JR stuck his oar in. Then what was supposed to be an easy meeting to take care of a few formalities turned into a declaration of war. But, I'm glad he spoke up. He brought up something that no one else had given much thought."

"Really? What was that?"

"He wants the OS wiped out before they go to Antarctica again. Says there's no point in going if they just show up again, with more troops this time."

"Oh, my gosh, Daniel, he's right!"

"Yeah, I know. The Board took it up right then, drafted a resolution to present to their various governments. It's kind of strong."

"Well good!"

"No, wait, you don't understand. Here, let me read it to you. 'We, the Board of Directors of the Rossler Foundation demand that the governments of the free world immediately and without reservation take all steps necessary to apprehend and detain every member and employee of the criminal organization known as The Orion Society on charges of murder and attempted murder, as well as any other civil or criminal charges that are warranted as a result of investigation. Our goal is to eliminate all traces of this organization to ensure the safety of peaceful citizens everywhere. We further demand that the organization's financial interests and other projects be exposed as they become known, and every effort be made to make reparations to all governments, organizations and individuals or their families who have been harmed by the activities of the Orion Society. Let it be known that if governments will not eradicate this threat, the Rossler Foundation stands ready to do so.' How do you like them apples?" he finished, whimsically.

"Wow! You couldn't veto that last sentence?"

"I tried. They overruled me."

"Let's just hope the governments respond. I'm not sure we're big enough to go after the OS, based on what we've learned of them in the past."

"Tell me about it. I don't have a clue how we could do it if governments can't or won't. It will take the cooperation of at least several of the major Western countries. But that's not the worst part."

"Are you serious? What could be worse?"

"It's on me to present this to Nigel Harper."

'Daniel, absolutely not! He'd consider it the worst insult, a demand like that. In fact, I can think of several countries who are likely to turn on us for this. How could you let this happen?"

"Sweetheart, you know that there are rules governing the foundation. We have to abide by them like everyone else. Even with our extra votes, I couldn't stop this. Our only hope, and this is why I called you, is to see what Luke can do."

"Oh, no, not again! Aunt Sally was glad to let him help save me when I was kidnapped, but you know she wants him to retire for good, even from the consulting work. What am I going to tell her?"

"That your husband may have his head on the chopping block if Luke can't see a way to do this right?"

"Great. She has to make a choice between her husband and mine? I don't like it Daniel. But, I can see your point. So I'm going to have to say talk to Uncle Luke about it, see what he says. If he's all in, I guess he'll help us deal with Aunt Sally."

"Sweetheart, you're the best. I'll give them a call, see if we can take them out to dinner. I'm sure you don't feel like cooking. How's Nick?"

"Nicky's fine," Sarah answered sweetly, knowing the diminutive of the baby's name would annoy Daniel just enough to let him know that she wasn't pleased. "I don't mind cooking. Tell them to come to the house. I don't think we should discuss something like that in public."

"Okay, thanks, sweetheart. I'll bet getting to play with Nick will soothe Sally's ruffled feathers."

"You'd better hope," she laughed.

Later that evening, around a meal that Sarah lovingly prepared with her own hands despite the financial ability to hire help, Luke listened carefully as Daniel laid out the problem. Sarah nervously glanced at Sally from time to time, but so far she hadn't posed an objection. Her attention was focused solely on her great-nephew, which probably explained it.

"So you see, Luke, I'm between a rock and a hard place. I can't just lay this on him, and I can't let it go much longer before letting him know. I'm sure the delegates are even now preparing to talk to their own governments. Letting Harper hear it through the grapevine would be even worse than just springing it on him."

Luke seemed to be in deep thought, so it was Sally who asked the obvious question. "What do you want Luke to do about it? Daniel, it isn't his responsibility, it's yours."

"I know, Sally, but I was hoping Luke would have some ideas that would help me do it the right way. A way that will gain cooperation instead of resistance. The Board didn't leave me much room to hedge my language."

"I say we just ask for a meeting with Harper and give him an apology first, then hand it to him," Sally answered.

"Would it really be that easy?" Daniel asked, taking Sally's suggestion seriously.

"There's some merit in it, but maybe I can soften the edges a bit," said Luke. "The head of the CIA is still a friend of mine, even though I've all but retired. Let me give him a call. Maybe if you go in with reinforcements, the wrath will at least be spread out a little."

"Well, I guess he can't yell 'off with his head' in any case," Daniel chuckled. "But I'll be glad of reinforcements."

~~~

In the end it turned out to be a little easier than Daniel had expected, because he got help from two quarters. First, Luke's CIA contact was all for it, and agreed to back him up in any meeting with the President. Daniel and Sarah both thought it would be best for him to go to Washington in person, rather than calling with this news, and he was on a plane that very day. The second was a stroke of luck. With perfect timing, the Israeli prime minister called as President Harper was seating Daniel in the Oval Office.

Daniel knew from Harper's side of the conversation and his widening eyes that the cat was out of the bag, but instead of blowing up, Harper quietly answered that he thought someone was there to talk to him about it right now, and he'd get back to his caller.

Daniel sat straighter in his chair as Harper replaced the receiver into the ornate old-fashioned cradle of the telephone on his desk. "Well, let's hear this infamous demand. Is it as bad as my colleague from Israel said?" Harper's eye shifted from Daniel to his CIA Director with a spark of humor. "I see you brought a bodyguard. It must be bad indeed."

It served to put Daniel at ease as he answered in kind. "It's a freaking insult, sir, but I agree with the sentiment if not with the wording." With that, he handed over the heavy cream-colored letterhead of the Rossler Foundation, with the demand printed in an ornate font. Harper read it, his eyes flashing dangerously as he read the word 'demand' aloud. Seconds later, he looked up.

"And this has gone to the head of state of every country represented on your Board?" he asked. The mild response disarmed Daniel completely, and he let out a sigh of relief.

"Yes, sir. The delegates were instructed to present it to the heads of their respective countries within forty-eight hours of returning home. I would imagine that there could be some who haven't received it yet, but they will soon."

"Very well. Since you've brought the right man for the job with you, let's get the show on the road. Director Lewis, tell me how you propose to comply with this, er, demand."

"Gladly, Mr. President. Before we make a move of any kind, we're going to have to clean house ourselves. Ever since the Rosslers put themselves in the hands of the Mossad rather than us, we've been working to root out any remaining Orion Society moles in the Agency. I have reason to believe that our job isn't finished, but I intend to flush out the rest of them using this campaign as bait. I hope you don't mind that I don't go into detail regarding

24

that plan with a civilian present, sir. No offense, Mr. Rossler."

"None taken," Daniel responded.

"Suffice it to say that we will be using a trusted contractor, one who is above suspicion, to assist us with the plan. Once we've exposed our mole, or moles, we'll pressure them to give up information about their OS contacts, and roll them up the line until we have the leaders. If other countries' agencies are cooperating, I believe we can strike quickly and effectively, making sure to preserve their financial data. We'll have our best forensic financial analysts on hand to track down their assets and seize them pending trial. Will that be good enough, Mr. Rossler?"

Daniel nodded. "As long as you at least cripple them before my expedition gets started. And warn us if you see any evidence that they've already dispatched people to our location. You know my brother had to take out six of them single-handedly last February. I'd prefer that not happen again."

"We will, certainly. Please give your wife and her uncle my regards. If you'll excuse me, I need to get some assignments made to get started."

"Just a minute, Lewis," the President said. "I want you to work with the other security agencies on this, and none of your silly internecine rivalries. Bring in the FBI, NSA and Homeland Security. I'll expect a joint report at least weekly and please make sure I hear about everything before anyone else. You know I hate surprises."

"Yes, sir."

Daniel happened to know that Sam Lewis's relationship with Sarah's Uncle Luke was much warmer than his parting remark had indicated. He'd been Luke's supervising officer during his CIA days, and had been instrumental in helping Daniel's group to escape back in the day. His formality had been part of a strict need-to-know mindset that saw no reason to reveal the closer relationship to the President, when it had no bearing on the current case. Once he had gone, Harper relaxed a bit, too.

"So, my friend. You were really going to come in here and demand I do something about the OS?"

"I would have preferred to put it in the form of a strong request," Daniel grinned, receiving a return grin from the President.

"What if I had refused?" Harper asked, a glint in his eye.

"Well, then I guess I'd have had to send my brother JR and my two Marine buddies to do the job," Daniel answered, barely suppressing a guffaw. "When are you and Mrs. Harper going to come out and go skiing with us?" he continued.

"Well, I should have time after the election," Harper returned. "You know it's a mid-term election, but I still need to stump for the party's candidates. I should be able to get some R&R in after the first of the year. It'll be good to have a chance to kick back and relax again. How does late January sound?"

"Sounds great! We'll look forward to seeing you." With that, Daniel rose, knowing President Harper had other people waiting to see him.

"Wait, Daniel, tell me a little bit about this new expedition. What's the purpose?"

Daniel filled Harper in, using some of Summers' language from his presentation to the Board to emphasize how important the foundation thought it would be to current understanding of previous cycles of history. Harper nodded thoughtfully.

"You know, I never thought when I took office that I'd preside over a nation that would be turned on its head over an old conspiracy theory," he quipped.

"And I never thought I'd be anything but a journalist and amateur archaeologist," Daniel returned. "Funny how things work

26

out." He shook Harper's hand and left, with another heavy sigh. It was up to someone else, now. His days of fighting the OS were coming to a close, and none too soon. After all, Nick needed a secure and safe future with both his mommy and his daddy. With the OS eradicated, the world would be one step closer to that ideal.

True to his word, Lewis set his own team in motion immediately, and spoke urgently with the heads of the security agencies in more than a dozen other countries as soon as he was able to reach them. Some answered immediately, others called back after speaking to their own heads of state. The plan was repeated, in Germany, England, Israel, France and Turkey, spreading out among the allies of those countries like a drop of water on a paper towel.

~~~

Back at home, Daniel was pleased to greet Luke early the next morning after flying back from Washington.

"Luke, glad you're here, I wanted to thank you for getting Lewis on board for my meeting with President Harper. It went well, and I have every confidence that the job will be done before October. Sam Lewis sends his best, by the way. Now, what can I do for you?"

"You know we've been reviewing our background checks ever since Misty Rivers was caught spying, yes?"

"Yes. Are we clean?"

"Not quite yet. We have a translation lab assistant who'd like to make a deal. Shall I just turn her over to the police, or would you like to interview her?"

"Another woman. Why did they choose mostly women?" he questioned.

"You should ask your baby brother that question," Luke

said, a grim line where his mouth should be.

"You mean..."

"Yes. They considered him the weak link. Misty was the first volley, so to speak. By the time she was exposed, that Brazilian scientist, Carmen, had broken training and was more focused on the man who attracted her, Robert Cartwright, rather than attempting to attract the one she was supposed to, JR. If she hadn't made that mistake, who knows what would have happened down there. You need to have a serious talk with JR."

"Is that really necessary?" Daniel hedged. "He and Rebecca Mendenhall seem pretty committed."

"Do you trust him not to cheat if someone throws herself at him?"

"I do, but maybe I'd better have a talk with him anyway. Man, I hate to get on his case again, now that we're on pretty good terms. He seems to have straightened out. I'll see what Rebecca says about it."

"Better safe than sorry. As long as he sticks closely to Dr. Mendenhall's side, I'm confident everything will be okay. It's when temptation comes calling that I worry."

"Okay, I'll talk to him. Anything else?"

"Yes, you never answered my question. Would you like to interview our suspect?"

"Oh. Yes, I would. When?"

"How about right now?" Luke stood and strode to the door, which he opened wide to gesture at someone outside, then stood aside as a pretty young woman sullenly walked in and took a seat without waiting for an invitation.

Daniel stared at her for a moment. She looked a little like Sarah; same coloring anyway. The brilliant smile was missing. It

28

frightened him to know that the OS knew so much about his brother.

"How do you pass information to your handler?" he asked.

She leveled a cool gaze at him. "Facebook," she said. "It's encoded."

"You'll keep your account open, and pass on some information that we'll give you. Or, you can go to jail. Your choice."

"What's it worth to you?"

"To have your cooperation? We can use it, but we don't need it. You're on your own for money. If you're any good at your job, you can stay and draw a salary until this is over. The question is, would you prefer to help us or go to jail? Again, your choice."

"They'll kill me," she said, dropping her cool act.

"They won't have the chance," Daniel responded, hoping he was right.

"Okay, I'll play. What do you need?"

"Mr. Clarke here will let you know exactly what he wants you to do. I imagine he'll also be keeping a very close eye on you. I wouldn't try anything underhanded if I were you. Jail is always a possibility, and I have no problem having you arrested immediately if Luke tells me you've been less than cooperative."

As they left, Daniel shook his head. He hadn't bothered to ask her name. With luck, he'd never see her again, because she would be turned over to the CIA to be used for their operation and then when it was over she'd be fired. He felt no remorse at the harsh reality that she would be left without either of her jobs. A girl like that, she'd do whatever she needed to in order to survive. She'd land on her feet or she'd go to jail. Thinking of all the people that her employers, the OS, had killed or put in jeopardy, he really didn't care which. The OS had messed with him and his family for the last time.

Chapter 5 - My code name is Latet

Luke wasted no time in using the girl's communications link, at the same time alerting Lewis at the CIA that they had a lead. It never occurred to him, nor in fact to the girl, that her contact was none other than the lead OS operative stateside. She didn't know his name or even where he was located, but Luke had designed her message to lure out anyone who had information to trade for their own benefit. Hopefully, the girl's contact would take the bait and then use their own method of communication to lure out the next guy, until they'd rolled up the entire organization.

Latet read the CIA memo with disbelief. It was over, or would be soon. Every major security agency in the world was after the OS, and with a cooperative effort like that, even they would soon fall. It made the message he'd received from the last remaining operative at the Rossler Foundation tempting. But, could he trust that? The private Facebook message read, 'Compromised. Agency offering immunity for information revealing leadership or substantial financial info. Turn yourself in. No further communications.'

Was it genuine? It had the required image file attached, a compass rosette. It was straightforward, and he couldn't imagine any hidden message within. He could take the advice to turn himself in for immunity, go underground with the money he'd skimmed, or take his chances and try to save the OS. This couldn't be a snap decision. Before making any move at all, he would check his assets in various offshore accounts.

To his dismay, online access to some of them was out of service. He opened a new window and checked world news. Venerable institutions in Germany, France and Italy were under some sort of cyber-attack and funds were frozen. Unless Andorra was secure, he was screwed. With the funds in his bank there, he could disappear and there'd be enough to stay hidden until the other funds were released. But these banks were OS controlled. Would the funds ever be released?

Latet first had a trusted friend in Andorra pick up a package from his bank and transport it to Madrid, where he opened a new bank account with cash in a bank that to his knowledge was not OS-controlled, in the name of a business that had a corporate address in Seychelles. Feeling secure though somewhat short of funds, with an account full of Euros that had a value of just over a million dollars, Latet then contacted one of the leaders of the Orion Society.

The OS was a cartel run by four families, each having one representative to the group that ran the ancient organization. Each representative bore a code name, based on the quarter of the world that he or she claimed dominion over. Auster, the oldest and therefore the avowed leader, was a sharply intelligent woman who had managed to oust one family and replace it with her own daughter.

Auster's code name meant 'South'. Her daughter was the relatively new Septentrio, meaning North. The previous Septentrio had died of a stroke while indulging in a fit of temper, leaving no heir to take over. The other members, Occidens, meaning West and Oriens, meaning East, were relatively weak, mostly agreeing to whatever schemes Auster and her daughter put forth.

When Latet contacted Auster, he found her in a temper because the banking systems the OS controlled had been crippled. He wasted no time in informing her of what he knew—that the CIA, aided by security agencies worldwide, was launching an attack on the OS. Latet wanted instructions.

"How exposed are we, Latet?" she asked.

"It's hard to say, but the fact that they've frozen funds in most of your banks isn't a good sign. What do you hear from your people in industry and the military? Am I the first to report in from security agencies?"

"You are. I've tried to contact your counterparts in Germany, France and Italy to find out what's going on with the banks, but they aren't responding."

"They're probably compromised. What are your arrangements for going to ground in a situation like this?" This was the real reason for Latet's call. The only reason the OS had lasted as long as it had was the secrecy with which it operated. As long as no one, particularly governments, knew of them, they could control their assets with impunity. Now that they were known, it was only a matter of time before they fell, given a concerted worldwide effort. Latet didn't intend to be on the losing side.

Auster wasn't a fool, but Latet was a trusted senior operative. She anticipated the secure communications network that the OS controlled going down at any time, as soon as any operative who knew of it turned to save his own skin. To maintain communications with Latet, she gave him the locations of the others as well as where she'd be hiding as soon as she could direct the counteroffensive to the bank fiasco.

"Latet, I expect to see you face-to-face as soon as you can make the arrangements. How will you communicate with me?"

Caught off guard because he was dependent on the secure videoconference link, he had to think fast. His arrangements with some of his operatives came to mind.

"Create a Facebook account, and send a friend request to this address." Quickly, he typed in a link and sent it via instant chat.

"What in the world is Facebook?" Auster asked.

"Ask your daughter. I've been using the Private Message feature to communicate with some of my people. It isn't immune to search warrants, but there are so many users, it would be difficult for the CIA to discover us. It will have to do until we re-group."

Auster agreed, then cut the communications link.

For a moment, Latet considered toughing it out and waiting to see who would win. But, his earlier assessment came back to him. The days of the OS were numbered. Cursing himself for a fool, he made the final decision and pressed the intercom button.

"Director Lewis, please. On second thought, can you pencil me in for a quick conference? I'll be right up." He listened to the answer.

"I assure you, he'll want to see me. Tell him I have confidential information about the Orion Society." With that, he looked around the office he was certain never to see again. Nothing of personal interest caught his eye. He strolled out, carrying nothing but his cell phone and the extensive knowledge of the Orion Society in his head. He'd help take down his employers on the condition of being accepted into the witness protection program. There were others who wouldn't take kindly to the news that he was a traitor. After all, the Orion Society wasn't the only criminal organization in the world who needed CIA moles. He needed to retire and get out of the line of fire, before it all went down.

"Director Lewis, thank you for seeing me. I have information I believe you'll appreciate. I'm Agent William Smith, counterintelligence. My code name in the OS is Latet. I have a proposition for you."

Latet talked for several hours, revealing what he knew of the OS, in return for the promise of entry into the witness protection program. He had no illusions that it would actually protect him from whatever remnants of the OS might be left after his betrayal. What it would do for him was allow him to disappear from his current life. Once he was safe from prosecution, he'd disappear from the new one as well and travel under his new credentials to Spain, where he would become someone else again. Perhaps the trail would go dead there and he'd be safe. It remained to be seen.

With Smith's help, OS communication satellites were identified and disabled, either jammed by high-tech counterintelligence technology or crippled by top secret space-based illumination designed to fry their sensitive electronics. The network of OS-controlled financial institutions and multi-national corporations was paralyzed, key points for movement of funds shut down and under surveillance for attempted access. Auster's premonition about the communications had come to pass, with the help of her trusted lieutenant.

With their communications crippled, the directors of the OS were left alone and vulnerable to discovery, unaware that Latet was supplying the information about their whereabouts to cooperating agencies in Wurzberg, Germany, Singapore, Rio de Janeiro and Turin, Italy. In Singapore, Oriens was found cowering under a secretary's desk. Latet broke the news that he'd been arrested to Auster.

"How did they find him?" she asked.

"I'm not sure. I'm afraid someone has turned traitor," he said. "Are you sure you should stay where you are?"

"I don't know about the others, but I've told no-one my whereabouts except my daughter and you."

"You're probably safe, then. Do you trust your daughter?"

"I'll let that pass, but don't ever suggest that my daughter could be a traitor again."

As they spoke, the fortified compound where Occidens was located erupted in gunfire, as the Agência Brasileira de Inteligência attempted to enter and arrest him. Backed by the Brazilian Army, their firepower overwhelmed the mercenaries that Occidens had gathered to protect him. The latter, since they weren't bound by loyalty, threw down their arms as soon as they began to take heavy casualties. Occidens was wounded, but was taken into custody and reports were that he was expected to recover.

Latet didn't receive that news until the next morning. By the time he reached Auster, she had heard it already and was livid when he opened the chat window in Facebook to let her know.

"Who is providing them with this information?" she demanded. Latet knew that if he didn't convince her it wasn't he, there would be hell to pay. He named an operative in Germany and asked if it could be him.

"I'll check with my daughter," Auster replied. "Is your position secure?"

"Yes," Latet lied. "They don't suspect me."

"I expect you to follow our traditional expedient if you are caught. You have the means?"

"Of course." Latet had no intention of committing suicide, of course, though his betrayal of the OS might yet have that effect.

Several days passed, while Latet nervously waited for the Agency to wrap up the operation to take the leaders of the OS into custody. Reports indicated that some of the corporations under suspicion of being OS-run were resisting efforts to seize their records. In more than one case, security guards in factories and oil refineries engaged in short gun battles with arresting forces before being overwhelmed. Latet spent each night in a different hotel, weapon at hand, expecting at any moment that OS operatives would arrive to accuse him of working with the enemy, or just to kill him without warning.

On the fourth day after Occidens' arrest, Lewis called Latet into his office.

"We can't get anywhere near the Wurzberg or the Turin sites. Do these people know you by sight?"

Latet had a sinking feeling that he knew what was coming, but the only way to secure his safety was to take out the leaders. "Yes, sir, they do."

"We need you to go in to pave the way for Special Forces. Can you convince them that you're there to tell them something of such importance it can't be entrusted to whatever communications you're using?"

"You know what communications I'm using. Agents have my account names and passwords; they're watching everything I do."

"Answer the question." Lewis had little use for a traitor, and the man in his office was a traitor to both sides. He couldn't care less whether he'd insulted the guy.

"Yes, I think so. Who do you want first?"

"I think the mother will be demoralized if we take the daughter first. She may even surrender."

"Don't count on it," Latet muttered.

"What was that?"

"I said, good plan."

"All right, then. Go home and pack. I want you on a plane to Germany this afternoon. You'll have a Special Forces squad to keep you company."

Just what I wanted, Latet thought.

Twenty-four hours later, he stood at the front door of a venerable manse, one of the historical homes of the city. Guards frisked him for weapons, and admitted him to the house, where he was showed to a sitting room and told that Septentrio would be with him shortly. Latet was still unused to the title referring to a woman.

When she appeared, Auster's daughter took Latet off-guard. She looked nothing like her mother, who was tall, regal and a redhead. Septentrio was a petite blond. Amazing that such an unprepossessing figure of a woman could wield the power that this young woman did.

"To what do I owe this unexpected visit, Latet?" she asked.

"You know that Oriens and Occidens have been arrested," he answered.

"Of course."

"I have reason to believe you are in danger here. I'm here to escort you to a safer environment."

"I appreciate it, but I think not."

Just then, a loud blast interrupted them. Before Septentrio could ask what was going on, Special Forces troops streamed through the front door, guns drawn.

Septentrio flashed a look at Latet as she was being handcuffed. "You! You're responsible for this!"

Latet grinned. "What are you going to do, tell your mother on me?"

With Septentrio in custody. Latet was flown next to Turin, where he planned to distract Auster in the same way he had distracted the daughter. This time, it wasn't so easy.

Three of the four supreme leaders of the Society had been identified and arrested with little trouble. The fourth, the middle-aged woman known as Auster and said to be the most powerful, barricaded herself behind her military style guard as the agents responsible for her arrest forced their way into her study, Latet among them. When she recognized him, she shrieked her anger and seized a gun from one of her guards. Before anyone could react, she mowed him down, along with several others, in a burst of semi-automatic fire. She and her guard went down seconds later as fire was returned from the surviving strike force.

The three members who were arrested, including the daughter of the slain leader, proved to be cowards, first trying to bluff with the 'do you know who I am' card and then trying to blame the others. Eventually, under harsh questioning, all three broke down, the two men crying like babies, and agreed to hand over records and documents that blew the entire organization open like a dropped watermelon.

Their interrogators and the investigators involved in forensic analysis of the records were shocked at the extent of the corruption. Literally hundreds of years of greed and power mongering had resulted in a network whose tentacles reached into a majority of international corporations. What was worse was the revelation that the organization controlled large portions of dozens of governments and military organizations, both major and minor. Even the Vatican was not immune, nor were quite a few other prominent churches. The list of names was extensive and appalling.

Slowly, it dawned on a stupefied planet that these monsters had truly thought themselves gods, untouchable and above the law. Some believed that they had to be crazy, deluded and in need of a reality check. Those were the naïve ones. The reality was that the four leaders of the Orion Society were neither crazy nor in need of a reality check. They and their forbears had for generations been untouchable and above the law. That the tides had turned did not erase the fact that, for hundreds of years, they had indeed been as gods.

International finance was in chaos as forensic accountants worked around the clock to sort out the convoluted scheme of money laundering that one spokesman described as 'a one-thousand-tentacled octopus'.

The Orion Society turned out to be major shareholders in more than half of the most profitable big-pharma operations, some of which had benefited from 10th Cycle knowledge, much to Daniel's disgust. In retaliation, the Rossler Foundation moved immediately to suspend all ties with them and bar them from receiving further information from the Foundation until they had paid full restitution to both business entities and users of their medicines. Stricter controls were subsequently placed on all pharma companies, with periodic audits to be held for assurance that the technology was being used beneficially and without undue profit.

The OS had operatives in high office in the Teamsters Union and several others, owned majority stock in the most profitable multi-national companies in the world including two major oil companies, and controlled nearly half of the banks in Europe. The news dropped the stock market 25%, rivaling the Black Friday crash of October, 1987. Confusion about whether company funds were legal shut down dozens of companies, putting thousands of people out of work.

President Harper was besieged in the Press Room by journalists feeding on a backlash that threatened to flip the expected outcome of the mid-term election. He urged calm. Naturally, they wanted to know if any of the names on the list belonged to members of his administration, or even he himself. The last question prompted a temper tantrum the likes of which hadn't been seen since Barack Obama's years in office. The reporter hastily apologized, but insisted that the names on the list be published. Her demand, - 'name them and shame them' - became a battle cry on the lips of both parties' spokespeople.

Elsewhere in the world, prime ministers were being forced to resign, while lower-level politicians were systematically arrested for corruption and graft. Many abruptly announced their retirement for 'personal reasons', either poor health or family obligations. The Tea Party in the US gained strength for the coming election, with the popular sentiment that all experienced politicians must be corrupt. 'Throw the bastards out' became their rallying cry.

How could this have happened? Everyone wanted to know why no one had tumbled to this massive conspiracy over the centuries. No one had satisfactory answers. More than one head of police and security agencies lost their jobs abruptly. Director Lewis barely retained his job, after testifying before Congress that he had been investigating and cleaning house for the past several years. At least he had known something was up, which was more than other countries' security agencies could say for themselves.

Appalled by what his Board had unleashed, Daniel nevertheless felt more secure about his family's safety than he had since learning of the Orion Society and their vendetta against him. That the world in general was safer, or would be once the dust had settled, was a given. It was the validation that they had done the right thing, irrespective of the consequences. He met with the Foundation employees to assure them that their jobs and the funds that paid their salaries were safe. They now had a little less than three months to mount the second expedition, and to that end, he requested that his employees return to their work and not let the chaos surrounding them distract them from the mission they'd all sworn to uphold: the fair and equitable distribution of the knowledge of the 10th Cycle Library, just as fast as they could translate, test and disseminate it. He received a standing ovation.

Chapter 6 – Team building

Since their return from Antarctica and in preparation for the next expedition, JR had spent the time productively, first taking a two-week between-semester course in project management at the Colorado School of Mines that strengthened his natural sense of order as well as what he'd learned about logistics in the Marines. As soon as he'd finished that, he decided to take Rebecca and visit his parents. Even though he'd seen them at the emotional reunion held for the returning expedition members in lieu of the memorial service for which everyone had gathered, the general chaos that prevailed with their return hadn't made for a satisfactory visit, and he wanted to present Rebecca to them as not only his colleague and doctor, but as his love.

JR expected that his parents would be crazy about Rebecca, and wasn't disappointed. Aaron congratulated him on snagging another good one and lamented that he couldn't find anyone half as special as either Sarah or now Rebecca. Naturally, JR sent him up with a remark that he of course didn't deserve anyone so special. A wrestling match ensued that alarmed Rebecca until she noticed Nancy laughing beside her. Rebecca had no brothers, so this display of brotherly affection was strange to her.

JR had made his decision. He hadn't particularly been searching for a wife since his college sweetheart had thrown him over and disrupted his life plans, but he knew that the search was over, anyway. There could never be anyone like Rebecca, and he was lucky beyond measure that she loved him, too. With the clear approval of his parents, JR began a plan of action to give them a second daughter.

Ben and Nancy made it no secret that they were happy for JR. Rebecca was very different from Sarah, but the two were already good friends. It didn't matter that Rebecca wasn't a particularly brilliant cook like Sarah. That she loved their son was all that was required for their approval, love and respect. The only thing that could have made Nancy any happier was for Aaron to find a woman as wonderful as Sarah and Rebecca.

~~~

JR and Summers had an unusual working relationship, often volatile, but strangely effective. Summers couldn't seem to remember that JR was no longer his assistant, but rather the director of the expedition. His clashes with LeClerc had often been the result of his controlling nature, and it started out that way with JR. JR, however, wasn't having any of it. JR had seen the danger that lack of a clear line of leadership had put the first expedition in, and he had no intention of following in LeClerc's footsteps. So, when Summers stated a preference for a line of prefab buildings that JR thought inferior, he put his foot down.

"I don't care if they're thirty percent cheaper. They're also at least thirty percent more likely to fail in a gale-force wind. This is going to be a semi-permanent installation. It makes no sense to install inferior buildings that we'll have to replace next year; that's false economy. We're going with Guerdon, and that's final."

Frustrated, Summers attempted to argue. JR merely crossed his arms and raised his eyebrows, as if to say, 'do you really want to do this?' Summers sighed and made a notation in his budget software. Since JR was the brother of the CEO of the Foundation, any budget overruns he insisted upon were on him, not on Summers. Secretly, he was pleased. He had originally preferred Guerdon's man-camp complexes, but he didn't think he could swing the funds for them. With JR taking the brunt of the political fallout, he could have his cake and eat it, too.

After that, things went more smoothly, with Summers

putting up only token resistance to JR's insistence on the best equipment and materials. It got to the point of being a game between them, so much so that both would have been disappointed if they got through a logistics meeting without a friendly argument.

On the other hand, JR bowed to Summers' previous experience in running archaeological digs. He admired the way Summers had divided the expedition into phases to avoid extra expense, knowing that they wouldn't need the bulk of the diggers for at least four weeks, probably six. The plan was to set up the camp, beginning with core buildings such as the mess and laundry facilities, infirmary and administrative offices. The scientists would each have small labs within the admin building, along with a conference room for any meetings that required more room than their small offices would accommodate. The first dormitory building would be for the use of the scientists as well. As soon as these buildings were up, the scientists would move from tents on the ice into more comfortable quarters, and construction would begin on dormitories to house the diggers.

At the same time as the initial few buildings were going up, a second construction crew under the supervision of JR and Robert together would begin tunneling a route through the cave system into the valley. Robert would be there for two purposes; one, to be sure that the route they took destroyed as little of the beautiful cave structure as possible, and the second to ensure a sound structure by evaluating the transition between the sedimentary and igneous layers.

With each completed phase of the tunnel, tracks would be laid for an electric rail line that would serve numerous purposes. It would be a people carrier, both for the further reaches of the tunnel construction and for delivering both scientists and diggers into the valley later. It would also carry any heavy equipment or other material into the valley when the digging started, and possibly would be used to convey overburden from the excavation site to a dumping ground out in the canyon. Summers hadn't decided about that yet, and would not be able to do so until he saw the ruins for himself.

One thing he brought up to JR was the necessity of cleaning up the bodies of the seven OS people that they hadn't had time or equipment to deal with last February. Strangely, it was Summers whose practical nature brought it up. JR knew he'd have to man up for the task, but the thought of seven half-decomposed bodies nearly brought on a waking nightmare. When he spoke to Rebecca about it, though, she assured him that by the time they returned, indeed probably within little more than two weeks after they left, the temperature in the valley would have rendered the bodies to their skeletal remains, even without the assistance of large animals or insects. Bones he could deal with. He didn't want to see faces. He returned to Summers and assured him that he and Robert Cartwright would be able to bury the remains, or if Summers preferred, transfer them into an out-of-the way room in the cave system that surrounded the valley.

JR was looking forward to seeing Robert again. The big Aussie was good company, almost always in a good mood no matter what. JR's own demons left him in a foul mood occasionally, but with Rebecca's and Robert's help, he'd try to shake them off. However, the excitement of being in on the planning stages of an important archaeological dig had him enthusiastic about his chosen field of study as he hadn't been since before he dropped out of college just shy of his graduation and joined the Marines. Not even the belated presentation of his undergraduate degree, for which he had earned sufficient credits before joining the Marines and Daniel had arranged to be presented in a special ceremony after the return from Antarctica, had given him this thrill.

With a far different attitude about this expedition than

44

about the last one, JR began to seem like his old self to his family and to Rebecca, who congratulated herself for it though she knew that being entrusted with the responsibility for the expedition went a long way toward restoring JR's self-esteem. By mid-August, he was interviewing and hiring the base camp and road construction crews, who, despite the OS being in shambles, all had to pass a rigorous background check. This time, Luke was determined that no saboteurs could slip through. Each new employee, whether based in Boulder or heading for Antarctica, was thoroughly vetted back to their childhood, and so were their parents.

Plans were coming along with good speed as August drew to a close and the scientists began gathering for final briefings before the planned launch date of October first, again going through a selection process similar to that of the first expedition.

Instead of being a challenging adventure, this expedition was almost a coveted vacation, with the exception that they would have work to do. Applications came in droves. Candidates were selected, vetted and placed in ethnic groups, from which drawings were held among the most highly qualified. At last, the core group of returning expedition members were joined by two new scientists, a botanist from Jordan named Haraz el-Amin, and a transplanted New Zealander, Nyree Dasgupta, a microbiologist specializing in ancient DNA genome sequencing. Each of the scientific fields represented also had one assistant, which included an Egyptian, a Turk, a Pakistani, and a Saudi, as well as a Chilean and a dark-skinned junior IT specialist from Georgia whose accent was so thick that only Cyndi could understand him.

With such a diverse group, it was to be expected that there might be friction. To prevent it from jeopardizing the expedition, Summers asked Rebecca to arrange for extensive teambuilding and sensitivity training exercises. They turned out to be so much fun that the participants almost felt as if they had been given a day off to play. Afterward, everyone understood that they were expected to respect each other's cultural differences and treat each other with respect at all times.

Chapter 7 – Meet the parents

The rest of the preparations went smoothly and quickly, with the previous expedition's plans to draw from. JR was to be sent ahead with the base camp construction crew to prepare for the arrival of the road construction crew and the scientists by leveling and packing the snow that covered the ice sheet and setting up the numerous tents that would shelter them until dormitories could be built. By the time the others arrived, the base camp crew would be finishing out the mess building, which would be delivered on October fourth, weather permitting.

Accordingly, the advance group was to leave Boulder on the twenty-eighth of September for an October first arrival at McMurdo. This time they wouldn't travel by ground, but would be dropped, along with the materials they'd need for the first week, by helicopter. If JR felt any apprehension at returning to the place where he and the others had almost lost their lives earlier in the year, he chose to say nothing about it.

Despite being fully involved in the planning and logistics, JR had other things on his mind. Now and then, he had to pinch himself to make sure he wasn't living in a dream with Rebecca. When he was tired, as he often was, JR could still doubt himself and worry that he could never be worthy of someone like Rebecca. She was beautiful, confident, obviously smart and on top of it all. He was a screw-up. And yet, he loved her with all his heart and knew that if he lost her, he'd never recover. Once was bad enough. Twice would be fatal.

One evening, he went to Daniel and Sarah in despair.

"Bro, I want to ask Rebecca to marry me, but I'm afraid," he confessed.

Daniel and Sarah looked at each other fondly. "No more

than I was," Daniel responded.

"You? No way! You guys were made for each other."

"We had our moments, though. Remember that Sarah lost her memory temporarily. She didn't even know who I was, and there I was hopelessly in love with her."

"Hopeless is right," Sarah laughed. "I thought I was going to have to pop the question myself." She nudged Daniel. "Just like Rebecca said..." Her hand flew up to her mouth to stop the words, but it was too late. JR latched on to the comment.

"What did Rebecca say?" he demanded.

"That she wonders when you're going to get your act together and propose," Sarah blurted, now that she'd slipped up.

JR was stunned for a moment, and then a slow grin crept over his face. "She does, does she?" Daniel and Sarah could get no more from him that night.

JR kept to himself the secret plans he had for the farewell at the airport. Unbeknownst to Rebecca, he had visited with her parents in Boulder to ask a very important question.

At first, the Mendenhalls had been less than pleased with their daughter's decision to take up with the handsome but, to their knowledge, mentally unstable JR Rossler. In the weeks since the pair had moved in together, though, her parents had come to respect JR's efforts to become a responsible man. Through Rebecca's eyes, they learned that he had been brought up well, was intelligent and resourceful as well as kind and fun-loving. Now he was seeking their permission to ask for her hand in marriage, which both greatly improved Mr. Mendenhall's opinion of their housekeeping arrangement and thrilled her mother with the prospect of a wedding in the family.

JR began by telling the Mendenhalls that he knew he had

problems, and that he could understand if they weren't sure of him. He went on to say that with Rebecca's help, he'd been working on his behavior, and that someday he hoped to be cured of the PTSD. With obvious sincerity, he told them he'd die before he'd hurt her, and that if they would entrust her to him, he'd prove that he could someday be worthy of her love.

Their permission obtained, JR went ring-shopping, with Sarah as his co-conspirator.

Rebecca was at the airport to see him off, along with JR's family and Sinclair, who had developed a soft spot for the troubled young man since his return in March. Sarah and Daniel, who were in on the secret, could barely contain their glee as the group gathered outside the secure area for final goodbyes. JR turned to hug Rebecca close and whisper that he'd miss her until she joined him in a couple of weeks.

"Be careful, love," she whispered back. Then she laid a kiss on him that had the others hooting and calling out 'get a room'. Suddenly, to her confusion, JR dropped to his knees, and, in front of both his family and the strangers who stopped to stare, along with Rebecca's parents and sister who came out of hiding at the prompt, declared his love for her. Rebecca's eyes sparkled with unshed tears, though her brilliant smile signaled to all and sundry that they were tears of happiness.

"Rebecca, please tell me you'll be mine forever. Will you marry me?" he asked in conclusion.

Everyone burst into cheers and applause, even the strangers, when she nodded. "Of course I will, Joshie," she answered, using her private endearment for him. He produced a solitaire that, thanks to Sarah's advice, was perfect on Rebecca's slender finger.

"Oh, honey, I love it!" she exclaimed, momentarily

becoming just a young woman in love rather than a cool, calm and collected MD.

All too soon, JR was forced to leave the rest of the party and make his way through security to join the construction crew, who had gone ahead. JR's insouciant grin was the last the family saw of him before he disappeared into the secure area. Rebecca couldn't help worrying about JR when he was away from her, whether it was for a few hours or a few days. This would be the longest separation since their friendship had blossomed into love last spring.

It didn't matter to her whether they were married or not. She had been committed to JR in her heart since he saved her and the rest of the expedition members on the previous trip. If she were honest with herself, she'd have to admit she had feelings for him before that, but he'd just made it impossible to get close to him then. Rebecca had no doubt that he was committed to her when he moved in with her. She had faith in his love for her. He might have been a player before, but she was certain he was faithful to her now. Besides, she was a believer in the concept that people lived up, or down, to the expectations of their loved ones.

As long as she had faith in him, he would live up to it. In JR's case, though, his sense of integrity had been so damaged by what happened during his hitch in the Marines that she worried about his state of mind when she wasn't there to monitor. If someone expressed doubt about him, he would begin to doubt himself. Someday, maybe he'd heal. Until then, she intended to be at his side, his rock in a stormy sea, and his vocal advocate in a crisis. Rebecca had worked herself into tears by the time she got back to Boulder, but packing for her own departure was a good exercise to dry them again.

The trip from Denver International to Boulder was easily an hour and a half, longer at rush hour. By the time the send-off party was home, JR, and the construction crew were half-way to Dallas, where they would board a connecting flight to Miami, thence to Chile, Christchurch, New Zealand and finally to McMurdo. It was a grueling trip, but thankfully some of the flights were short enough to stretch the kinks out of their legs before the next one. JR in particular had a difficult time on planes, especially if there were no first-class accommodations. His legs were longer than ninety percent of the American male population, and he figured he would be in the top one percent in height if the population of the whole world were ranked. At six feet, ten inches, he'd almost been good enough for the NBA, if his college girlfriend hadn't sent him into a tailspin.

The long flight gave all of them a chance to rest up from the going away parties. JR reckoned that he would sleep away a good portion of each flight. None of the construction crew had been to Antarctica, so between flights he gathered them into a tight circle and regaled them with tales of near darkness, unremitting daylight and howling winds. The last part was serious, even though he told his tales as if they were scary stories from around a campfire. On the previous expedition, one member had presumably been swept away by the wind when he failed to latch onto the guide rope. His body was never found. Fortunately, the winds weren't expected to be quite so fierce where they were going, but it was still fun to spook the men a little, now that they were committed to the journey.

When they reached Christchurch, JR recommended that everyone have a hearty and tasty meal, as it would be their last other than trail food until the mess building was up and the cook got to the camp. On the next day, they'd fly to McMurdo base, a facility that couldn't be described adequately to anyone who hadn't been there. None of these guys had even been in jail, that is, if their background checks had been accurate. That was the closest JR could come to describing an Antarctica base, having spent a few nights in jail on a disorderly charge for assaulting a cop before the last expedition.

~~~

Since they had to have a way to refer to the canyon where the base camp would be set up, JR had proposed Purgatory Canyon, as a contrast to Paradise Valley, the name the previous expedition had given to the hidden valley accessed through a system of caves. Though it wasn't official, the name had caught on. The construction workers got their first taste of Antarctica there, since their arrival at McMurdo was followed only a day later by their helicopter trip to the canyon. JR got a kick out of the comments he heard, all good-natured griping about the weather conditions.

"I thought it was summer? Where's the sun?"

"It's bleedin' minus sixty out here! What was I thinking?"

On the first day, JR and his assistant construction boss accompanied the heavy equipment transport and began surveying and laying out the camp as they waited the hour for the rest to arrive on the second helicopter. As soon as everyone was in place, JR called them together and set tasks. These two, including his assistant, would spray red lines on the snow to guide the equipment, those two would run the bulldozers to flatten the entire area, and two would begin setting up tents as soon as that section of the camp was leveled. They would first set up the two-man tents that would shelter everyone who was already here. The other five would take the first sleep shift as soon as their tents were set up. JR would be the sixth on the second-shift crew, but he would forego sleep until the first sixteen hours safely established the routines. During the sixteen hours of downtime while each man rested and his equipment was returned to readiness, he could sleep for any or all of them, and choose when to sleep and when to wake. All that was required was that they sort it out with their tent mates.

Every couple of hours, everyone on-shift would switch jobs after a break for a hot beverage and some food. The cold temperatures were debilitating, especially to humans who were working hard and burning the precious calories that they would have to replenish frequently. JR had already decided to use the cave as an informal shelter for the breaks. At minus thirteen Fahrenheit, it was almost warm inside compared to out in the open. He knew now that it was because of the heat leaking out of the hidden valley beyond the cave, and *that* was because of the volcano underneath it, a fact that still gave JR the hebejebes and had been suppressed in the media.

Until Robert arrived and had a better chance to study and evaluate the thermal wells within, it was assumed the volcano was asleep, if not extinct. Robert said if it were extinct there would be no heat, but JR didn't know that much about geology. As far as he was concerned, if it was hot down there, it could erupt at any minute, despite Robert's assurances that it wasn't likely. Still, there was no sense in spooking the construction crews, who were assumed to be ignorant of the finer points of volcanism as well. So, they just didn't tell them. If it all did blow up, they'd be dead and couldn't sue them anyway, JR reasoned with graveyard humor. Because of the dangers that were well-known, most candidates for the position weren't family men, either.

The first break came none too soon for any of the men, who filed into the cave with various exclamations of wonder and gratitude that they actually felt warm. Their cold-weather gear was state-of-the-art, or they wouldn't have been able to complete their assigned tasks at all, nor stay outside for more than a few minutes, without encountering severe hypothermia. Layers of insulating fabrics inside coveralls that looked suspiciously like moon suits, as one of the workers dubbed them, retained the heat that the suits manufactured using an array of small rechargeable batteries. Generators were scattered among the tents, with cables snaking into each tent, both to power heaters for warmth when the occupants were inside and to recharge the suits' batteries when they were off-shift.

Because from this day forward, the daylight would grow until there would be a couple of months when it was high all the time, no darkness to cue sleep, everyone had been issued a supply of melatonin and was encouraged but not required to take it. Each of the two teams would experience different 'days'. JR expected the entire construction project to take a month or less. He had planned for every eventuality, including generator failure, damage to the environmental suits and potential trouble among the men. If worst came to worst and everything failed at once, they could all retreat to the valley and wait for rescue, but he was determined to show Daniel and everyone else that he was on top of this. As the work commenced, he observed his crew with pride.

~~~

Five days after work commenced on the base camp, the second wave arrived. These ten workers, plus a couple of explosives experts, a mining engineer and Robert Cartwright to consult and supervise, would begin construction of the rail line through the cave system and into the valley. Their tents were ready, and the mess building had been delivered although it wasn't yet in operative condition. The next day would bring more material and supplies for the construction projects, along with the much anticipated arrival of the cook. Finally, they would have some decent food and a warm place to eat it.

JR and Robert greeted each other heartily. It had been months since they'd last been in each other's presence, but they had developed a bond in the shared dangers of the previous expedition and a warm friendship followed. Keeping in touch by Skype, they knew each other as well now as if they had been friends for years. An awkward hug in the bulky environmental suits and a on each other's back marked their reunion.

"G'day, Cobber. Ow-yar-goin'?" was Robert's greeting.

"Speak English, will you?" retorted JR, who had understood the greeting better than he let on.

Robert would share JR's tent until the scientists arrived, but of course would move into his own when Rebecca got there. He made a bawdy remark, then immediately apologized as he saw JR's serious face.

"Hey, mate, you know I was just arsing about. I'm sorry, didn't think. The last time I saw you, you were on the rebound from your latest plaything."

"True. I forgive you, but you need to know, I'm serious about Becca. She's promised to marry me."

"Congratulations, mate! And enough said. In fact, I'm looking forward to finding out if Cyndi is a goer to take up our fling again. We've emailed a few times, but I can't read her."

"She's been busy learning a couple of new technologies for her stint here. She's still responsible for the electronics, but now she's doubling as our IT and communications person. Raj, our IT director, has really been putting her through her paces."

"That's good then. Anything between them?"

"No, Raj is married to a knockout. Cyndi couldn't compete."

"Hey! Don't you slag off my girl, mate."

"Dude, I have no idea what you just said, but I stand by my opinion. We'll just have to agree to disagree, until you can get a look at Raj's wife. Then you'll agree with me."

"We'll see. Hey, when's lunchtime around here? I'm

starving."

JR looked at his watch, which thankfully behaved itself outside the cave. "Coming up on first shift break time right now. Let's go."

On the way, JR asked Robert how long it would take him to understand the valley, which Robert was now calling a caldera.

"Not long. I've had some luck with a new technology for seeing what's underground, and I got some time with one of your government's satellites for imaging. I can pretty much tell you what it's all about right now. I'm mostly going to be confirming my conclusions with some deep-core sampling, if I can figure out how to get a drill rig in there. If not, I'll probably be exploring the rest of the cave system to see how it all connects. I'm sure the thermal wells extend into the caves somewhere."

Oh great, thought JR. *So it's under where we take our breaks, too.* He forgot to guard his expression, drawing a laugh from Robert.

"Have you ever been to your Yellowstone Park?" he asked.

"Sure. Rite of passage for an American. I've been to a lot of the National Parks. Why do you ask?"

"Did you walk around wondering if there would be an eruption any minute?"

"No, of course not."

"Well, I'd say that's more likely than this one blowing. When you've got time, I'll take you through the geology. It's really pretty fascinating."

"Wait, are you saying there's an active volcano under Yellowstone?"

"I'm saying there's a string of them. If they ever let go at the same time, the US will be done for, and it may usher in a new Ice Age."

"Why did you tell me that, man? How am I going to get the nerve to go home?"

Robert laughed again at JR's rueful face, certain that there was more truth in his question than he'd want anyone to know. He was going to have to set the guy at ease and figure out when this one had last erupted. More likely, it was a long stretch of mountain-building through less violent lava flows. The depth of the dome from the top of the cone was one clue that the molten rock underneath had sunk substantially since then. He'd venture a guess that the last flow was at least tens of thousands of years ago, maybe longer. Maybe it had all ceased when the bit of Australia that crashed into East Antarctica had come to its final resting place.

With the arrival of the second construction crew and more material, work doubled for JR. He was no longer taking sixteen hours off, feeling the need to supervise both shifts. The eight when everyone was off at the same time became the normal 'night', so that everyone was on the same page with regard to the date. By the end of the day when the cook arrived, the mess building was in business and the camp construction crew began on the science building. When everyone had a place to work, they'd start on the dormitories so they could abandon the tents for sturdier housing.

Meanwhile, the mining engineer and Robert went into the cave to explore both routes that the previous expedition had discovered. They had a difference of opinion on the better way to go with the road. The route that Robert had pioneered, complete with a six-foot squeeze that would defeat anyone whose build was larger than Robert's, was actually the shorter, once the twists and turns were straightened out with tunneling. The mining engineer favored shorter, mostly because the sooner they finished, the sooner he could get out of this place. He'd been all for the adventure when he was recruited, but the strangeness of the surroundings made him nervous. All that white, punctuated only by the red of the tents and environmental suits. Okay, the buildings were a sort of gray-blue color, but still. He didn't like it.

Robert, on the other hand, felt that less damage to the cave ecology would be done if they simply enlarged the tunnel through which he and the others had crawled to freedom before. It was clearly in stable rock, since there were no supports in it. And, it opened on both ends to a very large space where they could stage the construction materials. The fact that it was so open also made it possible to have the crews working from both ends at the same time. Doing that in the other route left the potential for the two ends not to meet up. There wasn't a clear line of command for this decision, so the two of them took it to JR.

"I think you should follow Robert's lead," he said, once he understood what was being argued. "He's been through both routes into the valley, and he understands the caves as well as anyone does."

The engineer, in a huff, said that in that case his services weren't needed and he'd take the next helicopter back to civilization. JR wasn't accustomed to out and out mutiny in the ranks, and took offense to the man's attitude.

"Fine. You're relieved of duty. You can pack your stuff--the next helicopter will be here in about two hours

"Thanks for backing me up, mate," Robert said, when the other man had left.

"No problem, dude. That's what friends are for. And I do think you have the better grasp of the situation, anyway."

58

Aside from that issue, which remained small because JR took command of it without hesitation, the next couple of days went well, and all was in readiness when the next wave, the scientists and their assistants, touched down on the helipad exactly seven days after JR and his first crew arrived. Summers looked around and was astounded at the progress. Rebecca, on the other hand, ran straight into JR's arms to be immediately swept off her feet, dangling a foot off the ground.

The camp was laid out, some in red lines still as construction on the prefabs continued, in an efficient way; the tents nearest the cave entrance would give way to the dormitories as they went up. An environmentally sealed pathway between the operations buildings and the dorms was as wide as a city street, leveled and packed by the bulldozers, as was the helipad, which was furthest from the cave. On the other side, nearest the closed end of the canyon, were the operations buildings. The mess and science buildings were complete, while the admin building had only a few more hours of finishing before it would also be ready.

For now, everyone would continue to sleep in tents, but the dormitories would start going up next. JR explained to the scientists that he'd promised the construction crews the first building, as they'd been in tents the longest. El-Amin, with a bit of remaining entitlement issue, started to raise an objection, but was quelled by a look from Summers and Rebecca. He was still on probation and could easily be sent home, so he closed his mouth and said nothing.

The following day, the science team would go in through the existing tunnel under Robert's leadership, and begin assessing the work ahead of them.

Chapter 8 – Three passions at Paradise Valley

In JR's tent after a long first day, the two lovers clung together in their double sleeping bag, glad to be in each other's arms again even if the accommodations weren't all that comfortable. The cots on which the two halves of the sleeping bag were supported each dipped in the center, leaving a ridge in the middle that dug into JR's side as he snuggled close to Rebecca. The unacceptable situation was remedied by throwing the joined sleeping bags on the floor of the tent instead, with gratitude for their thickness and insulating ability.

Snuggled warmly inside the cocoon of their sleeping bag, JR took Rebecca tenderly into his arms, holding her tightly without speaking for long moments. Only when she stirred against him did he murmur against her hair.

"I missed you, sweetheart. I don't ever want to be without you for that long again."

Rebecca raised her face for a kiss, which stopped all talking for a while. JR's hands were stroking her back, her side, leaving heated flesh in their wake.

"Never, my love, I agree," she whispered. Her own hands busy, Rebecca sighed into his neck as JR nuzzled behind her ear. Giving herself to this man had completed her in a way she didn't know was possible. Their reunion was sweet and passionate, sealing their vows to be together more certainly than any words could.

"I should have come with you from the beginning," Rebecca said, later.

"It was cold, and the food was terrible. I'm glad you waited, even though I missed you," JR said.

"Silly, it's still cold. What if one of the construction workers had been hurt? I should have been here."

"Don't be ridiculous. No one got hurt, and if they had, I'm a pretty decent medic in a tight spot. We had a first aid kit on steroids. I could use the box for a house," he joked.

"I'm just saying. Next time I'm coming with you."

"So, you think there'll be a next time?" he asked.

"Don't you? I don't see you settling down to a desk job at the Foundation, or a teaching position once you finish your graduate work. You strike me as the action type," she said.

"You're right, there. I just don't know how many more discoveries we can make on this world, Becca."

"You might be surprised," she said, prophetically as it turned out.

JR gathered her into the crook of his arm, relishing the weight of her head on his chest and her leg thrown over his as they both fell asleep.

The lovers couldn't have known, but wouldn't have been surprised, that after they disappeared into their tent, two other couples were snuggling together in the privacy of their own tents, as well. Cyndi had waited until she could catch Robert alone before launching herself at him for a passionate kiss. Never one to waste such an opportunity, Robert responded enthusiastically. Discovering the same difficulty with the cots, they made use of the same solution. In their case, it was a first time. Cyndi and Robert had been attracted to each other during the previous expedition, but no opportunity had presented itself. Now they made up for lost time, Robert thanking his lucky stars that he had it right about Cyndi.

The American girl was a beauty, no doubt about it. On the last expedition, Robert hadn't taken much notice of her before their ordeal in the cave and finding the way out of the valley. He'd been desperate to crack onto the doctor. It had become manifest, though, even before they reached safety, that Rebecca had eyes only for JR. Odd pairing, that, but evidently it worked. The two were engaged, and Robert had to look elsewhere. Cyndi had shown an interest, and they'd stayed in touch. Neither had let on that they felt more than friendship, afraid to be embarrassed, especially when the ill-fated Carmen had practically thrown herself at Robert's feet on the first expedition.

Tucked inside the zipped-together sleeping bags now, Robert peeled Cyndi out of her sleeping clothes and skinned out of his own, pushing all of them out of the bedding before exploring her curves with his big hands. She was definitely a goer, this girl. He'd enjoy getting to know her in other ways, too. After all, Mum had been making noises about grandchildren. Maybe it was time to settle down and fall in love. Or fall in love and settle down. However that worked. Cyndi stilled his thoughts with a deep kiss, and then it was all soft moans and feeling his hands on her and hers on him. Oh, yes, she'd do.

In Angela's tent, Summers was preparing to take his leave. The pair had enjoyed a burgeoning friendship since the previous expedition. Ange had been loyal to Summers, even when JR took over the leadership of the escape plan, and Charles appreciated it more than he could say. He'd come face to face with the knowledge that he was a physical coward, humiliating beyond belief, and yet this quiet and gentle woman still looked up to him. A lifelong bachelor, Charles Summers had never had a serious relationship. Most women weren't interested in studious types, it seemed. They wanted derring-do and dashing looks, neither of which Charles could provide.

Angela was different. Not particularly a beauty, her face was nevertheless pleasant, a little round and serious, her fine gray eyes hidden behind wire-framed glasses and the whole topped with short-cropped curly brown hair. In his undergraduate days, an anthropology class had taught Charles that most couples were drawn together based on many factors, among them an equality in the level of beauty each possessed. You could see it if you people-watched for a while. You hardly ever saw a really beautiful woman with an ordinary-looking man, and if you did the explanation probably lay in other factors, like wealth. But in the masses of ordinary people, you'd find plain with plain, average with average, and beautiful with beautiful. That's why Charles was happy that Angela wasn't beautiful; because he wasn't, either.

It was true that Ange was ten years his junior. That didn't seem to matter to her, though. Her eyes shone when he talked about his love for archaeological discovery. She didn't seem to notice that his hairline was receding, or that his eyes were rather small or his nose rather large. She saw his intellect, and valued it, and that made Charles like her very much. He hadn't made any move to kiss her, yet, plenty of time for that. But he thought of her as his girlfriend and assumed she felt the same way about him.

Therefore, it was rather a surprise when she stopped him as he turned to leave.

"Charles, don't go yet, please."

"Why, Ange, what do you need?"

"To be quite frank with you, Charles, I need to know whether you like me at all."

Taken aback, Charles stuttered. "O-of course I d-do. What would make you ask me such a thing?"

"You've never tried to kiss me, Charles. Do you only like me as a friend? Because I'd very much like to kiss you."

Charles was thunderstruck. Feelings he'd long suppressed rose within him, doing embarrassing things to his clothing if the truth were known.

"I, I'd very much like to kiss you, too, Ange."

"Then why don't you come over here and do it?" she said, a shy smile playing around her lips.

And thus it was that Charles didn't return to his own tent that night after all, thinking that perhaps he'd better trade roommates with someone so that Ange could stay with him in his. A grin that he would have been horrified to see was pasted on his face. Who would have thought that an old confirmed bachelor like himself could acquit himself with such finesse in a single sleeping bag with a young woman?

Chapter 9 – The stele in the city

To make the most of their time, when the scientific crew went in through the ancient tunnel the next day, they took with them sleeping bags, food, clothing and paraphernalia for collecting scientific specimens, carrying out field tests and so on. Angela and her assistant were on deck for one of the important first steps, that of accurately mapping the valley. The other scientists were forced to wait for their entry until she was finished with the first few yards of her grid.

Robert and Cyndi would be missing from this foray for a couple of days while he accompanied her in climbing the peak on the outside to set up one of the communications links, an Iridium Pilot land station that would provide both data and voice communications for the site. Each of the little devices that resembled a three-legged stool would support broadband data speeds as well as up to three simultaneous voice calls. After much debate, the expedition was equipped with two of them. Because they were in a narrow canyon at the base camp, one would be set up at the rim of the caldera for communications within the valley, and the other in camp. Because it weighed nearly thirty pounds and because it was standard operating procedure that no one went out on the ice alone, especially in more hazardous conditions than were common in the canyon, Cyndi needed a companion for the task. Because he was an experienced climber and big enough that an extra thirty pounds in his gear wouldn't faze him, Robert was the choice.

By the end of the first week after the scientists arrived, much of the central valley had been mapped, though Summers and Angela had words regarding how to go about it despite their new-found romantic relationship. He wanted to proceed directly to the center square where the thickly-growing trees and vines had turned them back before, and penetrate the barrier immediately. He was convinced that whatever signs of humanity remained would be found inside. Angela agreed, but said that it would be more efficient to map as they went. Since he couldn't very well pick her up and bodily force her to proceed at speed to the center, Summers conceded with ill grace and barely contained his impatience for a couple of days while Angela went about it in her own way.

That consisted of bouncing a laser off the distant cliffs with the help of a transit theodolite, not an easy task when the distances were up to eight miles and there was a jungle in between. In some cases, it required JR's help to climb a tree and precisely calibrate the theodolite while it was precariously balanced on a high limb. However, with the aid of these modern technological marvels, she was able to enter the details on her electronic tablet, which began to display an accurate map within hours. Angela had sent her assistant and Cyndi's, borrowed for the purpose, to the opposite side of the valley by the quickest route to map the other side. When they met up and synched their programs, the central strip, including the mysterious square, would be complete. After that, she would accompany Summers inside the square for a more detailed map of the smaller area, while her assistant and JR completed the side strips of the map in the same manner.

The group was still stymied by the light in the valley, something they'd noted during their previous sojourn. Nothing in anyone's store of knowledge accounted for the even, bright white light that shone all the time. They knew that the sun was still barely above the horizon outside. By all rights, it should have been pitch dark in the valley. Yet, the white ceiling of mist emitted or reflected, they weren't sure which, the strange light. As soon as they saw it, el-Amin and Nyree Dasgupta fell into argument over whether the source was vegetable or biological in nature. Both were convinced it was one or the other of those choices, but they each assumed it was something to do with their own specialty. Summers was satisfied that their bickering would soon lead to the solution, since each wanted to be the first to explain one of the natural phenomena in this impossible place.

~~~

Finally, as they rose for the third time after sleeping in the valley, it was time to approach the square. Summers was more anxious than ever, as the schedule called for them to leave and report their data before going back in for another three days. Because work to enlarge it was now well underway in the large exit tunnel, someone would have to crawl through the more restricted passage with the squeeze area to halt the work so they could exit. Otherwise, they might be in the tunnel when blasts brought down debris on their heads, or even blew up right above or beside them. Angela, as the smallest, had volunteered. Summers thought it was fitting punishment for holding him up. Angela, unaware that he considered it any such thing, continued to glow in the newfound pleasure of their physical relationship.

Meanwhile, they had eight or so hours to work before their trek to the outside. The two had camped just outside the barrier in order to get an early start in the morning...if you could call it that when the light declared it noon all day every day. As soon as they began to push into the heavy growth, they realized that barrier wasn't just a word they'd been using to describe it. There was actually a plan to the way the vines had been planted and woven together between the tall, straight tree trunks. Summers couldn't believe it; now they would have to search all the way around the perimeter for the way in, or cut the vines, which would no doubt infuriate el-Amin.

Fortunately, they didn't have long to search. Though it slowed them down in getting around the perimeter, they elected to stay together rather than going in opposite directions. Since they had already walked around half of the square to the right last year, they decided this time to go left. That paid off when, in the middle of the next side, they found the entrance, a deceptive break in the barrier that led through a maze-like path until it let them out on the inside. Angela felt as if they'd fallen through the rabbit hole when they looked around. Before them, remarkably free of the ubiquitous vines, stood a miniature village, filled with domes and spires that were so fantastic in shape that both stood open-mouthed for an eternity before turning to each other in wonder.

When the shock had passed, Summers let out a whoop of triumph and grabbed Angela, twirling her above the ground as she laughed delightedly. When he put her down, she grabbed his hands and began jumping, until they were both cavorting like baby goats on a fine spring day.

"Do you know what this means, Ange, my dear? We'll be famous! I theorized this city was here, and I came to find it, just like Columbus setting out for the new world! We have proof, now, that the 10th Cyclers were right about other cycles before them! It's astounding!"

Angela rather thought Charles had made some huge assumptions, that the city wasn't 10th Cycle in origin among them. But she was very happy for him. Clearly he felt he had reason to make these statements, and indeed, it wasn't her specialty, so who was she to question? So, she smiled proudly, and agreed with everything he said.

The construction of the buildings before them was otherworldly, something out of a children's book of fairy tales, perhaps. Closer inspection revealed that they were built of what Summers would have called bricks, except for the fact that they were shaped more like small stones, about the size perhaps of cobblestones in a medieval street. The rounded shapes, captured in a matrix of cement, could be any shape the builder desired. Therefore, it seemed that whimsy had taken over, creating a playful, cartoon-like architectural style that made the two researchers laugh. For a while, they wandered between the shapes that were no taller than he, pointing out new ones to each other.

The spell was broken finally, when Summers stopped to photograph the buildings. That's when he noticed that they weren't tiny at all; that what they were seeing was the protruding roofs of a buried city. This expedition had just turned into an archeological dig. Now, far from being unhappy that they'd be leaving in a few hours, Summers couldn't wait to tell the others and give JR the go-ahead to call for the crews of experienced diggers that they'd put on standby. He was so gleeful that he practically skipped as he and Angela, now hand in hand, retraced their steps and hiked the four miles or so to the rendezvous point to meet the others.

Summers shuddered as Angela disappeared into the passage through which he, JR, Rebecca and three others had crawled to reach this valley last February. He had come a long way under Rebecca's care to overcome the claustrophobia that paralyzed him on the first trip. He hardly batted an eye when they'd come through the larger tunnel three days before. But that squeeze, an area where you had to creep like an inchworm through a space that made an MRI device look like a cathedral...he wasn't up for that again. Maybe never again. Fortunately, Angela didn't mind, and she would soon be back through the other entrance. While she was on her way, the others hiked around the mile or so to the larger cave opening.

While they waited for the all-clear from the tunnel crew, Summers couldn't keep the news to himself, even though he thought Angela would enjoy the celebration if he waited for her. He showed Rebecca and JR the pictures, and their expressions of surprise gave it away to the rest. Before he knew it, Summers was showing everyone. He felt remorse only when he saw Angela's face, unable to hide her disappointment that she hadn't shared in the fun. Still, she appeared to forgive him. He'd just have to be more careful in the future.

As soon as the crew was back at base camp, Cyndi copied the pictures from Summers' phone and his professional-quality camera to his workstation hard drive, and backed it up. Only then would she okay using the images in a slide show presentation that Summers prepared to report to the world. Naturally, the first to view it were the support team at home at the Rossler Foundation headquarters. Daniel and Sarah, Nicholas and Sinclair, were all on hand to have a first glimpse of the greatest discovery since the 10th Cycle Library itself.

Press releases were prepared in Boulder, but before they were released, Daniel called his good friend President Nigel Harper with the news, having emailed him a copy of the presentation.

"Congratulations, Daniel. This must be the culmination you've been looking for, after all the trouble last year," Harper said, after making the appropriate remarks about the interesting shapes in the photos.

"I can't say it doesn't help, Nigel, but I'm not sure it was worth all the lives we lost."

"Nonsense. Any great endeavor costs lives. Climbing Mt. Everest, making the world safe for democracy. Finding the information that a civilization from the vast reaches of the past left for our benefit."

Daniel knew Harper was trying to absolve him of the responsibility for lost lives, but it seemed to him that whenever he was involved in great discoveries, too many didn't make it through. Nevertheless, this was Summers' triumph, not his, and Summers deserved the accolades that would come his way because of it. To think, an impossibly old civilization, making their home within a hidden paradise in the middle of a frozen wasteland—humans living in Antarctica! It boggled the mind.

The full impact didn't reach the Rossler Foundation or Summers either, until a day or two after the press release. Then the world exploded with excitement. After four years, the news of older civilizations was passé, even when a new technology came out of the Library. A few days of excitement, and then another news story knocked that one out of the limelight and the attention-deficit masses forgot about it. This, however, was glamorous, exotic, the stuff of science fiction. The extraordinary beauty of the surrounding jungle coupled with the strange architecture kept this story front and center for days.

Things moved fast after they reported what they'd found. The first group of diggers, all of Middle Eastern origin, arrived in just under twenty-four hours, dispatched from a staging area in Indonesia where they had been gathered for the last few days in anticipation of being needed. Within two weeks, a second crew, this one all Spanish-speaking, would arrive from the opposite direction, staged at the tip of Chile where the last jumping-off point toward New Zealand was located. The crews had been chosen from among experienced archeological diggers, fifty from each area. Rather than mixing them and creating language barrier, diet and religious issues, they would all work among people whose culture was similar to their own, two weeks for each crew, with two weeks off while the other crew took over.

El-Amin would serve as translator for the scientists when the Arab-speaking crew was on shift, and Rebecca, whose Spanish was adequate for the task, would serve for the South American crew. JR knew a handful of Arabic phrases from his stint in Afghanistan, and hoped to expand his fluency while working among the first crew.

Work on the rail line stepped up, some of the camp construction crew signing on to stay once the last of the prefab buildings went up. They had built enough of them so that when all one hundred diggers were in camp, some coming and some going, everyone would have a decent bed. The first crew went in through the newly expanded tunnel on foot, no longer forced to crawl. While they worked their twelve on, twelve off shifts, the rails were being laid as quickly as possible so that the trip by rail car would eat up less of the work shift.

~~~

With fifty men working for him, Summers was confident they could make good progress on the excavation. While he directed that effort, the other scientists were also busy on theirs. El-Amin and Dasgupta had established a working relationship that led to their decision to determine the cause of the constant light, and were combing the cliff sides for a light-emitting plant, microbe, or mineral. Robert took the time to examine each bit of dirt or rock they brought to him, but nothing he knew of would emit light without also being radioactive, a hazard he devoutly hoped was not plentiful in the valley.

Robert's main goal was to confirm his theories about the valley. He wanted to first locate and test every thermal well, whether it be in the form of a hot spring, a fumarole or an open and oozing lava flow. He doubted the latter would be applicable, but the valley was large enough that no one had covered every foot of it yet. Fortunately, he now had an accurate map, on which he could mark the locations of any geothermal activity he found. To be methodical about it, he divided the valley into a grid covering a quarter mile square in each area. With the first square he explored situated at the cave opening where the rail line was nearing completion, he would fan out from there, moving from side to side as well as forward in the grid. After he and his assistant went over the first three squares or so, he hoped to break up their efforts so they could cover twice as much area at a time. He'd know as soon as he'd seen his assistant work.

Work was proceeding apace when Summers' attention was drawn to a commotion near the center of the square, perhaps one hundred yards from where he was working. JR was with him, consulting him about a detail in the rail line construction. When the shouting went up, both looked up, startled, but because of some of the building roofs in the way, they couldn't see what was going on. By unspoken mutual consent, they rose and began trotting toward the commotion, weaving in and around the spires between them and where the cries were coming from.

The city had been carefully divided into a grid, with work teams of five men each, consisting of a lead or foreman and four other diggers. Whenever one of the diggers made a discovery, he was to report it to his foreman, who would then evaluate whether it was necessary to bring it to the immediate attention of Summers, or wait until the work ended for the day. Due to the language barrier, it had been determined that only the most unusual or startling discovery would warrant an immediate notification. When JR and Summers arrived on the scene, they found the foreman of this crew and one of his workers shouting at each other in Arabic. JR could catch only a word or two here and there, as the men were speaking rapidly and with great passion. He stepped between them, making a placatory gesture, and said, in Arabic, "What's going on?"

Immediately, both men began rapidly entreating him to take their side of the argument, and his meager acquaintance with the language was again overcome. He pumped both hands, palm down, in the universal signal for 'quiet' and tried again. Addressing the foreman, JR repeated his question. This time he caught the gist of the argument. The other man had found something, but the word didn't mean anything to JR.

"Show me," he said to the worker. The man threw a triumphant look at his foreman and swaggered down the steps of the tiered excavation, leading JR with Summers following into the very center. Now that JR noticed, at the bottom was a partially-excavated monument of some kind, with the same or similar almost-familiar script that he and Cyndi had discovered in the cave so many months ago carved into it in bas-relief.

"Summers, look!" he exclaimed, but there was no need. Summers was already stumbling toward the monument with a look of awe on his face.

"A stele!" Summers breathed. "This could be the key to the city! Ask them if they can read it."

Neither Summers nor JR expected that the workers would be able to read the script, but it did bear a passing resemblance to Arabic as far as they could tell. JR posed the question, and the foreman who had followed the others down stepped up to peruse the carvings. His hand lightly touched the carved symbols, so lightly that even Summers could not fault his handling of the artifact. But, he was shaking his head. Disappointment flooded Summers, irrationally, since he'd had no expectation that the man could actually read it. It would take a couple of days, at least, to get Sinclair O'Reilly here, but it seemed that would be the fastest way to discover what the monument had to say.

JR suggested that they wait and ask el-Amin to take a look at it before calling for Sinclair's presence. After all, it would be most embarrassing if all the stele said was 'You are here.' Summers reluctantly agreed, and they went back to the spot where Summers had abandoned his walkie-talkie, a prosaic device that nevertheless was of great use inside the valley. El-Amin said that it would take him and Dasgupta about two hours to reach them from their current location, another delay that almost made Summers tear at his hair. When they arrived, el-Amin examined the stele with disdain.

"This is not Arabic," he announced.

Gathering all his patience, Summers explained that they were aware it wasn't Arabic, but that the 10th Cycle language had turned out to be very similar to ancient Sumerian, so he thought this script might be familiar enough to guess at. El-Amin made a sound of disgust and left, followed by Dasgupta, who had become his shadow. Nyree didn't care for the way el-Amin disrespected her, but she did admire his focus on his field of study, which mirrored her own focus. They had become partners of a sort, although their different cultural biases could never allow them to be friends.

JR now conceded that there was nothing to do but call in Sinclair. Meanwhile, Summers requested that the crew working in the grid that contained the stele focus on completely uncovering it, so that when Sinclair arrived, nothing would hinder his translation of the entire monument. They tried to take pictures of it to email to the foundation, but the uniform light in the valley made it difficult to pick out the carved symbols in a two-dimensional representation. There wasn't enough contrast. Nevertheless, they sent what they got to Sinclair, hoping he could get a head start.

Chapter 10 - That isn't Arabic, it's Aramaic!

The call from Daniel came shortly after dinner. Sinclair and Martha were relaxing with a second glass of wine each when the jarring notes of the phone made them both jump. Sinclair got up to answer the call.

"No, just relaxing, no worries," he said, with Martha listening curiously to try to pick up who was calling and what it was all about.

"How fast? How quickly can you book a flight?" Martha sat up straighter at that and tried to catch Sinclair's eye. When he glanced at her, she mouthed 'where are you going?' "Antarctica," he said aloud.

"I'm coming with you," she said.

"Daniel, hold on, I'm having two conversations at once. Let me deal with my bride."

To Martha, he said, "Dearest, you can't come to Antarctica. It's cold, and dangerous, and this is work."

Sinclair and Martha had married quietly, with only Daniel and Sarah as their witnesses and a few close friends, shortly after the drama of the previous March. Martha was in Boulder for the memorial service held for the members of the first expedition to Antarctica who were at the time missing and presumed dead. When the news came that six of them were alive, including young JR Rossler, the memorial service turned into a celebration except for one family, who didn't receive the same good news. In the aftermath, Sinclair escorted Martha home to Providence, RI, to pack up her things and move her to Boulder. The small wedding took place shortly thereafter, followed by a reception dinner with

Sarah's family, Nick and Bess Rossler, Raj and his wife and of course Daniel and Sarah.

However, plans for another expedition immediately went into high gear, and Sinclair had, with Martha's understanding, asked if they could delay their honeymoon until work settled down. She was looking forward to a couple of weeks in Cancun or somewhere now that the expedition was well under way. She hadn't counted on Sinclair joining it, despite his telling her that he had volunteered.

As Sinclair finished his conversation with Daniel, which included a description of why his presence was requested, Martha thought fast. Why shouldn't she go with him? She'd heard that the valley was a tropical paradise. She was as healthy as he, and he'd told her of his argument with Summers that people were now offering pleasure tours in Antarctica during its summer. When he hung up, her mind was made up. And when that happened, it wasn't easy to budge her. Martha gave the impression of being a sweet, white-haired motherly type, though she had no children of her own. But under the soft, attractive exterior was a will of steel.

Once he was off the phone, Martha began ticking off her answers on the fingers of one hand, speaking firmly.

"Four reasons why I am going with you my dear. First, if it's cold, you'll need me there to keep you warm. Second, if it's dangerous, I need to be there to protect you. Third, you know you can't relax from work if I'm not with you to take your mind off it, and fourth and most important, you owe me a honeymoon, you old coot. Either I'm going, or you're not going," she finished.

"Dearest," Sinclair began. She held up her hand, palm toward him.

"Talk to the hand. I meant what I said."

"But, they need me there. They've found a monument with script on it."

"Then go. But I'm going with you, and that's final." Not for the first time, Sinclair wondered what bus had hit him when he met the redoubtable Martha Simms. Long widowed, he wasn't prepared to fall in love again at his age, but fall he had, and hard. He could deny her nothing.

"Yes, dearest. Can you be ready to leave tomorrow?"

"We'd better get packing," she said, all sweetness now that she had her way.

~~~

In what seemed like both no time and forever, Sinclair found himself face to face with the stele, presumably left by the 9th Cycle society that had inhabited this valley. No time because he could barely remember the whirlwind of activity that culminated in the two-day trip to Antarctica. He and Martha had barely time to pack a few necessities before the limo deposited them at DIA, from whence they embarked on an ultra-long-haul flight direct to Australia with only a refueling stop in Hawaii. From Australia, they'd hopped to Christchurch, thence to McMurdo and finally helicoptered to what the expedition members were calling Purgatory Canyon. The first night they were there, Sinclair felt as if he had walked the entire way, as he and Martha paced the aisles of the aircraft to avoid getting blood clots from sitting so long. The sense of forever came from the deja vu. Staring at the stele, he was thrown back to the time when the final key had unlocked the 10th Cycle syllabary for the first time.

This script on the surface looked more like Arabic than the other. However, none of the work crew, who spoke a variety of dialects of the language but all read Modern Standard Arabic, had been able to read it, so he knew that the resemblance was superficial. Still, with the clues and techniques that cracking the

78

10th Cycle code had provided him, he thought he could read this one with only a little study and experimentation. Because of the simplicity of the final clue that had to do with the direction of the script, Sinclair first began by attempting to make sense of the individual elements as if they were written from left to right, opposite the direction that modern Arabic used.

When that didn't bring any enlightenment, he then tried reading in columns, from top to bottom and bottom to top. It was plain from the top-down direction that columns weren't applicable. This language had to be read right to left, left to right, or in alternating rows like the 10th Cycle language. Or, it wasn't Arabic at all, merely resembled it. This was going to require some computer manipulation. Sinclair missed Raj for that task, but he understood Cyndi had been studying with Raj for months. He would see what she could do with his request. He didn't consider that the language he was looking at might be in a code of any kind. That would have been very unusual on a public monument.

They began by taking photos of the script, using shade devices and more sophisticated lighting to bring out the stone-on-stone letters. They photographed both the stele and back in the cave, where the tunneling project had carefully preserved the script that was there. It was plain to Sinclair that the scripts weren't the same, though they bore enough superficial resemblance to fool a layperson. Cyndi, with some online help from Raj, did her best to divide the individual words by manipulating the photos, cutting each apparently separate word away from the whole photo and saving them in individual images. When she had done that, she called Sinclair into her office and showed him on the computer monitor what she had. Martha had come in, too, as she was interested in everything that was going on in this microcosm of scientific inquiry. She was deep in the memory of the time Sinclair had broken the 10th Cycle code and thinking fondly of her late husband Mark as she watched Sinclair's efforts absently. Both women jumped in alarm when Sinclair slapped himself on the forehead and shouted.

"I can't believe I didn't see that before! That isn't Arabic, it's Aramaic!" He rushed from the office, barely remembering to put on his outdoor gear, before dashing away from the building toward the cave.

Martha and Cyndi looked at each other in confusion before following, catching Sinclair as he ran down the tunnel where the rail line was almost complete.

"Honey! Wait, slow down," Martha called. "What in the world!"

"I have to see the original. Hurry." With that, he turned and began jogging again. Cyndi caught him easily, but Martha lagged behind as she was a little winded. By the time she reached the final destination, the stele, she was seriously annoyed with her new husband. However, the look on his face as he read the stele, his lips moving, washed away her pique.

"What is it, honey?" she ventured.

"It's a directional sign," he breathed. "This is so close to ancient Aramaic that I'm certain I'm getting it right. Look here, this should be 'library', and this has to be 'hospital'. He pointed at the words as he spoke the English translation. Then he turned to Martha with a comical look of consternation on his face.

"I'm slipping, dearest. I let the preconceived notion that this was like the 10th Cycle script in the cave blind me to the very obvious resemblance to Aramaic."

"It looks like Arabic to me," Martha said sturdily, as if to comfort him for the mistake.

"About the only resemblance is the diacritical marks, and they don't even mean the same thing. Don't try to comfort me, dearest. I screwed up."

"Well, it's all settled now. But what does it mean?"

Summers spoke behind her, startling all of them, who hadn't heard him arrive. "It means that we now know where the most important excavations should be, what to focus on first. Sinclair, did I hear you say 'library' and 'hospital'?"

"You did indeed."

Cyndi, watching from the sidelines, and Summers too, separately thought that it would be hard to say Sinclair had screwed up, when he turned and read the stele with ease right then. Both had of course heard the story about when he did the same thing with the 10th Cycle greeting. Watching it happen before their eyes was an awe-inspiring experience. Cyndi, especially, who wasn't accustomed to being in the midst of people who spoke multiple languages, much less those who could read several alphabets, was fascinated by the old man. She didn't care what they said back at home about how eccentric he was; in her eyes he was a genius.

"I'm going to redirect a couple of crews," said Summers. "Would you like to be on hand when they uncover the library? I think you can make the most of that. I'll get Rebecca and supervise the excavation of the hospital. I'll be in touch with Hakim, your foreman, when we find anything that requires translation. And you can have him let us know when your crew turns up anything. Fair enough?"

"More than, Charles. Thanks for inviting me down," Sinclair said, genuinely grateful to be in on this discovery. He would divide his time between fully translating the words on the stele and watching the progress of the excavation of the library. What a wonderful adventure! "Martha, my love, how are you enjoying our honeymoon?" he asked, his eyes sparkling.

"Very much, dear. I certainly couldn't ask for a more exotic or exciting one," she responded, lifting her eyebrow as she said 'exciting', so he'd know she wasn't only referring to his success in reading the script. Sinclair happened to be quite virile for a man just past his seventieth year, and she didn't care who knew it.

~~~

Once again, the expedition made world news as the report of the progress in determining exactly what the ruins contained was reported. By now, people who were interested in such things were watching for new discoveries daily, eager to be among the first to know of the wonders being uncovered. Daniel got a kick out of Sinclair's version of his early mistake, which of course Sinclair embellished, coming as he did from a long line of Irish storytellers. That didn't go into the press release, of course, though Harper heard it, mostly because Daniel understood that his friend loved a good joke—especially if it were on someone else.

The excavation efforts were stepped up, naturally.

~~~

Robert had confirmed that the soil on the valley floor was composed mainly of ash, with decomposing plant matter enriching it. The fact that it had nearly buried the buildings in the central square over the millennia spoke to ongoing volcanism of some sort, but he hadn't yet located a source for the ash. It certainly wasn't falling now. The latter fact made JR feel better, but Robert knew it meant nothing. However, what tests he'd been able to run led him to believe that the magmas beneath their feet were stable and unlikely to seek the surface. Nevertheless, he planted permanent seismograph stations throughout the valley at regular intervals. If the mountain started to rumble or the dome started to rise, immediate evacuation would be called for.

On the day after Sinclair's breakthrough in reading the

stele, he sauntered into the central square looking for a break from his work and a chat with the others to see what might be new and exciting. He found Robert outside the hospital site excavation, watching as the workers brushed away thousands of years of ash and dirt.

"Do you think they were more or less advanced than the 10th Cyclers?" Robert asked.

"From what we've seen, probably less. But remember, we have no context for when in their cycle they inhabited this valley. If we assume that our cycle is only six thousand years old, and add that to the twenty-six thousand years of the 10th Cycle, this city has to be at least thirty-five thousand years old. But it could be as much as twenty thousand years or so older than that. It boggles the mind, doesn't it?"

"Not when your field works in millions of years, instead of thousands," returned the geologist. "But it does make my head hurt, trying to think of the 10th Cycler's as so much more advanced than we are, despite living so many thousands of years in the past. Do you think we'll ever find the answers to where we are in our cycle? Or whether there were others in between, that didn't leave any trace?"

"Maybe, maybe not. But I do think we'll be able to get a feel for how far these guys had gotten before they abandoned the city. Do you think it was because the volcano erupted?"

"I doubt it. We'd be seeing the city covered by lava flow instead of ash if it had actually erupted. But ash is just as dangerous in great quantities. Were you aware that when Vesuvius killed Pompeii, it was clouds of ash that overcame most of the people? Everyone seems to know that Pompeii was destroyed by a volcano, but most are remarkably ignorant of how it went down."

"Actually, I've been there. Eerie," said Sinclair, with a shiver. Summers had noticed them and climbed up the terraces of the excavation to join them.

The three sat in companionable silence until a worker gave a short exclamation and held up what looked like a primitive surgical instrument.

"Ah," said Summers. "Now we're getting somewhere." He raised his walkie-talkie and called JR and Rebecca to join them at the hospital site. This should prove to be very interesting.

Not to be outdone, Sinclair returned to the library site and was reading several clay tablets that his crew had unearthed and brought to him with reverence. Martha sat beside him, incongruously knitting as he studied the ancient tablets. He wondered if the library were actually a museum of written artifacts as well, or if the people who'd lived here were no more advanced than the ancient Egyptians of the current cycle. The tablet he had in his hands seemed to be a poem or at least a series of couplets. He began to read, idly, and attempt to put it in a poetic meter as he translated.

Oh, children of [unknown],

Heed our sorrow.

We knew not the answer.

We could not help you.

Forgive us,

For we remain.

And you are all gone.

Gone from this place.

All of your blood.

Our children, too.

Those of our unions with you,

The ill-fated.

Woe is our companion.

We will not forget.

Martha spoke quietly beside him, tears in her eyes and her voice choked. "How sad! What do you think it means?"

"I don't know," he answered. "It sounds like an illness or something."

"It sounds like a tragic epidemic."

"Maybe. I wonder if there's more of the story somewhere here. Can you record it in my laptop t as I read? I can go through it faster that way."

"Of course! I've been wishing I could make myself useful."

Sinclair and Martha went through quite a few more clay tablets before it was time to break for the day. They didn't find any other references to the mystery that the poem presented, except for one tablet that referred to a plague that had reduced the population of the city greatly. The same word Sinclair couldn't translate that had appeared in the poem appeared in that tablet also. Perhaps the poem was about that plague. He set those two aside, intending to ask Summers' permission to carry them out so that he could do more research online to try to find the meaning of the word.

There was to be a celebration of sorts out in the canyon tonight, as the workers who'd been here for the past two weeks were to rotate out for their two-week break at home with their families, while the new set, all from South America, had presumably arrived on schedule and would start working tomorrow. JR had called for the cook to put on a feast to welcome the new workers, while sending the first crew off in style.

~~~

The change from the Middle Eastern workers to the South American crew wasn't as smooth as JR had hoped, but it couldn't be helped. He and Summers had combed both areas for a full one hundred qualified diggers, but they were competing with other projects and they couldn't very well mix two groups with such different cultural norms and languages. That there would be a language difference to adjust to each time the shift changed was a given. They hadn't thought much about the cultural differences, but they were there. The first group, most of them Muslim, insisted on observing daily prayer times. The scientists couldn't object. In addition to being heartless, it would have created quite a political stir.

Now, however, the South Americans wanted a siesta after lunch. As far as the work was concerned, it wouldn't have mattered. The light was uniform, day and night. However, it left the scientists to either work on without digger support and made for a long day by the time the diggers were through with their afternoon shift, or they would have to observe the tradition themselves. It came down to a challenge of sorts. Out of pride, several of the science group refused to succumb to the mid-day nap, while the others, who would have liked to take a siesta, instead pushed through their post-lunch grogginess and worked longer hours like the rest.

Thank goodness it was for only two weeks, JR thought. He would have been one of the nappers, given the choice. His work ethic had more to do with getting things done right in whatever time he had to do them, and less with watching a time clock. The irony was that clocks and watches wouldn't work inside the valley anyway. Robert said it had to do with the amount of iron in the layers below them, or maybe even within the surrounding cliffs. The magnetic qualities interfered with the electronics in watches, as well as with some of the scientific equipment. Other equipment was unaffected, but JR didn't bother with the explanation. Who cared why?

By the third day or so, work had begun to flow as normal, and the next two weeks went even faster than the first two. Summers and JR both thought that the transition wouldn't be as disrupting after the first time. Both crews now knew to whom they were assigned to direct their work, where they should be each day and what they were expected to do. Aside from the fact that progress in the excavation would have taken place when the first crew returned, they should be up to speed and ready to work.

Chapter 11 - What is it, Traci?"

Sinclair and Martha were to rotate out when the crew changed again, since no evidence had been found to indicate that any other language was represented in the ruins but the one similar to Aramaic that he'd first seen on the stele in the square. Translation of whatever was excavated in the library could wait until the artifacts or photos of them could be transported to his lab in Boulder.

Sinclair was thinking seriously of laying over for a couple of weeks in Hawaii on their way back to Boulder, to give Martha the kind of honeymoon she truly deserved. He had translated the entire first batch of tablets that the original work crew had brought him, and was waiting for Summers to decide whether they would be left here, where being kept in their long-time environment may preserve them better than removing them from it. The electronic records, of course, had already been transmitted back to the Foundation building in Boulder, and Sinclair had a copy on his laptop that he'd carried with him.

The mystery hinted at in the poem he found had been set aside when a tablet commemorating the arrival in the valley was unearthed. Piecing together the history as best he could with an incomplete record, it appeared that the armful of tablets were more or less contemporary with each other, and that they had all been inscribed about fifty years after the inhabitants had first found this paradise and built the city. A terrible plague of some sort had decimated their numbers, eventually running its course without the inhabitants ever learning how to cure it. How long the city had lasted thereafter hadn't yet been determined, nor what had caused the 9th Cyclers, if that's who they were, to abandon it.

It seemed like no time at all when JR came to their room and asked if they were ready to be picked up the following day. The crews were about to change, and this would be their last chance to catch a flight out until the next two-week rotation. They chatted for a while, and JR gave them letters to hand to his brother and sister-in-law in person; eyes-only reports about how the group was getting along. So far, so good, actually. Rebecca's team-building exercise seemed to have borne fruit.

Sinclair and Martha didn't know, because there hadn't been a head count of the incoming workers when the chopper lifted off, that they were leaving just as a problem developed for the expedition. They went on to Hawaii and had a more traditional honeymoon, before returning to chaos in Boulder two weeks later.

Meanwhile, at base camp, JR looked on in dismay as the group of workers sorted themselves into the same five-man crews as before. An entire crew was missing. He sent for el-Amin, his own Arabic not up to the job of getting a coherent explanation. When he had the story straight, he went to Summers.

"We're short five men," he explained. "Apparently they were too sick to get on the plane when it was time to leave, so the others left them behind. They say they will come along in a few days. Looks like we'll have to budget in an extra chopper run to get them here."

"Either that, or tell them to stay home and they can come the next time. We can stretch the workers we have here, without going to the expense of bringing just five in from McMurdo in the middle of a shift. Who's missing?"

JR turned the list of missing workers over to Summers and went to settle another issue on the railway construction, now

89

nearing completion. He would be glad to get rid of this contentious crew, who could not seem to get anything done without a fight. JR was tired of sorting them out and frequently told Rebecca he'd like to just wade in and knock their heads together. Too bad they hadn't been in on the team-building exercise.

By the end of the week, they had decided firmly that the missing five could just return for the next shift, as their presence wasn't worth the hassle of getting them to the valley for just the remaining week of the shift. Now that everyone was returning on the rail line at the end of each 'day', they were all well-rested from sleeping in a real bed in the dorm and eating the good food that the chef prepared each evening. On the Friday, the acknowledged weekend day for this crew, JR and Rebecca made a good-will tour of the dormitories to greet the workers and ask if they had any needs that weren't being met. They found many of the rooms empty, the occupants engaged in the day of prayer in the prayer room. In others, they found non-observant crew members relaxing, playing chess, and in some cases using Skype to communicate with their families.

El-Amin was one of the non-observant Muslims, though he frequently joked about his father being strict. JR and Rebecca were concerned when he didn't answer his door, but assumed that he could be sleeping, or engaging in some activity for which he wanted privacy. They went on to the next door and didn't think of it again until dinnertime, when he still didn't appear. A conversation with Nyree Dasgupta indicated that she expected Haraz to join her at dinner, which made their concern grow. After dinner, JR accompanied Rebecca to knock insistently on his door. His appearance when he opened the door shocked even the doctor.

"Haraz, what in the world? Are you ill?" she cried. The

90

Jordanian turned without a word and staggered to the nearest piece of furniture, where he sank gratefully to a sitting position.

"I'm sorry, I seem to have the flu," he said, a cough interrupting him.

"Why didn't you come to the infirmary?" Rebecca asked. "How long have you felt ill?"

"Only since waking this morning. I didn't think you'd be in the infirmary, since it is Friday." The misconception that she would take the same weekend day had delayed treating him by a full twelve hours or so, but Rebecca had JR help the man to his feet and guide him through the weather-proof connecting tubes to the building where the infirmary was located.

"I can't do much for you if this is viral," she said, "because when you have a viral infection, your own immune system is the best fighter. But let's start with an antiviral medication, since that's what it looks like. I have to warn you, they aren't always as effective as we'd like. Meanwhile, I'll take a throat swab and culture it for bacteria. I'd like you to stay in the infirmary where I can monitor you and I think we should hydrate you with an IV. Any objections?"

El-Amin shook his head weakly. "Thank you, Dr. Rebecca. I am most grateful for your care." It was a far cry from the arrogant and often fractious man who had wreaked such havoc in the team before they left Boulder. Rebecca almost mentioned to JR that she liked him sick better, but thought it wouldn't be very professional. Her night became even busier within the next few hours as, one by one, four of the scientific assistants were brought in by some of the diggers. Without el-Amin to translate, JR struggled to understand what the crew had to say, and eventually put it together that these four had been in prayer with the others until they became too sick to continue.

Rebecca was at a loss to explain why this handful of men were ill with the flu in a contained environment like their camp and the valley. Remembering that one entire five-man work crew was missing because of illness, she wondered if the illness had a long incubation period, long enough for these five to have been exposed by the missing men. What was puzzling, though, was how that could have happened when there was little contact between the botanist and the scientific assistants and the work crews. It had to have been at the prayer room, she thought, until she remembered that el-Amin wouldn't have been there. Still puzzling over the method of exposure, Rebecca was nevertheless too busy with five patients, whose conditions were deteriorating rapidly, to be able to follow her train of thought to a conclusion that made sense.

By the end of the second day, she had ruled out a bacterial cause for the illness and had made her patients as comfortable as possible. She took a moment to email Boulder and ask for help in locating the missing five crew members. If they could tell her the course of the illness and how long it took to recover, she might be in a better position to determine how to help the men in her infirmary. She also ordered a new supply of antiviral medications. They weren't as effective as antibiotics were on bacterial infections, but they were better than nothing. And if this thing turned out to be very contagious, she'd need more medicine for the next wave of it.

Already weary from checking on her patients around the clock, she returned to the infirmary to dispense water for those who would drink it, change IV bags and speak quietly to each man. El-Amin was the sickest, and she was quite worried about him. He had a fever that she couldn't break no matter what she did. All she could do was try to keep it below a level that might cause brain damage, and pray that an answer came through her email soon.

~~~

Daniel was up to his ass in alligators, as his North Carolina neighbors would have said. The aftermath of the demise of the OS had left world markets in chaos, and ongoing investigations had revealed a much larger than anticipated network of dummy corporations that unfortunately had ties with the Rossler Foundation. Sorting it out was still taking much of his time, months after the fall of the OS. At the same time, it was a PR nightmare and he was constantly having to put out media fires while at the same time the Foundation's expedition was a media darling. It was baffling and exhausting to juggle the hostile elements while entertaining the positive reporters. Despite having cut his teeth as a journalist, he had begun to hate the media with a passion. Now he knew why people wouldn't talk to him back in the day, though he'd actually had a pretty good track record compared to other journalists.

Rebecca's second email requesting information about the missing crew members reminded him that he'd delegated the inquiry to an assistant and hadn't heard back. He called her in.

"Traci, what have you heard about the sick workers? Rebecca's on my neck about the answer."

"I'm still trying to get some information, Daniel. None of them has responded. I just sent an inquiry to the agent who found them for us just this morning. You'll be the first to know, as soon as I do."

"No, I want you to email Rebecca first. Then you can tell me. I don't have time to be involved in this. Did you send her medicines yet?"

"Yes sir, three days ago."

93

Some hours into the following day, a very pale Traci knocked on Daniel's doorframe. He had a policy of keeping his door open unless he needed privacy for confidential matters. He looked up, took in her face and motioned her in.

"Sarah, I've got to go, something's wrong. I'll call you back as soon as I know what it is," he said, placing the receiver in its cradle when he'd heard his wife say she understood.

"What is it, Traci?" he questioned sharply. Daniel's temper was fraying with all the problems, and his employees knew it. They ignored his tone of voice most of the time, knowing it was the situations that caused his stress and that he didn't mean anything personal. This time, though, Traci shrunk, literally, before his eyes. Alarmed, he tried again, this time modulating his tone.

"Traci?"

"Daniel, they're, they're all dead. And their families are sick."

Daniel shot out of his chair, sending it crashing into the wall behind him. "What? Who? Those diggers?"

The frightened girl tried to stand her ground, but ended up stepping forward and sinking into a chair in front of his desk. "The agent finally got back to me. He had trouble because they were from three different countries, Egypt, Turkey and Saudi Arabia. They're all dead, and according to what I've been able to find out, about fifteen more are sick, mostly the families of our men. The local news media is beginning to take notice."

"Is anyone working on treatment?" Daniel had retrieved his chair and was seated on the edge of it, his elbows on his desk and head in his hands. "This is a disaster. Do they know what it is? Have you emailed Rebecca?"

It was all Traci could do to sort out the questions that flew at her. "I emailed Rebecca, yes. She got the medicine we sent. The agent I talked to referred me to a doctor in Saudi Arabia. He was too busy to talk to me, but someone in his office said that they don't know what it is, just that it seems to be highly contagious. I guess they've traced the movements of the first five, and have found a handful of crew members and passengers on their flights from Indonesia to their homes that are sick, along with some family members of the dead men. They're all in hospitals, receiving the best treatment available."

"Stay on top of this, Traci. And thanks for the update. I want a daily report."

"Sure, Daniel." Though she was still shaky, Traci left, while Daniel picked up the phone to call Sarah back.

Chapter 12 - We've got a situation on our hands

Rebecca could hear the phone ringing in her office, but she was too busy to answer it. Her patients were deteriorating, and nothing she did helped. Finally, the ringing stopped. When she'd changed all the linens and IVs and dispensed more useless medication, Rebecca went to see who had called. Her voicemail had a message from Daniel, and there was a new email from his assistant, Traci. Since the email was older, she read it before calling Daniel back.

'Five crew members deceased, their families sick. Highly contagious virus, doctors working on treatment. Do you need more medicine?'

Rebecca stared at the screen, unable to process what she was seeing. *All five* of the sick crew members had died? Her blood ran cold as she realized she had five more in her infirmary. Was there any chance that the illness was not the same? Highly unlikely, especially since the email went on to explain that there were fifteen more cases, all of which had been exposed to the illness by those first five. And yet, none of them had complained of symptoms before flying out to McMurdo. 'Highly contagious virus' was another phrase that staggered her. She had forty-five rotating crew in air-tight dormitories, not to mention the support crew, the scientists and the remaining assistants. She needed to get everyone equipped with face masks right now, if it wasn't already too late. And what about the South Americans that had rotated out last weekend? Were any of them sick?

Her mind reeling, Rebecca called Daniel back, hoping he had some answers for her.

"Daniel, it's Rebecca," she said, unnecessarily. He'd

recognized her voice even though the comms link was over satellite broadband.

"Becca, it's good to hear your voice. It looks like we've got a situation on our hands."

"Daniel, tell me that someone knows what this is. We've got an environment here that's almost designed perfectly for any disease to sweep through like a tornado."

"I know, Becca and we're on it. We're monitoring the situation in the home towns of those poor guys, and as soon as anyone gets a handle on it, we'll let you know what stops it. Are you doing okay? And JR?"

Rebecca heard the sub-text; is my brother sick? Daniel still hadn't gotten over almost losing JR after sending him here against his will last year. She was glad to reassure him that so far only the five she'd reported were sick. Maybe it wasn't even the same illness, she told him, though she knew better instinctively. She told him that Traci had offered another shipment of medicine, and that she hoped she wouldn't need it, but maybe he'd better send it as a precaution. The sooner an antiviral was utilized, the better the outcome. While she was thinking of it, she also asked for a supply of stronger antipyretics, since the high fever was of major concern. Even knowing that there was controversy in interfering with a fever, which is part of the immune response, she was concerned that the resulting brain damage was of more concern than the deleterious effect on the immune system.

After talking to Daniel, she located JR, who'd just come in with the work crew and scientists on the train from the valley. It was hard to believe it had been an entire week since el-Amin and the others had first presented with their symptoms. In another week, the shifts were supposed to rotate again, but she had grave reservations about bringing anyone else into the environment.

She'd need to express her misgivings to JR and Summers, who would have the authority to stop it if they thought her theory had merit. Meanwhile, she wanted JR to send to McMurdo for a large supply of face masks to try to mitigate the spread of this thing to the rest of the people in the expedition. With luck, they could contain it, and hopefully save these patients from the fate of their co-workers. Even as she planned for all eventualities, however, Rebecca understood that this was far more serious than a seasonal flu. It had all the markings of a killer.

JR and Summers didn't agree with the idea of putting everyone in face masks. Summers went so far as to say it was like locking the barn door after the horse had bolted. JR thought that if no one else was sick by now, they weren't going to be. Rebecca had her doubts, but at least she had enough face masks for herself and for JR when he went in to help her with some things that were proving difficult. The four devout Muslims were reluctant for her to touch them, even as sick as they were. JR had volunteered to give them their sponge baths and get them dressed in fresh gowns when their original ones became soiled.

Rebecca could manage the rest, now that IVs had been started. Even getting the sheets changed could be accomplished by rolling the men out of the way while gripping the edge of the soiled sheet, slipping a clean one underneath, and repeating the process from the other side to pull the clean sheet across. So far, she'd been able to allow the men to get up and roll their IV stands into the bathroom with them. If any became too weak to do that, she was going to need a full-time male assistant to help with bedpans. *Stop borrowing trouble,* she admonished herself. These men had been sick for a week, and they weren't dead yet. With luck, they'd caught the illness in time to save them, or it was a different virus. She checked on them one more time before scrubbing thoroughly and joining JR and Summers in the mess hall. They still hadn't talked about whether to bring in the South

American team.

Rebecca, Summers and JR discussed the options over dinner. They did have two dormitories, one of which was empty except during the shift changes. JR suggested thoroughly cleaning, disinfecting and sterilizing the one that stood empty now, to minimize any transfer of the virus, and bringing the South American crew in as scheduled. They would take pains to keep the crews separate, and to clean anything that the crew on deck now would have touched. After thinking about it for a minute, Rebecca conceded that viruses weren't usually transferred by touching inanimate objects anyway, as they typically needed a host vector to survive.

She began to believe that she was blowing everything out of proportion because she was so tired, having had little sleep for the past seven days. When JR insisted that Rebecca leave her patients for a few hours in the care of some of the support crew who would volunteer, she agreed. She needed some rest, or she'd end up in an infirmary bed herself, and then what would happen? Not for the first time in that week, Rebecca kicked herself for not requesting an assistant for herself. This pace was punishing, and if there were a second wave of illness, she would have no reserves to meet the demands it presented.

Thank goodness most viruses became weaker as they went from host to host. Unless they mutated; that could be a problem. But, *sufficient unto the day is the evil thereof*, she told herself again. They didn't even know what virus they were dealing with, so she shouldn't be assuming the worst-case scenario yet. It was good to snuggle into JR's arms, letting herself be the one to be comforted and pampered for a change. For the sake of her patients, she had to appear strong and confident, even for the Muslims who had no respect for her, as a woman. But now and then, she needed to be vulnerable, to be protected, and to have her man's strong arms around her and his love cradling her. Thinking these thoughts, she drifted off to sleep.

~~~

Despite the drama taking place on Rebecca's watch, work continued on the excavations and in all the other scientific inquiries, except for el-Amin's projects. Nyree asked after him, and Rebecca told her he was ill but under treatment. She maintained the same confidentiality about her patients as she would have in her office at home, in fact, telling anyone who inquired about any of them that they were resting comfortably.

Not only was she concerned about confidentiality, but she didn't want a panic on her hands if the bulk of the expedition members knew how gravely ill her patients actually were. Even Robert and Cyndi didn't know, and presumably Summers hadn't shared it with Angela, either. It was tough for her to maintain an air of normalcy when she encountered them, but she did a good job. No one except Rebecca, JR and Summers knew how sick the five were, and that was the way Rebecca wanted it.

Unfortunately, that state of affairs didn't last long. With her first five patients deteriorating in spite of everything she could think to do for them, now a steady stream of diggers with sore throats and sniffles were seeking some relief. She lost count within the first hour on Monday morning. She sent each one to his dorm with some antiviral and antipyretic medication and the admonishment to drink plenty of liquids and stay in bed unless they became worse. She didn't want any of them getting on the train to infect others, or trying to work when they would need all their strength to fight this thing off. The proof of that was her five initial patients, all of whom were struggling to breathe now.

In desperation, Rebecca sent for JR and told him she was going to need help. She demonstrated on el-Amin how to insert a cannula and start an oxygen feed, knowing all the while that if more became this ill, there wouldn't be enough equipment to treat all of them. This was the tenth day since the first five had become ill, and there had been no word yet from Boulder on what might help. As soon as she took care of the people who were now presenting with the initial symptoms, she planned to call Boulder and if they still couldn't help, she'd demand some phone numbers of doctors who'd treated the sick ones on the outside and talk to them herself.

As soon as JR arrived, he asked what was going on. More than half of the work crew hadn't reported for the inbound train to the valley, and Summers was up in arms about the excavation schedule. After all, they had a limited time here, and he couldn't afford to have his crew unavailable. Checking her records, Rebecca had to report to JR that in addition to the five gravely ill patients in the infirmary, she had sent eighteen to their dorms with the same initial symptoms. She assumed the course of the illness would follow more or less the same pattern, so she had about a week to get in more supplies of antiviral and antipyretic medicines, oxygen and equipment to deliver the latter. She told JR she was going to need more help in caring for them as well. She needed reinforcements, as soon as they could get there.

That evening when the work crew arrived back in the canyon on the train, ten more reported to the infirmary. At dinner, the mess hall was virtually empty, with one scientist, four assistants and twenty eight diggers confined to either the infirmary or their dorm rooms. Summers counted heads, aghast.

"We're down to one-third of my crew," he lamented. "JR, you need to bring the South Americans in early."

"Wait," said Rebecca, at the same time as JR said, "I doubt..."

"Go ahead," he deferred.

"I don't think we should bring anyone else into this situation until we understand what we're facing," she said. "Except some medical personnel. I need to talk to Daniel tomorrow and find out what's happening with identifying the virus those first five had. I was too busy today to do it."

"Maybe I can do that for you tomorrow," said JR. To Summers, he said that he doubted they could get the scattered South American crew back much earlier than their scheduled arrival on the next Sunday anyway. Rebecca was frowning.

"JR, thanks, but I'll probably have to talk to the doctors myself."

"Oh. Sure, babe," he said. "But I'll stand by to help however and wherever I can." He sent her a reassuring smile and squeezed her hand before returning to his meal.

As it turned out, the call was deferred until late in the afternoon on Tuesday, because all seventeen of the remaining crew members reported in sick during the night and the next morning. By the time an exhausted Rebecca had made them as comfortable as possible, with JR's help in the case of the thirty percent or so who wouldn't allow her to touch them, she was near tears.

"JR, what *is* this? How could this have happened?"

"I don't know, sweetheart, but one thing's certain; you need help or you're going to get sick yourself. In fact, I'm surprised you haven't already."

"Doctors tend to develop immunities, they're exposed to so much. But I'm worried about you, and anyone else who's been riding the rail cars with the ones who are sick. If everyone else here gets sick, I definitely won't be able to keep up."

"Babe, you can't keep up now. Let's go call Daniel."

Daniel, who'd delegated staying on top of the situation to his assistant Traci, was shocked to learn that the entire digger crew had been infected, but promised to get information to them by noon the next day and then to send whatever medicine and medical personnel needed as soon as they'd assessed the need. Daniel was deeply concerned that more workers were ill, but no one seemed to be getting better. While he wasn't given to alarmist thinking, he had a nagging feeling of unease that he couldn't explain or shake off.

The moment he hung up, he intercommed Traci to come to his office immediately.

"Traci, I thought I asked for a daily report on the situation with those dead crew members' family."

"Yes, sir, but I can't get one. They're stonewalling me because of patient confidentiality." Daniel had run into that once before, having been denied access to Sarah while they were engaged until her family okayed it. But he hadn't thought about it in conjunction with their current situation. He kicked himself for delegating it to Traci, who, while competent at most things, seldom took initiative. He would have to handle it himself.

"Get me the doctor's names and numbers, Traci. I'm sorry, I shouldn't have put this on you. I'll take care of it." And he would, though he didn't have a clue how. Fifteen minutes later he was checking time zones to determine whether he'd be able to reach the doctors at their respective hospitals. Unfortunately, it was late in the evening in all three countries, though he did try Egypt because it was an hour behind the other two. As he'd expected, no answer. Rather than leave a message, Daniel left the office with the intention of returning by eleven that night to begin trying to reach the doctors in Saudi Arabia and Turkey. He'd stay until he had some answers.

Sarah was surprised to see him home so early, but happy when he came into the nursery where she was playing with Nick, to kiss her and the baby.

"What are you doing home?" she asked. "Did you fire yourself?"

"I've considered it a couple of times," he answered, only half-joking. "I have to go back and may be there all night. Thought I'd come see you and Nick and maybe get a couple hours of sleep."

"What's going on, honey?"

"Rebecca's got a damned epidemic on her hands and she needs answers that I should have had for her last week. I need to get on top of it, and I probably should go down there myself."

"To Antarctica? Daniel, what can you possibly do, besides get sick yourself? I don't want you to go."

In answer, Daniel took Sarah into his arms, the baby squealing in delight between them. "Sweetheart, this happened on my watch. The buck stops here, you know?"

"But, it isn't like you failed in some way to keep them from getting sick."

"I know. But most of the sick ones are those diggers from the Middle East. You know how volatile those people can be. I need to make a showing at least, demonstrate that we're doing all we can. I'll take a couple of doctors and more supplies with me, probably. Anyway, nothing's been decided. I need to talk to those doctors that treated the first five men that got sick."

"The ones who died? Would they have done much about identifying the illness?"

"Yeah, I think so. According to Traci, all of their families were sick by the time they died. I need to find out how they took care of them."

"I see. Do you want some dinner before you take your nap?"

"No, sweetheart, I'm not very hungry. Maybe I'll take a sandwich with me when I go back. Just let me get a few hours' sleep."

Because of the time difference between the countries where the five had died and Boulder, it was just past midnight when Daniel persuaded a Saudi doctor that he didn't want personal details, only an update on the families because the first five were his employees. He intended to arrange a settlement for the deaths, even though it wasn't strictly speaking a company responsibility, he said.

In return for those assurances, the doctor told him that two patients had died, at about the same time as their families, totaling six people, had presented with the same symptoms. Those six, he said, were desperately ill, no treatment had halted the course of the disease, and he didn't expect them to survive. He had no information on other family members, and several dozen people who weren't related were now also ill. Shaken, Daniel took information on the precise count and promised to get back to the doctor if the others had found answers. It was the first that the doctor had known that more than his original two were involved.

Daniel's next call was to Turkey. This time he told the doctor that he had information that might be vital to the well-being of some of his patients. Again, he didn't necessarily need names, only general answers. Again, two of the patients who had died the previous week were under his care. Daniel wanted to know how many family members were now ill. Surprised, the doctor asked how he'd known. Daniel gave him the information from Saudi Arabia, including the doctor's name, and again took count of the ill. Seven family members and several dozen unrelated people. He repeated the process in Egypt within the hour. When he was done, he sat back in dismay.

To his knowledge, his five employees had died within two weeks of their scheduled return to Antarctica. Fifteen family members were also in danger of dying, as well as around seventy-five others in various stages of infection. No one had put it together on an international level as yet, but he was certain that it would hit the newsstands as soon as the three doctors began talking among themselves. There was nothing he could do until morning, but he stayed at the office for several more hours, writing notes to himself about what his next moves should be.

Chapter 13 – It means jihad

By the time Daniel reached Rebecca on Wednesday at around noon, she had established a routine. They had moved the patients that wouldn't allow her to care for them into dorm rooms on one side of the dormitory hall, with the remainder on the other. She had moved everything needed to care for those patients into the dormitory's day room, where JR and the cook's assistant, who had first aid certification, were holding down the fort. Rebecca herself was constantly monitoring her five original patients, none of whom was responsive enough now to object to her touch. Every hour or so, she crossed to the dorm to check with JR on the progress, or lack thereof, in helping the others fight off this seemingly innocuous, but deadly, bug. None of these patients had been told that it was likely to get worse before it got better.

When she wasn't actively caring for patients, Rebecca was either trying to rest for a few moments or praying for a miracle in the form of the arrival of something that would save the dying ones. Because it was apparent they were dying. They were all but comatose, unable to breathe without mechanical assistance from the oxygen pumps, and their fevers were approaching critical despite IV antipyretics and cool sponge baths. She needed an ice bath for them, but ironically, there wasn't one available. Transporting them outside where there was plenty of ice would have been fatal.

Daniel's call caught her in the deserted mess hall, cajoling a bowl of soup from the surly cook. She took the call there, with her back turned to the kitchen so she couldn't be overheard.

"Daniel, tell me you have good news."

107

"It would be a lie, Rebecca, I'm sorry." Her head dropped, knowing that he'd just given her patients a death sentence, without his knowledge.

"What have you learned?"

"You know the ones who didn't return to camp all died, right?"

"Yeah."

"And that their families were sick. I've confirmed that the sick family members are critically ill and not expected to survive."

"Oh, my God!"

"It's worse. Rebecca, I have confirmed that at least seventy-five others are sick in just these three countries. I tried to call the CDC this morning, but it needs to come from a doctor or Medical Examiner. We need to know if it slipped through anywhere else. How are your patients?"

"Dying, Daniel. Barring a miracle, I don't think they'll last through tomorrow. That means that as far as we know, this thing has a one-hundred percent death rate."

"I'm coming down. I'll bring another doctor, some PAs, and a virologist with me. We have to get to the bottom of this."

"Daniel, it's too dangerous. Send the medical personnel, but you stay home with Sarah and little Nick. She'd never forgive me if you caught this. I'd never forgive myself."

"I have to come, Rebecca. The buck stops here, remember? I can't give the impression that I'm leading from behind. I know I can't help much, but I have to be there to show that we're doing all we can. And out of respect for the dead. Expect us in forty-eight hours at the latest. I'm going to try to get there sooner. What else do you need?"

"More face masks, oxygen, as much antiviral and

antipyretic medications as you can get. I'll call the CDC and ask them to include you in the reporting loop. Daniel, please stay home."

"I'll see you soon, Rebecca."

Rebecca drank her soup rather than have the cook madder at her than he already was, then hurried back to her patients. El-Amin's eyes were open. "Haraz, can you hear me?" He turned his eyes to look at her without recognition. "We're getting more medicine, Haraz, and other doctors. Hang on if you can. Don't give up." Rebecca was fighting her emotions, not wanting him to see that she was afraid for his life. Slowly, his eyes closed, but his lips were moving, though little sound came out. She put her ear closer to try to hear what he was saying.

"Light," he whispered. "I...know..." When nothing more was added, Rebecca straightened and looked at him. He was gone. Choking back a sob, she hurried to each of the others. All were still breathing. She returned to El-Amin's bedside and gently drew the sheet over him. She would take care of everything else later, but right now she needed to report to JR, and more than anything, she needed his strong arms around her.

"JR," she called as she entered the dayroom. As she saw the other person in the room, she stopped abruptly. JR was getting up to come to her, so she stood her ground, and then when he got to her, drew him out of the room into the hall and threw herself into his arms.

"Babe, what is it?" he asked, fearing he already knew.

"Haraz el-Amin is gone," she said. Her mournful tone told him that she meant the man was dead. He squeezed her more tightly.

"You did the best you could, Becca."

"I know that! But it wasn't enough. And I've heard from Daniel." The rest of the story tumbled through her lips as fast as she could speak while trying to maintain her composure. "JR, please, please be careful about washing your hands, and wear a facemask anytime you tend to these men. I couldn't bear it if..."

"Nothing's going to happen to me, Becca. I'd be sick already if it was. But I'll be careful, and I'll make sure everyone else is, too. So, Daniel will be here in a couple of days with more doctors and medicine?"

"Yes. And I need to go and call the CDC to get them working on it, too."

"Okay. Do me a favor and fill in Summers, okay? He's probably sulking in his room because he doesn't have any diggers."

With no patience to spare for Summers' misplaced priorities, Rebecca snorted. "He's lucky he doesn't have this. So far, everyone that came down with it as long as fourteen days ago is dead, or dying."

With that sobering pronouncement, she went back to the admin building where Summers' office and her infirmary were located. She reported to Summers, who was in his office rather than his sleeping quarters, and then went back to her patients. The soft susurrus of the oxygen machines was comforting, until she realized that she had failed to turn off el-Amin's. Quickly, she went to each of her other patients, suppressing a scream as she found them dead, one by one. When she had ascertained that there was no mistake, she sank into a chair by el-Amin's bedside, shaken to her core. All five, gone within an hour of each other. What was this monstrous disease? And who among her close friends and colleagues would come down with it next? She clenched her hands into fists. No one, if she could help it. Not one more death to this evil would she tolerate. Turning to el-Amin, she uncovered his face, touched it briefly and poured out her sorrow that she hadn't been a good enough doctor to save him. Then she covered him again.

Somberly, she turned off the rest of the oxygen and performed those duties attendant upon death that she could manage on her own. Rebecca was too weary to remember the other preparations that would need to be carried out to honor these men's religious beliefs, but she would consult with JR. Somehow, they would have to get it done. With no more need to constantly monitor her infirmary patients, she turned out the light and walked dispiritedly to the dormitory building.

JR spotted Rebecca from the day room as she passed on her rounds. She looked worse than ever, alarming him. Fearing she'd become ill, he jumped to his feet and went after her, finding her in the first patient's room, adjusting the IV drip. The man was unconscious, JR noticed, as he put his hand on Rebecca's shoulder.

"Becca, honey, you look done in."

In answer, she turned into him, buried her face in his chest and, in almost a wail, told him the other four critical patients were dead. Grateful that the man in the room was unconscious, JR pulled Rebecca out into the hall.

"Honey," he started.

"I couldn't save them! Don't you understand, JR? What good is a doctor who can't save her patients?" She collapsed in tears as JR held her, sending love her way with every fiber of his being. She had worked herself beyond her breaking point—no one could have done more. He told her so, and reminded her that some things just couldn't be helped. Gradually, she gained control, and in a calmer voice told him she was too knackered to know what to do next.

JR reminded her that it would fall to the Foundation home office to notify next of kin, so they would need to make the call to the Foundation. He offered to do it, so she could lie down and rest.

111

With Daniel possibly en route, he wasn't sure who would handle it. The main thing that concerned him right now was whether it would be appropriate to store the bodies within the cave, which was quite a bit colder than a morgue would have been, though less so than the open canyon. He spoke aloud his certainty that the families would want the remains of their loved ones returned to them for proper burial.

"JR, that's appalling! Decomposition will have started by that time, and the bodies are infected with an unknown disease. We should do the right thing for them here."

"Let the Foundation determine what to do, Becca. You shouldn't have to worry about anything besides making sure the rest of these guys don't suffer the same fate."

"JR, at dinner time, I want you and—what's his name?"

"Jeff. You mean the cook's assistant? Jeff."

"I want you and Jeff to make sure everyone is comfortable, and then come to the mess hall. We have to decide what to do about the crew that's due here on Sunday, and I'm going to need your help with Summers."

"Okay, babe, I'll be there."

It was then that she realized she hadn't yet reported to the CDC. She'd get the night shift, but at least someone would be there to take her report. After that, it was a matter of waiting for someone to help her.

Her call to the CDC was as satisfactory as a call to a government agency ever is, that is, not. After being shuffled from department to department, she threatened to call the State Department instead, since all of her patients were foreign citizens. That got her transferred to someone who was prepared to deal with her without passing the buck again.

"Five dead, forty-five ill, you say?"

"Yes, but these aren't the only ones dead. Before we knew there was a problem, we rotated the entire crew home for two weeks, and five didn't return. We now know they have died and fifteen members of their families are ill, along with seventy-five or more others who were unrelated. My employer, Daniel Rossler, attempted to report this a couple of days ago and was told a doctor must do it. I'm a doctor."

"Two days ago! What took you so long?"

Rebecca took a deep breath to avoid losing her temper. "I have fifty sick patients in Antarctica, and no help. I've been a little busy."

"Sorry, Dr. Mendenhall. Do you have information regarding who treated those who didn't return to your base?"

"No, but my office does. Call the Rossler Foundation tomorrow morning and someone should be able to help you."

"We'll do that. Do you require anything of us in the way of direct help?"

"Not at this time. I understand that my employer is on his way with more medicine, equipment and medical personnel. We'll keep you apprised of the situation as it develops. Please let me know immediately if you learn of anything that can halt this."

"Yes, ma'am." After giving instructions on phoning her or emailing her, Rebecca rang off and looked at her watch. Time to beard Dr. Summers in his den. Or rather, at the mess table.

~~~

"It's out of the question, Charles. We can't expose that many more people to this, whatever it is. You'll have to halt the excavation until we have it under control," Rebecca was firm, even though she was too weary to have this conversation.

"But, that may be too late! It's already November. We simply don't have the luxury of waiting this out." Charles glared at Rebecca, while Robert, Cyndi, Angela, Nyree and JR looked on. The few remaining occupants of the mess hall were at a table by themselves several feet away, and the conversation at this table was taking place in intense whispers to avoid spreading panic.

"I'm afraid she's right, Charles. We can reevaluate when my brother and the medical people get here," said JR. "Until then, we can't risk another entire crew. I'm going to wave them off for at least a week."

"This will go in my report as your decision against my recommendation," warned Charles.

"That's fine," said JR. "I'm used to being a scapegoat." Protests broke out around the table, but JR kept his eyes steadily on Charles, until the other faltered.

"It's settled then. Robert, what help do you need with your experiments, any?"

"Nothing Cyndi can't help with, if she's willing. I'm sorry to hear about Hakim, though. He was a good assistant. Can't believe he's gone."

Nyree and Angela nodded, having lost their assistants, too. It wasn't that they couldn't conduct their studies without them, but that there wouldn't be time for as much. Just then, Rebecca remembered el-Amin's last words and asked Nyree about them.

"Nyree, Haraz said a few words just before he died, maybe you know what he was talking about. He said, 'Light. I know.'"

At that, Nyree burst into tears and ran from the room, with the occupants of the other table staring after her in as much bewilderment as those at her own.

"I'm sorry," Rebecca started. JR covered her hand on the table with his.

"Don't be. I was afraid of that. I think they became closer than either would have admitted. Just give her some time."

The table fell silent, each lost in his or her own thoughts, until Angela broke it. "Can we please talk about something other than illness and death?"

Everyone looked at her as if to encourage her to go on. "Robert, I can see you've marked a bunch of features on my map. What do all the symbols mean?" she asked.

"Oh, ah. You know we, er, I have been mapping the geothermal features as I find them." He sketched symbols on his napkin as he continued. "This means hot springs, and the number beside it is the temperature as I measured it when I found the spring. This one means fumarole. And this one, will mean lava ooze if I find any. So far I haven't."

JR let out a whoosh of breath, then grinned at the others. "I just don't like the idea of lava flows in the valley," he explained.

"I've told you and told you, you drongo, this thing isn't likely to erupt any time soon."

"Still," said JR.

"What's a fumarole?" Rebecca asked, to change the subject.

"You might know it as a steam vent," Robert answered.

"Are any of the hot springs something we could bathe in?" Summers asked, not to be outdone.

"Most are too small or too hot, or both," Robert said. "But if I find one that would make a good spa, I'll let you know. Charles, the first fumarole I found was thanks to your hospital excavation."

"Oh? I don't remember."

"One of your crew came and got me one day and led me to it. It was near the center; I can't believe you wouldn't have noticed

115

it."

"Do you mean that little crack, with the moisture and algae around it?"

"That's the one. Didn't you notice steam coming out of it?"

"Not really. Is it a lot? Does it come out all the time?" asked Charles, more curious now than he wanted to admit.

"Well, not a lot, no. But pretty much constant. That's why the edges are always moist."

"Interesting," Charles said, without elaborating.

As they got up to go their separate ways, JR spoke quietly for Charles's ears only. A moment later, Charles approached Rebecca. "Er, I'm sorry I was so insistent," he said. "I'm very eager to get this all done before anyone else has a crack at it, you know. But I shouldn't have taken it out on you, you're doing the best you can."

Surprised, Rebecca answered with equal grace. "It's all right, Charles. I know how much this means to you. I hope we have an answer soon so you can get back to work."

That night as she prepared for bed, Rebecca realized that no new cases of the flu-like symptoms had presented since Wednesday morning, almost forty-eight hours. That prompted her to take a mental catalog of everyone who'd been at mess that evening, everyone who wasn't sick, in other words, to make sure that no one was hidden in sleeping quarters, unable to call for help and not being missed. No, everyone was accounted for. No new cases, thank God. To be sure, she wrote down all the names of the symptomless occupants of the valley. Something struck her as she wrote them and checked them off. Not one Middle Eastern name was among them. Telling JR she'd be right back, she hurried to her office and checked her charts. She was right. Everyone who was sick was one of the work crew of Middle Eastern origin, though some had been recruited from the UK and the US. Not one who wasn't sick was Middle Eastern. But, since when did a virus target someone based on their ethnic group? That wasn't right, was it?

Rebecca returned to JR in their room. "I think I've discovered something, JR, but I don't know what it means."

"What is it?"

"This disease, this flu—it may only make Middle Eastern people sick. No one else here with us has gotten sick. What could that mean?" She looked up at his face. JR had turned white and was staring at her in shock.

"It means jihad," he said.

Chapter 14 - What kind of hell had they dug up down there?

In Boulder, Sarah was sitting in for Daniel, little Nick crawling around the office contentedly. Sally was due any minute to pick him up for a play date with the horses, but he was a good baby and Sarah knew she could handle things until her aunt arrived. Nick had found a plastic model of the Great Pyramid and was trying to eat it when Sarah took the call from the CDC.

"Sarah Rossler."

"Ah, Mrs. Rossler. I understand we are to communicate with you in your husband's absence?" Sarah repressed a sigh. She and Daniel were actually co-Directors of the Foundation, and her proper title was Dr. Rossler, but her nine-month absence while on maternity and new mom leave had undermined her visibility, it seemed.

"Yes, you may speak to me. Do you have anything to report on the nature of this disease?" she asked.

"No, ma'am, that hasn't been determined. I'm calling to update you on the death toll and the number infected, now that we have an accurate count. We were able to trace the movements of the index cases. It's rather unusual to have five, but as nearly as we can determine, all five died within a few hours of each other. We had to assume that they all encountered the virus at essentially the same time. In addition to their families, they infected several people on their commercial flights home, including two flight attendants."

"Just a moment. How do you know it's a virus?"

"All doctors treating the patients initially tried antibiotics, except in several cases where they examined blood samples for the microbe responsible. The antibiotics were ineffective. The microbe resembles the classic form of a coronavirus. RNA hasn't yet been determined, so we can't say for certain what virus we're dealing with, but there's no question it's a virus."

"Thank you for explaining that. I'll take the numbers now." Sarah expected more than one hundred, since that had been known last week. She almost dropped her pen, though, when the answer came back. "One hundred and thirty-five known dead, four hundred and five infected."

"God in Heaven," she breathed.

"Indeed, ma'am. If it continues at this rate, thousands could die."

"Thank you for the update. And so far you know of nothing that will stop it."

"No ma'am. We can't develop a vaccine before we have a complete DNA sequence, but keep in mind that having the sequence doesn't guarantee we can develop a cure. We're working on it."

"My husband should be arriving at our expedition site in Antarctica any time now. He's taken a virologist and an assistant with him, as well as a couple of medical doctors. I'll make sure they report anything they learn to you."

"Thank you, ma'am. And, may I say, we all appreciate your husband putting this together before it got any bigger than it did. He's probably saved thousands by his quick actions."

Sarah appreciated the praise on Daniel's behalf. She was fully aware that the report would have been even sooner if the red tape surrounding it hadn't caused a two-day delay. She thought about that for a few minutes and tried to do projections in her head, but her distraction proved too much to handle for that kind of math. She picked up the phone and called Raj.

At her request, Raj came to her office immediately, bringing his special, high-powered laptop with him. When he heard her request, he told her that all that power wasn't required, and asked to use her desktop instead, so they could save the work to her hard drive. After a few false starts as Sarah faltered in describing what she wanted, he had the skeleton of a spreadsheet, ready to put the initial numbers in for a projection tool that would show them the extent of it.

Using the data Sarah received from the CDC, he quickly established a timeline and extended it horizontally to show future weeks. He added a cell for a what-if number and asked Sarah if she knew how many people on average each patient infected. Using three, because fifteen had become ill after being exposed to the first five, Raj plugged in the variable, which instantly populated the weekly projections. As he read across the row, he asked Sarah what week they were in.

"I think the fifth or so since the first few got sick."

"Four hundred and five," he read. "Twelve hundred and fifteen, three thousand, six-hundred and forty-five," he read aloud, growing paler with each word. He stopped speaking.

"What is it?" Sarah said, from her place on the floor, changing Nick's diaper.

"You'd better come and look."

Sarah finished her task, pulled up Nick's tiny britches and got up, walking over to where Raj had his finger pointed at her screen on Week Eight.

"Over ten thousand!" she exclaimed, running her eyes to the end of Raj's projection, Week Seventeen. "Oh my God!" The last number she saw in the row was two-hundred and fifteen million.

"Sarah, I may be wrong, but I think that's more than the Spanish flu killed, back in 1918."

"God help us," she said.

When Sally arrived, she found a white-faced Sarah staring at a screen full of numbers in shock.

"Sarah, what...?"

"Tens of thousands, maybe millions. God help us, Sally!" Sarah said, unable to say anything but repeat the desperate prayer of a few moments ago.

Sally struggled to understand what Sarah's words could mean, while Sarah herself got up and picked up her baby. She held him tightly enough to make him squirm as she buried her face in his neck and sobbed.

When she was able to regain her composure, Sarah told Sally what she'd learned. She couldn't keep news of this kind to herself, and she had enough foresight to know that when it hit the media, there would be trouble.

She handed Nick over to Sally, along with his diaper bag. "I'll come for him when I can. Sally, it could be a few hours. I have to make plans. Raj, can you stay here for a few?"

"I understand, honey. I'll take good care of him, won't I, Nicky?" The baby laughed and patted Sally's cheek, then made a grab for her glasses. "Wanta go see the horses?" Sally dropped a kiss on Sarah's cheek as she left, carrying a squirming Nick and his gear. "Call Luke, honey," she said. "You don't need to go through this alone."

When Daniel and Sarah had formed the Rossler Foundation, they'd received some flak from people who didn't think there should be so much nepotism in the staff. Sarah's uncle, Luke, was the head of security, Daniel's grandfather, Nicholas, the head of research. Now Sarah was happier than ever that she had older and more experienced people, people she trusted with her life, to help her hold things together while Daniel was gone.

She sent for both of them, told them the situation and then turned her computer's monitor to show them the numbers. At first, they couldn't believe it. Raj took them through the rather simple formulas, one cell at a time, until they saw that there was no mistake.

Luke saw the security risk. Yes, he was appalled at the numbers, which indicated over one thousand people sick by next week, nearly four thousand by the following week. If it went longer than that, it reached five figures: nearly eleven thousand more people sick by the third week from now. But, he could do nothing about the sick and dying. His concern was the safety and security of the people within this building, which would probably be under siege when it got out that the first patients were all expedition members. What kind of hell had they dug up down there? And how was he going to maintain security when it became known?

Nicholas, Daniel's octogenarian grandfather, sat down heavily, stunned and grieving for the potential loss of life. When he realized that two of his grandsons were in harm's way, it bowed him in worry. Sarah wished she hadn't sent for him, hadn't selfishly leaned on the old man in her panic. But, as she watched, Nicholas visibly pulled himself together and straightened his massive frame. "We'll beat this, sweetie. Daniel's smart as a whip, and JR's tough as nails. They'll figure it out. We just need to keep the home fires burning."

Sarah didn't think she'd ever heard so many clichés in one sentence before, but she appreciated his effort, and she was relieved that he'd rallied. "Of course, Grandpa," she said. "We'll do that." When the men had left her office, Luke saying he needed to make some plans for a security response, Sarah sighed deeply and called Antarctica. She desperately wanted to hear Daniel's voice, but she wasn't sure he was there yet, and this couldn't wait. She would talk to Rebecca instead.

~~~

That morning, Rebecca had confirmed that there were still no new cases, but she was discouraged to find that the course of the illness wasn't varying. All forty-five of her remaining patients were worse, and if Daniel didn't arrive today, some would die sooner because she didn't have enough oxygen equipment to keep them all breathing. When JR brought her a phone to take the call from Sarah, she sounded harried.

"Hi, Sarah. I don't have much time."

"I know, hon. Listen, I've got CDC info for you, and then I'd like to speak to Daniel if he's there."

"He's not here yet, Sarah. I'm praying he gets here any minute. Some of these people don't have long without the medicine and equipment he's bringing."

"I'm so sorry."

"I know. What's the news from CDC?" Rebecca knew there was probably an email with the same figures in it on her computer, but she hadn't had time to check within the past few hours. Sarah gave her not only the figures, but her calculations.

"Okay, here's the way it's breaking down. There were five index cases," she started, using the medical jargon as if she hadn't just heard it an hour ago. "It looks like they're infecting an average of three each, and so far the death rate is one hundred percent. We're looking at over ten thousand affected within the next three weeks." Sarah's voice had been steady until that moment. Then it hit her that her husband was heading into ground zero. "Are, are you and the others, JR, all…"

"I know what you're trying to ask, and I think we'll be okay. Sarah, don't say anything yet, but we haven't had any new cases

123

since the workers got sick. Either they all got exposed somewhere else, where we haven't been, or we're somehow immune. As soon as Daniel gets here with the virologist, I'm going to test everyone here and see if we can find some answers."

"Be safe, Becca. And take care of my Daniel, will you?"

"You know it, Sarah. After all, he'll be my brother-in-law soon." Rebecca wasn't as certain as she'd led Sarah to believe, but she hoped it had given the other woman some comfort. She didn't know what she'd do if she and JR were separated while one faced an unknown danger. It was bad enough facing it together.

Eventually, Rebecca found time to check her email and found the spreadsheet with the projection extended out for several months. As she read the figures for weeks sixteen, seventeen and eighteen, she paled and felt lightheaded. This was a nightmare, and unless she and the CDC could find a solution soon, it appeared that the entire population of earth could be wiped out within months. Surely the 100% death toll couldn't continue. She'd never heard of something so uniformly deadly to those who contracted it. And why weren't she and the other scientists sick? They'd worked closely with the patients who were now dying. What could it mean?

With the figures in hand and expecting reinforcements any time now, Rebecca decided to jot down summary notes of everything she could think of that might help the virologist. She started with the five who never returned from their first rotation home. Where in the valley had they been working? Did they contract the illness here, or on the plane? Rebecca suspected here, because el-Amin and the other four who died next hadn't been on any plane with the first five. Then five more, followed within three days by the other forty. Where had they all been that she, JR and everyone else hadn't?

Summers would know. Unfortunately, he was in the valley, stubbornly excavating at the hospital site on his own. In fact, besides the support crew and JR, she was alone here. All of the scientific personnel were in the valley. It dawned on her that whatever the sick ones had encountered, it had to be in the valley. Frantic, she flew through the passageway to reach JR.

"JR!" she cried breathlessly. "We have to get those guys out of the valley!"

"What? Babe, calm down. What are you saying?"

"I've been figuring out where they got sick, and it has to be in the valley! We've got to get the scientists out."

"Wait a minute, Babe. You and I, Summers, Robert, Cyndi and Angela were all in that valley for thirty-six hours or so last February. We didn't get sick."

"I know, but it couldn't have been anywhere else. The workers were the first, and then they went home and everyone's thinking maybe the plane, but Haraz and the others weren't on the plane. It has to be here, or in the valley."

"Slow down, Becca. Okay, let's say it's in the valley. The scientists been in there almost every day since everyone got sick. If it was going to make them sick, it would have already. Besides, didn't you tell me that a virus can't live without a host? We haven't found anything alive in there but the vegetation. Can you get a virus from a tree? Or a vine?"

Rebecca began to catch her breath, and calm down with JR's rational breakdown of the facts. "You're right. Maybe those first five got something on the plane here that took a long time to incubate. But, JR? I'd feel better if we shut down the projects until we've figured out where it came from. Can you do that for me?"

JR expected that it might be an uphill battle, but to help Rebecca cope with the overwhelming strain she'd been under, he agreed to propose it. If he could get the support of one or two of the others, it could work. Once she showed him the spreadsheet, a shaken JR was willing to do anything to stop the inexorable progress of the disease.

"JR, we need to make sure everyone coming in puts on a face mask, too. I know you think we're okay, but the others haven't been exposed yet, and I don't want them to be."

"Okay, Babe, I'll meet them in the airlock and make sure they put masks on as soon as they take their cold-weather masks off."

He made good on his promise an hour later, when Daniel arrived with the promised virologist, Ben Epstein, and two young doctors, Beth Proctor and Janet Smith. Rebecca's heart sunk when she saw that there wasn't a male to help with patient care. She should have mentioned it, but she wouldn't now. She showed the virologist to the infirmary, where he would set up a lab, and then helped supervise the unloading of the medical supplies so the new doctors and JR could start the worst of the patients on oxygen. She left JR to brief Daniel on what they'd learned since he left Boulder.

Chapter 15 - It's about to hit the fan

Rebecca was busy bringing the virologist up to speed on patient history and her attempt at investigation, apologizing that she hadn't had time to make more progress on studying the disease itself.

"I can't imagine that you could have done any better, Dr. Mendenhall. You had quite a crisis on your hands."

"Have, and please call me Rebecca. I've got forty-five critically ill patients, including five who would have died by morning without the oxygen you and Daniel brought. I'd call that a crisis."

"Just so. I'm Ben, by the way. I didn't mean to downplay what you're still up against. But from what you've told me, there's little likelihood that you'll have any more cases, once these die."

For a moment, all Rebecca could do was stare at Ben, her mouth open in readiness to say something that her brain wouldn't supply. "I would hope that we can save them," she said, finally.

"You can hope. But the truth is, by your own records, they have less than a week to live. I can't imagine that we'll make enough progress in that time to avoid the outcome. Unless this larger sample proves that we don't have a one-hundred percent death rate after all."

"Try," she snapped, knowing she was taking out on an innocent bystander her days of worry, grief and exhaustion. She wouldn't give up on these men, not if it took the last reserves she had. She didn't appreciate the newcomer's seemingly casual acceptance that all of them would die.

"I will, but please, Rebecca, you have to be realistic."

"Fine. What can I do to help you?"

"Walk me through what you know of the progression of this disease. Then I'll need a blood sample of an infected patient, so we can take a look at the bug."

"All right. The first five became ill after they left on a two-week rotation leave. We don't know exactly when their symptoms started. When the rest of them, all of these who are sick right now, came back, those five stayed behind, and we were told that they were too sick to come. Five more, who all died last Wednesday, never left the area. On the Monday before that, the others started reporting in sick, and by Tuesday morning the entire work crew was ill, all with the same symptoms. We know from the five who died here that antibiotics don't help, and we've verified that it's a virus, though I don't think we know what type yet."

"What was the experience of the five who died here?"

"They presented with sore throat, mild respiratory distress and slight fever, which is why we thought bacterial infection at first. It was only when we sent for information about the five who didn't come back that we put it together. By that time, those five were dead, and the ones here were worsening daily. Nothing that we did helped, and they all died within hours of each other, approximately two weeks after they became ill."

"Was there any contact between the sick ones and the work crew that's ill now?"

"No, not really. They were in the infirmary, and the work crew didn't start coming in there until a week later. They'd been here a week on their second rotation."

"So, you haven't determined the vector?"

"No. One thing I have noticed, though. There haven't been any other cases since these forty-five became ill. So everyone that's left here is either immune for some reason, or we haven't been where they've been."

"Is there any way to determine where they've been?"

"Yes, here in Antarctica there is. Where they were before, I don't know if we can track that down. Probably not in a hurry. But, Dr. Summers will know where the work crew was assigned. I believe he had the workers divided into five-man crews for their excavations."

"Five. And you say the first to die were five, and then five more."

"Yes, but the second five weren't work crew. One scientist, our botanist, and four assistants working with several different scientists, including Dr. El-Amin. They wouldn't have all been in exactly the same area of the valley."

"All right, that's an anomaly for now. How about the rest. Was it all of them at the same time?"

"All within a twenty-four hour period."

"Were these men ever together in a group?"

"Yes, on the train into and out of the valley each day, in their dormitory and at mess. Some of them in the prayer room. Fifteen or twenty are devout."

"So, we don't even know if they all were exposed to one source, or if some infected others."

"No, not yet."

"All right, let's go talk to Dr. Summers."

"I'm sorry, but he's in the valley. All of the scientists and the remaining assistant are there. They'll be back shortly, at the end of the day."

"Then let's get that blood sample."

Rebecca led the way to the dormitory. Epstein decided that he'd like samples from several patients. The likelihood that there was more than one virus working was remote, but the virologist was thorough. With five samples from five randomly-selected patients, he returned to the infirmary that was now his lab to examine them. It was fortunate under the circumstances of the remote location that 10th Cycle technology had replaced bulky electron microscopes with a much more portable device; otherwise something as small as a virus would not have been visible. In short order, Epstein had prepared each sample for cultivation. When the virus had time to multiply, it would form plaques, or colonies. Rebecca watched, fascinated, as he worked. She had a basic understanding of the process.

Once the virus had been introduced to a medium of growth, colonies called plaques would grow until they were eventually visible to the naked eye. From the plaques, various methods would allow for DNA and RNA sequencing, which would identify the specific virus at fault. The 10th Cycle microscope would allow Epstein to get a look at an individual virus cell, which in itself could narrow down the family of virus they were dealing with. However, none of this could be done instantly. They had to be patient while the plaques grew. Rebecca was acutely aware of the passage of time, knowing that her patients were worsening hour by hour. Epstein was methodical and would not be hurried. Better to do it right the first time, he insisted, than hurry and perhaps get the wrong result.

When all the samples were prepared, Rebecca suggested they move along to the dining room and wait for the others to arrive. Epstein continued to question her, asking insightful questions and exploring more questions that the answers brought up. He'd just begun to understand that the illness was confined to one ethnic group when JR and Daniel arrived, with Summers and the science crew on their heels. As soon as the group had served their plates from the cafeteria line, Epstein addressed Summers.

"I understand you would have records of the locations in the valley where each of the men have worked, is that correct?"

"Yes," Summers confirmed. "But, do you think this illness originated in the valley? How can that be? I've been there every day since we arrived; well before the work crews got here, and I'm not sick. Same goes for everyone here," he said, waving his fork around in a circle to indicate the entire table.

"It's just one avenue of investigation," Epstein answered. "However, I understand that Dr. Mendenhall has applied some logic to the puzzle, and does have some concerns about the valley. Frankly, I'd like to see this miraculous valley."

JR interrupted. "Daniel and I have been talking, and we think it's prudent to shut down work in the valley until we know more."

He in turn was interrupted as Summers, Angela, Robert and even Nyree protested. "We don't have time. We've only got about three months before we have to button it up for the winter," Summers said for all of them.

"I'm sorry, but the decision is final. Anyone else going into the valley will have to wear protective gear, and it will only be in support of Dr. Epstein's investigation."

Before more discussion could ensue, Daniel also had something to say. "We have other issues to deal with right now. I've been in touch with our agent in Indonesia, who has notified the families of the crew we still have ill here. They are demanding that we send them home."

Rebecca gasped, clapping her hand to her mouth. Daniel looked at her, waiting for her to voice her thoughts. "That's a death sentence! They're too ill to be moved, and they're contagious! It would be irresponsible."

"I'm afraid we have no choice. We can't hold them here against their wills, and they've all asked to be repatriated. McMurdo will be sending both helicopters first thing in the morning. I'll send one of the doctors with each helicopter, but that's all we can do."

"What about our investigation?" Rebecca asked.

Epstein answered her. "I have all I need from these men. I agree we should send them home, where they can get better care and be with their families. It's the humane thing to do, especially if they're all fated to die."

With that, Rebecca realized she had no chance, and indeed no right, to keep the patients in camp. Of course, they should be with their families.

Hours later, lying in JR's arms with the expectation of her first uninterrupted night of sleep since the whole ordeal had begun, Rebecca had a feeling that she was missing something, something important. But, her exhaustion overtook her before she could examine her mind for it. Her uninterrupted sleep was not to be, however. At about three in the morning, a knock on the door woke JR, who went quietly to see what the matter was. He returned in a moment and gently woke Rebecca.

"I'm so sorry, sweetheart, but it's one of the doctors Daniel brought with him. She has bad news."

~~~

Rebecca, Daniel and JR were on hand to see off the two helicopters the next morning. Rebecca's exhaustion was almost unbearable, and JR intended to insist she go back to bed to get the sleep she'd missed last night. The three a.m. wake-up call had been to go to the bedside of one of the ill workers, who had taken a dramatic turn for the worse. Despite all she and the other doctor could do, they were unable to lower the man's fever, and his kidneys had shut down. By the time his fever reached the fatal 108F mark, he'd died in convulsions. Four others were in similar circumstances before he died, and the three doctors had lost all five men by eight the next morning. Now Rebecca and the two

Rossler brothers watched as the helicopters took off, each bearing an exhausted doctor and twenty gravely ill men toward McMurdo and a chartered flight to Indonesia.

From Indonesia, the men would be sent to the four corners of the globe, almost. Nineteen were from Middle Eastern countries ranging from Iran to Egypt and points in between. Four were residents of the United Kingdom, and seven were to be sent to the US. The other ten lived in various European countries.

Daniel had learned the previous day while communicating with Sarah that the death toll outside of Antarctica had risen to over four hundred, with more than twelve hundred now suspected of having the same virus, exactly as Raj's spreadsheet predicted. Some countries in the Middle East, where most of the cases were located, had put quarantine procedures into place. News media was reporting it as a new strain of MERS, or Middle Eastern Respiratory Syndrome, a flu-like viral illness that was first reported in Saudi Arabia in 2012. Unlike the current outbreak, MERS wasn't particularly quick to spread, although the first four hundred or so cases, most of which were confined to the Arabian peninsula, produced about a thirty percent death rate. The obvious fear was that the virus, of the type coronavirus, had mutated to a more deadly form.

When the helicopters were out of sight, JR insisted on taking Rebecca to their room for some much-needed sleep, despite her protests that she needed to be available to help Ben Epstein, or to be on hand in case anyone else became ill. JR assured her that he would come and get her if she were needed in either capacity. When she caught sight of herself in the mirror as she brushed her teeth, Rebecca was grateful for his interference. She was a mess, her hair in need of a shampoo and black bags under her eyes, her skin sallow and loose, as if she had lost ten pounds. Hopefully, eight full hours of sleep and then a shower would go a long way toward restoring her to normal. JR stayed to be sure she actually got in bed after her shower, and tucked her in with such care that Rebecca's last thought before succumbing to the exhaustion was of how tender he was. She went to sleep smiling.

JR joined Daniel in the dayroom of the science staff dormitory, a smaller building than either of the crew buildings. There he found Summers in near-mutiny, with almost all of the others supporting him. Robert, with Cyndi standing sturdily beside him, was urging that they just be patient for another day or two.

"JR, I'm glad you're here," Summers said, though why he thought JR would switch sides was a mystery to JR. "Tell your brother we have to make more progress here. We can't just stop. It would be like, like those men dying in vain."

JR was fed up with Summers' intractability. It seemed the man did nothing but whine and worry about his precious excavations, caring not at all for the loss of life that was taking place even now. "Charles, you need to stand down. There's more at stake here right now than making progress on your excavations. That goes for all of you. The virologist says the virus plaques will be ready to read later today. Let's at least wait until we know if it's this coronavirus they're talking about, and whether or how we can protect ourselves. I'll ask Epstein to give us a layperson's understanding of it at dinner. Fair enough?"

With Summers still grumbling, the party broke up, most to go to their labs to attempt to make use of the time. Daniel and JR went to JR's office.

"JR, I want to let you know I'm proud of the way you've held it together here," Daniel said.

"Wish I hadn't had to send for my big bro to rescue me," JR said. Daniel could tell there was more truth to the statement than JR's light tone meant to convey.

"Hey, that's what big brothers are for. Seriously, JR, you guys weren't equipped to handle any of this. You wouldn't believe how fast things are going downhill outside. Quarantines are in effect in half a dozen Middle Eastern countries, and this thing is spreading like wildfire in spite of it. I guess it's very contagious. It's funny—I've relied on Raj for data for years, and for the first time ever, I hope he's wrong. I don't want to think about even 5% of that happening, much less half of it."

"I know, dude. Rebecca has a theory about that. If she's right, it's lucky for us, unless the damn thing mutates. But it could get dicey out there."

"What do you mean?" Daniel asked.

"All the cases that broke out here were Middle Eastern. And none of the non-Middle Eastern people have been sick. It's too early to say for sure yet, but it looks like this thing's targeting by ethnic group."

"Oh, shit," said Daniel.

"Yep. It's about to hit the fan," JR returned. But, even he didn't realize how quickly his prophetic statement would prove true.

Chapter 16 – "What's coming is bad"

As soon as Sarah had spoken to Rebecca, she took action to stay on top of media reporting about the epidemic. The Rossler Foundation had a PR firm on retainer for those times when a particularly interesting discovery in the 10th Cycle library required media coverage. What she wanted now was daily reports on the news stories, particularly from the Middle East, and an appropriate response for when someone put it together with the Rossler Foundation expedition. She was savvy enough to realize that Daniel wasn't the only competent journalist in the world. It was *when*, not *if*. There were likely to be unpleasant repercussions, and a proactive approach would be best.

By the next day, she had dozens of electronic news clippings in her email, and it was clear that a few sources had begun to realize the scattered cases in different countries were related. Once they tracked down how they were related, it would be too late for the Foundation to be proactive; they'd be in full defensive mode. She wanted Daniel's agreement, though, before she made the announcement that the first cases had come from their expedition. To her, it seemed best to accept accountability, but it wasn't her decision alone. However, because the expedition was on McMurdo Station time for convenience, and McMurdo was on New Zealand Standard Time, it was currently four a.m. on Wednesday morning for Daniel, eighteen hours ahead of Sarah's time zone. She would let him sleep a while longer.

In anticipation of his agreement, she called the Foundation's agent at the PR firm instead.

"Mary, thanks for getting that info to me so quickly. I may need you to update it more often within a few days. But, what I'm calling about is something else. Do I have your word that what I'm about to tell you is strictly confidential?"

"Of course, Sarah. Haven't we worked together long enough for you to trust us?"

"Yes, Mary, I do. However, this is explosive, and it's going to take all your skill and that of your firm to keep us on the positive side of the news."

"Are you kidding? Everyone loves the Rossler Foundation. I love the Rossler Foundation. You guys helped cut my electric bill by ninety percent."

"Thanks, Mary. Maybe that's an approach to take. Weigh the good against the bad. But what's coming is bad."

"You're scaring me. Has there been a leak? Terrorists have something dangerous?"

"No, Mary. It's that disease. I'm pretty sure the first cases were diggers from our expedition. We've unleashed a disease on the world somehow, and there doesn't seem to be any way to stop it. I've run the numbers. Within the next few weeks, unless we find the answers, we're going to have a pandemic that rivals the Spanish flu back in the nineteen hundreds."

"Holy shit, that's why you wanted those stories?"

"Yes. I need you and your firm to start working on how we tell the truth and give the facts without getting our building burned down. And Mary, not a word to anyone that might leak it to the press. It's vital we keep it contained, at least until we have a response."

"I understand. I think I'll start updating that feed every twelve hours, just for my own information. I'll send it along to you, too."

"Thanks, Mary."

"Sarah, wait! Is there any danger here? All those stories seem to have come out of the Middle East."

"That's because the diggers were Middle Eastern, I think. I don't know, but it's conceivable they exposed everyone on their flights. Why they didn't all get sick when our employees' families did is one of the mysteries. With global air travel, I don't know that you can contain something this contagious, though."

"Thanks for reassuring me," Mary said, the dry delivery coming across even on the phone.

"Sorry, Mary. I'm trying to think several weeks ahead. It isn't helping me that Daniel's down there, he and his brother and some very good friends of ours, and that's ground zero. I'm going out of my mind with worry."

"Oh, Sarah, I'm so sorry! Well, count on us to do everything we can on our end. Keep me posted on Daniel, will you?"

"Sure."

Sarah's next call was to Nicholas. After a restless night, she had woken up in the morning with the idea that the answer might lie in the 10th Cycle Library, in the medical sections. She wanted him to put all possible resources on it, including having Raj do an electronic search for any and all references to respiratory illnesses. She found that he was ahead of her, having done that as soon as he left her office the previous day.

"Grandpa, what would we do without you?" she asked, pleased that the old man's brain was as sharp as ever.

"You'd figure it out...eventually," he said. She could visualize the mischievous twinkle in his eyes, and felt a rush of love for Daniel's grandfather, her favorite in the family after Daniel, though she would never admit that to the others.

"You'll let me know if you find anything?"

"Of course."

"Thanks, Grandpa. You're the best."

Sarah thought she heard something like, 'and don't you forget it' as she returned the receiver to its cradle. Next, she called Sinclair, just back from his two-week Hawaiian honeymoon with Martha.

"Good morning, Sinclair! Welcome back," she said.

"Good to be back, though that's the most fun I've had in years," he answered.

"Do you mean the honeymoon part or the Antarctica part?" Sarah teased.

"Ha, you won't catch me! It was all honeymoon," he said.

"I'm so happy for you and Martha," Sarah said. Then, because she knew of no way to ease into it, she asked if they were both feeling well.

"Never better. Why do you ask?"

"Have you seen the news yet, about that flu that's sweeping the Middle East?"

"Caught something about it on TV last night. Why?" he asked again.

"I don't know how to tell you this, but we think it came out of that valley."

"What!? How so?"

"I don't know if anyone is sure of how yet, but the first five cases that we know of were diggers from our expedition. The next few were their families, but now it's breaking out in earnest, and it's bad, Sinclair."

"Bad, in what way?" he said.

"Every way. The latter stages are very painful, and so far there's a one-hundred percent death rate. No treatment anyone

139

has tried has been successful. And, it's very contagious. I'll send you Raj's spreadsheet and you can see for yourself. This is going to be a disaster of epic proportions if we can't help find a cure."

Sinclair's heart constricted as he thought of his Martha afflicted with such an illness. In typical human fashion, he didn't expect to be a victim himself, but the thought of his loved one vulnerable sent him into frantic worry. "I'd better check on Martha," he said.

"Do that, but first, let me tell you the other reason for my call. I need you to divert translators from their current assignments when Raj locates medical references to the symptoms. Maybe the 10th Cyclers knew of this, and maybe they had a cure. It's worth looking, but we need to find it fast."

"What are the symptoms?"

"Similar to flu. A sore throat, cough, followed by respiratory distress, high fever and death."

"Good Lord! How will anyone know it's this and not just seasonal flu?"

"That's the other reason we need to hurry. It's flu season. If people think they're just sick with ordinary seasonal flu, they might not get treatment in time—if that's even possible."

"Right. I'll get on it, right after I call Martha."

"Thanks, Sinclair. Let me know of any progress you make."

"Wait, Sarah, I may know something, though I'm not sure it's of use. While I was down there, I translated a poem that seemed to refer to an epidemic, and we later found a tablet that referred to a terrible illness that killed many."

"Did it talk of a cure?"

"Not that I recall. But, I'll see if I can put my hands on the records again and make sure we get everything we need from it. If nothing else, maybe we can sync it with the 10th Cycle records and find something."

"Good idea, Sinclair, and thanks."

Sarah decided to have an early lunch and then it would be a reasonable time to call Daniel. She had done everything she could think of to help from this end, but she suspected that unless the 10th Cyclers had an answer, it would be up to Rebecca and the virologist Daniel had taken with him to literally save the world. One last glance at the open spreadsheet on her monitor, looking ahead a few weeks, made her shiver. In 1918, fifty million people worldwide had died of what the history books called the Spanish flu in a single year, more than the Black Plague had killed in Europe in the four years from 1347 to 1351. If Raj's projections were correct and everything remained the same, this disease would kill over seventy million in the next three months. It was enough to ruin her appetite, but she went to eat anyway, knowing that starving herself was not the way to save those people.

An hour later, with a cup of coffee at hand, Sarah reached Daniel. The sight of his face, even with less than perfect video quality, reassured her like nothing else could have. He looked good, if a little tired.

"Hi, Sarah, my love. I'm glad you called. Of course, if you hadn't, I'd have called you."

"I couldn't wait, honey. I almost called you at four a.m. your time."

"You probably would have found me awake. I didn't sleep well, worrying about this thing."

"Same here. Any news yet on what it is? How's Dr. Epstein working out?"

"He's made some strides. Listen, Sarah, I have some potential bad news."

"Potential?" Sarah was bewildered. It was all bad news, wasn't it?

"Yeah. I mean, I know this illness is bad, but JR told me something yesterday that could mean real trouble on the political front."

"I've already got our PR department working on it. Daniel, I think we get the facts out before someone works it out and we have to go into defensive mode."

"No, love, you don't understand. It's something else. Ben hasn't confirmed it yet, but we're all supposed to have blood tests today, and then we'll know for sure."

"Daniel, are you saying you may all have it?"

"No, love, stop reacting for a second and hear me out. So far, the only people we know of who have become ill are Middle Eastern."

"Okay."

"It looks like this thing might target just one ethnic group. I think it would be a very bad idea for the Rossler Foundation to accept accountability for something that looks like genetic warfare."

Sarah literally felt the blood drain from her face. "Daniel, what have we done?"

"Whatever it is, it's something we couldn't have anticipated. Ben thinks the reason it's so lethal is that no one has immunities to it. I'm going to let Rebecca explain that to you. But the real mystery is how a virus could have survived in that valley for so long with no host; long enough to make anyone ill, no matter who it was. A virus usually requires a host, and there's nothing here that could do it that we know of."

"I've set everyone looking for anything in the library that can help," Sarah said.

"Good, that's what I was going to have you do. Tell Mary to craft a response, but don't go forward with an announcement that it's our fault. You know what that could mean if extremists take it literally."

"Yes. It's why I wanted to talk to you before I gave the go-ahead. But, Daniel, how are you going to determine if what you say is true? About it only targeting Middle Eastern people?"

"We'll know more after the blood tests, love. Try to be patient. You might want to talk to Luke about security."

"Already done."

"See? That's why we're so good together. We've got the same brain."

"Just the one between us?" Sarah said, trying for a lighter tone.

"Oh, I think we deserve more credit than that. Listen, Sarah, Ben's calling me for my blood test, and you know how much I like needles. I'll talk to you later today."

"You stay well, Daniel Rossler."

"Yes, ma'am."

Chapter 17 - We all have it

Daniel held his arm out to Ben, who pushed it down on the table next to Daniel's chair. "This will sting a little."

"Do I get a lollipop afterwards?" Daniel quipped. In truth, he hated needles. They always said 'sting', but it hurt like a hot poker branding his skin, and the sight of the vial filling up with his blood made him queasy. It was funny, he never worried about a bruise or even a cut. Blood on his head from cutting it open while wrestling with his brothers as a kid, no big deal. Even the blood from his Marine buddy's nearly-severed leg hadn't fazed him. No, it was something about the vial. That blood was always darker, too, like something was wrong with it. He turned his head away as Epstein expertly wrapped a rubber tourniquet around his arm and slipped the needle in.

"Done," said Epstein.

Hmm, Daniel had barely felt that. He kept his eyes averted from the vial, though. JR was in the doorway a jibe on his lips if Daniel said anything wimpy, or horrifyingly, fainted. Then it was JR's turn for the needle, and Daniel prepared to send him up for any display of weakness. It was one thing to dread or fear something, and quite another to actually show it. Try as he might, he couldn't help but think a bit less of Summers for his paralysis with claustrophobia, for example. There was no way in hell that he himself would show anyone that he disliked needles.

Finished with JR, Epstein said that he should have results for everyone by late in the afternoon, and the brothers left on errands of their own.

Epstein prepared the samples, which he'd drawn from everyone who'd been into the valley. If these results were inconclusive, he'd also have to sample the support staff, but logic suggested that it was something inside the valley. How that could be so, when everyone claimed there were no animals, birds, reptiles or even insects, was a mystery that he'd have to tackle if he could confirm that it was inside the valley. He didn't want to go in there himself.

It hadn't escaped his notice that all the previous victims were Middle Eastern, and though he was third-generation American, his grandparents had left Israel for America shortly after arriving in Israel in the first place. It was a far cry from their native Germany, a dream of all observant Jews. "Next year, in Jerusalem" the prayer at the end of the Passover Seder had come true for them. They had loved the concept of Israel, but not the reality, nor the prospect of endless warfare.

It was true that the Middle Easterners who'd become ill were Saudi, or Turk, or Jordanian; in other words, all Arabs. But, in truth, though Arabs and Jews had a history of bitter enmity, they also shared a genetic heritage that made them all cousins, if not brothers. If he had to go into the valley, he would do so in a biohazard suit, to protect himself from exposure to whatever was killing his cousins in the Middle East. He had taken to heart the suggestion of the good doctor, Rebecca Mendenhall, that all newcomers wear face masks infused with germicide at all times. It was an inconvenience, but getting this dreadful flu would have been much more inconvenient, to make a laughable comparison. Now that the sick had all been gone for a few days, he'd stopped wearing the face mask except in the lab. He was more careful in his makeshift lab. In addition to the microfiber face mask, he also wore a plastic shield that covered him from forehead to below his chin.

Once the samples were prepared, it was a matter of placing them into the device that he still called a microscope for the sake of convenience. "10th Cycle Refractory Visualization Device" was much more unwieldy. Ben Epstein held his breath unconsciously as he put his eyes to the lenses that would deliver a highly magnified and probably brilliantly colored image of the blood sample, complete with any viruses that might swim there.

There it was: definitely a coronavirus. Almost beautiful in its intricacy, and matching exactly the images from a similar exercise performed on the blood of the random sample of patients before they left. There was no question that this subject had the virus. Who was it? Summers. And yet, Summers had been here from the beginning, and wasn't sick. What was the difference? Or was it just that the illness had a longer incubation period than they'd thought?

Epstein put aside the first sample and took up another. Same result. This one belonged to the cartographer, Angela Brown. One by one, Epstein examined each slide. Everyone in the scientific crew of the expedition had the active virus in their blood. How was it that they weren't sick? Was it just a matter of time? Or was it a confirmation that there was a genetic component to the course of the illness? There was one slide left, Daniel Rossler's. He had arrived with Ben and had not yet been into the valley. If he were free of the virus, it may mean that it wasn't as contagious unless it was creating symptoms, or perhaps it would mean that long incubation period again. Epstein put his eyes to the lenses. There it was. Daniel also had the virus. Good lord, how long would it be before everyone here was dead?

With a dread he couldn't acknowledge and remain sane, Epstein took a sample of his own blood and prepared the slide. Taking a deep breath, he forced himself to look. The relief was palpable when he found his blood to be free of the virus. His precautions had paid off. To be certain, he drew another sample and confirmed the first test. He was virus-free. But everyone else in the camp was infected, though not sick as yet. It was all the more important, then, that he take the utmost care to remain

146

uninfected. To contract the virus might very well be his death sentence. Now that he was certain, he went to report his findings to Rebecca.

"Rebecca. I'm ready to give you my report. I'm afraid it isn't good news."

Rebecca looked up. The olive tint to Epstein's complexion was more sallow than she remembered. This must be very bad news, to cause that. She waited as he drew a fortifying breath.

"Everyone whose blood I tested has virus cells in their systems, including you, JR and Daniel," he said. "Everyone, without exception, except me."

Rebecca paled. The immediate implications didn't need to be explained to her—they were carriers. They could not risk infecting anyone else, and the only way to make sure to prevent it was to quarantine themselves. That meant that no one could leave this base.

~~~

Bowing to Epstein's expertise in lab work, Rebecca had volunteered to comb the history of viral epidemics online to see what she could learn about how or why particularly virulent strains spread rapidly, anything that might stand out about the symptoms as similar or different to other epidemics and basically anything that might help understand this outbreak.

Sarah's report of the spiraling growth rate of affected patients had scared her to death, particularly in view of her suspicion that there was a genetic or ethnic component to how it selected its victims. It was one thing, horrible though it was, to project a death rate of seventy million in four months among the world population of some seven billion. It was quite another to project it onto the perhaps three hundred million population of the Middle Eastern countries. If allowed to run to week seventeen at the current rate of growth, it would essentially wipe out all Middle Eastern peoples. The thought was staggering.

When Epstein came to give her his report, it reminded her that shared genetics meant other peoples in the region and indeed worldwide were also at risk. She suggested that they contact the CDC and have two more experts flown in, an epidemiologist and another virologist. Epstein agreed that another virologist was a good idea, but pointed out that they had made the epidemiologist pointless by sending the majority of the sick back home. Rebecca's eyes widened, and, leaving a bewildered Epstein standing in her office, she sprinted for JR's, where she expected to find Daniel.

"Daniel!" she cried, as soon as she saw him. "We should have kept those patients here! And we've got to find the South American group and have them tested. And Martha and Sinclair!"

"Becca, slow down, sweetheart," JR admonished. "What are you talking about?"

Rebecca brought herself up short. She should start at the beginning, because JR and Daniel didn't yet know what Ben had discovered.

"We're all carrying it, the virus. I don't know why we didn't get sick, but exposure to us exposes anyone we're in contact with."

"How do you know that?"

"We have to assume it. If we leave here, we may contribute to the spread of the virus. We have to quarantine ourselves."

Daniel and JR looked at each other with dismay. That meant there'd be no going home for Daniel or anyone else, not until they got this thing stopped.

"That's not the worst of it," Rebecca went on when she understood that they'd figured out the implications. "At the rate it spreads, it's going to wipe out every one of its favorite target population in less than four months. We can't stop it from spreading—we have to find a cure."

Daniel sat down heavily. His first thoughts were of his beloved wife and baby son. When would he see them again, if ever? It didn't bear thinking of, he simply had to find a way to go home, but without putting them at risk. Rebecca was right, they had to find a cure. Then he remembered she had mentioned Sinclair and Martha. There was no time to waste; he had to let Sarah know right away. It was after nine in the evening in Boulder, but Sarah would be up. If she and little Nick hadn't been around Martha or Sinclair, they couldn't risk any exposure until the older couple was tested. He nudged JR away from his computer and brought up Skype. Please, God, he prayed, let Sarah be close enough to the computer to hear the ping.

While he waited for an answer, Rebecca and JR spoke quietly in the corner and she conveyed her request for another virologist.

"But, JR," she said. "We have to make sure that they understand. If we can't stop it and we can't cure it, we may not ever be able to leave here. We might have to make that valley our home and literally start repopulating the world."

JR shook his head. "I don't know if that's sustainable, sweetheart. We just have to cure it, that's all."

Daniel had connected with Sarah, much to his relief. He brushed away her dismayed response to his frazzled appearance.

"Sarah, this is extremely important. Have you had any personal, face-to-face contact with either Martha or Sinclair?"

"No, they're coming to dinner on Friday so I can welcome them home. Why?"

"Ask them to go into voluntary quarantine until they can be

tested for this virus. Honey, sit down."

"I am sitting," she observed.

"Good, because there's no good way to say this. We all have it. Everyone here is carrying the virus that killed all those people."

Sarah froze, before a wail tore from her throat. "NO!!! Daniel, no, no, no. Please don't die!"

"Honey, calm down. We're not sick. No one quite understands why, yet, but some of us are carrying it even though we haven't become sick. Everyone who has become sick is Middle Eastern. I don't think any of us here are going to die, but we can't risk exposing anyone else until a cure is found. You're going to have to be strong, my love. I can't come home yet."

Sarah's wails had softened as he spoke. Her Daniel wouldn't die, she caught that part. But, what was the part about him not coming home? Still softly weeping, she asked him.

"For how long, Daniel? I need you. You promised to be home for Christmas. Nick's first Christmas! When can you come home?"

"I don't know, sweetheart. It could be awhile. But we've got Skype, and we can talk every day. Bring Nick to the screen so I can talk to him tomorrow, okay? Be strong, we'll figure it out."

It was all very well to say 'at least we have Skype', she thought. But Skype couldn't put his arms around her, hold her when she was worried and frightened, like right now. Skype wouldn't provide a brother or sister for Nick. They'd talked about having another when Nick was between eighteen months and two years. This wasn't an acceptable turn of events. As she pulled herself together, Sarah tried to smile for Daniel.

"Yes, we will. We have to, Daniel." She didn't want to let him go when they'd exhausted the thoughts they had on what to do next and then said all the 'I love yous' and 'I miss yous', the secret endearments that meant so much to each other. At last, though, Daniel said he had vital tasks to complete there, and Sarah knew she needed to call Sinclair and Martha. A last tearful goodbye was their final communication of the day.

It was past ten, but Sarah had to let Sinclair know not to come into the office until he and Martha had been tested and given a clean bill of health. As an afterthought, she emailed Rebecca to send a picture of the virus, so doctors would know what they were looking for. Then she called the O'Reilly residence.

"Sinclair, it's Sarah."

"Sarah, what's wrong?" It crossed her mind to wonder why he would immediately assume something was wrong, and then realized she'd probably caught them in bed, or getting ready to be.

"Sinclair, I'm sorry to call so late, but it's important you know this right away."

"Don't worry about that. What is it?"

"I've just talked to Daniel. Sinclair, everyone in Antarctica has that virus we talked about this morning. The ones who are left there aren't sick," *yet*, she mentally added. "But they've discovered it doesn't take much to spread it, just a few seconds' contact. I'm so sorry to have to tell you this, but you and Martha need to be tested for it. They think it comes from Paradise Valley."

Complete silence from the other end of the phone made her begin to wonder if there had been a better way to communicate the news. "Sinclair, say something. Are you all right?"

"Yes," came the gravelly answer. Sinclair cleared his throat. "Yes, I understand. Well, Martha's feeling fine, and so am I, but if you can have it and not have symptoms, I guess you're right, we should be tested. Where should I go?"

"I'll have a picture of the virus by email in the morning, I'm sure. I'll send it to the lab in our provider network. Call them in the morning and tell them you're coming in, and that someone in protective clothing needs to meet you outside with masks. They'll handle it from there."

"All right. Sarah, why did I insist on going down there? I'll never forgive myself if Martha..."

"Let's not borrow trouble, Sinclair. I'm sorry to give you bad news right at bedtime, but I thought it was important that you not expose anyone else if you have it."

"Ah now, there'll be the divil to pay if we're spreadin' it, lass," said Sinclair, a form of whistling in the dark by affecting an Irish brogue. "All those people on the planes, and in Hawaii."

"It may not make any difference at all in the end, Sinclair. Just hope for the best and get tested in the morning. And call me with the results, please."

Chapter 18 – That's the real McCoy

In Turkey, a brother of one of the recently evacuated men sat beside his bedside, watching his brother die. There was nothing the doctors could do, and no hope. With his last breath, the dying man asked for his death to be avenged. It started there.

It had been six weeks since five people home on rotation from the Rossler Foundation archaeological expedition had begun to feel symptoms of an illness that eventually killed them. Now over one thousand people across the Middle East were in the same shape as Hamid's brother; dying, with no hope of a cure. Where had this evil arisen? In a remote location, chosen by a group of Americans who had specified that all their workers be of Middle Eastern descent. How could this be other than a deliberate blow against Islam?

Hamid was not a highly intelligent man, and he knew it. However, he could find no flaw in his argument that his brother and many others had been deliberately killed because they were Muslim. Everyone knew that Americans hated Muslims. Their every action demonstrated it. Nevertheless, Hamid was a humble furniture maker, and did not know what to make of his thoughts. Rather than put them aside after his brother's death, he visited a scholar, who assured him that his concerns would not go unnoticed.

In the same way, word trickled from the relatives of the sick, before they themselves became ill, to the larger community and eventually to Muezzins and leaders in mosques and coffee houses alike. From there, first one journalist, and then six more and finally many latched on to this perfect conspiracy and wrote stories in their newspapers and blogs that white infidels had finally done it; that a jihad had been mounted against Islam via a deadly disease that was rapidly consuming the Middle East.

Sarah saw these articles, gleaned from around the world and translated by Mary's team, and bode her time. Daniel was considering how to address the dangers, and she could now see his point about not rushing to take accountability. What she saw in the articles frightened her. Not reasoned essays about how the epidemic might have been accidentally unleashed, but leaps of emotion to the conclusion that it was deliberate. Nothing could have been further from the truth, she was certain. None of the Rosslerites would have even thought of such a thing, much less have put it in motion. However, the time was coming, and coming rapidly, when their response to an out-and-out accusation would be required.

Week six passed and with it over twelve hundred virus victims. Another thirty-six hundred some-odd were now ill, and it had spread from the Middle East to the UK and the US, with isolated instances in other countries. Sarah would have liked to point out to the radical journalists whose stories were growing more and more vicious that not all of the victims were Muslim. Still, the overwhelming majority were of Middle Eastern descent, and in many Americans' eyes, it was basically the same thing. Now those Americans who always seemed to take up a cause without thought or understanding were also clamoring for an answer to the ethnic cleansing that they insisted was taking place. A scapegoat would be named soon, and unless Sarah missed her guess, that would be the Rossler Foundation.

Mary reported that they did indeed have a campaign ready to refute any accusations, so Sarah waited for Daniel's decision.

Daniel called Summers, JR and Rebecca to meet with him concerning who else should be notified of their discoveries so far.

Rebecca had already made her report to the CDC and was awaiting an answer on getting another virologist on board. The fact that it could be a one-way trip complicated matters. Who would volunteer to go to Antarctica when there was every likelihood they wouldn't be able to go home, either because they were quarantined or because the virus could kill them? She wouldn't want to have to make that choice herself.

The big question in Daniel's mind was containment of the political repercussions. He and JR both knew quite well that some elements in the Middle East would view this as a deliberate attack. Those same elements had demonstrated for decades that they had no compunction about killing innocent victims to call attention to their grievances. Hell, they even gladly committed suicide to do it, assured of their reward in the afterlife for being a martyr in the cause. Neither had fully explained his thinking to anyone else, but it was time to make some decisions.

There was no question that the resources of the world should be brought to bear on the crisis. On the other hand, would retaliation come to those at home in the US? Would it be out of the question to find themselves confronted by armed soldiers? How could they warn the world, get help with finding the cure and at the same time, protect themselves and their loved ones from the consequences of a radical response?

Daniel asked JR to explain the political climate in Afghanistan, since he'd been there most recently. Even he was sobered by JR's take on it. Afterward, he suggested what he'd been thinking, which was that they needed to inform the President. When he shared Sarah's synopsis of the media storm, everyone was in agreement. It was too big now to expect to find a cure themselves, and besides, they had no right to choose for the world. If it took the resources of the entire world to contain the crisis, so be it.

They didn't have time for pride or the desire to fix what

they all felt they had broken. In a series of meetings that they opened to the rest of the scientific staff at Purgatory Canyon and set up as a video conference with Sarah and her inner circle, they gathered their facts and the conclusions they could draw from them.

Their first conclusion was that it had somehow originated in the valley. They weren't certain of where, but Summers reported that the first five were the workers he'd assigned to the 9th Cycle hospital site when the stele was translated. They wanted to give Epstein all the support he needed to discover the vector, so a mission to the site, the first since Daniel had arrived, was planned.

The second conclusion was that they had made a fatal mistake, literally, in sending the frankly ill people home. The first five had been asymptomatic when they left, so that couldn't be laid at their door. But the forty that went home in the second week of their symptoms were likely to be directly responsible for one hundred and twenty more deaths, and those for countless more.

Sarah's team was tasked with gathering as much information as possible about the life cycle of the illness, while the Antarctica group went in search of the vector. They would meet again in eight hours to take up anything else they found out.

~~~

The hospital site was the target of the first investigation, carried out by Summers, who was assisted by Daniel, JR, and Rebecca. Knowing the danger, Rebecca insisted Ben stay in camp. In spite of the urgency of locating the vector, Summers insisted that the excavation plan be honored, and the others agreed. It was unlikely they'd have to dig too far for the clues, in fact. The Middle Eastern diggers had encountered the vector somewhere in the previously excavated portion of the site, or nearby. The fact that the group at hand didn't know what they were looking for made it more difficult, but not impossible.

Summers' original excavation plan had laid out a grid of one meter by one meter, but the diggers had started at a corner that Summers designated A, and were fanning out from that corner to expose one four-inch layer at a time in the first and then adjacent squares of the grid. At the center of the grid was a spire that Summers had assumed was near the center of the hospital building, or perhaps the campus. He had paced off a good-sized area around the spire and set up his grid assuming that they would find buildings within that area, and possibly interior rooms if the weight of thousands of years of dirt and ash hadn't collapsed the buildings.

Within the four weeks or so that the diggers had been on this particular site, the top two layers had been removed from the entire grid, and several more layers were removed in step fashion from corner A to the center spire on a diagonal pattern . The result looked like a trench, with the lowest area just wide enough for an adult to walk in without tripping over the four-inch deep and eight-inch wide steps that angled upward from either side. That is, Summers remembered it looking like that.

When the group arrived though, an area just outside the grid boundary adjacent to Corner A had collapsed except for a small opening in the center, perhaps the size of two hands spread side-by-side. Corner A's stepped excavation had collapsed as well. Summers rushed to it in dismay.

"Who has been in here? The dig is compromised!" Summers shouted. JR assured him that no authorized parties had been inside the valley since Rebecca called for the site to be shut down. "Who would sabotage my dig?" Summers insisted.

The others looked at Summers and then at each other, but no one could conceive of such a thing. "Is it possible some of the support staff came in?" asked Rebecca.

Daniel was examining the opening in the caved-in section just outside the grid. "Look here. There's steam coming out of this hole, and the ground around it is wet," he observed.

"Is it very hot?" JR asked.

"Hot enough to vaporize water, but it isn't coming out rapidly, and doesn't seem to be under pressure. Look, it's just drifting."

"This is one of the geothermal wells that Robert's been mapping. I wonder if he has this one on his map."

Rebecca came over to look, and noticed something that looked like algae under a thin overhanging rock. "I think we'd better get him in here to take a look. If I'm not mistaken, that's algae. I wonder if anything could live in such a hot environment. Like fish?"

"Someone will have to go and get him; the train's at this end," JR said. "I'll go. Rebecca, are you coming with me?"

"I think I'll stay here and keep looking, JR. We don't have a lot of time before the next conference call."

JR left at a ground-eating lope while the others split up and searched both the grid and the undergrowth nearby for anything out of the ordinary.

Two hours had passed with no sign of JR and Robert when Daniel said, "Tell me again why we aren't using motorized vehicles in this valley?"

"The idea was, no gasoline-powered vehicles; nothing that could emit exhaust. The valley is too small, and the walls too high, to permit hydrocarbon-based fuel in here. It would destroy the ecology."

"Oh, yeah," said Daniel. "But what about electric carts?"

"We didn't have the budget for them; too much else was

critical. Next year," answered Summers.

"If there *is* a next year," Daniel said, just as Rebecca returned from her last foray into the surrounding gardens.

"Oh, there'll be a next year," she said, misunderstanding what Daniel meant. "There just may not be any people."

Daniel knew the situation was grim, but he hadn't spent any time looking at the calculations. "Surely this virus couldn't kill everyone on earth in just a year," he said, catching Rebecca's meaning.

"Ever hear of that old IQ test math story problem?" she answered. "Almost everyone gets it wrong."

"No, what are you talking about?"

"If an encroaching vine doubles every day, and it takes ten days to cover half a dam, how long does it take to completely cover it?"

"Twenty days."

"No, you fail. Eleven days. You should look at Raj's spreadsheet again, Daniel. Assuming this virus continues at the rate it's going, and that it will eventually kill anyone it infects, it could completely depopulate the planet in around five months."

"Seven *billion* people?" Daniel said, aghast. "But, you said it only targets Middle Eastern people."

"You seem to be laboring under the misguided illusion that all of us are pure this, that or the other," Rebecca said. "What would you think if I told you that virtually everyone on earth today has between one and four percent Neanderthal genes? At some point, *homo sapiens* and *homo Neanderthalensis* intermingled for thousands of years. Clearly, they also interbred. Eventually, Neanderthals died out, but their genes live on in us. Who's to say that whatever is making Middle Eastern people vulnerable to it doesn't exist in small quantities in all of us?"

"Are you saying that this virus only attacks Neanderthal genes?"

Rebecca made an erasing gesture, impatient that she hadn't made it clear she was just using an example.

"No, not at all. But, in the human genome there's about ninety percent of the DNA that contains no instruction codes for making proteins. We don't know what that's for. They call it 'junk' DNA, but it has to be for something. In fact, around eight percent of it is endogenous retroviruses. Basically, it's leftover fragments of ancient viruses."

"Retroviruses, like HIV?"

"That's a suspected one. We just don't know, Daniel. What I'm saying is, there could be something about Middle Easterners, something more prominent in their genetic makeup than in ours that makes them vulnerable to this virus. But it might not be exclusive, and on top of that, viruses have a tendency to mutate. When they run out of their preferred host, there is a good chance they'll mutate to take advantage of some weakness in the rest of us."

"But then, wouldn't we be sick, too?"

"Maybe it takes longer. Maybe some other factor neutralizes it. Whatever the case may be, we may not have time to discover it and craft a response." Rebecca fell silent, her body bowed with the weight of her understanding and even more so with the weight of what she didn't yet understand. Daniel put a hand on her shoulder to steady her.

"We'll find it," he said. "We have to." He turned in surprise as a thudding sound behind him announced that JR had arrived, with Robert Cartwright on his heels.

"Crikey, have you ever tried to keep a fast pace for this

one?" he asked of no one in particular. "Near ran my legs off. Where's this fumarole you've found?"

"Is that what it is?" Rebecca asked.

"Bob's your uncle. Hole in the ground, steam coming out. Abso-bloody-lutely. That's the real McCoy."

Everyone crowded around as he examined the fumarole. "Nice one. Probably opens out a little ways under. This is probably what powered your hospital, or maybe just supplied hot water and such. What else can I tell you about it?"

Remembering her earlier question, Rebecca asked, "Can anything live in that?"

"Oh, yes. I'm no biologist, you need Nyree. But various little creepy crawlies can live in that environment. Some too small to see. See here, algae's growing, and all kinds of little whatchamacallits and thingamabobs feed on that. Be careful if you want a sample. The ground around it could be undercut. You don't want to fall into one of these. Unless you fancy being instantly cooked."

With nothing else of obvious interest and because time was now running short to get to the next video conference, Robert used a long extension pole to collect a good-sized sample from the algae and another from the wet dirt on the other side that didn't contain an obvious algae bloom. Then the group started back for the rift in the valley wall and the train that would carry them quickly back toward the outside.

Chapter 19 – Time to tell the President

Epstein and Nyree had hurried to her lab, which had more equipment for examining biological specimens, after collecting the imaging device he'd brought with him to take with them.

Nyree lamented the loss of her friend Haraz el-Amin, whose knowledge of botany would have helped them with the first examination, that of the algae. But the main thing they wanted to know was whether there were any microorganisms living on or within the algae. The next thing was, if so, what were they? If they actually found insects, it was very likely that those were the vector. It was well-known that insects and their viruses had developed more or less synchronously. How a virus might have gone airborne from such a vector was a question they weren't prepared to answer yet.

At the appointed time, Daniel, JR, Summers and Rebecca were gathered in the conference room for their next video conference call with Sarah and her advisers in Boulder. No one was surprised to see Luke with her, or Nicholas, but Sinclair's presence was a shock. Before anyone in Antarctica had a chance to ask or comment, Sarah broke into her famous smile and spoke first.

"We've had wonderful news! Sinclair and Martha are free of the virus."

Everyone on both ends of the video link broke into applause at that. Not only was it good news personally, but it gave them a clue about how the virus had gone active and spread. If neither of the O'Reilly's had the virus, it meant that no one had been contagious in Antarctica until the second five victims contracted it.

The first five had shown no symptoms until after they left

the valley. This meant that the virus probably wasn't contagious until symptoms appeared, at least until it had gone airborne, which they surmised because they all carried it, even those who hadn't been directly exposed to the sick diggers.

Sarah was able to report the course of the disease after symptoms began. Questioning several doctors who were dealing with patients in the Middle East had revealed that symptoms started with a sore throat, following which patients experienced moderate symptoms similar to seasonal flu; that is, sore throat, coughing, headache and body aches. Instead of beginning to improve at the seven to ten day mark, though, symptoms worsened. The patients' lungs filled with fluid, leading doctors to believe at first that the patients had contracted a case of pneumonia secondary to the respiratory aspects of flu.

Around the ten to twelve day mark, a high fever set in, resisting all efforts to lower it until the patients' organs were affected. Most patients died of acute and cataclysmic kidney failure. A few died when their fever reached one-hundred and seven or above before organ failure, in which case they died of brain aneurysm when their blood pressure shot up because of the fever itself. Death always occurred between twelve and fourteen days after symptoms began.

Investigators that Sarah had hired had also confirmed that all known dead were of Middle Eastern origin, and that no one not of Middle Eastern origin was thought to have the same flu. The latter was made more difficult to determine because it was 'flu season' in the northern hemisphere, and several strains of virus were causing outbreaks of similar symptoms to the early stage of the deadly strain. That meant that anyone with flu symptoms had to wait at least a week to determine what it was.

In view of the fact that all of the non-Middle Eastern expedition members were carrying the virus without symptoms, Rebecca recommended that all flu victims, no matter what strain they or their doctors thought they had, be tested for what they were now calling the 9th Cycle flu. The cost would be staggering when multiplied throughout the world, but they couldn't take the risk that carriers would infect more Middle Eastern people. There was also the concern that the virus could mutate at any time. It had gone airborne in record time here in Antarctica, and that showed its superior ability to adapt.

Both Sarah and Rebecca made notes on the science matters. Rebecca for the purpose of conveying the new information to Epstein when the call was over, and Sarah because the next agenda item was the political climate. She understood that the time had come to warn the President.

There was no question that not only the President of the United States but also world leaders in every country must be informed, the sooner the better. They had to be given a chance to respond to the crisis proactively, even though Rebecca was convinced that no conventional response could avert the growing disaster. Not to tell them would be irresponsible and in addition would be political suicide, not only for the Rossler Foundation, but for the US, as the host and major supporter of the Foundation.

The issue was exacerbated because of two factors. Many of the fundamentalist Muslim leaders in the Middle East had taken the stance that the 10th Cycle Library was the property of the Middle East rather than the Rossler Foundation. This despite the Foundation's stated goal of making the information available to everyone so long as it wasn't something that could be made into a terrorist weapon.

The second factor was that, because of the prevalence of terrorist organizations throughout the Middle East, some supported by governments, no Middle Eastern country was represented on the Foundation board. Israel was the only one, and of course that added to the bitter enmity of the two factions. The bottom line was that the Middle East, in general, had a deep suspicion of the Rossler Foundation and could easily be influenced by any whisper of conspiracy.

Before the Rosslerites had an idea what to say, therefore, the entire group would brainstorm the potential consequences, so that they could put together a presentation for the President and Board that would show they'd left no stone unturned.

JR insisted, backed up by Daniel, that the worst consequence after the mounting death toll was going to be the tendency of radical Islamic elements to believe that this was a deliberate attack. It was likely that they would claim it was engineered by the Rossler Foundation, or the Western world in general. Even if the leaders of those elements, the Shiite Ayatollah or imams in the affected countries, didn't believe it was deliberate, they might very well say it was, just to take advantage of the situation to further their agenda. No one in the group questioned that, though mainstream Muslims were peace-loving, the radical elements had total world domination as their goal. Their tactics for the past few decades had intimidated some world powers into appeasing them at any cost.

Unfortunately, there were elements on the other side of the question that would use any excuse to wipe out the terrorists even at the cost of innocents. Since before September 11, 2001, the world had been perpetually on the brink of widespread warfare, with the US leading the way in taking their grievances to the battlefield in the Middle East. This disease, if the world were to believe it was a deliberate attack on Muslims, could turn the tide of what was left of positive popular opinion against the US. If the Middle Eastern countries united and pressed a military response against the US, there was every likelihood that countries previously neutral in the question, or even leaning toward the Middle East, could join them. Some of those countries had nuclear weapons.

Sarah could take no more of this talk. "Have you all forgotten the 10th Cycle warning?" she asked. "You're talking about the cataclysm that could end this cycle, and that's if the entire world population isn't wiped out by the disease! We can't be planning a military solution! We have to find a cure."

"Sweetheart," Daniel said, leaning into the screen as if he could reach through it to take his beloved in his arms. "You don't understand what we're saying. It won't come to nuclear war everywhere. As soon as they understand the virus came from here, there's every chance that the President will be forced to nuke this valley to appease the Muslims. They'll also think it will wipe out the source of the virus, but that ship has sailed. It's out of confinement already, and nothing can stop the spread."

Sarah had turned white at Daniel's matter-of-fact discussion of their group being the target of a nuclear blast. She felt like throwing up, but for the sake of the rest of the group, suppressed the urge. With a superhuman effort, she steadied her voice to respond.

"Then we must find the cure soon. Now. What do you need?"

Rebecca spoke up. "We need at least one more virologist. If Ben contracts it, we'll lose the ability to work on a solution. But, you just heard why the CDC is reluctant to send anyone. They may not have figured out that we may all be in danger of elimination, but they know we've put ourselves under quarantine. We can't afford to infect anyone else, and now that we know we're carriers, it would be highly irresponsible for us to leave here. Unless we can find a cure, anyone coming in is probably making a one-way trip."

Sarah shuddered. She had urged Daniel not to go, but his sense of responsibility forced it. Now they may be separated

166

forever. It was too much to bear, but she must bear it. For the sake of their son, for the sake of the Foundation, and for the sake of saving everyone they could, she must hold it together and lead the Foundation.

"I'll find someone who will volunteer," she answered, though she had no idea how to do it. She would cross that bridge when she came to it. "Now, what do we tell the President, and the Board?"

Together, they crafted points to convey in their report to the President. After showing it to him, they would call the Board together on an emergency basis and inform them as well. It wasn't out of the question that the President would take it straight to the UN, but in any case, the Rossler Foundation would do its part. They decided to leave out any speculation about a nuclear solution. Instead, they would first present the facts, including the projections of the spread, the confirmation that only Middle Eastern people got sick from the virus, the theory that non-ME people were carriers and could infect others, and that the death rate among those who got sick was 100%.

They would recommend that anyone presenting with flu symptoms be tested for 9th Cycle virus, and that quarantines be put into place for anyone found to be carrying it, until a vaccination or antiviral medication that would kill the virus was developed. Finally, they would put in a well-reasoned warning about the concern that the Muslim world, ninety-nine percent of people originating in the Middle East, might easily be persuaded to believe that it was a deliberate attempt at ethnic cleansing, to wipe them out, in other words, genocide.

~~~

Raj was dispatched to create the PowerPoint, while Luke made arrangements to wake the President and give him the report as soon as it was ready. Daniel was standing by to be the spokesperson for this momentous occasion, knowing that Sarah had to get some rest and see the baby. He doubted if she would sleep until exhaustion overtook her. No one was sleeping well in Antarctica, except the support staff, who knew little of what was going on.

Meanwhile, research continued in the biology lab, and Daniel was pleased with the progress in combing the 10th Cycle library for any reference to the expedition that had found this valley.

The next thing to do was try to find any information in the archaeological site. Most likely, it would be found either in the hospital archives or in the library. Unfortunately, they had no diggers, so they would have to make do with who and what they did have. They wouldn't even consider having the South Americans, who were no longer standing by in any case, come back. Aside from the additional virologist they'd requested, no other human being would be asked to make a one-way trip to camp. Even their supply runs would now have to be carried out by airdrop.

JR called together the support staff and scientists alike, except for Ben Epstein and Nyree, to inform them of the situation and solicit help with the digs.

"I want to assure you that if you are not already sick, you probably won't be. Everyone here is carrying the active virus in our bloodstreams. We've determined that it isn't likely to make you sick unless you're of Middle Eastern ethnic origin. However, it means that we can't leave here, not even when winter sets in. We need to find a cure before that, and before the people who have already left here infect too many more people outside.

"I expect all of the scientists to put themselves in Summers' hands for assignment on one of the digs we'll be pursuing in an

168

effort to find some reference to this disease and how to stop it. Yes, that includes you, Malik. I know you're Cyndi's assistant, but now you're a digger, just like the rest of us.

"I'd also like volunteers from the support staff. Some of you are sitting around with nothing much to do, since we don't have fifty extra people to clean and do laundry for. I assure you there is no danger in what we're asking you to do. Who'll step forward?"

With some low discussion, everyone but the cook and his assistant stepped forward. That was just as well; they still had quite a few mouths to feed. JR named two janitors and a laundry worker to stay behind for support of the remaining group, and had the others follow Summers for a crash course in how to dig an archaeology site. At Summers' insistence, because doing anything else would destroy the site forever, they were going to try to do it properly even though speed was of the essence.

Tomorrow, everyone but the skeleton crew in the camp would head for the center of the valley, hoping against hope to find the answers they so desperately needed.

~~~

Raj had worked fast. Within an hour, he had a beautiful PowerPoint presentation ready for Luke to convey to the White House, thence to the President's computer. Daniel was standing by with his copy cued up. A Secret Service agent was tasked with waking the President.

Within minutes, President Harper's face appeared in the video conference screen. Daniel wondered how he managed to look not only alert but also put together, his hair combed, a silk scarf wrapped under his robe, presumably to conceal his neck and pajamas.

"What's this all about, Daniel?" he inquired mildly. For a man who'd been awakened at two in the morning, he was remarkably calm.

"Mr. President, I'm speaking to you from Antarctica. I'm afraid I have some bad news. I have the unenviable task of telling you of a critical threat to national security," Daniel answered.

With that, Harper sat up straighter, a look of consternation on his face. "The hell you say. I think you'd better get on with it, Rossler."

Daniel didn't fail to note that Harper's tone and mode of address were less friendly.

"Sir, if you'd have your aide turn on your computer monitor, we've prepared a presentation to make it easier to grasp the main points. After we go through it, if you have more questions, we'll do our best to answer them."

One by one, Daniel took Harper through the facts. Trained to hear out a report of this nature without interrupting, Harper nevertheless let out an oath of dismay when the projection of the numbers came up. Like many Presidents before him, Harper's political persona concealed a sharp intelligence that allowed him to grasp the implications even before the slide changed. However, he remained silent as Daniel turned to the concerns about the political climate. Nodding his head, he agreed with each of the points they had prepared.

When Daniel was finished with the presentation, he remained silent. The President didn't need to be invited to present questions. If he had any, they'd be forthcoming soon. Harper remained in intense thought for several minutes. At last he raised his head and looked Daniel in the eyes through the video screen. Daniel met the gaze forthrightly.

"On your honor, you swear that this was inadvertent on your part, the part of the Foundation."

"Yes, sir." Daniel didn't add 'how could you doubt it'. Right now, the President wasn't his friend, he was the sole protector of

170

the United States, and the person on whom the shit-storm would fall when this news was released.

"Even when you sent all those sick people home?"

"Yes, sir. We didn't understand that the disease was so highly communicable at the time, and we didn't have the resources to care for them. Besides, their families and governments were demanding their return. We had no choice. However, it was a grave error, and we will take full accountability for making it."

"Dr. Mendenhall, I take it you treated all the cases that originated there at your base?"

Rebecca, not really expecting to be addressed by the President of the United States, stammered, "Y...yes, Sir. Mr. President."

JR squeezed her hand surreptitiously and Daniel nodded at her encouragingly, so it was with more confidence that she answered his follow-up questions. "Yes, I believe the projections to be reasonable, if not optimistic. No, I found nothing that would halt the illness, nor have the Middle Eastern physicians I've spoken to. No, sir, we had no choice but to send the sick ones home, given the demands of their families and governments. Yes, it is indeed terrible, sir."

"Very well. I'm going to have to call in the National Security Council, and some of them may have questions for you. Will you be available?"

"Yes, sir. I'll stand by. The rest of the group is going back into the valley to see if we can find some answers."

"Good. I have no doubt I'll be talking to you soon, Daniel. Thank you for getting this to me as soon as you could."

Daniel was grateful to hear his given name on the lips of the President again. He still felt accountable for the disaster at hand, but the President had given him the gift of understanding that it had been unavoidable. If the rest of the world were as understanding, Daniel could face death if necessary. It was the loss of respect that would grieve him, and the stigma that would follow Sarah and little Nick.

Chapter 20 - This is what we're going to do

Despite the early hour, Harper convened an emergency meeting of the National Security Council. Everyone was somewhat used to being called in the middle of the night, but what the President had to tell them was going to be a shock to rival any since the inception of the Council in 1947. In twos and threes, the members entered the conference room and sat in their usual places, waiting without speculation for an explanation of why they'd been called in.

The Council consisted of the President as its chair, the Vice-President, Secretary of State, Secretary of Defense, National Security Advisor and the Secretary of the Treasury. In addition, the Chairman of the Joint Chiefs of Staff was present as the statutory military advisor to the Council, the Director of National Intelligence as the advisor in that capacity. Although Harper didn't immediately see a role in this matter for him, The Director of National Drug Control Policy, as a statuary advisor to the Council, was also present.

Due to the widespread consequences of this particular situation, the President had also invited, if a command order could be considered an invitation, his Chief of Staff, his Counsel and his Assistant for Economic Policy, along with the Attorney General, the Director of the CIA, the Director of Homeland Security and the Director of the CDC.

This formidable group wielded power of awe-inspiring proportions, and their advice and decisions would shape the official response of the United States to the crisis, which until this moment, no one had known of but the CDC. Thus, the wrath of the President for having been informed by a private citizen rather than the director of that agency fell upon the hapless man. Taken by surprise, he could only say that his department had not confirmed the assumptions of the Rossler Foundation scientists.

"I'll expect your resignation when this crisis is over. For now, you'd better get your department in gear. You're dismissed, but report back here in six hours to tell me what progress you've made. I may have more information for you by that time, but I assume the Rosslers are reporting to you directly."

"To one of my department heads, actually," said the man, sealing his fate. The President hated any supposed leader who threw his juniors under the bus or passed the buck. If Harper hadn't already demanded his resignation, he would have done so now. Instead, he turned his attention to the Secretary of State, who had hurriedly called in her foreign policy advisors for the Middle East. They would arrive shortly. She asked to defer that discussion until that time.

Harper nodded, then gazed at his Assistant for Economic Policy. "What's this going to do to the stock market?" he inquired, with deceptive mildness.

"There's no way to project for sure, but I think we can all agree that it's likely to plummet. I'd advise that we get in touch with Securities and Exchange and have them suspend trading immediately."

"That would mean we would have to also immediately make a public announcement. Are we ready to do that?"

Homeland Security spoke up, since the appropriate responder had already been summarily dismissed. "Mr. President, we're going to have to do that very soon anyway. From what you've told us, we need to institute quarantines. The only way to do that effectively is to let the public know what's going on. I agree it's going to cause panic, but I don't see a way to avoid that. We'll have to activate National Guard units to maintain civil order, and we'll have to put all doctors under some sort of official control."

"All right. Just a moment." The President took a moment to call in the Press Secretary. When he arrived, they'd have to bring him up to speed and get him working on a speech for the President to present to the nation.

Defense, NS, HS and the Chairman of JCS had been talking quietly amongst themselves while the President called the Press Secretary. They were hammering out who would be responsible for what aspect of the response even before the foreign policy advisors arrived. There was no question in any of their minds that there would be rioting in the streets as soon as the President imposed quarantines.

Contrary to Harper's intent, which was to quarantine people carrying the virus, these men had assumed that there would be a nationwide quarantine of any person of Middle Eastern descent. The precedent had been set in World War II with the internment of Japanese-Americans. That history had harshly judged that decision was immaterial to them.

By the time the foreign policy advisors arrived and the Secretary of State had informed them of the crisis and received their input, almost everything else was in place. It was time for everyone to take up the question of what the Middle East would do.

They might as well have asked JR. Every point he'd made and had inserted into the presentation was brought up by the experts. Anti-American sentiment in Middle Eastern countries was already at an all-time high, fueled by the modernization brought by world-wide dissemination of American culture and American innovation.

Traditional leaders could see their influence being undermined by the internet, expanded world travel and a secularization of their constituents. Radical leaders responded with hatred and violence, sparking a military backlash, which ratcheted up the distrust and dislike for the invading power even further. Even nominal allies like Saudi Arabia had over ninety percent unfavorable ratings of the United States. The strong support of Israel by the US wasn't helping the situation, either.

The bottom line was that the experts agreed—when the crisis reached the proportions the projections showed in the next couple of weeks, with nearly fifty thousand dead or dying of a virus that only attacked Middle Easterners, the radical response would be explosive. Even more important, it would take only a month more to wipe out virtually the entire population of those countries. The Chairman of the Joint Chiefs of Staff ventured the question that several others of the same opinion were hesitant to.

"Why would we not just let this thing run its course? These people have been a thorn in our sides for decades. Give it a couple or three weeks and they won't be able to give us any trouble. Problem solved."

Harper, his Secretary of State and her staff, along with several others openly gaped at the man. Could he really have just proposed genocide as a solution? Harper's stomach roiled, repulsed at the thought. He was going to have to call for another resignation. He'd be lucky if he even had a government by the time this was resolved. His weary voice took on a ring of leadership and power as he answered.

"We will not just let it run its course because that isn't the right thing to do. That option would be as evil as what they're going to accuse us of. We unleashed this thing, indirectly as it might have been. I will not stand by idly and watch while fellow human beings need my help. That is not the America I serve. Besides, do you really believe you can stand in a burning forest without getting scorched? We must stop it, at all costs. And, we have a moral obligation to offer our help, our all-out efforts, to the countries affected, whether or not they are our enemies."

Most of the room burst into applause, as the Press Secretary hastily wrote down the words. They would form the core of the President's public speech wherein he announced his government's response to the crisis.

After hours of meetings, everyone had a task to accomplish. The President wanted control of the airwaves at noon Eastern, and his speech had to be ready. His advisors scattered, Harper called Daniel.

"This is what we're going to do..."

~~~

One piece of the big picture was deliberately left out of Harper's return call to Daniel. It wasn't because he didn't trust Daniel—he did—but it was top secret and couldn't be revealed. In fact, Harper had been reluctant to approve it, particularly after his top military adviser expressed his desire for a permanent solution to what he inelegantly called 'the Arab problem'. Placing such power in the hands of a bigot wasn't his first choice, but at the urging not only of the military, but also of the foreign policy advisers and the Secretary of state, he signed off on it, knowing that doing so made him complicit in an international crime.

The idea was to place a number of satellites in geosynchronous orbit above the region. The spy satellites he had no problem with, nor with the increased communications capability. However, those with laser anti-missile capabilities, a modernization of the old Star Wars plan from the Reagan years, gave him pause. He was reasonably certain that those were a violation of international treaties forbidding the weaponization of space.

His advisers' assurances that everyone else was doing it and had been for years just made him weary. What good were treaties if even the good guys violated them? He was still smarting from the humiliation of having to admit to a US biological warfare program of which he'd known nothing beforehand.

Almost the last straw was the military's insistence on deploying some satellites with nuclear strike capability. There was no hedging about this certainty. It was a clear violation of treaty. It was also touted as the first line of defense if diplomacy went south, as it was very likely to do.

Not only would Daniel and his group not hear of it, neither would any of the Allies. It was strictly "Need to Know", and no one needed to know that the US had just joined the ranks of criminal regimes. God willing, it wouldn't come to a pass where the weapons were needed, but if they were, better to have them than not. With his logic clearly in mind, Harper gave the okay and the birds were soon on their way to roost in the skies above the Middle East.

~~~

Before Harper went public, he owed his allies a heads-up. And before any other, he owed Israel advance warning. There was no hope of keeping what was coming a secret, though of course he wouldn't publicly speculate on the Muslim response. The proper way to do it was through the UN Security Council, and that would come as soon as possible. But, not everyone on the Security Council was an ally. He'd get his ducks in a row first. There was simply no time to delay his press conference, not if he hoped to contain the virus that was already reported to be within his borders. According to a call that had just come in from the CDC, there were twenty-one known cases. He had to get them, and anyone they might have exposed, quarantined at once.

Harper reflected that there were silver linings to almost every cloud. The fact that he was a lame-duck president was the silver lining to this one. He could act without thought to the political repercussions. Sure, his party might suffer, but that couldn't be helped. At least he would know that his actions were free of thoughts of the next Presidential campaign, a little over two years hence.

When an aide came to inform him that a line had been opened to Israel, Harper was as ready as he ever would be.

"David, this is Nigel Harper. I have some important news."

David Yedidyah listened closely as Harper detailed the facts as he knew them. Israel faced a double threat. Until it was established that there was no one within the borders that already had the virus, he must assume that his entire population was at risk. There was almost no chance that no one had it.

Despite their differences, many Arabs still lived in Israel. Relatives from Syria and Jordan especially regularly crossed the borders. The fact that Israel had not been able to stop suicide bombers from entering made it almost certain that infected people had come in, either by chance or by design. Yedidyah had decided to close the borders before Harper even came to the question of a Muslim backlash. No country knew better the lengths to which fanatics would go to express their hatred.

When Harper fell silent, Yedidyah thanked him for the early warning. "Is there anything we can do to help you, my friend?" he asked.

"Pray," said Harper.

While Harper called each of America's closest allies, beginning with Great Britain, Yedidyah wasted no time in acting. He closed the borders, allowing anyone who wished to leave to do so, but refusing all inbound transportation without explanation. Airlines were in chaos as their planes were forced to find other destinations. Suspicion grew, but Israel refused to explain her actions.

A news blackout was imposed as military teams went house to house collecting blood samples, but there was no containing the outcry on the internet. Soon every conspiracy blogger on the planet was speculating about an epidemic in Israel! Ironically, they failed to relate it to the one that was overtaking the Middle East, despite some radical leaders ranting about a designer disease.

Within two hours of his call to Yedidyah, Harper was addressing the UN Security Council. Reaction of the members ranged from shock and grief to outrage. Harper took it in stride. The important thing, he insisted, was not to lay blame but to find the cure. When the meeting was dismissed, all fifteen members raced to inform their governments, and an announcement was made in the General Assembly.

In Boulder, Sarah had called a meeting of the Board. They would not learn of the crisis before their respective compatriots in the UN, but her responsibility was to inform them personally. To her gratification, even those that she might have thought would be troublemakers expressed concern first for the expedition members in Antarctica. Sarah assured them that as yet, no one had come down with symptoms since the last worker group had been sent home. However, they were under self-imposed quarantine. No one would be allowed in or out until an answer was found, except for a volunteer virologist that had still not been located. It was a sobered group that broke up their meeting just in time for the President's press conference.

Most stayed in the Foundation Boardroom to take in that speech. Sarah left the head of the table to take a seat more conducive to viewing the large screen hanging behind her seat there. The familiar tones of the Emergency Broadcast System announced the beginning of the press conference. "We interrupt this program to bring you an important message. Please stay tuned."

The screen switched from NBC's noon programming to the image of the President, standing behind a podium and backed by the blue of the Presidential pressroom wall, the seal of the United States centered behind his head.

"My fellow Americans, I am here today to tell you of a grave threat to humanity and to our national security. Please listen closely as you will be asked to respond individually to this crisis, in order to avert it."

Sarah imagined the ripples of shock and dismay across America, akin to the wave of emotion that had swept the country on the morning of September eleventh, 2001. This time, though, it wasn't a foreign terrorist that threatened a few thousand, but a medical condition set loose on the modern world by the Rossler Foundation's expedition. She had to hold herself tightly in control as the President went on.

"It has come to our attention that a deadly virus has been infecting hundreds of people in several Middle Eastern countries. Scientists have determined that everyone who comes into contact with this virus is infected, without fail. However, certain characteristics mark those who actually become ill. At this time, we must ascertain who might be carrying this virus and isolate them to avoid spreading it any further. I have been in contact with world leaders this morning to gain their agreement that our response will be universal. As of this moment, I am declaring a state of emergency for all of the United States and our territories or protectorates.

"These are your individual instructions. If you have no symptoms resembling flu and have had no contact with anyone who has flu symptoms, we urge you to stay at home as much as possible, or to protect yourselves with anti-microbial face masks and frequent hand washing if you must go out. Otherwise, if you have had even casual contact with anyone you observed to be coughing, sniffling or complaining of flu symptoms, you are required to go to your local hospital to be tested for the virus even if you do not have symptoms.

"If you yourself have any of the common symptoms of flu, that is, sore throat, cough, body aches, respiratory distress or a high fever that will not respond to medication, you are instructed to call your local emergency number and report yourself as sick. Medical personnel will come to you with the appropriate protective gear. Do not leave your house, on pain of arrest. All residents with flu symptoms are under quarantine, effective immediately. If you are watching this broadcast from somewhere other than your home, proceed to your home without delay or detour. If you require something you do not have at home, such as groceries or medications, they will be brought to you."

"I want to assure all residents that these measures are merely precautionary except for certain individuals whose special circumstances make them vulnerable to becoming ill from the virus. We are trying to avoid a mutation that will release it to the general population. At this time, only individuals of Middle Eastern descent are known to develop symptoms. If you are of Middle Eastern descent, you are particularly vulnerable. Please take all precautions to avoid contact with any person exhibiting flu symptoms, no matter their ethnic heritage, and if you are currently experiencing symptoms, do not delay in calling your local emergency response number.

"Finally, we are working to set up a call center. A toll-free number will be published later today so that if you have any questions, you will be able to get immediate answers. In addition, the CDC will be publishing the latest outbreak list as well as full information about the virus as it becomes known.

"My fellow Americans, in times of crisis throughout our history, our citizens have risen to the occasion. It is vitally important that you do so once again, whether you are a citizen, a resident alien, or a guest, invited or uninvited. Help us keep you safe. If you are so inclined, pray for our neighbors who are fighting for their lives, and pray for our nation and the world to come through this crisis unscathed."

As soon as the President ceased speaking, pandemonium broke out in the press room, but Harper was turning to leave. There were no other questions that would be prudent to answer, even if he could. He could only hope for a few more hours of peace before the world-wide announcement of a pandemic affecting only Middle Eastern peoples caused a backlash of those peoples. And then, God help us all.

~~~

As the Friday that marked the beginning of Week 8 of the outbreak by Rebecca's count dawned, what had been a quiet rumble in the countries most affected by the spreading illness became a roar. The latest statistics were over five thousand dead, nearly eleven thousand infected, with most of the latter beginning to show symptoms. In addition, it had slowly become apparent to the general public that this virus killed all of its victims.

Hospitals were flooded with panicked people who had sore throats and other symptoms, whether from the virus that officials were calling the H10N7 Influenza A or some other strain. What was defeating the researchers searching frantically for a cure or at least a medicine that would effectively kill enough of the virus for immune systems to do the rest, was that there had never been an H10 before.

JR found it difficult to follow Epstein's explanation, especially the part about mutation, so he asked Rebecca to break it down for him.

"Why H and N?" he asked. "And what do the numbers mean?"

Rebecca tried to find a way to make it clear. "These virus designations derived from the protein spikes on the virus cell's surface that helped it invade healthy cells, hemagglutinin and neuraminidase," she said. "That's where the H and the N come from."

"Okay, that makes sense."

"So, before this, we knew of nine hemagglutinin proteins, and sixteen neuraminidase. So viruses could be named anything from H1N1, to designate what kind of protein spikes they had, to H9N16, right?"

"I guess."

"Look, each virus cell has one type of H protein and one type of N protein. So, that makes one-hundred and forty-four potential strains of flu."

"Okay, I get it. But they're calling this one H10N7. I thought there were only nine hema-whatisis proteins."

"That's what everyone thought until now. The hemagglutinin protein in this strain doesn't match any of those nine. It's a new kind. Or more likely, a very old kind that hasn't been seen in thousands of years."

"It was the reason everyone was so concerned about mutation. Now there could be one-hundred and sixty strains; sixteen more strains than before, each using the new H10 hemagglutinin protein and one of the sixteen neuraminidase proteins. With this development, if H10N7 didn't kill everyone, one of the other fifteen might finish the job," JR observed.

JR made this leap of logic at once, and Rebecca confirmed his conclusions. Then she gave him a mini-course on influenza pandemics.

"Historically, Influenza A pandemics resulted from a cross-over of a strain that hadn't previously infected humans or had disappeared for some reason; and therefore no one had immunities to it. That's what some researchers think happened with the Spanish flu, why it killed more young people than old, when it's usually the other way around."

"What do you mean?"

"They think that the very old had some immunities to it from childhood, but then it disappeared for thirty years or more. That was the H1N1, by the way, which we saw recur just a few years ago. We think that the flu vaccines we've developed since then prevented the same kind of pandemic. In any case, the young people had never been exposed to anything similar, so they died in droves, like the victims of our virus are doing now."

"So, this one disappeared and no one has immunities? Why aren't we sick, then?"

"That's the big question. In this case, it's the new hemagglutinin protein that's the problem. Or so the scientists think."

The other question was where it had come from, Rebecca knew. As she explained to JR, all strains of Influenza A had previously been proven to exist in wild birds around the world, but if this one existed in a wild bird, it hadn't been found yet. Scientists were fascinated, but frightened. At the rate this was growing, they wouldn't have time to find the answers before the entire population had been infected. Now that they knew everyone got it but only Middle Easterners developed symptoms and died from it, they suspected a genetic component—but how would they locate it in time?

~~~

Leaders in the affected countries called in their science advisors and demanded answers. The only answers that the scientists had were that this was something new, something no one had seen before, and that it attacked a single ethnic group exclusively. The logical conclusion was that it had been engineered to do so. The leaders consulted each other and determined that they needed to locate patient zero and find out where he had been when he contracted this virus. That search took almost a week, but at the end of the week, they all knew. The first five cases had all come home from an archaeological dig that an American team had opened. The team was from the Rossler Foundation, which had sole access to information from the now famous 10th Cycle Library. Therefore, they concluded, the Rossler Foundation had used their exclusive knowledge to engineer a disease designed to wipe out Middle Easterners, or, more likely, Muslims.

Within a day, the Ayatollah that currently dominated the most conservative factions of Iranian politics had made a public announcement on National Iranian Radio and Television, the official media arm of the government. Westerners had developed a 'genetic bullet', a disease that was killing thousands now on a daily basis. Other radicals took up the cry and soon even moderate Muslims were beginning to wonder.

News from internet sources that claimed Muslims were being rounded up and interned in the US evolved into claims that they were being deliberately infected with the virus. Communications back to Muslim groups in the US urged them to hide and not comply with the quarantine order. Outbreaks in other countries were being reported, though the numbers were fewer than one hundred in most places, as opposed to the thousands in the Middle East.

Somehow, news leaked from Israel that they had no cases, fueling the claims that Zionists were behind the disease along with the Americans. When someone let it slip that the virologist who was in Antarctica with the expedition was one Ben Epstein, a Jew, the outcry began to infect even the most resistant Muslim leaders. Iran was the first to call for a concerted response, followed quickly by Pakistan. It was now a race to find a cure before someone rattled a nuclear saber.

186

Harper watched these developments via hourly updates from his advisers. It was what he'd been led to expect, but it was happening far more quickly than he'd hoped. To Harper's dismay, the technological network he'd envisioned wasn't up to snuff, adding to the general panic of the citizens. They hadn't anticipated the volume of calls to the helplines, so not enough had been set up, which resulted in people having to wait in the queue for up to three hours. Many were impatient for answers, and instead of waiting, called 911, overwhelming that system.

Naturally, the usual auto accidents, fire, people having heart attacks and babies, all the normal emergency calls were still going on as well, but because the system was overwhelmed, some of those calls went to voice mail. As a result, there were preventable deaths and an outcry about the inadequacy of the system. No one could have predicted the chaos that would ensue just from the information being out there. Harper despaired that there would be a complete breakdown of civil order if the disease actually got a foothold in the US.

The added complication that several organized groups were actively resisting his quarantine orders was something he didn't need, but he couldn't dwell on it. He was expected at a UN Security Council Meeting where he would no doubt be grilled about the US bioweapons program. The program that he'd only just been told about. He was livid.

The report from the CIA that no one had told him before because he had no need to know almost gave him a stroke. Such programs were highly illegal; that the US continued to carry out research was unacceptable, and that was the mildest word he could think of. When he'd reprimanded everyone responsible for the deception, the observation of the Chairman of the Joint Chiefs of Staff that everybody did it, only no one could prove it, infuriated him to the point of nearly striking the man.

Now he would be forced to admit to the wrongdoing and allow the UN to send inspection teams to all the National Laboratories. That it was a terrible breach of security didn't matter. The only way to avert immediate censure and possible siding with the Middle Eastern countries on the part of Russia, China and several smaller countries was to come clean. That all of those countries undoubtedly had bioweapons that could wreak havoc if unleashed in the US notwithstanding.

The British Prime minister had even given him an unwelcome history lesson when he recalled that a South African cardiologist, one Wouter Basson, had been thought to be working with the Israelis on a bioweapon to target blacks, during the apartheid years. It couldn't be proved in court, but there was plenty of circumstantial evidence, and it was widely believed among people who remembered that better evidence had been suppressed by several governments, including the US.

Harper was prepared to swear categorically that the H10N7 strain of influenza had not been developed by the US, nor by any entity within the US, nor by Israel as far as he was aware. However, he had no doubt that he was in for a figurative beating at the hands of the Security Council members. His only defense was to call on all US allies to make their scientists available for questioning as well, and to either repudiate the accusation of making the virus, or admit it if they had. It wouldn't be enough to completely dispel suspicion, especially with the entire Arab world up in arms, but it was all he had.

Before the meeting was scheduled to begin, the first of the suicide bombers breached the gates of the US embassy in Turkey and killed fifteen people.

~~~

More than a week had passed since Ben Epstein's arrival on

site, and he was still virus-free. It was a matter of great relief to Rebecca, as well as to the man himself. It was Ben who had first discovered the extra hemagglutinin protein on the surface of the virus, and had reported it to the CDC, which disseminated the information to everyone worldwide who was working on the problem. However, something nagged at him. No one, Middle Easterner or not, had immunity to this virus. It should have been making everyone sick. The hemagglutinin protein didn't explain the selection of only one ethnic group for illness. There had to be something else.

In the valley, excavation was proceeding rapidly. As the library team unearthed more and more tablets, it became clear that the 9th Cycle civilization represented by this site was not as advanced as the 10th. Summers compared their level to that of ancient Egypt, around 3500 years before the birth of Christ. Therefore, they were losing hope that a medical breakthrough would be made with the translation of these tablets. Nevertheless, photos of each and every tablet were transmitted regularly to Boulder, where Sinclair and his team were working frantically to translate them. In the other department of the Foundation, Research, Nicholas and his team were combing the already-translated records and the index for 10th Cycle mention of anything resembling this flu.

Rebecca's leap of logic that theorized the virus had gone airborne was confirmed by researchers in the Middle East, who, whether they had political opinions or not, were at least still willing to communicate with the expedition. They had worked out an incubation period of seven days while the patient was symptom-free, followed by seven days of mild illness and then an average of seven days of excruciating deterioration before death. Some delay could be accomplished by keeping the patients in an ice bath with IV fluids being administered, but since this was almost as painful as the symptoms leading to death, the patients were always given the choice. Few could endure it. No one had yet determined whether the virus would run its course eventually if the fever and consequent organ failure could be alleviated, since no medication at their disposal achieved that.

Ben chafed at the relatively primitive lab setup that he had. Convinced that there was a genetic key to the puzzle, he desperately wanted a gene sequencer. And a Middle Eastern victim to examine the difference between his genome and that of, say JR's, or Robert's. He had to settle for the DNA sequence from one of the recently dead victims being emailed to him, along with images from an electron microscope, since the researcher who was cooperating with him didn't have a 10th Cycle device. On a morning late in the eighth week, Rebecca appeared in the biology lab.

"Ben, I've been reading about these retroviruses, or parts of retroviruses, that make up so much of the human genome. I ran across an old Wall Street Journal article that talked about remnants of some really old viruses being activated under some circumstances and causing some bad stuff to happen, like cancer growth. I followed up with queries of some later work and found that there's been some progress in that theory. Is there any chance that what we're seeing is a gene, or an expression of a gene, being activated in Middle Eastern people somehow that makes them vulnerable to this virus that would otherwise be harmless?"

Ben sat back on his stool. "You could have something there. To test that theory, we're going to need a number of samples from infected but still healthy people to compare to a random sample of the victims, to see what may be active in the latters' DNA that isn't in the formers'. The greatest concentration of infected but still healthy people that I know of is right here in this camp. Do you think the others will cooperate by giving samples? We'll have to figure out how to get them out to the US for gene sequencing."

"I have no doubt that they'll cooperate. Whether anywhere in the world will be prepared to accept them is another question."

"Is there any chance your Foundation would send us a DNA sequencing machine?" Epstein asked, with little hope of a positive answer.

"Only one way to find out. Let's ask them. But it will take a minimum of two days to get it here, and we'll have to figure out a delivery method. I'm assuming it shouldn't be dropped from a helicopter."

"Probably not," was Ben's dry response.

The next conference call with Boulder brought good news and the opportunity to propose that a DNA sequencer be sent to Antarctica. Rebecca explained why they needed it and emphasized that it probably wasn't a prudent idea to send samples of DNA that might also contain virus cells back to the USA for sequencing. Sarah said that if they could secure one quickly enough, the new virologist could bring it. That would solve the delivery problem. The helicopter would set down far enough from camp to offload both the sequencing machine and the scientist, and Epstein, as the only virus-free individual in the camp, would pick them up in a Sno-Cat.

As relieved as Rebecca was at the news that they had a volunteer, she cautioned that he must be prepared to maintain absolute sterility measures to avoid contracting the virus. "He's not Middle Eastern, is he?" she asked.

"*She* is not. We made sure of that. She can be ready to leave as early as tomorrow."

"We need that sequencer almost as badly as we need her. I'd rather she waited for it."

"We'll get both of them there as quickly as possible."

"What's the sit-rep there?" Daniel asked.

"Not good. We've got the Eastern bloc nations demanding to see our National Laboratories to be sure we aren't making bio-weapons, and the military resisting because we probably are. The Middle East is ready to explode, and your Dr. Epstein is at the center of one controversy. We could see open warfare soon, Daniel."

"What does Epstein have to do with it?"

Rebecca and the others listened in growing astonishment as Sarah described the theory put forth by the Ayatollah Kazemi of Iran. "Ben is Jewish and a virologist, therefore he synthesized this virus in order to wipe out all Muslims."

"What? That's ridiculous! In the first place, he didn't even get here until the first fifteen were dead. Besides, if he contracted it, it would kill him, too," said Rebecca.

"You know that, and I know that. But the radical elements in the Middle East don't care anything about the truth. All they care about is that they have a plausible reason to call for jihad. Ask Daniel. Ask JR. They called it in the first place, and now it's happening."

"She's right," said JR. "We knew it, as soon as we realized it only made them sick, not us." He felt a prickling between his shoulder blades, the sensation of a gun, or rather a nuclear warhead, pointed directly at his back.

Chapter 21 - I'm here to kill it

Within days of the announcement Harper made to the UN, most developed countries had instructed their scientists to put aside political differences and work toward a cohesive response to the threat of disease. While it was true that the bulk of the cases were still confined to Middle Eastern countries, dozens of other countries were seeing small outbreaks here or there, the size dependent on the number of Middle Easterners represented in their respective populations. The ninety-one cases in the US by week eight was the largest group outside the Middle East. In every country, though, the death toll was still 100% of the Middle Easterners who contracted it, irrespective of where they were receiving treatment. Even though the US, for example, had much better medical facilities, the outcomes were no better than in the poorest village in Yemen.

With unprecedented cooperation among agencies responsible for disease control in all of the countries that wished to be involved, the American Centers for Disease Control, or CDC, was allowed to assume leadership. It was quickly decided that dividing the research among countries, with several working on one of four goals, would be the most efficient way to address the growing peril.

The US, Great Britain and Australia would bring all their resources to bear on learning everything possible about the structure of the virus. Following a tip from Rebecca Mendenhall in the ill-fated Antarctica camp, they would also look at how the virus might be acting within cells, after attaching and before making the victim ill. That is, what was going on during the incubation period?

France, Germany and Italy would be working on creating a vaccination. Until a victim survived long enough to develop antibodies, though, this effort was for the future, assuming there was a future. At the current rate of spread, virtually every person of Middle Eastern descent would be wiped out in a matter of weeks.

Russia, China and Japan would put aside their differences and work on understanding why existing antiviral medications failed to halt or even slow down the course of the disease. Rebecca had used both amantadine and rimantadine against it, which should have prevented the virus from entering new cells once administered. This effort would require close cooperation with the countries studying the structure of the virus, since that would have a bearing on what changes to make to the medications to increase their effectiveness.

All Middle Eastern countries were busy treating the patients, but doctors were requested to report to the CDC, as the central clearinghouse, any treatment that delayed the worst of the effects. That knowledge would then be disseminated in an attempt to keep the living victims alive until the other efforts bore fruit.

As week eight drew to a close, the political climate world-wide was less cooperative by far. Not content with his first speech proclaiming a 'genetic bullet' aimed at the heart of Islam, the Iranian Ayatollah made daily announcements concerning the signs pointing to the return of the Twelfth Imam, a figure that many Muslims believed was to return toward the end of the world. Like the second coming of Jesus that Christians looked forward to with a mixture of dread and rapture, the return of the Twelfth Imam was to be ushered in with various signs and portents of violent and dreadful nature. Radical elements who followed the Ayatollah with slavish devotion were all too happy to assist in creating the chaos described.

The coming of the Twelfth Imam, also known as the Mahdi, was prophesied to occur after a period of great turmoil and suffering upon the earth. No one now living in a Middle Eastern country could doubt that this period had arrived. Before too many days had passed, most devout Muslims were actively praying for the relief to be granted when the Mahdi reappeared; that is, the final defeat of Judaism in particular, the establishment of a new world order wherein Islam was to be the only religion practiced, the rediscovery of the Ark of the Covenant which will in turn prove that Islam had been the correct religion all along, and the distribution of enormous amounts of wealth to all Muslims, among other desirable outcomes.

In Iran, the Ayatollah was preparing to reveal himself as the Twelfth Imam as soon as conditions were right. He had even secured a white horse, which was being secretly nurtured and groomed for the greatest beauty imaginable, upon which the Ayatollah would ride to the location of his revelation. Unbeknownst to him, several other imams in various Middle Eastern countries were devoutly considering whether they were in fact the Twelfth Imam. One or two, fancying themselves to have supernatural power by virtue of their stature, visited the sick and dying, to effect a cure, only to succumb to the disease.

In the West, responsible media was urging calm cooperation with medical edicts, while the rabble-rousers were having a field day quoting the inflammatory speeches coming out of Iran and to a lesser extent out of other Middle-Eastern countries. Talk show hosts who had been predicting jihad for years now shouted 'I told you so' from their bully pulpits. Some advocated the same thing that had so disgusted the President when issued from the mouth of his Chairman of the Joint Chiefs of Staff; why not just let the virus run its course and get rid of the problem once and for all. Secure in their hubris that nothing could touch them in their privileged Western life, they spewed hatred until the most vocal of them was found beheaded in his own home, after which most toned down their rhetoric.

The UN Security Council argued daily about what response to make to these provocations, with some members advocating arrest or assassination if necessary of the Ayatollah and others opining that the US journalist who had lost his head received exactly what was coming to him. Still others, who prevailed, urged patience as the medical world was focused on one thing and one thing only: stopping the pandemic.

~~~

On Monday, the middle of the ninth week as Rebecca was tracking it, Ben Epstein suited up and drove the Sno-Cat to the mouth of the canyon, where one of the McMurdo helicopters set down to deliver one Hannah Price, CDC virologist, and her equipment; another 10th Cycle microscope and two gene-sequencing devices. To Ben's utter shock, Hannah turned out to be a small woman in her seventies.

"Hi, Ms. Price, I'm Ben," he said, reaching awkwardly in his cold-weather gloves to shake her hand, also gloved.

"Call me Hannah, young man. Let's get on with it. You can fill me in on the way." With that abrupt statement, Hannah climbed with agility that belied her age into the Sno-Cat.

Ben was consumed with curiosity about his new partner while he drove back, explaining what he, Nyree and Rebecca had done so far, what they were thinking, and what remained to be done. As he explained Rebecca's theory that there was something active or inactive in the Middle Eastern victims' genetic makeup, their genome, that was the opposite in the non-Middle Easterners, Hannah nodded continuously.

"You're thinking that this virus turns on a gene or an allele that makes them particularly vulnerable to the replication of the virus. Or turns it off, with the same effect."

196

"Precisely." Ben wanted to remark on the woman's age and the likelihood that she would be up to speed on such cutting edge work. However, it would have been very rude, and he was not a rude man. He would simply have to observe and determine in that way whether Hannah would be useful or not. Why a woman of her age would volunteer for such a mission was another question that he couldn't ask directly.

"Have you determined where in the gene sequence this mutation would be?" Hannah asked.

"No, because we haven't had the equipment to do so. Thank you for bringing it with you."

"It was sent without my involvement, it just came at the same time."

Hannah's abrupt manner was surprising, but Ben needed the help so badly that he determined to just live with it and adapt. But he couldn't help being more and more curious about her.

"Tell me how you propose to proceed," she demanded.

Ben explained that they had three sets of blood samples on hand. The first were samples preserved from the dead Middle Eastern patients and those of the sick ones that would permit it before they were sent home. The second were samples from the rest of the people in camp, who had been exposed to the virus and now carried it but had not become ill. The third was his blood, the only non-infected sample in camp. He proposed to sequence each sample and then run a comparison to determine differences. After that, they would examine the differences to see if they could spot the trouble. Without the equipment Hannah had brought with her, it would have been next to impossible, and with it was still a monumental task.

"I'll contribute as well," she said. "But, given that the worst expression of the disease occurs in Semitic people, I propose that we also look at the differences between yours and mine first, and

197

focus on those differences as we examine the others."

Ben was thunderstruck. Not only was it a brilliant suggestion, but it showed that Hannah had done her homework well. Having been isolated in Antarctica while work continued on the outside, he felt as if he were far behind current events. He hadn't realized that it was common knowledge that the disease only sickened those of Middle Eastern descent, though he should have known if he'd thought about it.

"Good idea," he returned, revealing nothing of his thoughts. "In fact, what do you say to the idea of taking blood samples from you daily? It could reveal how long it takes for a person not of Middle Eastern origin to contract the virus.

"Of course! That's a brilliant idea."

Ben was more surprised than ever. His suggestion that she would contract it despite taking precautions hadn't even fazed her.

"One of the things we've wondered is whether people of mixed ethnic origins are vulnerable, and if so whether to the same or a lesser extent."

"I suspect that those who have the genetic mutation we're looking for would be, and those who escaped it would not," Hannah answered.

"Wait, this is only a theory," Ben started to protest.

"It's a very good one, and it's our task to prove it," Hannah said, her pronouncement firm and final.

"Yes, ma'am," was Ben's only choice of answer. Besides, they had arrived at the airlock, and it was time to show Hannah how to get in. Hannah would don antimicrobial face masks and gowns, gloves and shoe covers to avoid exposure to the virus. Strict protocols had been put in place to protect Ben, who had allowed them to slip as the weeks went by, since they were quite inconvenient. They would now be followed by Hannah as well, as much for the opportunity to observe a non-infected non-Semitic subject as for her health.

As soon as they had taken these precautions, Ben ushered Hannah through the other side of the airlock, where Rebecca awaited them.

"Welcome, Dr. Price. We're so glad you volunteered to come." If Rebecca had any curiosity about the older woman, she didn't reveal it. But once again, Hannah surprised Ben.

"I suppose you're wondering why an older woman like myself was willing to come here," she said. "I have no family, and have lived a long and productive life. When they said it might be a one-way journey, I knew it was my duty. Rest assured, I'm qualified. Since I had no one to spend my retirement years with, I've continued to work."

In just a few sentences, Hannah had answered all of Ben's unspoken questions, explained her abrupt manner and triggered his compassion. If at all possible, when this was all over, he would take the place of her missing family and friends. Maybe as they worked, she would say more about how she'd come to this state of affairs. Trailing behind the two women, Ben couldn't help but compare Rebecca's youthful step with Hannah's, and was gratified to see that Hannah was sprightly and sure. His misgivings about her age began to melt away with the observation.

Work on the project began immediately, with Ben drawing Hannah's blood sample and the two of them preparing each other's samples for sequencing. Within a few hours at most, they would have a start on proving Rebecca's theory, that there was indeed a genetic component that explained the virus' behavior. Meanwhile, it was time for Hannah to meet the other remaining members of the expedition. She wanted to interview them herself to see if she could spot anything they had been too close to the matter to see.

<center>~~~</center>

Ben took it on himself to introduce Hannah to the rest, who each welcomed her. Some, like Summers, were too distracted with their experiments and documentation, to be especially warm. Others, like Daniel, though busy, had naturally welcoming personalities and were therefore more demonstrative in their welcome, pumping her hand and smiling. Hannah greeted everyone with the same abrupt reserve, but seemed to Ben to be pleased that she was appreciated.

He had saved Nyree for last, because he wanted Hannah to have more time to understand the work he and Nyree had been doing with the samples of algae from the fumarole at the hospital. He hoped that they were on the verge of a breakthrough in determining where this thing had come from, and wanted Hannah's opinion.

Ben didn't know what Nyree's stake in the matter was, other than the chance to get out of this camp and home eventually. Nevertheless, he appreciated that she was working tirelessly to culture numerous samples of the bloom, in the hope that they would be able to spot a microbe in it that looked promising. The lack of any other vector they could imagine in the valley made this their best bet for finding where the virus originated. That the first five to become ill had been assigned to the excavation there at the hospital where the fumarole with its algae was found made it even more promising.

After the introductions, Nyree explained her methodology and the next steps she would take, both refreshing Ben's understanding and bringing Hannah up to speed. Nodding, Hannah indicated her approval.

"Have you been able to see anything yet?"

200

"Not yet, but it's early. I hope to have large enough colonies of whatever the algae harbors to analyze the individual cells by tomorrow."

"Excellent. Please inform me when you do. I'd like to see it for myself."

Nyree turned to Ben with raised eyebrows. At his nod, she answered, "Of course."

By now it was time for the mid-day meal and everyone gathered in the mess hall for it. Rebecca, as usual, announced the latest numbers she'd received from Sarah. Over 32,000 new cases had been reported to the CDC, with a total of almost 50,000 either sick or deceased. The speed of the increase was staggering, even though Rebecca had a predictive spreadsheet that had forewarned her. That it was very accurate said two things; one, that they had estimated correctly that each new case would be responsible for an average of three more, and that at least that number wasn't accelerating. Raj's spreadsheet was easy to modify if a sudden surge indicated an unfavorable mutation, but so far it was proving remarkably stable. However, that was cold comfort when the next week's projection indicated over 140,000 dead or dying, 98,000 of them new cases. Under any other circumstances, it wouldn't have been suitable mealtime conversation.

Since they hadn't seen anyone but themselves for two months, Hannah's arrival constituted a reason to celebrate despite the grim reason for it. The cook had baked a cake with a welcome message on it, and to Hannah's intense discomfort, everyone expected her to make a speech before she cut it, though she wouldn't be able to enjoy it, or the rest of the meal, until she was ensconced in a makeshift positive-pressure environment to avoid breathing the contaminated air.

"What should I say?" she said in a whisper to Rebecca.

"Why not talk about your credentials and why you volunteered to come," Rebecca answered sotto voce.

Encouraged, Hannah began.

"Thank you for the opportunity to tell my story," she said. "I was born in 1945, to parents who remembered the terrible toll of the Spanish flu as well as the more recent tragedy of the Holocaust. They raised me to believe I could make a difference, no matter what my chosen course in life might be. In those days, it wasn't a foregone conclusion that a bright young woman might choose career over a family. In fact, it was rather rare. But, the stories my father told about his older brothers dying of the flu and his parents' grief because they were left behind made me want to do something about illness.

"By the time I was twelve, great strides in discovering the causes of several viral diseases were being made. When I started college in 1960, the virus that causes hepatitis B had not yet been discovered. And I had determined that, rather than becoming a doctor treating diseases, I wanted to eradicate their causes, before they made people sick. I obtained my PhD in virology in 1968, when it was still very much a new field of study.

"You may ask, why, almost fifty years later, I'm still doing this. The answer is simple. Like most women of my generation, I married and expected to have a family. My husband, however, was involved in an automobile accident in 1982 that changed our lives. He was so severely injured that he required three units of blood, which we later understood was infected with HIV. In those days, we didn't have much to fight AIDS with, nor much understanding of all the ways it could and couldn't be transmitted.

"As a virologist, I knew enough to protect myself, and because we had no children I was able to nurse my husband through his illness and death. Suffice it to say, I hate all viruses and especially retroviruses. My parents were gone by that time and I had no siblings, my husband had been an only child as well and his

202

parents were also gone. There was nothing left for me but to spend the rest of my life understanding viruses, their origins, their actions within cells, how to kill them or at least prevent them from replicating.

"That's why I'm here. This virus is another hateful thing, something determined to erase an entire ethnic group from the face of the earth, just as HIV seemed determined, before we understood it, to attack homosexuals and that vermin Hitler to attack Jews. I'm here to kill it."

Her last, simple statement sent a thrill of hope through Rebecca. This valiant woman, with twice the experience of Ben, Nyree and Rebecca put together, was their last resource, but what a magnificent resource she was! A fighter, with reason to hate every aspect of the virus they were up against. Standing, Rebecca led the others in applause that brought the cook and his assistant out to see what the ruckus was.

When the noise died down, Hannah continued in her normal manner. "That's it, then, let's get to work." She, Nyree, Ben and Rebecca were the first to get up and leave for the labs, where they hoped to see the gene sequences from the first two samples completed.

The rest of the scientific group stayed behind.

"What do you think of her?" Daniel asked the group at large.

"Feisty lady," Cyndi said. Being somewhat feisty herself, this amounted to high praise. Angela nodded her agreement.

"Think they can pull it off?" Robert asked.

"If they can't it won't be for lack of effort," Daniel replied, with JR nodding his own agreement. "We've got a top-notch microbiologist, two highly qualified virologists, and Rebecca, who just happens to be brilliant. They have to pull it off. There's no other choice."

It wasn't necessary for anyone to recapitulate what they knew was happening in the outside world; the numbers spoke for themselves. Having been there, Daniel and JR knew all too well what the scene must be like in the relatively primitive medical facilities of much of the Middle East. They didn't need to see the pictures to understand that the hospitals would be overwhelmed, the resources for taking care of the dead unable to cope with the sheer volume of corpses. They didn't need to be told to know that by now, there would be rioting in the streets as hospitals locked their doors and turned away new patients, as the word went out for families to care for their sick at home, and deal with their remains themselves.

It was true that the same conditions wouldn't apply in the West, at least not yet. Fewer numbers and better coordination meant that hospitals would be able to handle the influx of patients, as long as the virus didn't mutate. In that case, even the West would descend into chaos.

Chapter 22 - Heterozygous and Homozygous

In the science building, Nyree excused herself to examine her cultures while the other three went into the infirmary to check on the sequencing progress. It was progressing, but not yet finished. Hannah took the opportunity to question Rebecca about her theory.

"Where did you learn about virus fragments in our DNA?" she asked.

Rebecca responded with a bit of embarrassment. "In an old article in the New York Times, actually," she responded. "I was searching the internet for anything that could be relevant while Ben was studying the cultures and determining who had the virus in their bloodstream. I came across this article that said scientists were speculating that fragments of ancient viruses might be responsible for cancer and some other illnesses when they got activated somehow."

"But, you don't think this virus was present in your index cases, became activated somehow and then spread from there?" Hannah asked.

"Well, I haven't thought about it like that," Rebecca admitted. "That would solve our problem of what the vector is. We haven't been able to determine that, with the idea that the virus was present in the valley."

"Is there anything in the valley that's unusual enough to make you think it might have activated a genetic virus?"

"Well, let's see. There's a light source in the valley that no one has been able to understand or locate. Our botanist, who died of the virus, said something as he was dying that made me think he had a theory, but Nyree was working with him on it and she doesn't know. Otherwise, nothing."

"Hmm. Doesn't sound like something that could cause this. We'll look into it, of course, if Nyree's cultures don't yield an answer. Nothing else, you say?"

"Not that I can think of. Ben?"

Ben shook his head. "I haven't been inside the valley, so I wouldn't know. Hannah, what makes you think an unusual light source couldn't cause it?"

"It wouldn't explain the contagion to people who have never been exposed to the light source," she answered. "I won't rule it out if we can't make headway with the studies you've already undertaken."

"Am I correct in believing more work has been done since that Times article?" Rebecca asked.

"Oh, yes, absolutely. I've been involved in some of the studies myself. Very astute of you to pick it up, Rebecca. It's one thing that could account for the fact that only one ethnic group is affected. Ben, what's your particular expertise in the field?"

"Identification of the strains and prediction of the effect of mutations on human populations. Also vaccine development," he answered. He didn't need to explain to Hannah, as he had to Rebecca earlier, that virtually all strains of seasonal respiratory viruses were transferred from birds to humans, from whence they mutated wildly, presenting new challenges each year as they migrated around the world.

Ben's expertise was to analyze the H and N strains that were cropping up in each season's virus and determine who might be vulnerable based on the history of which strains had been encountered year after year. Once a vaccine had been formulated for the new strain, target populations were warned so that they could take preventive action.

"Excellent. I've done work in vaccine development, but more recently I've been working on gene replacement to attack ancient virus fragments that are present within the patient's DNA. As Rebecca has so aptly discovered, we now know that these fragments can act very much like a stick in the spokes of a bicycle wheel. Activate one, and it creates a cascading effect on hormones that are responsible for immune response along with other biochemical reactions.

"We're fairly certain that viruses cause the conditions under which several different cancers thrive, and we know that certain genetic expressions can code for susceptibility to the herpes viruses. I wouldn't be a bit surprised to learn that there was either a nearly-universal genetic sequence that, depending on its activation, makes an individual susceptible to this virus, or an ancient viral fragment present in Middle Eastern peoples that was somehow activated in your valley. Determining which and what to do about it will be our focus."

Just like that, Hannah assumed leadership of the investigation, with Ben's willing cooperation. If Rebecca's theory was correct, they'd recruited exactly the right virologist, and he would follow her lead. His discovery of the new hemagglutinin was sufficient contribution to assure him his place in history if they could stop this thing. If not, it wouldn't much matter.

While they waited for the gene sequencers to finish with the first two samples, Ben also showed Hannah a number of slides in the 10th Cycle microscope, to familiarize her with the structure of the H10N7 virus as it looked when viewed with that equipment. Hannah had seen the virus under an electron microscope, but the resolution and color differentiation of these slides made her exclaim with pleasure that it was almost like having a 3-D model of the virus. She spent some time turning the images from side to side, flipping them from front to back and up to down, memorizing the face of her new enemy.

In some ways, it was beautiful, looking like a close-up of some globe-forming flower that boasted many colors in each petal. In other ways, it was chilling, foreign, like nothing she had seen before. Where had this thing come from? What caused it to attack Middle Easterners only, even as it infected everyone who came into contact with it? What would kill it, or at least halt its ability to kill? All the questions must be answered, and not necessarily in that order. Hannah would be content to find an effective gene therapy or even a vaccine, and let others answer the other questions.

~~~

Now that Hannah had raised the question, Rebecca couldn't get it out of her mind that the strange light could have something to do with either activation of the virus or some other aspect of the disease that had caused it to attack the Middle Easterners. With el-Amin gone and Nyree consumed with culturing the algae and any microbes to be found within it, she went to Robert with her questions.

"Robert, did Hazar or Nyree ever confide their findings to you with regard to the light in the valley?"

"No, they brought me a few specimens to see if they would fluoresce and cause the light, but none did. Why?"

"Just a theory I'm working on. Do you have any thoughts about what could be causing it?"

"Not really. Is it important?"

"It could be." Rebecca took time to carefully explain the background to Hannah's question. "If we could determine the source of the light, we might be able to determine whether it had anything to do with activating the virus or not. Or at least eliminate it."

"If it will help, I'll do some investigation. Is Nyree busy?"

"She's culturing that algae you took from the fumarole, but it's like watching grass grow. She could probably stand to have something else to do for a few hours. What did you have in mind?"

"Well, it isn't safe to climb with just one. I was thinking I'd belay her while she climbs up to investigate the higher reaches of the canyon walls, if she's willing."

"Why don't we ask her?"

The two walked through the halls to Nyree's lab, finding her napping on a cot. She woke as the door opened, though, and told them they weren't disturbing her. Nyree's work had revealed something in the algae, but it wasn't the coronavirus that caused the illness they were studying. On closer examination, it appeared to be a form of adenovirus. Since it seemed to bear no resemblance to the target microbe, Ben continued his work without considering Nyree's virus to be important. The vector for the N10H7 virus remained unknown, and Hannah wasn't informed of Nyree's discovery.

When Robert suggested his plan, she eagerly agreed, with the stipulation that someone had to check her cultures every hour or so to see what else, if anything, was growing. Rebecca promised to send Ben to do it, and Nyree went to her room to get her cold-weather gear for the trek to the cave opening.

"We'd better clear this with JR and Charles," Rebecca said, belatedly wondering if they were overstepping their bounds by planning to enter the valley without authorization. While Ben went to his own room, Rebecca sought out JR, who was with Daniel and Summers in Summers' office.

"Hey, guys," she said, entering the office, "how's it going?"

"About the same," answered Daniel, whose eyes were glued to a computer monitor that had several open windows tiled for simultaneous viewing. One showed a ticker-tape style stream of information from world markets. While the stock exchanges in the US had been closed since the declaration of emergency, some countries had declined to follow suit, with the result that global markets were down as much as eighty percent. Another window was open to CNN, which was broadcasting from the floor of the UN General Assembly, muted with subtitles rolling across the screen. From a quick glance, it appeared that if the volume had been on, nothing but shouting would be distinguishable. Several others were open to live streaming media sources, from Reuters to AP to the most critical, National Iranian Radio and Television, NIRT.

Leaving Daniel to his monitoring of world status, Rebecca gestured to JR and Summers and took them aside. "Robert and Nyree need to go into the valley," she said.

"I thought..." JR started.

"Hannah has brought up an interesting question, and the only way to answer it is to settle the light source dilemma once and for all," Rebecca continued, throwing JR a look of apology for interrupting him. "She thinks it's possible something in the light source activated the virus, which might already have been in the Middle Easterners' genetic code. If that's the case, it's why the virus only attacks them, and it lets us off the hook, since it's already inside them. Mind you, Hannah doesn't think it's a strong possibility, but while we're waiting for everything else, I thought I'd ask Robert if he had any ideas. He wants to take Nyree in and have her climb to heights she and el-Amin didn't get to before, while he belays her."

JR was inclined to grant Rebecca's request, but before he did, it wouldn't hurt to check with Summers to make sure the man's feathers didn't get ruffled. He looked enquiringly at

Summers. A mutinous expression was on the face of the archaeologist, but he was clearly considering his answer. JR and Rebecca didn't have long to wait for it.

"If it will provide an answer that will let me get back to work before the season is over, I'll agree to it," he said. Wordlessly, JR and Rebecca exchanged a look that spoke of their opinion of Summers' single-mindedness in the face of global disaster. Then JR nodded.

"Go for it," he said.

Rebecca left to inform Robert and Nyree that their mission was a go, while JR, unable to contain himself, confronted Summers.

"What's wrong with you, man? Tens of thousands are dead, and all you can think about is your precious excavation?"

"Did it ever occur to you that there might be records of this disease in the hospital ruins?" Charles answered. "Maybe even records of a cure?"

"They didn't find it in the library," JR countered.

"No, but that's no reason to assume it wouldn't be in the hospital. Come on, JR, it's been weeks and none of us are sick. Let me take a few of the support personnel in there and continue to excavate."

"You're willing to take the risk?"

"Yes."

"All right. But we have to inform anyone who proposes to go in that we can't guarantee they won't get sick. And we can't force them to go if they don't want to."

"Fair enough," said Charles. It was late enough in the day that, although the sun was still high, he preferred to wait for the next day to start. With little thought to how he would get his workers in if Robert and Nyree hadn't returned with the rail cars, he went to recruit some, with JR following to make sure the situation was explained to them in terms they could all understand.

Robert and Nyree wasted no time in heading into the valley. By now, Robert was familiar with every face of the canyon wall that surrounded the valley. He thought it might be necessary to rappel down from the top to find any artificial source of the light, but that would require considerably more effort in climbing the outside slope of the ash cone in the Antarctic environment. If they could check some easily-accessible ledges inside first and find something there, it would be preferable. Nyree and el-Amin had already covered some of the lower reaches, but not being expert climbers, they hadn't ventured further than easily climbed tumbles of rock had allowed; the highest being some one hundred feet or so above the valley floor.

From the top of the roughly circular canyon to the edges of the valley floor averaged some eight hundred feet. Since Nyree was small and wiry, Robert felt he could safely guide her to climb some areas to approximately halfway up. If she found nothing, he would either have to teach her more advanced climbing techniques, which would take more time than they had, or recruit JR to spot him as he rappelled from the top.

Robert and Nyree made their way in silence around the canyon wall until they came to the first waterfall, which emanated from a fissure in the canyon wall about two-thirds of the way to the top. It had carved a path that consisted of several steps where water collected and then flowed over the lip to the next protrusion. The canyon wall was broken nearby, with both vertical and horizontal cracks and ledges that Robert thought would be a good introduction to free-climbing.

Nyree would harness up and carry a length of rope with

212

her. Any chance she had, she would loop it around a sturdy protrusion or crack so that if she needed him to, Robert could lower her quickly. When she couldn't go any further or became concerned about her safety, he would lower her and then try to retrieve the rope. It wasn't the most efficient way to accomplish their goal, but was all they could do with the resources at hand.

"What am I looking for, Robert? Your best guess," Nyree clarified. She and el-Amin had been looking for plants or insects that fluoresced in colonies to reflect off the constant mist at the top of the canyon. The heavy mist, a product of the intersection between the intense cold of the outside and the rising warmth from the volcanic understory of the valley, prevented the sun from shining into the valley even at summer equinox. It also prevented anyone inside the valley from seeing the sky. The light seemed to come from the mist, but common sense told them that it was a reflection. The only trouble was, no one had yet found what could be casting light up to the mist to be reflected.

"Honestly?" Robert answered, "I don't have a clue. If it were lava flow, the quality of the light would be different, and I'd think it would spill over and we'd see it on the walls. It's probably more in your bailiwick than mine."

Nyree nodded and turned to the wall. "Here goes," she said, placing her hands as high as she could reach, one foot on a crack about three feet from the ground. She heaved herself upward, climbing easily from crack to ledge to protrusion.

"Pace yourself," Robert warned. Nyree responded by slowing her upward progress, resting a bit as she placed the rope in its first secure place. Pitons really would have been better, Robert reflected, but then he would have had to instruct her in their use. Free-climbing was all right, as long as she was careful in where she placed her weight. He watched anxiously as she made her way upward.

When she had climbed as far as she could, Nyree was still a few feet short of her goal, what appeared to be a broad overhang that suggested a ledge above it. She called down to Robert for suggestions on how to proceed up and over the overhang, but he was unwilling to risk her safety on a technical move like that.

He asked her to see if she could move horizontally, either from where she was or anywhere she could comfortably see below her perch. In answer, she began to spider sideways, away from the waterfall, until she found a narrow crack that followed the trajectory of a ledge that was mere inches wide. Placing her hands into the crack, she steadied herself as she inched along the ledge, which traveled upward and still further away from the falls.

As she'd hoped, the ledge on which she stood intersected another that led up and back toward the falls, eventually becoming the overhang that had stopped her before. In a heart-stopping maneuver, she transferred her handhold from the crack, which was now below her shoulder level, to the intersecting ledge, and prepared to make the transition with her feet as well. Below her, Robert watched in horror as she slipped, catching herself with her hands only, and her feet scrabbling for purchase on the ledge from which she was trying to transition. When she caught it, she was stuck, stretched to her limit, on tiptoes and with her hands still holding much of her weight close to the wall.

There was nothing Robert could do but climb to her rescue, even though that left no one to belay them down. This had been a foolhardy venture that could yet end in tragedy for one or both of them. But, he had no choice. He couldn't simply leave her there, and she wasn't likely to be talked down after a close call like that. Nor was the belay rope in position to let her down. It took him mere seconds to analyze the situation and begin climbing, making better progress because of his superior height and climbing experience. When he reached her, he straddled her body, taking a precarious balance on his toes and steadying himself with his left hand jammed securely into the crack. Gently, he removed her hand from the upper ledge, holding her body steady by pressing his into her.

"See if you can put your hand in the crack, lovely," he said, unconsciously using the term that he always used mentally for any woman.

Reassured by Robert's calm voice and steady presence, Nyree complied, finding the crack after a couple of passes. "Okay."

"Now the other," Robert directed. This time, she found it more quickly. "I've got it."

"Good girl. I'm going to swing back to the left, now. You wait here until I'm out of the way."

"Okay."

When he'd performed the tricky move, which required all the strength in the fingers of his left hand to steady himself in a lopsided position, Robert retraced his climb, placing his feet easily on the same places where he'd come up. He wouldn't ask Nyree to do the same, though. The belaying rope was a few feet below her present position. Before climbing all the way down, he secured it in the crack they'd been using, inserting a camming device first, through which he fed a sling fastened with a carabiner, wrapping it around the rope.

Then he scrambled to the bottom and told Nyree to let go and push away from the ledge. At first, she was paralyzed by fear of the drop, but as Robert talked, explaining what would hold her up, she relaxed. Without uttering the critical words 'on belay' to indicate she was going to put all her weight on the rope, Nyree swung free. Robert wasn't caught off guard, though, knowing her inexperience and probable fright, he took her weight easily and let her down slowly, directing her to push away from the wall with her feet if she got too close. When she was down, she threw her arms around him and burst into tears.

"Here, now, you did fine. No need for this."

"You saved my life," she answered.

"Only after putting it in danger in the first place. We're going to need another person before we do this again. Let's see if JR can spare a day."

~~~

After seeing Robert and Nyree off on their mission, Rebecca returned to the infirmary, where the gene sequencer had finally finished its work. Before looking at the results, Ben and Hannah prepared two more slides, this time with samples from a deceased patient and from Rebecca, whom they assumed to be carrying the highest number of virus cells because of her role as doctor to the patients. Once they had the machines working on the next slides, they each took a copy of both the original sequences and began to compare them against each other.

Ben took the methodical method of comparing chromosome by chromosome, while Hannah went straight to the loci of several genes she suspected of implication in the disease. Therefore, she was first to find the first difference, an allele, that is, a variant, of the CCR5 gene that in Ben's sample was heterozygous and on hers was homozygous. Since the CCR5 gene has an important role in resistance to infection, this was a significant discovery.

The kicker was that the CCR5 gene made some individuals more vulnerable to certain viruses, and at least one common genetic mutation, the CCR5-Delta32, actually protected individuals with homozygous expressions of it from certain other viruses, specifically several strains of the HIV virus. Hannah would have to think about this, whether it could be the key or not. She would also have to analyze Ben's anomalous CCR5 gene for the genetic deletion and compare it to known mutations like the Delta32. Then she'd have to examine the action of the mutation in attracting or repelling T-cells, the body's infection fighters.

Before settling on this particular difference to investigate, Hannah compared several other locations for other genes associated with immune response, including CD4, the prototype marker for T helper cells, CD8, the marker for cytotoxic or killer T cells, both important in fighting infection, and IL10, an anti-inflammatory cytokine important to immune response to inflammation. However, she found no other areas of suspicion.

It made perfect sense to Hannah that a defective or ineffective CCR5 gene could mean the difference between contracting the virus and dying from it or contracting it and not even becoming ill. What she didn't know was whether Ben's heterozygous expression of the gene was an individual trait, or the ethnic trait they were looking for to explain the difference between desperately ill or dead Middle Easterners and presumably healthy others. The opposite could also be true. Perhaps her homozygous expression of the gene was an individual trait, not necessarily shared by all the members of the expedition and by extension, all non-Middle Eastern peoples. The sample was too small for true discovery. If it turned out to be a promising line of inquiry, they would have to turn it over to the CDC and their multi-national partners to prove it.

The fact that the remaining members of the expedition were still healthy nine weeks after the first sign of illness led her to believe that they would continue to be so. She knew of no virus with an incubation period of nine weeks, except perhaps herpesviroids or the small number of others that could go dormant within an organism's cells only to attack again if the cells were disturbed. The dichotomy of this virus indicated it was not of that type, or so she could hope for the sake of her new friends and indeed for the sake of the world population.

Hannah's next step would be to determine whether the

fatalities' CCR5 gene was heterozygous as well, but to do that she had to wait for the sequencers to finish their next set of samples, at a minimum. Meanwhile, while Ben patiently continued to compare the chromosomes, Hannah started looking more closely into the CCR5 allele that represented what she thought of as the anomaly in Ben's blood sample.

As Hannah's agile mind lined up her mental to-do list, Daniel walked in looking for any sign of progress that he could report to the President in his next call. With Hannah looking pleased and Ben positively excited, Daniel thought they must have made a breakthrough, and indeed, they had, though the investigation wasn't yet finished. Hannah started to explain it to Daniel, but was soon stopped by his upraised hand.

"You might as well be speaking Greek, or maybe Swahili," he said, so thoroughly confused that he had a flashback to his school days.

Hannah drew a breath and calmed herself, realizing that she must simplify it all for Daniel. More slowly, she began again.

It was a matter of high-school biology to understand that an individual's chromosomes contained copies of genes from each of his parents. When the genes' DNA matched in sequence, they were said to be homozygous, or alike. When they didn't, they were said to be heterozygous, or different. When a gene was expressed in different ways, the way hers and Ben's were different, the individual expressions were known as alleles—variations on a theme, to borrow an expression from music. That was a simplification, of course, but Hannah knew she was going to have to explain this to people who couldn't be expected to know or remember it. Mentally, she drew a diagram known as a Punnett square diagram that would illustrate what she meant, using the common brown-eye versus blue-eye phenotype as an example. Yes, that would do to illustrate to the expedition leaders what she had discovered in at least the first two samples. It would be better to have a larger pool of subjects, but they would have to make do with what they had.

By now it was time for the evening meal, and Ben was at a stopping place. They walked together to the mess hall, Hannah explaining what she would say to the others. As far as she was concerned, they were on the right track and it would only be a matter of process of elimination to discover the reason for the virus's behavior.

"Do you think it's as simple as that?" Ben asked.

"Not very likely. In the first place, we need more samples to determine if it's completely normal. Even if it isn't, the fact that you have a heterozygous pair means that one of the alleles is dominant and the other recessive. It isn't very likely that every Middle Eastern individual has the exact chromosome you have. We still have a long way to go before we can even mention it to the CDC at home."

"What are you going to tell them here?"

"That we have a lead, but we have a long way to go."

"Good enough. I'll follow your lead in what to say and not to say," Ben affirmed.

When they got to the mess hall, only Robert and Nyree were missing. Ben asked about them, and Rebecca explained that she had sent them into the valley to again try to determine what the light source was, saying that it would save time in eliminating that as a factor. Hannah nodded, pleased at Rebecca's initiative. Too bad the girl was a practicing doctor. She'd make a great researcher with that kind of methodical mind.

Chapter 23 - Death to the Infidels

Although it was already Monday evening in Antarctica, it was again only about three in the morning on Monday when President Harper's Chief of Staff woke him with another crisis. In Alabama, a mosque had been bombed, taking out several occupied residences nearby. Eleven people were dead, members of the Muslim community that worshiped in the mosque were outraged and demanding reparations already, though the incident had just been reported within the past hour.

The worst part was that a mob of angry rednecks was facing down the National Guard unit that had been rushed to the scene. They wanted to finish the job of destroying the mosque, citing a rumor that there were plans afoot to mount a local jihad to avenge a handful of Muslims who had recently died from the N10H7 virus. With a crowd of upset Muslims on one side and the redneck mob on the other, the Guard unit was requesting orders regarding how to defend themselves and threatening to allow the combatants to just have it out.

Harper rose with his usual ability to come to full attention from a sound sleep. This was just the first in what he expected to be many skirmishes across the country. He didn't have enough National Guard to contain it if it spread, and for a moment he considered allowing this unit to do just as they threatened. Knowing it wasn't a viable answer, he sent for the Secretary of Defense to help him sort out what would be. While he waited for SecDef to appear, he once again cursed the bumbling idiot in the CDC who had delayed their response by failing to report what was happening. If only they'd had just a little more warning, perhaps the pandemic could have been delayed by stronger quarantine orders.

Harper was fully aware of the accusations from the Middle

East that his orders were to round up all Muslims and infect them with the disease. Of course he denied it, but his denials had no effect on the raging lunatics who were using the situation to further their own agendas. It also didn't help that some conservative religious denominations were actively citing passages from Revelation, interpreting them to mean that the pandemic was the fulfillment of prophecy.

One passage he had heard only that morning was from Revelation 6, verses 7 and 8: *And when he had opened the fourth seal, I heard the voice of the fourth beast say, Come and see. And I looked, and behold a pale horse: and his name that sat on him was Death, and Hell followed with him. And power was given unto them over the fourth part of the earth, to kill with sword, and with hunger, and with death, and with the beasts of the earth.*

The preacher who quoted it followed it up with the opinion that 'the fourth part of the earth' referred to the Middle East, and that any attempt to interfere with the natural course of the disease was in direct opposition to the will of God. Naturally, he then railed against all measures intended to halt the spread of the disease and urged his flock to defy the quarantine order. That meant that leaders on both sides of the issue were doing their best to make sure the crisis became even worse.

There were already rumbles in the UN that the Antarctica site should be nuked to eradicate the source of the virus. Only Harper's friendship with Daniel Rossler and his steady, logical refutation of the emotional desire for revenge among the more vocal of those elements was standing against that eventuality. The fact that the virus was now out and spreading rapidly through the Middle East made it foolish to nuke just the small area of Antarctica from which it was only supposed to have come. Why not nuke all of the Middle East, if wiping it out that way was the objective, he argued, but was quick to say that the very idea was ludicrous.

In fact, he would argue next, the handful of scientists there at ground zero seemed to be light years ahead of everyone else in figuring it out. Harper paused in his mental recitation of his reasoning to consider the idea of shipping all of the researchers to Antarctica and telling them they had to stay until they figured it out. Smiling at his own whimsy, he shook his head. No, there would be no nuking of his people in Antarctica while he was President. But what the devil was keeping SecDef? He should have been here by now.

It seemed longer than it actually was before SecDef arrived in response to Harper's call. As soon as Harper had explained the situation, he gave orders to send reinforcements to the embattled Guard unit in Alabama.

"Mr. President, I think it's time we brought our regular troops home from the Middle East. We're doing no good there, and we can use them here."

Harper thought he would never hear such a suggestion from his war-mongering subordinate, but he fully agreed. The remaining personnel in the Middle East would be sitting ducks when it erupted over there, and as SecDef had observed, they were needed at home. He exercised his privilege of executive order to make it so.

By the time most Americans rose later in the morning, hundreds of young soldiers were sighing with relief that they were going home. No matter what was going on at home, it couldn't possibly be as bad as what was going on where they were deployed. They had no idea that soon dozens, then hundreds of supposedly Christian leaders of the most conservative denominations, especially in the South, would begin urging their congregations to take matters into their own hands to help eradicate the Muslim presence in the Land of the Free.

Since he was up, Harper decided to call Antarctica and see what progress they were making for himself. Then he would have his Press Secretary set up a televised press conference to inform his constituents that everything possible was being done.

"Good morning, Mr. President. A bit early for you, isn't it?" Daniel asked. He was bleary-eyed with fatigue and ready to go to bed for some much-needed rest, but this call was important. At any moment, Daniel was prepared for a call from Harper telling him that the nukes were on their way. He didn't dare miss the call, because his last act would be to call Sarah and say goodbye. Thankfully, this wasn't it.

"Good morning, Daniel. It's getting a bit hairy out here. Wondering if your folks have made any progress."

"As a matter of fact, our new virologist did tell us at dinner that she has a possible lead. She said they've got some work to do before it will be confirmed, though."

"That's still good news, my friend," said Harper. "Any idea what she's looking at?"

"I didn't follow it all, but she's identified an anomaly on a certain gene between the sample of her blood and the sample of Ben Epstein's. If you'll give me a moment, I'll get Rebecca to come and give you the straight skinny."

"Ben Epstein, that's the Jew that all the rabble-rousers are saying engineered the virus?"

"Yes, sir, but that's patently absurd. He didn't arrive until after the first fifteen cases were dead."

"You know that, and I know that, but the man is going to be a target for whatever's left of the Middle East if he ever gets out of there. Those guys won't let a good story be confused by the facts."

"That's unfortunate, Mr. President. He's working tirelessly

to find the answer. You know he is at risk, too. No matter how much they hate each other, Jews and Arabs are all genetically Semitic. He'd probably die just like the rest of them if he contracted it. Speaking of which, how's Israel doing?"

"So far, so good. We warned them as soon as we knew, and they closed their borders. I've heard there were some pretty harsh quarantine conditions, but Yedidyah accomplished his objective. As far as I know, there are no cases there."

"Mixed blessing," observed Daniel, who knew exactly what the enemies of Israel would say about it.

"True," responded Harper, who also knew. "But there's also a news blackout, so hopefully it won't get out. If it does, they may find nuclear weapons pointed at them."

"Speaking of which," Daniel said.

"Just rumbles so far, Daniel. You know I'd give you a heads-up. Not that it would do you any good, but at least you'd have time to..."

"Just so," Daniel said, before Harper could spell it out. "Thank you. We couldn't ask for more."

"It wouldn't be my choice, Daniel, you know that."

"Yes, sir, but if it will prevent Armageddon, we both know what you'll have to do."

"I'm glad you understand. Push your scientists to work as fast as they can, Daniel. I don't know how long I can hold off, and I don't want to ever have to face Sarah if..."

"I know. We're doing our best."

Depressed by the turn his call had taken, Harper took a few minutes to have breakfast with his wife before getting in touch with his Press Secretary. "I've just spoken to Daniel Rossler, dear. What a fine man he is."

"Yes, we've always thought so. What brought on that observation just now?"

"We spoke of a potential for their site to be destroyed, and them along with it, to prevent global nuclear war. He understands. He told me so without so much as a quiver in his voice. Esther, how can I even consider it?"

"Nigel, when I married you, I knew you would always put the good of the nation before yourself, and the good of the world before the nation if it came to a choice. You've never let me down. You'll do what you must, but only when all other options have been exhausted. And you'll be able to say, 'I did my best.'"

If only his best were good enough, Harper reflected. Good enough to save his friend while also saving the world. How would history view him? He was a President who had successfully negotiated the return of the great treasure of the Tenth Cycle Library knowledge to the US and had led the world-wide effort to destroy the evil Orion Society, but was also the President who was helpless to stem the tide of viral death that threatened to destroy the Middle East, and with it, the world. Would there even be a future from which to look back on this history? Harper gave his wife a wan smile, knowing she would support him to the jaws of hell if she must. He only hoped it wouldn't come to that, but barring a miracle, it would.

~~~

Harper's report to Daniel that President Yedidyah of Israel had managed to contain all news coming out of Israel was already out of date. Israel had imposed a news blackout with armed Shin Bet operatives standing in the wings to impose swift punishment of any reporter who defied the order. No news of any kind regarding the H10N7 virus was to be reported, neither bad nor good. Firewalls had gone up in all server farms of internet service providers, and the government considered the blackout complete. Mossad and Shin Bet both knew, however, that the blackout was permeable. Numerous peer-to-peer solutions for circumventing internet censorship by repressive regimes meant that they had to employ constant surveillance for keywords such as the name of the virus, including several cruel nicknames like 'the Arab solution'.

Just as they had known, word eventually leaked out. In the tenth week of the virus outbreak, an Israeli citizen, unaware of the havoc he was about to cause, got word to his son at an American university that he was well, and that the country had been informed that there were no cases of the virus there. The son, young and hotheaded, blogged the information and his opinion that the virus was a plague that God had inflicted on the Middle Eastern nations whose political objectives included wiping out the Jewish state. Within forty-eight hours, the blog had been tweeted and re-tweeted on Twitter, discussed extensively on Facebook, flooded with angry comments from people with Middle Eastern connections and finally shut down by the platform provider because of excessive traffic.

But, the damage was done. The assertion that Israel was free of the virus was another arrow in the quiver for radical elements. Ayatollah Kazemi urged his constituents to demand a nuclear response to the notion that Israel was complicit in the development of the virus. Within seven days of the leak, even the most moderate of the Middle Eastern nations had agreed to join an assemblage of affected countries. As an ally of Iran and supplier with a large arsenal of nuclear weapons, North Korea was invited to join the assemblage as well. Chillingly, the hastily-formed group was called *In'a'al Mayteen Ehlak*, which means Death to the Infidels. North Korea, Iran and Pakistan among the participants all had nuclear weapons.

As week eleven dawned, nearly three hundred thousand new cases were reported, over ninety percent of them residing somewhere in the Middle East. This constituted a total of more than four hundred and forty thousand cumulatively. In terms of previous pandemics, it didn't yet rival the Black Death of medieval times, or even the Spanish flu, which had taken an estimated fifty million lives between 1918 and 1921. However, the more rapid spread of the disease meant that it would surpass the seventy-five million of the Black Death within another five weeks if not checked. Across the Middle East, support for the radicals was snowballing, and the voices of those crying out for revenge were becoming louder by the day.

Even as he deplored what was being said and done, Harper could understand the reasons. The medical situation had become so desperate that mobs were now burning hospitals, their spokespersons saying that if they couldn't save anyone, they might as well not exist. Even among Western nations, the drain on medical facilities was beginning to reach crisis proportions.

In the Middle East, with no choice but to treat ill family members at home, the sick treating the sicker, and everyone in a household condemned to eventually contract the illness and die, despair set in. An intolerable stench hung over the most highly populated cities, entire families sometimes being found dead and decomposing in their homes because no one was well enough to perform the death rites. Indeed, had there been someone well enough, there was no one to dig the graves. Among the poorest neighborhoods, corpses were turning up in the streets; with no one to collect them, conditions began to resemble those of medieval Europe during the black plague.

Throughout the early days of the crisis, governments had only haphazardly imposed quarantines, especially after that became the demand of the imperialist Western states. What might have saved many lives was instead denounced as a Western ruse to once again crush the Middle East under the heel of imperialist nations and kill them all. Listeners in every Middle Eastern country were pledging their lives and resources to the Ayatollah Kazemi, the Twelfth Imam, for only he could save them now.

The only thing that saved Israel from nuclear attack that week was the caution from moderates that any nuclear strike would invite retaliation from the West, which would surely wipe them out even more rapidly than the virus was doing. Before taking such a step, why not consult with doctors and scientists to determine if the West was just giving lip service to their search for a cure?

Listeners in the US and Europe breathed a sigh of relief as the vote was taken and common sense prevailed for another week. No nuclear action for at least one week, was the decision. North Korea, always overconfident in their ability to strike a killing blow to their bitter enemy, the US, was the only dissident. They would bear watching, lest they decided to act alone.

~~~

As soon as he had received the morning brief from his staff, Harper sent for the head of the CDC. Knowing he was expected to resign after the crisis was over, he nevertheless was doing everything in his power to make up for his blunder in not calling the virus to the President's attention before a civilian did. He was prepared to explain what progress they were making, even though he had to admit it was all on the backs of the two virologists in Antarctica, thanks to an innocent question by a civilian doctor. That fact alone made his organization look like a bunch of Keystone Kops, running around with much sound and fury and little effect. However, they did have access to a larger pool of unaffected blood samples, and the analysis was beginning to show some progress.

Without asking whether Harper would want the detailed scientific explanation, he launched into a loosely-organized report of a gene known as CCR5, its usual action in the body, its dual nature, the anomaly in Ben Epstein's blood that had led to research about a genetic mutation of it now designated Mu36. By the time he reached that point, Harper had heard enough to know

228

that someone would have to draw him a picture before he'd understand it. He cut the other man short.

"It's lucky for you that I'm talking to Dr. Rebecca Mendenhall on a daily basis, otherwise you'd have to bring me up to speed on all that. As it is, I've got the basics."

The director stood in shock for a moment, wondering why he'd been summoned then. Foolishly, he asked the question.

"I'm just trying to understand," said Harper, "why with all the latest equipment, dozens of the finest minds in medical research, and an almost unlimited budget, it's a couple of virologists and a civilian doctor stuck in Antarctica that are making the biggest discoveries."

Since he didn't have an answer for the question, which he suspected was rhetorical anyway, the director didn't try to explain.

"What do you want me to say, Mr. President?"

"Just tell me if we're making progress."

"Oh, yes, sir! Absolutely. We're working on a gene therapy that should stop the deaths, if not the infections."

"How long?"

"It's hard to say. It's our sole focus, and we know what we need to do. Our only problem is a delivery method that can be applied in the massive numbers we'll need. Then the manufacturing...I'd say less than a year, sir."

Harper exploded. "Have you even looked at the predictions? Do you know at what rate this thing is spreading? What planet have you been living on? We have less than two months before the entire population of the Middle East is wiped out. We probably have less than two weeks before they start taking the rest of us out with nuclear retaliation! Good lord, if it mutates the entire world population could be gone in six months. Get me the cure in a week, or we're all dead."

A shaken CDC Director arrived in his office half an hour later. He called in his first assistant director and formally handed over the reins, then went home and resigned by handgun. Harper didn't have time to mourn him.

Chapter 24 - It's important and urgent

Hannah and Ben had been hard at work, analyzing every sample they had. First, they double-checked Ben's first findings. Every remaining healthy member of the expedition had viral cells and antibodies in their blood. Every sample that Rebecca had preserved from those who had become ill had viral cells but no antibodies, a fact that gave Hannah a clue about how the disease could have so overwhelmed the patients as to cause death within three weeks.

Despite all precautions, Hannah's blood was also now showing both viral cells and antibodies, as was Ben's. The latter fact created some confusion, which they hoped to clear up as they sequenced the DNA in each sample. None of the other people of Middle Eastern origin had developed antibodies.

Because they had only two machines and the sequencing took up to eight hours per sample, it was slow going. Preliminary results showed that Hannah's suspicions were probably correct. Ben's heterozygous CCR5 genes were the only ones to be found that had characteristics of both Middle Eastern and non-Middle Eastern strains. All of the victims' CCR5 genes were homozygous copies of the Mu36 variation. Everyone else's were identical to Hannah's, all of which was found to be the norm in both her small sample of Middle Eastern and non-Middle Eastern individuals and a larger sample hastily tested through the CDC's home laboratory.

Ben was the anomaly. Why did he have one copy of the normal gene, and one of the abnormal? Was that why he had been able to develop antibodies for the infection? Would it be important in the discovery of the cure? The first question was the most urgent for Hannah. The answers would tell them how to direct the CDC in their testing.

"Ben, what do you make of this?" Hannah asked him, when all of the samples had been sequenced and the results charted.

"I don't know. Maybe my parents would," he remarked. "The only thing I can think of is that my grandparents escaped the Holocaust and migrated to Israel, then to the US when they couldn't adjust to the desert climate. Maybe there was intermarriage somewhere back in my lineage that let me inherit that normal allele. Lucky for me. Otherwise I'd be dead by now."

Lucky indeed, no matter how it had come about. Hannah asked him to check with his parents as soon as the time difference lined up so that his parents would be available to Skype. Meanwhile, she tuned the Tenth Cycle microscope to an even greater magnification and began to painstakingly map the Mu36 allele for how its sequence differed from the normal gene. There were several approaches that the cure could take, one of which wasn't a cure at all but an attenuation of the virus so that victims could recover. Hannah preferred a more proactive approach, one that would prevent people from getting the virus in the first place. Now that it was out in the world, there was no putting the genie back in the bottle, but perhaps a vaccination could be devised.

Best of all, in her opinion, would be gene therapy, but doing that on a massive scale would be cost-prohibitive as well as leading to other problems. One of them would be that, having already determined that this virus was engineered to attack them, how many of the potential victims would line up to be deliberately infected with another, which was required for the gene therapy vector? Neither of those issues was of interest to Hannah, though she acknowledged them. Her job was to find what was broken and fix it, bearing in mind that by fixing it she could break something else.

It hadn't escaped her notice that one genetic mutation of this very gene conveyed some protection against HIV. What advantage did this Mu36 mutation bring to the table that it would have spread so uniformly in Middle Eastern genetic heritage? Unfortunately, there was no time. Unless they stumbled on it by accident, they wouldn't know unless and until the genetic cure began to backfire.

Communication with CDC confirmed that of all victims sick from the infection worldwide, and every deceased patient whose DNA samples they could access had homozygous copies of the CCR5-Mu36 gene. That had to be the key. Something in the DNA of the gene was missing, the part that helped attract the killer T-cells that would fight the infection, maybe. In addition, it was preventing the creation of antibodies to the virus, resulting in a massive replication of virus cells that overwhelmed the body in a short period of time. If that something could be replaced, this virus would become harmless, not even as detrimental as the common cold.

Ben reached his parents within hours of his conversation with Hannah about his anomaly. "Mom, do you know about anything in my genealogy that would account for having Gentile genes?" He knew that was a huge simplification, but his mom wouldn't have any clue about how genetics worked.

"Not on my side of the family," she insisted. "But your dad's people, maybe they intermarried."

"Can you find out? It's important."

"Of course *bubbe.* I'll call your grandmother tomorrow."

"Mom, it's important and urgent. Can you call her today?"

"All right, all right, if it's that important. Anything else you want me to do today, Ben?"

With a flash of inspiration, he thought of something else, but wasn't sure he could secure her cooperation. "Yes, Mom, and this is also important and urgent. I need you and Dad to contact my work and have them come out and take blood samples."

"Blood samples! *Oy gevalt*, are you sick, Ben?"

"No Mom, but I should be. My blood is protecting me. I need to know if yours or dad's is the same. Promise me you'll do this for me?"

"Yes, but then I want the whole truth from you."

"Yes, Mom, okay. Will dad cooperate?"

"Yes, even if I have to threaten to cut off..."

"Mom!"

"I'll talk to you later, son."

It was past midnight in camp, and Ben was exhausted. He wanted nothing more than to go to bed, but Hannah was putting him to shame. She seemed ready to stay up until they got to the bottom of this thing, despite her age. Ben tried to read some of the charts she was developing, but he could hardly keep his eyes open. At last, defeated, he told her he had to get some sleep and retired to his room. Hannah stayed up another couple of hours, until her eyes wouldn't focus, and then went to bed herself. Though neither knew it, they were on the verge of a breakthrough of sorts.

~~~

Rachel Epstein was a woman of average intelligence who made up for her intellectual disadvantage with her husband and son using keen observation and knowledge of human behavior. Ben's assertion that he wasn't sick but should be, coupled with his sudden trip to Antarctica, had to have something to do with this terrible flu the President warned about. Rachel, a good citizen, didn't venture out of her house for anything less than an empty refrigerator, and recently not even for that. The family belonged to a synagogue, but they weren't particularly observant, so as soon as the President said 'stay home', both Rachel and Paul stopped going at all. Consequently, Rachel wasn't aware that an outbreak of the flu had occurred among some of her acquaintances. She didn't learn of it, in fact, until she called her mother-in-law, Ruth Epstein, to ask Ben's question.

"Why would he want to know that?" Ruth complained. "It's old news." Her accent, forged in Germany and scarcely softened by years in the US, was as familiar to Rachel as her own mother's flat Bronx utterances after being married to Ruth's son for nearly forty years.

"I don't know, *Oma*," responded Rachel, using the name Ben had always called his paternal grandmother. Why her in-laws insisted on keeping some of their German language alive, she would never know. It was an insult...but that was not what she was calling about. She would let it go. "He told me it was important and urgent."

"Is he sick?"

"That's what I asked. He said no, but he said he should be. That his blood was protecting him, of all things."

"We don't speak of it," Ruth responded, "But my Benjamin was conceived out of wedlock, with a German woman, a *shiksa*. His father insisted that his wife, my mother-in-law, take him in and raise him as her own. She only told him when they were preparing to send him out of Germany, may she rest in peace."

"Let me get this straight. Paul's paternal grandmother was not his father's real mother?"

"No, she was not. She was German."

"So, if Ben's blood is protecting him, it must be his German blood," Rachel concluded.

235

"'*Az s yyr'anyq*, ironic," was Ruth's pronouncement.

Ironic indeed, given that both of the older Benjamin's parents were victims of Nazi genocide. Rachel dreaded telling Paul that his father was a half-German bastard, even though it was apparently saving their son's life. But first, she needed to report that to Ben, and then to call the CDC as Ben had instructed.

Hours later, after Paul had come home from work and both had submitted to cheek swabs and blood draws at the hands of Ben's colleagues, Rachel dropped her bombshell on her husband. His response puzzled her, since she thought he would be horrified, or at least in shock. Instead, he calmly said, "Rachel, my love. You must not set foot outside this house. I will do the shopping."

By morning, Ben had both his answers. He was part German, and his parents' blood samples bore out the theory. Mom's had two CCR5-Mu36 genes, while dad's had the same heterozygous qualities that Ben's did. One normal, one Mu36. That meant that anyone of mixed heritage that had one normal gene would probably not become ill, based on his experience. It was good news...great news in fact. Ben and Hannah reported back to the CDC that massive sequencing should begin if they could gain the cooperation of equivalent Middle Eastern agencies. There had to be some number of the Middle Eastern population who would prove immune or at least resistant to the disease. The next question was, what percentage? And would it be enough to stave off nuclear war?

The new Acting Director of the CDC wasted no time in calling the President with the good news. Though he couldn't say yet what percentage of the Middle Eastern population was not at risk, that any might be was a ray of light in the midst of the political thunderstorm. That Americans had discovered it was even better.

236

It remained only to convince the scientists in the affected region to trust the information enough to do the testing that would determine the numbers.

As Harper remarked, that was a whole different kettle of fish. It would require finesse, and because it wouldn't help save lives already at risk, Harper directed the CDC to leave it to the State Department to determine how best to break the news. Then he sent for the Secretary of State to bring her foreign policy advisers for the Middle East and formulate a way to insert the good news in such a way as it would not seem to be a ruse. That delay proved to be beneficial later.

Chapter 25 – Ben is sick

After the first attempt that had nearly resulted in a bad fall for Nyree, Robert was reluctant to pursue the light source unless they could also recruit JR for the venture. More than a week had passed before JR found the time to do it, but at last his duties as expedition director were more or less at a standstill. Daniel was handling communications regarding the virologists' progress with their testing, there was no more need to cajole the support workers into giving their blood and cheek swab samples, and Summers had persuaded a few of the support people to work on his dig, so everyone was occupied. He was ready to help with the climbing.

The three climbers accompanied the workers on the rail line, but the two groups split up upon arrival in the valley. Not for the first time, JR pondered the suspension of reality in Antarctica. Here it seemed timeless, especially in the valley, with its uniform light, night and day, presumably summer and winter, though they hadn't experienced winter here yet. Even though they were in constant communication with the outside world, it still didn't seem real. The world was on the brink of a nuclear holocaust, and this little part of it could still be the first target, yet all seemed peaceful except in the lab where the virologists worked. He had to consciously bring to mind the date, now mid-January.

Christmas had passed unnoticed and un-celebrated in their single-minded search for answers. Hannah had arrived that week, which also distracted them from the date. Sarah and Nick had video-conferenced with Daniel so he could watch the baby tear the wrapping paper off his gifts, but JR had left the room when tears began streaming down Daniel's face. The disappointment of missing his son's first Christmas was bad enough, but subsumed in the knowledge that he might miss all the rest of Nick's firsts, it overwhelmed him. JR couldn't bear to witness his brother's despair. Instead, he'd gone to Rebecca and held her close, whispering his Merry Christmas to her. At least they were together. They had that. What anyone else did, he didn't know. There was no special meal, just their normal fare.

Now, almost three weeks later, it was as if time had completely stopped. Outside this place, nearly half a million people would die of the 9th Cycle virus this week, and another eight-hundred thousand or more would wake up with a death warrant in their blood. But here, time was suspended.

While JR harbored these grim thoughts, Robert and Nyree chatted about trying the same spot again. She never had made it to the broad part of the overhang, which was hidden from the spot where she lost her footing. If there was anything on top of that overhang to give them a clue about the light source, they'd missed it. Robert was considering it, but to do it, he would have to climb, leaving JR to belay him. It was risky, since JR wasn't very experienced, but he was more familiar with climbing than Nyree. He also had huge feet, the better to balance his six-foot-ten frame. Robert wasn't sure JR would be able to get a purchase on the narrow approach ledge, even in climbing shoes. Interrupting JR's silent musings, Robert asked for his thoughts on the climb.

"Dude, if you're willing to climb up there, I'm willing to watch you from down here," JR said, his small joke bringing him out of his gloom.

"Thanks, mate," Robert said, heavy on the sarcasm.

It was decided then. Robert would climb, placing anchors for the ropes so that Nyree could follow him. JR would stay on the ground and follow instructions. Robert began his climb with the belaying rope trailing behind him, but fixing a climbing rope to anchors every few feet for Nyree's sake. Even though she had climbed this pitch freestyle before, she'd lost her nerve with the near disaster, and would be more confident if she had somewhere to clip on when she felt the need. It seemed like no time before

Robert was at the transition point where he would have to let go of the crack in favor of the ledge at his shoulder level.

This was where Nyree got in trouble before. The ledge was above her sight-line, since she was several inches shorter than Robert. In looking up to see where to put her hands, she'd lost her footing and barely saved herself by grasping for the ledge. Robert, however, could see that there was an even better handhold further back from the edge, and was able to pull himself up without difficulty. The rope he placed there for Nyree's benefit helped her over the transition and onto a broad ledge. Looking around, Robert noticed that it continued well past the location of the waterfall that tumbled out of the living rock below it, and as far around the canyon wall as he could see on that side. A section had fallen away right where the transition point was, but the ledge continued on the other side of the gap, again as far as he could see.

"I'll be damned," he said to himself, just as Nyree scrambled to a standing position beside him.

"What is it?" she said.

"I could have saved myself some trouble if I'd done this first thing," he answered. "Now I know how the valley was formed."

"Really? Just because of this ledge? How do you figure?"

"It's a cinder cone," he replied. "I've known that all along. But I didn't notice, when Cyndi and I climbed up outside, that the opening at the top is broader than at the bottom of the valley. It's going to be a series of steps where later eruptions partially filled the valley until just the small area it has now was left. We're standing on one."

"Hmm," she replied. "What does that mean for our search?"

"That if we don't find what we're looking for on this step, we may want to take the other approach, and search from the top down."

"Well, I don't see any plants up here," she answered.

"No, and I don't think we'll find any further up, either. For one thing, it's going to get colder as we approach the rim, and for another, I'd bet my last dollar that everything in the valley was imported by the first people to settle it."

"The 9th Cyclers?" she asked.

"I don't think that's been completely established," he said, "but yes, if they were the first."

By mutual consent, they began to amble along the ledge, though they didn't want to go far because they couldn't see JR, nor he them from where he stood close to the wall at the bottom. After half a mile or so with no luck in finding any likely source for the light, they turned back until they reached the gap in the ledge and then shouted down to JR that they needed to climb some more. A faint echo of his voice shouting back at them let them know he understood, and once more Robert took the lead.

The next step was another two hundred feet or so from the previous one. Upon gaining it, Robert estimated he was some six hundred feet above the valley floor, and the temperature had dropped noticeably, though it still wasn't cold. As he looked left and right along the ledge where he stood, Robert could see that this step was more promising. To adequately explore this step before they had to climb down and return to camp, he needed help, so he got down on his stomach, hung his head over the ledge, and called to Nyree to come up.

They decided to go in opposite directions, Nyree clockwise and Robert counterclockwise, back toward the waterfall again, though it was still far below them. If anything that looked interesting or out of place was found, they were to shout for the other. Robert kicked himself for not thinking to bring walkie-talkies, but there it was. They didn't have them and would have to make do. Thus it was that he turned back upon hearing Nyree's high clear voice singing out. Striding as quickly as he dared back along the route he had followed, he soon came to Nyree, who was standing in front of something that looked like a klieg light surrounded by natural stone. What the hell?

As Robert approached, he saw with alarm that Nyree was stooping to pick up one of the glowing rocks at the edge of the pile. As soon as her hand touched it, the light in it went out. She dropped it in alarm and Robert ran to cover the last few feet between them. Nyree heard his footsteps and turned to him, a confused look on her face.

"Robert, what could this be?"

"I don't know, let me take a look."

Robert picked up the rock that Nyree had dropped and examined it carefully. To his trained eye, it looked like a tiny cooled lava bomb, with a high concentrate of iron ore embedded in it. He couldn't see a damn thing that would account for it throwing out the equivalent of a laser-beamed flashlight, nor for the light to have gone off when Nyree picked it up. Careful not to look directly into the broader beam that was directed upward, Robert examined the rest of the pile as well as he could. It seemed to be composed of many of the same type of rock, piled into a large cairn, all emitting a strong blue-white light so that the beams joined and streamed as one into the mist that collected at the rim. But, how was it possible? What had caused the rocks to emit light, and why were they still doing it, assuming it was a man-caused phenomenon, over 35,000 years later? And why did handling them turn them off?

Robert and Nyree discussed it briefly and decided to bring just the one rock back with them for laboratory analysis. Whether it would tell them anything, since its light was gone, was a question they couldn't answer. He placed it in his backpack and helped

Nyree climb over the edge of their perch, then followed her on the ropes. By the time they reached the valley floor, JR had stretched out for a nap, which was why they couldn't raise him by shouting to belay them down. Between the noise from the waterfall and the four hundred feet of vertical distance, their voices were lost. When they did reach the bottom, Robert felt justified in kicking JR to wake him up, but regretted it when JR leaped to his feet and charged, still not fully awake. Only Nyree's scream brought him back to himself.

"Sorry, dude. I should have told you not to wake me like that. When I'm asleep, I'm sometimes back in combat."

"It's okay, mate, I get it. No harm, no foul. I won't do it that way again." Robert remembered a time when JR was on the edge of out of control most of the time. That he'd made enough progress to even say the word 'combat' was fantastic. It had to have been Rebecca's influence. With that passing thought, he let it go and started telling JR what they'd found, beginning with the nature of the valley in which they stood, which caused JR to shiver with the knowledge of the volcano beneath their feet again. The part he liked was that they'd discovered the source of the light, though the discovery raised as many questions as it answered. He looked up at the glowing mist far above their heads in awe.

"You mean, these rocks just, shoot light out of them like a laser beam?"

"Something like that, though it isn't as focused. But, look here," drawing the small rock from his backpack. "I saw this one go out when Nyree picked it up."

Nyree ducked her head and blushed when she saw JR's frown, but it wasn't directed at her. It was a frown of puzzlement. "How...?"

"I don't know, mate, that's why I'm taking it back. I'll have to examine it under one of those fancy microscopes that Rebecca

243

and Nyree have." Then, thinking twice, he turned to Nyree. "You have no idea what caused that?"

"No," she reminded him, "my specialty is microbiology, I don't know a thing about rocks. I'm pretty sure that of the three, animal, vegetable or mineral, those fall squarely into the mineral category. Your bailiwick, Robert."

"Maybe so, but this is like nothing I've ever seen."

"Well," said JR, "The thing to do is look at it under magnification, take a picture and send it back to the Foundation. Let them find someone who can explain it."

"That'll do 'er," Robert replied. They continued to the rail line terminus to wait for Summers and his crew to appear, and then everyone left the valley for the night.

~~~

Examining the Mu36 mutation of the gene from fifty-one samples took time and infinite patience, not to mention both 10th Cycle microscopes. Therefore, the next morning when Robert requested some time with one of them to examine his rock, an incredulous Hannah flatly refused to relinquish either of them. Ben hadn't appeared at breakfast, but she expected him at any moment, and he would need the one she wasn't using. If and when they finished their task, Robert could have one for his project. JR agreed that the virus study took priority, and Robert understood, though he was disappointed. He resumed cataloging his soil samples instead.

It was two hours later when Hannah, absorbed in her examination, realized that Ben still hadn't made an appearance. She didn't begrudge him his rest, but it seemed that he never got to the lab as early as she, nor stayed as late. Accordingly, she took a break and found Rebecca.

"I'm concerned about Ben. He seems more tired than he should be," she stated.

244

"What's he doing?" Rebecca asked.

"Well, actually, I don't know. I haven't seen him all day. I assume he's sleeping."

Alarmed, Rebecca questioned Hannah about Ben's demeanor on the previous day. What she heard worried her as well. She told Hannah she would take care of it and went to JR.

"Honey, I'm afraid Ben is sick," she announced.

JR was sitting at his desk, reading the news feed that Sarah had forwarded from Mary's firm. None of it was good news. When Rebecca appeared and made her statement, he looked up in surprise. "Well, is he or isn't he?"

"That's just it, he hasn't come into the lab this morning. I'd like you to go with me to his room."

JR stood, stretched, and looped his arm around her shoulders. "Lead the way."

When they reached the dormitory, they consulted the handwritten directory for the correct room, then knocked on the door. There was no answer.

"Where could he be?" Rebecca fretted.

"Let's make sure he isn't here, before we mount a search," JR responded. He tried the doorknob. Locked. Taking a master key from the key ring at his waist, JR unlocked the door and opened it a few inches, sticking his head in cautiously before uttering a muffled oath and flinging the door open for Rebecca to see. Ben lay in tangled sheets, a sheen of sweat on his face and breathing raggedly.

"Oh, no," Rebecca sighed. "This is the virus; he's showing symptoms now. Damn it, JR, this could mean it's mutated."

By now, JR was almost as familiar with the behavior of viruses as Rebecca and the virologists were. He knew that by going unprotected into the room, he and Rebecca had likely been exposed to a mutated version. There was no help for it now, though. They needed to get Ben to the infirmary and begin treatment as soon as possible. With difficulty, they roused Ben and asked how he felt.

"Lousy," was the answer. "So much for my bastard German blood."

JR sat with him while Rebecca scurried back to the infirmary for a mask, informing Hannah as she scooped it up that they had found Ben and he was quite ill. For the first time, Rebecca saw a look of regret and compassion cross Hannah's wrinkled countenance. Maybe she had a heart after all.

Half an hour later, they had supported Ben while he took a cooling shower after determining his temperature to be 102F. They dressed him in a fresh hospital gown, gave him a mask to avoid infecting anyone else in the hallways, and helped him to the infirmary, JR taking most of his weight as they walked. Once he was comfortable in a bed, Hannah and Rebecca cooperated in getting an IV started, blood samples drawn and antiviral medications administered. Though none of this treatment had helped before, Rebecca was determined to fight for Ben's life. When she had him settled, she urged Ben to rest, sleep if he could. When it was time to speak with his parents on the other side of the world, she would wake him. Obediently, he closed his eyes.

"Hannah, why would this happen now? He's been here for weeks!"

"I can't account for it, Rebecca. We know too little about the disease. However, I will know soon if the virus has taken on a new form. We must pray that it has not, or everyone here may be doomed."

Rebecca appreciated the sentiment, though she reflected

that they may all be doomed anyway. But, how could one live with the constant threat of death raining from the sky? It wasn't possible to be normal and worry about a nuclear bomb all of the time at the same time. Therefore, she put it firmly out of her mind, trusting JR and Daniel to deal with it while she dealt with her patient.

      With Ben out of commission, Hannah withdrew her objection to Robert's use of one of the 10th Cycle microscopes, not realizing that she could have called on Nyree to help her with her work. Robert didn't think of it either, in fact, no one did. The oversight delayed discovery of the viral vector, though it had already been some weeks since Nyree unwittingly had the key in her hand.

      Robert worked quickly to prepare slides of shavings from his rock to view under the powerful imaging tool. What he saw puzzled him further. Where he had expected an amorphous form of the iron, due to the presumed high heat of the lava with which it was mixed, he instead found a crystalline structure which also exhibited highly magnetic properties. It was as if the ferrous content of the basaltic lava of the rock had been reheated and forced to form a crystalline structure on the atomic level. His first thought was that it looked man-made. Robert had some knowledge of artificial crystalline structures, but it wasn't his specialty. This was outside his knowledge base. After carefully preserving the record photographically, he returned the microscope to the infirmary. Afterward, he sent his findings to a friend in Chile who was one of the foremost solid state chemists in the world.

Chapter 26 - Ten thousand suicide bombers

Harper's foreign policy advisers suggested that the best place to convey the positive news that some Middle Eastern people may have natural immunity to the virus might be Turkey, rather than Saudi Arabia. While both were nominally allied with the US, it was becoming moot as both countries had set aside their differences with Iran and joined the Death to the Infidels consortium of countries. It was a peculiar institution of diplomacy that an ally might smile at you one minute and stab you in the back the next, Harper reflected. While his advisers dithered about which country to approach, or perhaps to approach both, he received a discouraging call from Daniel in Antarctica.

"Mr. President, I understand the CDC has informed you that our virologist may have offered a modicum of hope for Middle Eastern people of mixed heritage," he said, without preamble.

"Yes, it was good news."

"It was premature. Ben is ill, and its confirmed H10N7," Daniel stated. Because of the unremitting stress and his forced separation from most of his loved ones, Daniel had lost his ability to soften a blow. Harper peered at his friend through the video link and was saddened to see that he had aged ten years within the past few weeks. He made a mental note to call Sarah to try to comfort her, but doubted that anything would.

"Oh, shit," was his only comment.

"Indeed, sir. I'd hold off on announcing it if you haven't already."

"We haven't. Keep me posted on your virologist's health. The First Lady and I will be praying for his recovery."

"Thank you, Mr. President."

Harper called his people back in and forbade them to say anything to anyone about the potential mixed-blood solution. As of now, it appeared to be nothing of the kind.

His heart was heavy as he consulted his calendar and noticed that another meeting of the UN Security Council was scheduled for the following Thursday. He fully expected to be ordered to take drastic measures on his citizens, no matter what the damage to the irreplaceable resources in the Antarctic and no matter how senseless it would be. Grave doubts about what he would be expected to do included what would happen when megatons of ice were melted in a nuclear blast. What kind of flooding would it create for nearby New Zealand and Australia, perhaps South Africa?

Would it trigger a tsunami that would devastate Indonesia? Harper would make these arguments, and more, if his advisers could come up with any. But, if nothing persuaded them, he would be forced to act before nukes were aimed at his major cities. Wildly, he thought of several dramatic but ultimately futile threats. He would refuse and then resign as President. He would go to Antarctica himself and dare them to do it, knowing that if they dropped a nuke on a US President, war would ensue. Whatever it took, he couldn't do it. He wouldn't do it.

Unable to bring himself to call Sarah Rossler in his current state of mind, he sought the First Lady and asked her to call, telling her he was busy but worried about their friend.

~~~

On Thursday, January 23rd, Harper stood before the UN Security Council attempting not to appear defeated. His arguments against a nuclear strike on Antarctica were marshaled, and he hoped to prevail by common sense, though he knew that the emotional impact of this week's numbers was arrayed against him.

Over eight hundred thousand new cases. Nearly a million and a half now doomed. And no cure or even temporary solution was in sight. The actual numbers were down slightly from the projections, but only because of strict quarantines in developed countries.

Medical resources in the Middle East were completely overwhelmed if they still stood, and nothing helped anyway. Therefore many, mostly poor, were going untreated except by their families. They were crowded together in rapidly-deteriorating camps in many countries, and even in those countries whose wealth was able to provide better accommodations the stench of illness and death was beginning to hang over the facilities with no hope of eradicating it. There was almost no chance conditions would improve without massive action by volunteers who weren't of Middle Eastern origin. However, the murders of several such volunteers by radical groups hindered the recruiting of more.

To add to the misery, food supplies in the most affected countries were getting low. Of course, all Western embassies were now closed, even those that had survived the suicide bombings. Persons with white skin took their lives in their hands if they went into public in a Middle Eastern country. Most had fled. It was a dilemma no one knew how to solve. Help from the West was the only hope, barring a miracle, but the radicals made it impossible for help to come.

As Harper had expected, the first Security Council member to address him was the elected non-permanent member from Turkey. "President Harper, despite your claims to the contrary, all evidence points to an artificial manufacture of this hell-spawned virus by citizens of your country, aided and abetted by Israel. You have been urging patience for weeks now, while my countrymen have been dying in their thousands. It is time for you to accept accountability and eradicate the source. I demand that you destroy the base camp where the criminals are hiding with nuclear force, which should wipe out the source of the virus. Let me add that I convey this demand upon orders from my government, and that your failure to act may result in my country withdrawing from NATO and joining forces with the Arab League."

"Representative Demir, let me first offer my deepest condolences for the loss of your citizens, indeed for all the losses that your region has suffered. It grieves me that we are still discussing bioweapons when thorough searches by an international task force has found no such programs in the US. While we stand ready to try our citizens for whatever crimes you care to charge them with, they are in fact innocent until proven guilty. It goes against our entire history to execute them without fair trial."

"This is an extraordinary circumstance," Demir retorted. "And it seems to me that you had no compunction when it came to executing Osama bin Laden without trial."

Harper was outraged at the comparison of this situation with the bin Laden fiasco. With difficulty, he reined in his temper to speak rationally. "Representative Demir, there are fundamental differences between the bin Laden case and this one. Though I have no need to justify our actions to you, I will explain them to you. First, bin Laden was not a US citizen; he was an avowed international terrorist who admitted to the cowardly and heinous attack on our innocent civilian citizens on 9/11 as well as others. When we raided his compound, it was in an attempt to arrest him and bring him here for a fair trial. He elected to resist arrest. Unfortunately, we sometimes must use deadly force when a criminal resists arrest. The Rossler Foundation expedition has not done so. They are actively working to find a cure for what you so eloquently termed this hell-spawned disease. Bin Laden *was* a hell-spawned disease."

"Why then are they not here to answer our charges?" Demir asked, wisely deciding that the bin Laden card wasn't going to play.

"They are under quarantine, as are any other individuals

who exhibit infection, whether or not it has made them ill. I might add that they voluntarily quarantined themselves before the rest of the world was aware of the danger. There is no practical way for them to leave in any case. They are more than two hundred miles from the nearest base and without transportation. Any attempt on their part to reach the base without air transport would be suicidal. Rest assured, they are not coming out. What you suggest is the killing of innocent people, people who might very well be able to find the source, and perhaps the cure, for this flu.

"When we have stopped the spread of the virus there will be plenty of time to bring them here for trial. Let us leave this line of discussion. There are other compelling reasons why what you demand is imprudent. Even before the current crisis, the ecological impact of rapidly-melting polar ice was being discussed among scientists as an inevitable and unstoppable potential disaster. Coastal cities and low-lying countries world-wide have already seen the impact, and Asia is seen as the region most likely to be disastrously impacted over the next two hundred years. If anyone were to deploy a nuke there, you could expect it to disrupt the stability of the dormant volcanoes, which could have the effect of melting the ice cap even more rapidly. The strike itself could potentially set off a tsunami that would inundate Indonesia, Malaysia—essentially all of the Pacific Islands and low-lying coastal countries like Bangladesh. That might not affect the Arabian Sea, but the rise in overall sea level would, eventually.

"Furthermore, deploying a nuclear weapon has global consequences, no matter where you do it, particularly if it is a surface strike. I submit that your desire for revenge would have severe and unintended consequences for millions of innocent people, the majority of them from your region of the globe." Harper sat down, confident that he had dispelled any notion of a nuclear strike.

"If not a nuclear solution, then we must send military forces to secure the area and execute the criminals."

"Again, there is no need, and there will be no executions without a trial. The members of the expedition have voluntarily quarantined themselves, and indeed they were the first to call our attention to the coming crisis."

"So, you propose to do nothing and you expect us to accept what is happening without the satisfaction of seeing the miscreants punished?"

"I think you have not been listening carefully. I have a proposal, and that is that we stop this senseless discussion and work together to prevent the deaths of millions more people. I am sure you are intelligent enough to know by now that if we don't stop the virus there will be no one left to exact your revenge. I am amazed that, among all this death and disaster and human misery, the only thing you have on your mind is to go and bomb a few innocent people in Antarctica. If you can explain to me how that is going to stop millions more from dying I am happy to listen. So are you going to work with me to stop this virus or not?"

With that, the chairman called for a vote, and by a narrow margin it was decided that Harper's arguments were valid. For now, there would be no action taken. Common sense had prevailed again, but for how much longer? Several members suggested that a deadline be imposed for an answer, and that if the deadline passed with no progress, the US would be expected to send a military presence to ensure the expedition would not leave Antarctica. To this, Harper agreed, seeing no harm in deploying troops to ensure what the expedition was voluntarily doing in the first place. That the deadline was only three weeks away virtually ensured that he would have to do it. By that time, the world-wide death toll would be approaching that of the 1918 outbreak of Spanish flu, and the following week would double it.

~~~

Aside from the cost to human lives, which of course was the most disturbing, this crisis had disrupted world trade as international transportation ceased due to quarantines. If the stock markets hadn't been closed, they would have fallen in a crash that would have put 1929 to shame. There was no doubt that a global economic Depression was beginning and would likely last for decades. Harper's advisers couldn't even begin to estimate the toll.

Again because of transportation limitations, localized areas of hyperinflation were starting as commodities became less available. Even in the prosperous US, hunger could become the norm as food supplies, long supplemented by foreign agriculture, became depleted. As January drew to a close, only the Deep South could count on growing their own food rapidly, but of course even that would be impossible in the largest cities. For the north, spring planting season was weeks away, and even further to harvest.

Harper reflected bitterly that it was moot anyway. As nearly as anyone could tell him, the world population was about eight weeks from total annihilation at this rate and if the virus mutated in such a way that it began affecting everyone. The news that the Rossler Foundation virologist was ill had struck fear into him that it had, in fact, mutated. Perhaps everyone would die, and then any future problems wouldn't matter.

Harper's worst fears didn't take into account the unrest in the Middle East as he pondered the impact of the virus. It wasn't that he was stupid, nor was he uninformed. He was just focused on the wrong hazard. There was something that could annihilate the world population even more rapidly and certainly than the virus, and that was nuclear war.

Middle Eastern diplomats were angry, but they still followed diplomatic norms, using words to convey their anger rather than weapons. Middle Eastern radical religious leaders had no such limits. Iran's Ayatollah, the acknowledged leader of the people as well as the power behind political decisions, had been spewing hate-filled rhetoric with references to world cleansing by the Twelfth Imam for a month. As a result, the faithful were flocking to their local mosques to volunteer in the coming jihad.

The first target would be Israel, but Ayatollah Kazemi was in contact with numerous terrorist organizations to determine a way to wreak the most havoc in the West. Al-Qaeda, Jundallah, Komalah and the People's Mujahedin of Iran had to be wooed and drawn together in support of Kazemi when he declared himself the Twelfth Imam. With that accomplished, he could command radical Muslims globally. In his quest to unite the terrorist organizations, Kazemi was aided by a man whose background was not completely known to him.

The man, whose name was Ahmad Ahmadi, was a Harvard-educated strategist. His cunning, ruthlessness and excellent command of English made him invaluable to al-Qaeda's leader, who had loaned him to Kazemi when the coalition was being formed. Third in command of the Right Hand of the Twelfth Imam, Ahmad Ahmadi had invaluable insights into the minds of the infidels, especially of those in the United States. The part that Kazemi didn't know was that Ahmad Ahmadi was also a CIA agent..

Kazemi's task was made more complicated by the fact that the organizations he was trying to unite frequently fought among themselves and occasionally even a single organization could be rendered ineffective by dissension within itself. Had that not been the case, the first wave of organized attacks in the West might have occurred even earlier. As it was, a coordinated attack in five European capitals didn't occur until the morning of January 30.

On that day, suicide bombers in London, Paris, Berlin, Rome and Madrid succeeded in killing or maiming a total of seven hundred people, many of them government officials arriving for the morning's business in the mainland countries. The London strike, coordinated with the others, wasn't as effective, since it occurred earlier in the morning than the others. Nevertheless, the damage to the Underground station that was hit not only injured seventy-eight people, but also crippled transportation networks.

As morning dawned in the US, reports of the strikes reached the ears of President Harper in his morning briefing.

"Who's taking credit?" he asked.

"Something called the Right Hand of the Twelfth Imam. We've never heard of them," his Chief of Staff replied.

"Wait, I know something about this Twelfth Imam, don't I?"

"Yes, sir. You were briefed on Islamic culture when you took office. The Twelfth Imam is supposed to be the Islamic messiah, I guess you could say. There are a lot of prophecies and signs and portents, but it seems that the Ayatollah Kazemi in Iran has seized the opportunity to declare that he is the very one. You have an appointment with the foreign policy group in an hour. Right now they're trying to track down who this really is. The attacks were too coordinated and professional to be a new group."

"I'll never understand why people would be willing to voluntarily blow themselves up to make a point," Harper muttered.

"You know they've been promised all sorts of privileges in the afterlife, in which they believe literally," his assistant answered, revealing unwittingly that he perhaps didn't have a literal belief in it. "We have intelligence that perhaps as many as ten thousand suicide bombers have already volunteered since the radicals started spouting jihad. This Ayatollah Kazemi, especially, has been talking about how it's every Muslim's duty to join in the war."

"Ten thou...that's insane!" exploded Harper. "If that's true, no major city in the world is safe. That can't be true!"

"I'll get that confirmed, sir, if you'd like."

"All right, do that. We have to devise a response. Are any of my counterparts in the affected countries available? I'd like to send our condolences and support."

"Yes, sir. I have the Downing Street Chief of Staff's assistant standing by for your call. If you'll pick up the phone on my signal, the Prime Minister will speak with you."

"Good job." Harper despised the protocol that kept him from simply picking up the phone and dialing himself. Apparently he was too important to be kept waiting, and so were the heads of state with whom he wished to speak. A call like this typically took six people or more to execute. What a waste of manpower to save him a few seconds and make sure no one's nose got out of joint by having to wait for someone else.

Harper picked up the handset on the designated phone and uttered a strong 'hello'. A refined voice on the other end spoke.

"Good morning Mr. President. Thank you for your call."

"Harold, good morning. Though from what I hear your morning wasn't good. How many injured and killed?"

"No one killed, thank God. We have seventy-eight injured, some critically, but at present we believe that all will recover. What do your people make of this, Nigel? I understand that these bastards hit four other capitals at the same time. You haven't had any incidents there?"

"No, none has been reported. I expect to know more in about an hour, and I'll have someone get back to your people with our analysis as soon as we have one. I just wanted to express my condolences."

"Thank you. I must say, Nigel, I believe it has something to do with this damnable virus your scientists have loosed on us. Don't they have a cure?"

"Harold, I assure you, our scientists had nothing to do with it. Whatever happened was inadvertent and no, they don't have a cure. It's something that has lain dormant for perhaps thousands of years, and I don't pretend to understand it. We're working on it, is all I can say."

"Well, work faster, my friend. This on top of everything else, the quarantines, the economy...this is the last straw. There are some in my government who are asking why we're not finishing the job with nuclear weapons."

"Harold, not you too! I'm barely restraining the UN from demanding that. It's no solution, I swear to you."

"Very well. I must go, I'm needed elsewhere. Good to hear from you."

"God be with you and your country, Harold."

Harper failed to understand at that time what his counterpart was up against. Like many in the US, he had dismissed rabble-rousing warnings of the impact of radical Islam in the US, where religious freedom was a way of life. Busy with other crises for much of his tenure, he hadn't paid much attention to those briefings that warned of the creeping danger of Sharia compliance among the citizens of the US. It was even worse in the UK, where Sharia law had been formally recognized in 2008 and incorporated into the court system.

It created an environment where Sharia courts were free to issue rulings that contradicted the UK's common law, as well as European Union laws. By 2011, Muslims in the UK had begun demanding that in towns with large Muslim populations, including Birmingham, Leeds, Leicester, Liverpool and Manchester among others, Sharia law replace UK common law and become the only law in those neighborhoods.

The devastation of the H10N7 virus in those neighborhoods had led to suicide bombings against any remaining non-Muslim companies and threats against women who weren't compliant with Sharia law in wearing the Muslim veil. In fact, in some of these neighborhoods, conditions were as bad as in the Middle East; worse because of the proximity of targets for the revenge of radical vigilante groups. Harper was soon to learn the truth of it.

Before he had a chance to contact any of the other countries, his advisers arrived for the hastily-called meeting.

"What can you tell me about this Right Hand of the Twelfth Imam?" he said, rather unnecessarily, to open the meeting.

"Mr. President, as nearly as we can understand it, the Ayatollah Kazemi has managed to bring several rival terrorist groups together for one purpose. We've been bandying about the phrase Islamic jihad for decades. It's now upon us."

"How are they traveling? There's a global interdiction on travel."

"We're certain that the strikes in the European capitals have been carried out by long-embedded operatives who were activated by phone or email. However, no country on earth has the police power to stop all travel. Even in our own country, people are still traveling across country. It would take martial law to stop it."

"How many cases of the flu do we have here in the US, now?"

"Just over fifteen thousand," replied the Chief of Staff.

"Relatively few, then," Harper responded, though horrified at the thought that fifteen thousand dead or dying could be referred to as 'few'. Still, in comparison with the Middle East, that was the correct assessment.

"Yes, sir. We had fewer index cases here, seven I believe, and we got them quarantined pretty quickly. However, there are still cases coming in. It seems that the guards in the camps and healthcare workers are infecting others as they go about their business. The more people we send in to care for the sick and infected, the more silent carriers we have. It's going to get out of hand soon, and we don't have a solution for it."

"Put everyone in hazmat suits if you must, but see to it that the spread stops. Consider that an executive order."

"Yes, sir."

"Now, what are we going to do about these terrorists?"

"We're gathering all information we can with help from the CIA, who has moles in the organizations, but there are some pretty sophisticated countermeasures in place," said one of the advisers. "I think the Director told me they'd had three or four moles go silent in the last week. I'm afraid they've been compromised and possibly killed."

"Get the Director of the CIA over here ASAP," Harper directed the Chief of Staff. To the advisers, he said, "What should I be doing to help this situation? Would a press conference be of any use?"

"I guess you could go on TV and tell people to be on the lookout for suspicious activity," one said, with a dubious expression on his face.

"Wouldn't that just result in a bunch of people turning in their neighbors for no good reason?" Harper asked.

"Probably," was the dry reply.

"All right. Thanks for the update. I'll expect a brief every four hours until further notice. You're dismissed."

Director Lewis of the CIA arrived in short order, knowing that he was about to be grilled as to why the attacks hadn't been averted. The problem was that he had no assets in the office of the Ayatollah Kazemi, since he hadn't previously been associated with terrorists, but rather had taken a hard line against the US in his influence within the Iranian government. That didn't fall under the definition of terrorism, so they'd had no reason to infiltrate his office, or so they thought.

Lewis's analysts were just beginning to get traffic indicating an unlikely coalition of terrorist organizations being brought under one command center. Evidently, Kazemi had assets of his own that were used to activate cells in the affected cities for today's attack. It was as if they had all been given their orders by mental telepathy. There had been no voice traffic at all before the morning attacks. As soon as he was ushered into the Oval Office, President Harper indicated he should sit and then waited for Lewis to speak.

"Mr. President, I assume you want to know why we weren't on top of this." Seeing the President's raised eyebrows, he ploughed on, explaining it as he had put it together in his mind on the way.

"I have analysts brainstorming every possible manner of communication to make sure we miss nothing else, sir, but I cannot guarantee we will have the answer in time to avert more attacks in the next forty-eight hours."

Harper paled. "What about that clever thing that the Rosslers did with email accounts and draft messages?"

"That's the trouble, sir. We know it can be done, but there is no way to intercept the messages, because they aren't sent over the internet. There could be thousands of messages sitting in email draft folders that reveal all the bad guys' plans, but we have no way to find them. That's why it was so effective for the Rosslers."

"Are we completely vulnerable then?"

"No, sir, not completely. We do have eyes on known or suspected terrorists, but of course they're like cockroaches. For every one you see, there are hundreds more hidden. All we can do is watch the movements of the ones we can see, and try to intercept or disrupt any missions they might be involved in. We're also handicapped because our assets in the area had to have a Middle Eastern ethnic background, for their camouflage. Many are missing and presumed to have succumbed to the virus. It's also possible," he admitted with reluctance, "that the rhetoric has persuaded them to change sides."

"Good lord, Sam, how has it come to this?"

"Mr. President, that's a question for wiser men than I. I'm very sorry we've failed, and if you require my resignation, you'll have it immediately."

"Don't be silly, Sam. I can't fire you for not doing what no man can do. Just do what you can to keep this country from going up like a house afire, and keep me posted. I'll let you get back to business."

"Thank you, sir. We'll do our best."

Harper had full confidence in Lewis's command of his agency. But what he'd just learned gave him cause for deep concern. If the terrorists were using an undetectable method of communication, no one was safe.

His thoughts turned out to be prophetic when, at six-thirty-five that evening, an armored security vehicle drove straight into defensive fire from Secret Service Uniformed Division officers, running over two of them and killing them before crashing into the barriers and blowing up. Over fifty bystanders were killed or injured, but it was nothing compared to the similar but much more devastating scenario that took place in Tel Aviv eight hours later. Later, the question of how the truck carrying the explosives made it all the way to the US Embassy front door steps would not be easily answered, because all witnesses, along with more than half of the embassy personnel, were dead. The building was left in rubble, a complete loss, as were commercial buildings on either side.

For the second morning in a row, President Harper woke to devastating news, this time news that hit home. His ambassador to

Israel was dead, the mission crippled because of massive losses of life as well as the total loss of the building. He would have to recall the survivors, but first he wanted to speak to Yedidyah, lest his action be misinterpreted.

"David, I'm just devastated by the news of what occurred this morning in Tel Aviv."

"Nigel, I, too am devastated. Forgive me for not calling earlier."

"I understand. David, I'm going to have to recall the survivors and try to determine what to do about an embassy. I want you to know that we in no way blame Israel. It's merely to take care of our people and get organized. I trust we will be welcome when we've named a new ambassador?"

"Let's take that under advisement, Nigel. I'm not sure we can guarantee the safety of your citizens, nor can you assure me that more terrorist strikes against your country within the borders of mine will not occur if you return. Can we say that once the medical crisis we face is resolved, you will then be welcome?"

"David, our country has a long history of supporting Israel. Are you now saying that it will be better not to engage in diplomatic relations with each other? Because, if you are, I'm not sure Congress or the taxpayers will be happy about ongoing support."

"My friend, I would not put it so strongly. But we must face facts. Neither of us is in a position to create diplomatic policy right now. When I was in your country for a semester of foreign study, I learned a quaint saying from your southern states. When you're up to your ass in alligators is not the time to try to drain the swamp. Before we drain the swamp, we're going to have to fight these alligators, do you see?"

"I see what you're saying, but I don't like it, quite frankly David. My decision stands. Our people need to come home. I guess you and I will be talking another time about when we'll be welcomed back. I hope you haven't made it impossible for us to stand behind you."

"I'm sorry, Nigel. This wasn't my decision alone."

"I see. Goodbye, David."

Harper gently placed the handset of the ornate old telephone into its cradle, and then indulged in an expression of profanity to match his anger and disappointment. Surely this was the last blow, however. They said bad things come in threes. The flu, the terrorist strikes and now a rift with one of his strongest allies. How could it get any worse?

~~~

One more circumstance in America was on the brink of creating disaster. In certain areas of New York and Michigan, where the highest concentrations of Americans of Middle Eastern descent resided, civil disobedience threatened to accelerate the spread of the H10N7 virus. Especially for those whose roots in America were shallow, news coming out of Iran, Saudi Arabia and Turkey in particular was more trusted than that of the major US networks. The more bombastic the pronouncements of the self-proclaimed Twelfth Imam, the more his listeners believed that the medical crisis either didn't exist or was engineered for the purpose of ethnic cleansing. That the coordinated suicide bombing strikes had been such a success only gained the Ayatollah more support, both at home and abroad.

That it couldn't be both ways was beyond the capacity of an angry mob to understand. Groups began to congregate in the streets of Detroit where a large Muslim population lived, infecting the healthy faster than projected under the terms of the quarantines. The only response the government had was deployment of National Guard units. Sooner or later, it was bound to get ugly.

That day came when a grief-stricken woman threw a softball sized stone at a line of Guardsmen trying to break up a rally. Retaliation was swift, and the battle was enjoined. By the time order had been restored, several of the protesters lay dead of gunshot wounds and a number of Guardsmen and protesters alike were forced to go to hospitals for treatment of minor to serious injuries.

News media, ever on the lookout for inflammatory stories, reported it as misuse of military power by the government. Soon every Democrat in the US was calling for lifting the quarantine. In Colorado, the largest concentration of Arab-Americans was found in Aurora, a suburb on the southeast side of Denver. When the news came out that the first cases of the virus known were those of workers hired by the Rossler Foundation, headquartered in Boulder, several mosques sent representatives to a committee that started laying plans to mount a protest there. The protest was scheduled to take place on the first Monday in February, weather permitting. That day marked the mid-point of the fourteenth week of the virus.

Emma Clarke had moved into the guestroom of her daughter's home to care for little Nick as Sarah spent more and more time at the office, working to hold the foundation together even as more and more countries formally withdrew their support. On the morning of February 3rd, faced with the reality that her husband and the others in Antarctica would have to leave within the next three weeks to guarantee getting home before the Antarctic winter set in, she was frantic for any kind of news. But, since the foundation had no medical labs of its own, Sarah was forced to rely on the CDC, Rebecca and the virologists in camp and on second-hand news from other labs working on it around the world. The news was grim. No one had ever seen this virus before; there were no records of it anywhere in the medical literature.

Even the search of the 10th Cycle library hadn't turned up much as yet. With millions of records to search, only a fraction of which were translated, progress was slow. Sarah was staring blankly out her office window when she noticed a disturbance below. As she looked on, hundreds of people began streaming from the parking lot and then from the street leading to their building, abandoning their cars in the street when the parking lot filled up. They carried signs, and now she could make out a chant from the people who were gathering. Alarmed, she intercommed Luke.

"Luke, what's going on outside?" she asked.

"What we've been expecting for weeks. Those people are demanding that the Rossler Foundation turn over the cure for the virus."

"But, we don't have any such thing! What are they thinking?"

"Sarah, you know what they're thinking. It's all over the news, and Daniel and JR warned us of it weeks ago. They think we engineered it."

She knew he was right, but facing it was almost beyond her ability to cope. "Should I go and talk to them?"

"NO! Absolutely not. I'm sending out some of our security guards, and we've sent for the police. Stay put...it's dangerous for them to see you."

"Someone has to tell them we didn't engineer it. Those poor people...and what about the quarantine? Aren't they all risking catching it?"

"Yes, they are, and they're in violation of the quarantine. We need to sit tight until the proper authorities have straightened it out. Call your mother and let her know it might be a long day."

"Okay, Uncle Luke, but please, let me know when it's safe

to leave. I need to hold my baby."

The protesters today were fairly peaceful. No one fired a weapon, no one picked up a rock to throw. But it took hours to disburse the crowd. By the time it was safe to leave, Luke had called in some favors and learned where they came from. He appeared at Sarah's door with a report.

"These folks are from several mosques in Aurora," he reported. "Unfortunately, Arapahoe County has a fairly large contingent of Muslims. I'm sure we can expect more of this, and if we don't have a breakthrough soon, it's going to get worse."

"How can we convince them it wasn't us?" she asked.

"You had a PR campaign ready to go, didn't you?" Luke asked in return.

"Oh, yes, I did. I'll call Mary. I'm not sure it will help. We never expected it to get this far. I can't believe it," she moaned, looking at the projection spreadsheet that was open on her computer monitor. "Nearly eight million new cases this week. Why can't anyone figure it out?" It was a rhetorical question and Luke knew it, so he didn't answer. He didn't have an answer in any case. That was up to the scientists and doctors. When this was over, he would retire if there was anything left of the world. This would be his last battle against the enemy.

Chapter 27 - The time is upon us

From his office in the elegant columned Niavaran Palace in Northern Tehran, Kazemi stared out at a cool, dark sky. He had prepared carefully for this day, the day he would announce his plans for the coming cleansing of the world by fire. By now, he had convinced himself that he was indeed the Mahdi, having traced his lineage to Ali ibn Abni Talib, Mohammed's son-in-law. Even his given name, Amir, foretold his true identity as it meant prince, ruler or commander. He had gathered millions to his cause, all of whom waited only for his announcement to follow the prophecy by engaging in armed revolt to bring the kingdom of Allah to earth at last.

Kazemi had consulted with Ahmad, who was proving more and more valuable, as to the best date and time for his announcement. It gave him great pleasure to think that with the current plan, all attention would be on him until the missiles reached their destinations. Far better than taking credit for the strikes after the fact. Announcing that it was coming would strike fear into the infidels, but would precede a nuclear strike against Israel by minutes, leaving too little time for the infidels to react. Once Israel was eliminated from the earth, even America must sit up and take notice.

Of all his advisers, Ahmad's voice was the strongest in support of his plan. He urged that Kazemi take his rightful place as soon as the plans could be formed. All the world, indeed, all the universe was poised for this moment, his destiny. Henceforth, he would not be known as Amir Kazemi, but by his rightful name, Muhammad ibn Hasan al-Mahdi.

To lend the announcement its proper weight, his throne would be backed by the leaders of every revolutionary group he led, now enhanced by groups from Turkey, Egypt, Pakistan and

Jordan. He'd heard from groups as far-flung as the UK and Canada, Russia, the Sudan and even Argentina. Once he'd proved not only his intent but his ability to carry it out, more would come under his protection and influence. So single-minded was he in his quest to bring about the chaos described in the prophecy that he failed to consider what revenge the countries of the West might take on Tehran. Nor did he consider that his missiles might be inadequate for the task, especially in view of Israel's highly sophisticated anti-missile technology.

Whether or not missiles reached Israel, though, Kazemi's objectives would be met. His only goal was to precipitate war, in order to be able to rise from the conflict as the 'man of kindness' and 'perfect human being' who would bring about a new beginning, rebirth and resurrection. Kazemi, if he had ever cared in the first place, had ceased to care about the millions of people sick or dying in his region of the world. Their plight was merely the excuse for the execution of a plan he'd hoped to put in motion since his boyhood. Of course, his rhetoric would cite the ethnic cleansing, but in truth, it wouldn't have mattered what started it. The point was that he would be left in sole control of all the people on earth.

From that vantage point, he would be able to bring about the correct order. There would be no more education of women, whose proper place was in the home. Women would return to the modest practice of covering themselves completely. The disgusting use of alcoholic beverage would be banned. There would be no more unholy study of the mysteries of Allah's works in the name of science, rather, scholars would ponder His nature. The faithful would once more rely on their religious leaders to heal their illnesses and injuries. The world would then be at peace, secure in genuine life.

The time was at hand. In the time-honored way of those who favored sneak attacks, Kazemi marshaled his lieutenants behind him and prepared to broadcast his announcement at four a.m. on February 13. His focus was on the television cameras, so he didn't notice that Ahmad was not among them. The others were just as happy that Ahmad was missing...they were jealous of his growing influence with the great man.

"It is written that at a time of great need, Imam Al-Mahdi, the Twelfth Imam, will arise and lead the world to peace and prosperity through a cleansing conflagration. The time is upon us. Accordingly, I, Amir Kazemi, proclaim myself to be Al-Mahdi. It is my will that the infidels who hold our most holy shrine be wiped from the face of this earth in fire and perdition. Infidels everywhere may escape this fate only by submitting to the will of Allah and following the correct path of Islam. Let this day be a lesson to heed. By the time this announcement is aired, missiles will already be on their way to Israel. It cannot be stopped."

At four a.m., as the broadcast day began, watchers in Iran and around the world received the news according to their beliefs. Many in the Middle East were as horrified as the West on hearing the last sentence. Israel was still asleep, two hours behind Tehran's time zone. Western news media picked up the announcement during daylight hours of the previous date, though it was past midnight in most of Europe and Africa. All major American networks interrupted prime time programming to carry the recording in its entirety, while ordinary citizens prayed for something to go wrong with the Iranian missiles, wondering how long it would be before the news of the Israel's fate was announced.

Harper made an immediate call to Tel Aviv, but the phone went unanswered.

~~~

At the Pentagon, within the Joint Operations Center of the Joint Chiefs of Staff, all was in readiness. Despite President

270

Harper's caution and reluctance to escalate a shooting war in the Middle East, the JCS had been expecting an announcement like what they'd just heard for weeks. That it might come from any quarter was inevitable. That it would come from an Iranian Ayatollah was not surprising.

Given the nuclear capabilities of Iran, supplemented as they were by North Korean and Pakistani technology, neither was it surprising that such an announcement would accompany a nuclear strike at Israel, other Western allies or even the United States. With the ability to launch missiles from seaborne platforms had come the potential that an Iranian strike might reach the western shores of the US, and of course Hawaii, American protectorates or territories such as the Philippines, American Samoa and Guam among others and allies such as Australia were all vulnerable as well.

From the beginning of the crisis, at the time Harper had called all of his advisers together at once after Daniel's initial call, capability for a military response had been carefully designed. As soon as it was in place, observers and analysts were tasked with twenty-four/seven monitoring of all Iranian, Korean and Pakistani missile sites, whether nuclear capability was suspected to be there or not.

There may have been a handful among them who wished that all these preparations would pay off in the end with total annihilation of the countries that had invited war for so many decades. Most, however, tensed with worry. No one had any illusions that this was a minor action. In fact, it was the critical moment for which they'd prepared since the first World Trade Center bombing, early in 1993, and some of them from before even that. A successful nuclear strike on just one of their targets would put the entire Muslim world at Kazemi's feet. With the standing of a minor god, Kazemi might direct his worshippers to do anything, unthinkable things. He had to be stopped at any cost.

The Joint Chiefs had already briefed the President about what must happen if this day came to pass, and what assets were in place to defend home ground. A plan of action had been hammered out and approved against today's eventuality, and drills had honed it to perfection.

The first line of defense would be Israel's own air defense system, assuming the strike were aimed at Israel, which all felt it would be. If nukes were aimed at other allied countries, the same plan would go for them. If they were aimed at the US, the plan would depend on where the launch originated and what the target appeared to be. The US would not reveal its space based assets unless forced to.

The second line of defense would come into play only if the country's own defense systems failed to stop the missiles prior to a critical point. If they got past a carefully measured and calibrated point that was unique to each potential target, the laser weapons on the top-secret geosynchronous satellites would fire and presumably take out the missiles before they reached their targets.

The problem with that plan was that the lasers had never been tested from space, nor on the missiles that were available to Iran. Doing so would have revealed the top-secret weapons. Some might have called it Catch-22, after the standard phrase in the novel by Joseph Heller. No matter what it was, what you couldn't do without an unacceptable consequence invoked Catch-22. The powers that be had determined that revealing the existence of the weapon would be worse than having it not work when needed. Not everyone agreed with the philosophy.

Naturally, if anything got through, a retaliatory strike on whoever started this unholy mess would have to occur, to cripple their ability to follow it up with more of the same. Say someone in Iran did throw some nukes at Israel, or the US, and one got through. That someone would have to be wiped out, no matter what the collateral damage was. Following a strike on Tehran, preemptive strikes on its allies, North Korea and Pakistan would be necessary, to prevent them from doing it to us.

There was always the possibility that Iran and North Korea would act in concert. A coordinated strike, with Iran's missiles aimed at Israel and North Korea's aimed at the west coast of the US would be most devastating, due to the fact that the time to reach their targets was almost identical. If the objective were to destroy Israel's government and that of the US at the same moment, North Korea's missiles would launch a mere ten minutes earlier. If Iran were to divide its targets between the US and Israel, the difference in travel time for the missiles would still be negligible.

Everyone who had a crucial role to play in this drama knew all of the facts, plans and contingencies. Now it was at hand, and they were prepared to carry out their assignments. They just weren't prepared for the emotional burden. The young captain who would be forced to push the button to launch the strike on Tehran shook as he watched the satellite image of the missile site outside of Qom. Next to him, a female counterpart thought of her grandparents in LA. If she saw missiles aimed there rising from North Korea, they would be in imminent danger; there would be no time to call for evacuation. In that case, she would have no qualms about pushing her button. It's true that the female of the species is always more ruthless than the male, especially if she is called upon to protect those in her care.

~~~

President Harper in the White House and analysts in the Pentagon alike held their collective breath as they waited to learn whether Israel's anti-missile strategy had been deployed and whether it had worked. If so, giant drones located in Azerbaijan should have destroyed the missiles while they were still on the launch pad. After launch, there would be thirty minutes during which everything else in Israel's arsenal could attempt to intercept and destroy the incoming strikes. Failing that, though they had never admitted that they had nuclear weapons, Israel would use its last breath to launch a counterstrike in revenge. No one but the President and his military advisors, though, knew that the US had a trick or two up its sleeve for Israel's defense as well as its own.

The first news came in through satellite imagery of a massive fireball near Qom, Iran, minutes after the beginning of the Ayatollah's announcement. However, on the screen it was evident that three missiles were unaffected and remained on course for their targets. Two were apparently headed for Israel, the other for Los Angeles. The President was informed immediately.

"Get ready for a retaliatory strike," he directed his informant, who swallowed hard before saying "Yes, sir."

The colonel who had reported as instructed to the President immediately passed the buck to his commanding officer, where it went up the line to the General of the Air Force.

"About time we did something about those sand..."

"Ian, let me remind you there are other ears nearby," interrupted his counterpart, the Fleet Admiral, forestalling a politically incorrect epithet that could have sunk his friend's illustrious career. The two entered the war room, expecting final orders within the next ten minutes.

A satellite feed had been opened for screens in the JOC as well as in the White House, but it was too dark to see much. A faint streak appeared in the lower right quadrant of the screen, and Harper's breath hitched. Five minutes passed with nothing but the eye-straining black screen with what looked like a meteorite traversing it. Then, a brighter streak came from above, the two converged and a bloom of orange and red burst into view, so bright that Harper instinctively threw his arm in front of his eyes. As soon as he realized what it was, he dropped his arm and yelled,

'Hell yes!' His sentiment was echoed wherever the feed was active in the West. Israel was safe... the last missile had been intercepted and exploded safely far above ground.

In Israel, the colonel with his finger on the button received a tap on his shoulder and an order to stand down. The Prime Minister, standing surrounded by his generals in the Ops room, asked, "What happened?"

The Chief of the Mossad, smiling, said, "I will explain it to you later, sir."

That it would spread nuclear fallout below it was of concern. Jordan's prevailing winds were from westerly to southwesterly, meaning that Israel's citizens, along with those of Egypt and beyond, would still suffer the effects. The missile from Iran had come dangerously close to Israel's air space, evading Israel's own defenses. Within minutes, the explosion would have been over Israel, wreaking almost as much havoc from fallout sickness as the explosion itself would have caused. Only slightly less was to be expected now.

The crisis wasn't over, though. The screens immediately switched feeds to track the progress of the second missile, which was nowhere to be seen in the live feed. A few minutes passed while the analysts who were watching the Qom missile site were consulted, and the recording was played back from the beginning. Seconds later, Harper watched the orange bloom that signaled the death of the second missile, which death-star satellites had intercepted over the border of Iran and Afghanistan.

Once again, Harper considered the radioactive fallout problem. He knew from previous briefings during which a nuclear strike against Iran had been considered, that this one was going to affect even more people, some three million in Afghanistan, Pakistan and India could die within the first two weeks. Another thirty-five million would be exposed to carcinogenic radiation, if indeed there were that many left alive by the virus. This had been a costly mistake on the part of the Ayatollah Kazemi, or whatever he was calling himself now.

The Pentagon would remain alert, lest North Korea decide to get into the act, but for now the threat of nuclear holocaust was averted.

Moments later, a phone was brought to Harper and he was told that David Yedidyah was calling. That was just the man he wanted to talk to. He owed Yedidyah an explanation.

"David, I trust you slept well?" Harper said in lieu of 'hello', not without humor.

"Perfectly, thank you," deadpanned the other man. "By the way, you wouldn't have any idea where that Superman missile came from, would you? Like the Man of Steel himself, it came just when we needed it."

"I might. But, like Clark Kent, I'll deny any knowledge of exactly what happened. I trust you'll back me up when I announce to the world that the US is very happy that Israel's defenses averted the strike?"

"I will, on your assurance that none of your illegal satellites are pointed at us," said the Israeli Prime Minister. Harper frowned slightly at the adjective, thinking that Yedidyah was rude for bringing it up, considering the US had just pulled Israel's figurative bacon from the fire.

"Of course they aren't pointed at you. They were only placed there to protect you, and to keep your neighbors' missiles out of our airspace," Harper retorted. "Are you trying to tell me that you have none of your own?"

"If we had, we wouldn't have needed yours. I'm sorry if I offended you my friend. We are indeed very grateful for your assistance."

"How about allowing us to reopen our embassy, then?"

"I'm sure that can be arranged, as soon as our borders are opened. Unfortunately, our efforts to keep the virus out of our country must leave them closed for the moment. However, I will speak to my advisers about making an exception if you would like to send a contingent in Air Force One, with all passengers screened for antibodies. We cannot allow carriers into the country, I'm sure you understand."

"Of course. It will be a while before I can screen a candidate, introduce him to Congress and get approval, all the red tape involved in naming a new ambassador. Perhaps this damnable crisis will be over by then."

"As my sainted grandmother would have said, 'from your lips to God's ear'."

"You've succeeded in keeping the virus outside your borders, then?"

"Except for some isolated cases, yes. As soon as the symptoms showed, we quarantined them, along with anyone with whom they had contact. Their caregivers were instructed to wear hazmat suits when caring for them, and we kept them in negative-pressure rooms to keep any airborne microbes from getting out. We've had a few deaths, but we're keeping the caregivers in quarantine until a vaccination is developed. Our finest minds are at work on that."

"Ours, too. I trust you're getting all the up-to-date information from our central clearinghouse?"

"Oh, yes, our scientists work well together. Nigel, I am happy that our countries will be able to resume their long friendship."

"Me, too, David. Me, too. Now, what are we going to do about this lunatic in Iran?"

"If I had my way, we'd give him a taste of his own medicine."

"I'm afraid the UN would never approve. Especially since I've been telling them desperately for weeks that a nuclear strike carries global consequences, and I don't just mean disapproval from the rest of the world. I'd like to avoid that. Why don't you talk to your Mossad guys, and I'll talk to my CIA guys, and see if they can come up with a solution?"

"Very well. I don't promise that my people won't employ their own solution before that."

"I couldn't blame you if they did. I won't delay too long."

"Thank you again, Nigel."

"You're most welcome, David."

Harper turned to his Chief of Staff. "Well, that was exciting," he deadpanned. "What's next on the agenda?"

"You're scheduled for a press conference, sir. In fact you're a few minutes late. The major networks wanted to air your remarks right before their ten o'clock news broadcasts. You've got less than fifteen minutes."

"Time waits for no man, eh? I trust there's a speech ready for me. What am I going to say?"

"Just that a severe security threat has been averted, thanks to the quick action of our military. You'll name the perp. We left out what you are going to do about it in retaliation, since we didn't know."

"Good. I still don't know myself. But I'll be discussing it with the Joint Chiefs first thing tomorrow. I hope we'll have a response within the week that doesn't include nuclear force, but it hasn't been ruled out."

"Then tell them that, sir. The enemy will be listening.

Hearing that nukes are still on the table may make them pause."

It turned out that the networks had been running 'breaking news' stories almost since the immediate crisis had begun, thanks to an internet shockwave that hit during Kazemi's broadcast. The President addressed a terrified nation in a televised speech that pre-empted the beginning of the ten o'clock news. Among the most relieved of his constituency were the broadcast journalists who'd been asking, futilely, what was going on for the past hour. It is a peculiar talent of broadcast journalists that they can take one statement and one picture and weave an hour-long suspense drama that can compel their viewers to keep watching even while saying nothing more than 'something's going on but we don't know what.' The majority of Americans, either assuming it was over or oblivious in the first place, went to bed that night thinking that the world must be a safer place.

Nothing was further from the truth.

~~~

Ahmad had expected nothing less than the disaster that the launch became. From the bunker in which Kazemi and all of his lieutenants, watched the drama unfold, Ahmad watched too, planning his next move.

Kazemi was a fool if he thought that Iranian technology, indeed any and *all* Middle Eastern technology, even supplemented with North Korean, was any match for what the US threw on the trash heap every day. He'd been looking for a way to bring America down since his time as a student there convinced him that it was them or his people—there was no way that they could occupy the same world peacefully. His disgust for the wastefulness of Americans when his people starved in some countries fed his hatred, which had been nurtured in his cradle and fed all his life by his father's teachings about the great Persian Empire under Cyrus

279

the Great. The restoration of which, every true Persian should aspire to.

When the opportunity to study the enemy's ways had presented itself in his early manhood, Ahmad went willingly. Nothing he saw or learned in the US changed his mind about the decadence. Though he wasn't a particularly devout man, Muslim beliefs and cultural practices were as much a part of him as his skin. He came to hate Americans and what they stood for—disregard for other peoples, arrogance and conspicuous consumption. He hid his revulsion well, though, and the reward was that, near the end of his senior year at Harvard, he was approached by a nondescript man in a bad suit and offered a job.

This was what his father and those who had raised money to send him to school in America had hoped. If he took certain courses and made certain moves that attracted the attention of the CIA, perhaps he would be recruited. From within the infidel's own spy network, he could do more harm to the US than as a gun-toting soldier of al-Qaeda. He accepted the job, juggling his few assignments with as little harm to his real friends as possible with the full cooperation of al-Qaeda leadership. Even the death of their founder, Osama bin Laden, would not stop al-Qaeda from accomplishing their ultimate goal—destruction of America and all her allies. Ahmad was to feed the CIA what disinformation he could, and report to his commander what information the CIA wanted him to give them as well as anything he could pick up on his own. In fact, he was virtually a sleeper agent, as the CIA wanted to save his talents for a crisis.

When the medical crisis reached critical mass, Ahmad saw an opportunity in the gathering of his and other resistance groups under Kazemi's leadership. Until he understood what leverage it might give him, he would keep a low profile and cease all communications with his CIA handlers. They would think him dead, probably. Al-Qaeda would lose the advantage of knowing where the CIA was looking, but other advantages would replace it.

On the morning of the abortive attack, while others ranted and displayed their tempers over the destruction of Iran's nukes, the Ayatollah sat stunned. Ahmad observed from the rear of the room, waiting to see if Kazemi's temper would erupt as well. After all, he'd been the last person to assure Kazemi, who he knew very well was not the al-Mahdi, that today's strategy was sound. One never knew what an angry ayatollah might do. Perhaps he would pretend that this was not unexpected, so as to save face. Perhaps he would order any of his advisers who encouraged the strategy to be stoned, or even beheaded. If it began to look like a scapegoat would be required, Ahmad had plans to slip out unnoticed and disappear into the crowds in the streets.

Ahmad needed a Plan B, one that would leave him rich, or in power – or both. The man in whom he and the others had placed their trust was a fool, and he should have known it as soon as the plan to nuke Israel began to surface. By the time he knew of the extent of it, Ahmad could do nothing to stop it without bringing suspicion on himself, so he pretended to go along, even encourage the futile gesture. He had two choices: he could, if the Ayatollah weren't inclined to cast blame on someone else, remain in the ranks, but work subtly to learn anything of use to the CIA to win their trust again. That would give him the opportunity to later worm his way into the Rossler Foundation to steal back whatever of value could be found in the 10th Cycle Library, which the infidels had stolen from the Middle East in the first place. Or, he could assassinate the fool himself and take over the organization. Of the two choices, he preferred the former. Less chance to get his own hands dirty, more chance to gain both wealth and power.

Ahmad instantly stopped thinking to closely observe as Kazemi rose to his feet and hushed the bickering men in the room.

"My friends, the struggle for our supremacy has just begun. Our first blow did not land as we expected, but that does not mean we are defeated. Our enemy has turned our own weapons upon us, we know not how. It is now time to use our numbers to overwhelm the infidels among us and drive them out of our lands. We will push the Jews into the ocean! Once our land is cleansed, we will fight to erase from the face of the earth those who refuse to worship Allah. Allah is with us! All who are true to the Islamic faith must now take up arms, whether rifles, knives, stones or poison, and kill the infidels. I, Muhammad ibn Hasan al-Mahdi, decree it! He who kills an infidel will not suffer punishment, but will assure himself a place in Paradise!"

So, the man was not as great a fool as Ahmad had thought, but still a fool. He would curb his temper and keep his lieutenants close, while recruiting masses of expendable soldiers with his rhetoric. Ahmad could appreciate the strategy, especially since it left him at the center of the action. Within hours, Kazemi had again taken to the airwaves, this time to urge every true Muslim to do his duty and take part in jihad.

North Korea and Pakistan had also been waiting for the Ayatollah's response to the debacle. As soon as the broadcast was over, Kazemi received calls from both governments pledging their support, their nuclear weapons, and their armed forces to Kazemi to advance his war and utterly destroy the infidels when the time was at hand.

During the following seven days, the immediate result was the murder of more than a dozen Western physicians who were treating victims of the virus. As soon as the broadcast was picked up by both Western news media and security forces, every Western country withdrew their diplomatic missions from the Middle East and urged their citizens to leave with all possible speed. Other murders had less impact on the course of the virus, but inflamed the victims' families and governments to the brink of formal declaration of war. By Feb. 21, just a week before the nominal travel deadline in Antarctica that could trap the remaining expedition members for the winter, more than seventy-one million new cases of the flu had been reported, bringing the total sick, dead or dying to over one-hundred million. Twenty thousand of the faithful volunteered for suicide bombing missions, but fewer than half that number would be well enough to carry out their missions by the time they were called.

Chapter 28 - Let Rebecca tell you He's cured?

Harper was fully aware that his deadline was at hand. On the next morning after the unsuccessful Iranian strike against Israel, he had stood before the Security Council again, determined to use the barely-averted crisis as a reason the UN should not carry out its threats against the Rossler Foundation expedition. Once again it was Representative Demir from Turkey who demanded punitive measures against the Rosslerites.

"You have done nothing to stop this plague," he ranted. "It is time for the UN to act."

"When we last spoke, I agreed to send US troops to ensure that the expedition members stay where they are until they can be brought to trial. I am ready to do that. There is no need for UN intervention."

"On the contrary, President Harper. I demand that observers be allowed to accompany your troops. I'm not sure we can trust you at this time."

Deeply offended, Harper with difficulty restrained himself from answering in equally insulting terms. Through his teeth, he growled, "That will be fine. I will instruct my military to make it so."

"In addition," Demir said, "Turkey is resigning from NATO. We are also closing all US embassies in Turkey. You have twenty-four hours to get your embassy staff out of our country, and forty-eight to move out all US troops and other US citizens. Turkey's borders are now closed to America. After the forty-eight hours have expired, Turkey will confiscate all American air assets and jail any US citizen remaining within our borders."

Harper was stunned. This was an act of war. Surely Demir

and his government had not thought this through. He did his best to alleviate the situation on his own, knowing that otherwise he would have to act in kind. "Hakim, I don't understand why your country is reacting in this way. There is no threat from Antarctica. The people there can't get out, and they even voluntarily quarantined themselves as soon as they understood what was happening. Please, speak to your government. Urge them to reconsider. Our countries have been allies for too long to throw it away in a virtual act of war."

At the word war, Demir drew himself to his full stature. "It is America that has committed an act of war. An act of genocide. Our decision stands."

With a face like a thundercloud, Harper stalked out of the conference room, unwilling to interact more with the Turk. Once, he might have had more to say to the man, but his time in office had taught him not to give his temper free rein.

Upon his return to the Oval Office, Harper sent for the Secretary of State and the Joint Chiefs. It seemed he would be forced to sever diplomatic relations with Turkey, if not prepare for war. Then he instructed his Chief of Staff to convey the orders for a squad of Marines to be sent to Antarctica, sick at heart for his friend Daniel Rossler and the men and women of his expedition. Harper understood that the virus was not a biological weapon, but a time bomb left from some unimaginably long time ago. That his friend was going to catch the fallout was terrible, but someone had to be the scapegoat for the loss of what, by the end of the next week, would approach one-hundred million lives.

The least Harper could do, though, was warn Daniel. At mid-afternoon, Harper had a Skype session opened to look his friend in the face when he told him that armed troops would soon be there to essentially place the entire expedition under house arrest. Because he wasn't as familiar as the Rosslerites were by now with the deadlines imposed by the continent's weather, it didn't occur to him that the order would trap the expedition in the valley itself to withstand the Antarctic winter, since getting fuel to the camp would be impossible for the next six months.

"Daniel, have you seen the news?" Harper said, as soon as greetings were exchanged.

"That Iran tried to nuke Israel and the US? Yes, we saw it. Terrible thing. Lucky Israel was ready, and thank God you stopped the others early." Harper let that go, since it was still classified that it had been America that was ready.

"I'm afraid there's more, Daniel." Harper choked back his next words, wanting to break the news as gently to Daniel as he could. But, there was no good way to say it. As Daniel waited for the rest, Harper blurted, "The UN is demanding we send troops to keep you there."

Daniel's face reflected disgust at the stupidity, rather than anger. "That's ridiculous, Nigel. We're not going anywhere." Daniel had forgotten in his emotional response that he'd reverted to calling the President by his formal title, despite their friendship and Harper's urging to first-name him several years ago. Harper didn't even notice. He was a down-to-earth man, which was why he himself called Representative Demir by his first name when appealing to him as a human being rather than as a representative of a hostile government.

"I know, which is why I agreed to it, but only to keep them from dropping a nuke on you."

Daniel paled visibly, even across the unimpressive Skype interface. "They wanted..."

"Yes, Daniel. They've been demanding it for weeks. You called it yourself when all this started. This is the price of them holding off."

"Then I guess that's good news. But, how many are you

sending? We're trying to lay in food supplies for the winter, and it will have to be adjusted. Plus, Summers is going to have a fit about the ecological damage to the valley. We can't stay in camp, because we won't be able to get enough fuel for the generators for that long."

"Don't worry about food. I'll make sure they bring their own, and that they're prepared to be under your guidance as to the impact to the valley. I'm thinking a squad of Marines will be more than sufficient, but they'll have some UN observers with them."

"Oh, good grief! Well, make sure none of them are Middle Eastern. I don't want to think what might happen if any of them get sick and die. You might also want to warn them that it could very well be a one-way trip, and that it could get a little warmer than anticipated if the nuclear bomb advocates get their way."

"Good point. By the way, how's your virologist?"

"We're cautiously optimistic. We were able to keep his fever down, and it appears he may recover. If so, it will be a step in the right direction for figuring this thing out. Every other person of Semitic descent has been dead before this point."

Daniel's statement of this news was so low-key that Harper nearly missed the significance.

"Wait, he's cured?"

"Not cured, recovered. Here, let Rebecca tell you."

Rebecca, who had walked in at that moment and wasn't sure to whom she'd be talking, was shaken when she saw the President's face on the monitor. Daniel repeated Harper's question for her.

"Since no one's survived before, we don't know what the course of his health will be after this. It could be like the herpes viruses and hide in his cells, only to make him sick again later. Or, he could be immune now. We just don't know," Rebecca explained.

"Good heavens, I hope it turns out all right for him!"

"We do, too, believe me. He's a good guy, Mr. President," she replied.

Chapter 29 - Nigel I have the commander here

Time had virtually stopped for Rebecca when Ben Epstein reported to the infirmary with the virus. Aside from the fact that they desperately needed him to help study it, Ben had become a well-liked member of the team. The thought of him dying from the very illness he had come to study made her sick at her stomach. She was determined to do everything in her power to keep him alive.

It helped that they had by then established it was the high fever that made the virus so deadly. Rebecca reasoned that if she could keep Ben's fever down, he might be able to fight off the virus on his own. Unlike the others, he did have some antibodies circulating, and perhaps they would be aided by her antiviral medications. Accordingly, she enlisted JR and Daniel in a round-the-clock rotation that had them packing Ben in ice cut from the permafrost outside on a twenty minutes on, two hours off schedule. Twenty minutes was about all Ben was able to stand, and still it was very painful, leaving him shivering uncontrollably. Essentially, the virus tried to cook him from the inside even as his caregivers tried to freeze him from the outside. At times, he wept when one of them told him it was time for the ice. But, Ben wanted to live. If this torture would help him survive, he would take it as long as he could.

During the first week of symptoms, the course of his illness was typical. His symptoms were worrisome only because they knew it was the deadly H10N7 virus, but they were tolerable with normal care. It was at the beginning of the second week, when everyone was worried about the threat of violence to the Boulder group, that the worst of the symptoms began to show up. Rebecca could do little about the vomiting, in spite of giving Ben antiemetics. When she couldn't help him keep his food down, she started IV nutrition. Between that and the ice treatments, by the third day of the second week, a point at which all previous patients had entered comas or died, Ben began to improve. It was another week before his fever broke, and he began to exhibit signs of hunger. His three caregivers were exhausted but exhilarated when he woke up on the morning of the eighteenth day of his symptoms to declare himself hungry for real food.

Ben had lost twenty-eight pounds, and most of his hair would now grow in white, but he had become the first to survive the virus. It was cause for celebration. Even as Daniel and Summers worried over stocking enough food to last for six months and where they would house everyone within the valley, JR was asking the cook to put on a feast to commemorate Ben's recovery.

Of course the good news was reported to the CDC as well as to Harper and Boulder, but because no one knew what was different about Ben's immune system, other than the genetic anomaly, the announcement wasn't made worldwide. Still, a handful of scientists were set to the task of studying every component and every protocol Rebecca had used to see if they could identify a successful treatment.

Hannah had been taking blood samples from Ben every day since he turned the corner toward survival, convinced that the anomalous CCR5 allele was somehow responsible for the devastating course of the illness in Middle Easterners. If she could only figure out how and why it made a difference, they might be able to develop a gene therapy that could be delivered far more quickly and more effectively than a vaccine.

On the nineteenth day after Ben's symptoms began, unexpected guests arrived, along with the expected troops. Encouraged by the breakthrough of Ben's recovery, the CDC made arrangements with Harper to have five patients of mixed ethnic heritage at the beginning stages of illness sent to Antarctica for care. Rebecca was speechless with anger, not only at the risk to the patients' lives but also because she didn't have the manpower to care for them properly. She felt they could have consulted with her before presenting her with a fait accompli. But, there was no way to send them back.

Keeping Ben cooled on a schedule that saved his life was hard enough. Rebecca had no idea how she was going to manage five. To cope while Daniel and JR were busy making arrangements for winter supplies and storing what came in, she pressed Cyndi and Angela into service as practical nurses. Hannah, however, was happy to have a larger sample of a mixed genome to work with. Her immediate response was to take blood and cheek swab samples from each patient.

The Marines and their UN observers were a different matter. They were Daniel and JR's problem. The Rossler brothers were trying to come to a reasonable working relationship with Cmdr. Jack Neville, a man who was supremely unhappy at finding himself in command of only fourteen men, a job for a corporal at most. That he and his command were also stuck in an Antarctic wasteland for the winter was infuriating. Neville's first act was to commandeer the empty dorm building for his barracks, where Rebecca would have preferred to house the new patients until their imminent move to the valley. The infirmary was too small for all five, and she didn't want them disturbed by the comings and goings of expedition staff.

When Daniel had first told JR that the troops would be arriving, JR's reaction was to withdraw, working through his emotions in silence and with no help from anyone. His struggle was the dichotomy between being in charge of the logistics of the expedition and knowing that a superior officer was about to arrive. JR had achieved the highest non-com rank he could as an enlisted man who didn't anticipate a career in the Marines. As such, he was addressed as sergeant, holding the rank of E5. Sergeants of this rank were often heard to bark at any of their men who dared address them as 'sir', saying, "Don't call me sir--I work for a living!" It had been an officer's decision to send his men into the situation that was responsible for his PTSD, so officers were anathema to him.

However, by using some techniques that Rebecca had taught him, JR was able to come to terms with the idea that yet another person would be there to usurp his authority. Not that Daniel meant to do it—it was just natural for him, since he was the older brother and the head of the foundation. Still, he now shared his authority with Daniel. It wasn't what he'd expected when he signed on. Well, he would stand up to this Cmdr. Neville. The man didn't have a clue about Antarctica, probably. He'd have to follow JR's directions or risk his men. Accordingly, as soon Rebecca came to complain, he sent for Neville, immediately putting him in an inferior position as he met with JR in his office.

"Neville, do you know why you're here?"

"That's Commander Neville. And yes, I'm fully aware of why I'm here. What do you want?"

"First, I'm neither in the Marines any longer nor under your command. You'll do well to stand down, because this continent will kill you and your men if you don't pay attention to how things work around here. Second, I don't think you do know why you're here. You were sent here to appease some radical Muslims, nothing else. You were no doubt told you're here to enforce a quarantine. Were you told that as soon as you breathed the air inside the compound buildings you would be exposed to the virus as a carrier, and unable to leave yourself?

"Furthermore, if you get a funny feeling between your shoulder blades, it's because of the nuclear missiles that are pointed at us. For your information, at the last three UN Security

Council meetings, nuking us was voted down by only two or three votes. If the radical elements in the UN have their way, you've been sent on a one-way trip, along with your men. There was no need to enforce the quarantine, because Antarctica itself is enforcing it."

"What? There must be some mistake. No one informed me that we wouldn't be leaving again as soon as the travel season was over. We came to observe, and make sure none of you slip away."

"Don't be an ass. You've seen the weather conditions out there, and they are only going to get worse. Furthermore, we're more than a thousand miles from McMurdo and more than two hundred from Amundsen-Scott, which itself is going to be socked in for the winter in another ten days or so. No one is going to 'slip away', believe me. Nor are you going anywhere. The situation is bad enough out there without sending more silent carriers into the mix. You could pick up a pack of cigarettes at your local 7-11 and twenty-one days later, the Pakistani clerk would be dead of the virus and his family all sick. Nope, can't risk it. Use your head for something besides holding your ears apart. You're here for the duration, or until the Middle Eastern countries get tired of waiting for a cure and nuke us."

"I don't believe you."

"Are you calling me a liar now? Dude, I have no problem kicking your ass." JR started up from his chair, taking Neville by surprise by grabbing his lapels. Rebecca, who had been there at the beginning, had seen from JR's face as soon as the other man challenged him that they were likely to come to blows. With JR distracted, she'd slipped out of the office and had gone to get Daniel. They arrived together just in time for Daniel to put his arm between JR's enraged face and the commander's outraged one.

"What's going on here?" Daniel asked.

"He called me a liar," JR said, still fuming.

293

"I need to call my commanding officer and have him confirm what your brother just told me," Neville answered at the same time.

"What did he tell you?" Daniel asked, with deceptive mildness.

"That we are now quarantined with you and unable to go home. He even had the nerve to claim we might be nuked while we're here."

"That's about the size of it."

"That's preposterous. I would have been told."

"Listen, Neville. I came here to stop my brother from physically taking out his frustration on you, but you're beginning to annoy me, too. So which of us do you want to fight? JR, or me?"

Neville had no answer for that. Abruptly, he sat down. "I would still like to have a conversation with my commanding officer."

"That's no problem. But, if he won't tell you, don't call my brother a liar, call your captain that. Except, he might not have been told either. Tell you what, you go ahead and talk to him, and if you're satisfied then, so be it. If not, we're not going to allow you to make life any more difficult for us here than it already is. You'll sit in on my next conversation with the President. By the way, how did a Navy commander end up in charge of a squad of Marines, anyway?"

Neville was beginning to wonder if these men were indeed telling the truth, and he'd asked himself the same question. Slowly, he spoke as he thought out loud. "I'm not sure. Except, I've been here before. I'm not allowed to talk about it."

"Here? Here in this canyon?"

"No, on the ice near McMurdo. Really, I can't talk about it."

"All right, suit yourself. Before you call your captain, do you want to have Summers show you around in the valley, see what we came here to do in the first place? You're going to have to follow his lead in where you billet your men when we move inside."

"What do you mean, move inside? What's wrong with these barracks?"

"Aside from the ambient temperature being around minus 50 degrees when we run out of fuel and can't get more? Nothing."

"Shit," Neville said, forgetting the presence of a lady. "What else didn't they tell me?"

"I'll ask Summers to take you in, maybe he can answer that question. But, consider this. What would you have done if they'd told you the truth?"

~~~

Neville elected to talk to his captain first, and as Daniel hinted, the man knew nothing of the real situation. That wasn't for the attention of the lower-ranking officers, who simply carried out orders that came from above without explanation. Away from the imposing figure of JR Rossler, who he definitely did not want to fight, Neville's confidence returned and with it his tendency to consider civilians as less than himself. He presented himself to Daniel to call his bluff, with a demand that if he indeed had the president's ear, he wanted to hear it directly from the Commander in Chief. The smirk on his face gave away his true thoughts. Clearly, he didn't expect to actually speak to the president.

Daniel checked the time. It wasn't too late to call the president, and his eyes sparkled with amusement at the trick he was about to play. Inviting Neville to sit down, he dialed a number and put the line on speaker.

"White House operator, how may I direct your call?" Neville's eyes widened.

"I'd like to speak to President Harper, please. You may tell him Daniel Rossler is calling."

"Just a moment while I transfer your call." Neville began to sweat.

"Oval Office."

"Clarissa, its Daniel Rossler. Is he available?"

"I think so, let me check."

The next voice was Harper's, instantly recognizable to most Americans because of his Southern twang.

"Daniel? How's it going?"

"We've had a little issue with the troops you sent down here, Nigel. I have the commander here. Do you think you can clear up some of his questions?"

Neville's face had drained of all color when he heard Daniel call the president by his first name. He had no doubt he was about to be relieved of duty by the Commander in Chief himself, for doubting the man's friend. He swallowed convulsively as he listened to the Harper's next words.

"What are your questions, Cmdr. Neville?" *Oh, shit! The president knew his name. That couldn't be good.*

"Er, no questions after all, Sir. Er, Mr. President. I'm sure Mr. Rossler can answer any I have in the future."

"Very well. Just so there's no question, I expect you and your men to cooperate in every way with the Rosslers and their expedition staff. This stupid idea that they needed minders in their quarantine was not mine, but those are your orders anyway. Do you understand?"

"Yes, Mr. President."

"Carry on, then. G'nite, Daniel."

"Good night, Nigel," Daniel answered.

"Would you be interested in that tour of the valley, now, Jack?" Daniel could hardly keep the glee out of his voice. After weeks of bad news, a little harmless fun was just what he needed to feel more cheerful for a while. When Neville got back from his tour of the valley, JR could tell him what he was going to do for Rebecca. Those Marines would be a great help in the round-the-clock care of her unexpected patients.

"Yes, please," was the subdued answer from a thoroughly shaken Neville. If he got out of here, he was going to go for early retirement and a nice, stress free job at home. Walmart greeter, maybe.

Daniel accompanied Neville to Summer's lab, where he was consulting with Angela and poring over one of her maps, deciding where the group could set up camp inside the valley with the least ecological and archaeological impact.

"Charles, I'd like you to meet Cmdr. Jack Neville, US Navy. He's in charge of our babysitters. Would you mind taking him into the valley and showing him the ruins? While you're there, if you've decided already, you can show him where he and his men can set up their camp and store their food."

"Not at all. We haven't actually decided that, but we can take a look at some places we're thinking of while we're in there. Ready to go now, Cmdr. Neville?"

"Won't it be too dark?" Neville asked. Summers and Daniel looked at each other and chuckled.

"I doubt it," Summers responded, without further explanation. "Come on, there's no time to waste. Angela, would you like to come with us?"

"No, I think I'd better finish our project. You go ahead."

Moments later, Summers and a very confused Neville were bundled into cold-weather gear and approaching the rail cars that would take them into the valley.

Upon arrival within the square where the ruins were located, Comdr. Jack Neville stared at the spires and domes, remembering a video in a cold conference room. He'd been told to forget he ever saw it, and now the real thing was before him, as fantastic and strange as the video footage had been. Eleven years had passed, during which his previously stellar military career had stalled like a junkyard car. Even though the temperature was warm, impossibly warm, he couldn't suppress a shiver. And what the heck was lighting the place up like mid-day? Dr. Summers didn't notice his reaction.

"I'm curious, Comdr. Neville. I haven't had much contact with military personnel, but I haven't been under the impression that they are particularly interested in archaeology. What's your interest here? Besides containment, of course."

Neville paled. Even though the world now knew of this place, he had no reason to believe he was free to speak of classified information. With a wan smile, he fell back on a silly saying that had become popular because of spy movies.

"I'd tell you, but then I'd have to kill you." A dry chuckle for effect, and Summers was mollified.

"Classified, eh?" Summers joked. Neville saw no reason to answer.

"Shall we go?" Summers asked. "Or would you like to see where we think the virus originated?"

"No need for that," Neville said. His hasty answer amused Summers.

"There's no need for you to be nervous; you can't be made

298

ill, and you're already exposed. You're stuck with the rest of us until the quarantine is lifted."

Neville had a rather more frightening understanding of just how stuck he was, but there was nothing he could do about it now. He and his men were here, not to keep sick people from getting out. The poor bastards they'd brought with them had little hope of that. No, he and his men were here to keep the *well* ones from getting out, perhaps permanently. And if a permanent solution were required, he now understood that he and his men would be victims just as surely as the people they guarded. At least he now knew why he'd drawn the short straw. Neville reflected on his career while following Summers back to the train. What had he done to deserve this? He was well and truly up shit creek without a paddle, and had been for the last eleven years.

~~~

Daniel was acutely aware that in a matter of days it would be impossible to expect any more supplies from McMurdo for the next six months. Already, the weather was worsening, and the constant sunlight of December had become a dull red glow on the horizon only for those who had business at the mouth of the canyon. Within the narrow Purgatory Canyon itself and at camp, it was already perpetual darkness. On a personal level, he was already depressed, knowing he'd miss being with his family for Nick's first birthday, and that communications might be spotty. The most advanced comms network in the world was no match for the winter winds of Antarctica, though Robert assured him that he and Cyndi had thoroughly secured their Iridium Pilot unit at the top of the volcanic cone when they'd arrived. In the face of the worldwide tragedy, now approaching a death toll of over one hundred million with seventy million more falling ill, it was trifling, but to Daniel it was everything.

Nevertheless, he had a duty to his people to hold it together, help JR make sure supplies were adequate while they could still get them, and keep a calm demeanor regarding the Marines in camp. No matter how ridiculous it was that someone had thought it necessary to send them, they were still a threat to normal operations if they weren't given something constructive to do. It was time to have a talk with Rebecca and see what they could do about the five new patients the CDC had saddled them with. Shaking his head at the shortsightedness of sending those patients here at this time, Daniel agreed with Rebecca's anger, but needed to curb it for the sake of peace while they were all trapped here.

Knocking on Rebecca and JR's door, Daniel entered at Rebecca's invitation. JR wasn't there.

"Rebecca, what have you decided about the patients?" he asked.

"Well, so far we're doing okay caring for them in their rooms, but next week is going to be a problem. I guess we're all moving into the valley?"

"Yes," he answered.

"It's too hot there, it will drive their fever up. We're going to have to put them somewhere on the edge of the valley, but close enough to the cave system to move them there for their cold treatments. I guess it won't be like packing them in ice, but I don't see how we can move enough ice inside to get it done. Could you get Robert or someone to find a spot with a mean temperature of about sixty-eight degrees Fahrenheit, but close enough to carry them to a cooler room?"

"I guess we can have him look. What's your backup plan?"

"I don't know. Maybe load them on the rail cars and run them back to a spot where the temperature stays around fifty. I don't want to freeze them, but we've got to keep their fever down on a consistent basis."

"Okay, I'll get Robert started on that project. Summers is

working with Angela to locate less ecologically fragile areas for the tents. We have to get moved soon, preferably by the end of the week, but definitely before mid-March. Our fuel supplies will be completely depleted by then."

"I'd like to go ahead and move my patients this week, if that's okay," Rebecca answered. "I don't want to wait until they're in the worst part of it."

"Good idea. I'll notify Summers."

"Daniel, I'm sorry I made it more difficult with Cmdr. Neville," she said. Daniel waved off the apology.

"Never mind that. He was too arrogant about it. But since JR and I had our little chat with him, we seem to have come to terms now. I'd suggest you press his men into service to help you care for the patients. The president made it clear to him that he should spend his time here helping instead of interfering."

"I'm glad. Is there anything else you need?"

"Yeah, I'm not clear on what Hannah's doing. She's not the best at explaining it to a layperson. Do you know what she's up to?"

"When Ben first got here, he and I talked about an article I read that said our genome was made up of about ninety percent what they call junk DNA. It's mostly fragments of old viruses, retroviruses, that don't have any function. The article said that some scientists were exploring the idea that some of them were responsible for certain diseases, like cancer and some diseases that have an autoimmune aspect, like rheumatoid arthritis and MS. Do you follow?"

"Yeah, so far. We're all carrying DNA that's not good for anything but making us sick."

"Well, no, we just don't know what it's all for. Anyway, now that we've got a survivor in Ben, and all these new people to use as test subjects, Hannah's looking for something in that DNA that is prevalent in Middle Easterners and not present in others, or that responds to the CCR5 allele that Ben has in common with Middle Easterners. She thinks that if she can locate it, the steps to create a gene therapy are already well-known and will work faster than a vaccine."

"Oh. Well, when you put it that way, it makes perfect sense. But didn't she say that the CCR5 gene has something to do with immune response?"

"She did. However, that can be a double-edged sword. CCR5 can help make you sick just as fast as it calls white blood cells to attack the illness, because that's what causes fever, and the fever is what's killing people."

"Damn, that's confusing."

"I know. Try not to think about it, that's what I do," she laughed.

"Okay. So, will you keep me posted, so I can inform the president?"

"Sure, but Hannah's in touch with the CDC daily."

"That's as may be, but did they tell her they were sending these patients before they arrived?"

"Well, no."

"Then why would you think they'd keep the president in the loop the way he wants to be? I'm beginning to wonder about the damn CDC."

"Join the club."

That night was the first time in weeks that Rebecca hadn't been under too much stress to even think about romance. When JR arrived in their room after his long day, he found her freshly showered and dressed in a sexy nightgown he hadn't seen since Haraz el-Amin got sick. Surprised, he stopped short.

"What's this?" he asked.

"This is a sexy nightgown," she answered. "I trust you remember what that means?"

"Hmmm, I'm not sure," he deadpanned. "Can you give me a hint?"

"How about this?" she purred, reaching for his shoulders and pulling him down for a long kiss.

"I'm beginning to remember," he whispered, as he moved to a more comfortable position on the bed.

She hoped he'd also remembered to lock the door, but asking was now impossible because he had her lips covered in another kiss. And then she stopped thinking about it as the bliss of once more being wrapped in the arms of her hero overtook her.

~~~

The logistics of moving the camp for winter were complicated by the needs of the various groups who were involved. The last-minute arrival of the military, a squad of thirteen Marines, Neville and two UN observers plus five flu patients had thrown Summers' and JR's planning into chaos. True to his word, Harper had arranged for the military to bring their own food. They would be eating MREs for six months, a fact they were bitter about considering that the expedition had much better food. Harper hadn't taken into account food for the flu patients, an add-on that the CDC sprung on him with no time for arrangements to be made. It was true that they would not be eating much for the two weeks while their illness ran its course, and he'd probably assumed they wouldn't survive. Rebecca, though, had other ideas. She intended to save them.

Summers' task was to find spots that wouldn't impact the

ecology to pitch tents for fifty-two people inside Paradise Valley. Per Rebecca's directions, five of them would need accommodations close to the entrances to the cave system, where they could be moved in and out to keep them cool enough to survive their fevers. In the end, it was decided that the camp could be strung out along the edge of the valley in groups of two or three tents between the cave opening and the waterfall, which would supply both their drinking water as it fell and their bath in the pool below. One by one, every problem of logistics was solved.

Summers was ecstatic, because without other distractions, his work could continue uninterrupted. Most of the other scientists felt the same, though they understood that the inconveniences would probably get old. The only regret that Robert had, and Nyree with him, was that they hadn't determined what made the substance they'd found on the ledge near the waterfall glow as it did. The hadn't had an answer from Robert's solid state chemist friend after he acknowledged receiving the rock they'd sent him and said he didn't have a clue what it was either. Last they'd heard, he intended to send it along to Caltech, to a colleague there, to have it further analyzed.

Chapter 30 - There you are, you son of a bitch!

With the window of opportunity quickly closing and the rest of her lab already moved, Nyree decided to take another look at the algae cultures she'd been growing and studying for several weeks now, this time under the more powerful 10th Cycle imaging device. Each time she'd done this before, she had seen nothing out of the ordinary. This time, there was a difference. Puzzled by what she could see in the attached monitor, Nyree thought back over the previous tests. Not one had shown any foreign substance within the fine structure of the algae. This one must have been contaminated by something. She selected another sample.

After verifying that every sample had the same "contamination", Nyree sat back on her chair and thought hard about the structure of the substance she was seeing. It was a microbe of some sort; that was certain. And the shape was so familiar...then she gasped.

"My God, I've found it!" she whispered, almost reverently. For another moment, she hugged the knowledge to herself, then ran shrieking down the hall.

"Hannah! Hannah! I've found it—the vector!"

Doors flew open throughout the area. Summers and Angela were inside the valley, but Daniel, JR, Rebecca and Cyndi came running, arriving at the door of the lab Hannah had taken over at about the same time. She had just registered that someone was calling her name, and was in the act of flinging open the door when everyone converged on it.

"Wha...?"

"I've found it!" shouted Nyree again. "Come, come with

me. You have to see this. I've found the vector!" Catching her excitement, the whole crowd followed her to her lab, where, on the screen, they could see an entire colony of the H10N7 virus, looking very much like the head of a dandelion after it had gone to seed.

"This came from the algae that Robert collected from the fumarole," she said. "It took all this time to culture it, but there's the proof. Every single sample has it."

Hannah was nodding her head vigorously. "Yes, there's no doubt. That's where it came from. Congratulations, Nyree."

Daniel spoke from behind them. "Does that mean we can develop a cure?"

"Oh, no," Hannah said, unwittingly dashing his hopes. "We still don't know why this little bugger makes Middle Eastern people deathly ill and doesn't even cause symptoms in us. No, there's something else at work here. I'm still looking for it. This just confirms that the origin of the virus was in the valley; the workers didn't carry it here. " Hannah strode rapidly back down the hall to her own lab, leaving the others staring after her in dismay.

Daniel, in particular, was thinking that they had just swept the rug out from under their own feet. That was one of the arguments Harper had made against nuking the valley, and now it was gone.

As one, the rest turned their stare on Rebecca, who had some idea of what Hannah was doing, and the monumental task it was without Ben's help. To help them understand what was still left to be done before they could develop a cure, she explained in the simplest terms she could, drawing a simplified diagram of the DNA molecule on a whiteboard to help her explain.

"You know that Ben discovered one gene, the CCR5, which has two different forms. One form is normal for us, and one that's normal for Middle Easterners, but different from ours. You remember that he had a heterogeneous form of CCR5, with a mismatched pair that had one of ours and one of theirs, right?"

The others had all been told of Ben's discovery, but those whose expertise wasn't in the field of biology or medicine had not had a clear understanding of it in the first place, so they had put it out of their minds. With Rebecca's reminder, they were listening curiously for the other shoe to drop.

"So, Hannah and I talked about an article I read awhile back, about a lot of fragments of inactive DNA, some of which appears to be borrowed from old viruses, in the human genome. Remember, Daniel, we talked about that the other day. Hannah contacted her colleagues at the CDC to learn who was working on that, and they more or less told her it was a long shot and she'd be wasting her time. That made her realize that no one else was researching the possibility that something had activated some of those fragments, so she took it on herself.

"She and Ben narrowed down where on the sequence they might find differences in that material between us and them, and started comparing them visually. It's a huge job—human DNA has more than three billion base pairs. Obviously they couldn't look at every one of them, but the function of some huge sections are already well known, so like I say, they narrowed it down. She's maybe halfway through. What she hopes to find is a section of that junk DNA that's active and doing something in the Middle Easterner's specimens and inactive in ours. If she does, that will explain why they're sick and we're not, and will also give her a target for gene therapy."

"Is there any chance she'll find it before they're all gone?" Nyree asked.

"Not at the rate she's been going since Ben got sick. Unless she just stumbles on it. It could be anywhere, so who knows?"

"I'd better help," said Nyree, surprising everyone.

"How could you help?" Rebecca asked.

"At least I know how to use the machine, and distinguish between two things that don't look the same. I'm going to see if she'll show me how to help." With that, Nyree followed Hannah, and Rebecca shooed the rest back to their work. Daniel and JR lingered with her in the hallway.

"What chance do you give that?" JR asked.

"Hard to say. First, they have to find it. Then they have to devise the treatment and a way to deliver it. It's hard to conceive of that happening in the next two, two and a half weeks."

"Two weeks?" asked JR.

"That's how long we've got before the Middle East is virtually depopulated," Rebecca responded. Unlike the others, she watched Raj's spreadsheet daily, despairing over the accuracy of it. If only they *could* find a therapy that would save those who were sick now, and halt the spread. The numbers would still be appalling, but the population of the Middle East would recover eventually.

Even as she spoke, Hannah was listening to Nyree with astonishment. How had she missed that the 10th Cycle imaging device they were using had automated analytical capabilities? Nyree was showing her how to instruct the machine to computerize the examination of all or part of the samples' DNA sequence and alert the user to differences. Naturally, it had to be fine-tuned to avoid alerting at gene pairs that they expected to be different; those that coded for eye color for example. However, with Hannah's sample as the control and Ben's as the one being compared, they hoped to find the junk DNA that they suspected had been activated to cause his illness. Then they'd check that against one of the samples from the deceased members of the team. Hannah's previous experience had been in manually advancing the image of an electron microscope as she compared visually. This 10th Cycle device would not only be faster, but also more accurate.

Both women held their breath as Nyree set the analysis in motion. Hannah watched as the image moved in a blur, until the device signaled and stopped advancing the image so she could examine what it had found. Ah...the CCR5 gene. They already knew that was different in these two; but they also knew there was something else, at least if their theory was correct. Hannah clicked the command to start again. Moments later, another signal brought Hannah back to the monitor. On the screen was an entire section of gene pairs lit up on Hannah's sample and dark on Ben's. What could this be?

Hannah scanned the graphic for clues. On the upper left was a legend that indicated where in the gene sequence this section was located. It wasn't a familiar area to Hannah, so she turned to her computer and brought up the standard reference work that would tell her what, if anything, was known about it. Moving quickly through the index, she located the chromosome and then the first gene pair that was different in the sample. Nyree stood by, wanting to ask but afraid to distract Hannah. She could see that Hannah had discovered something interesting, maybe even exciting.

Hannah checked twice, looking back and forth between the legend on the screen, and the reference index. There was no doubt about it. This section was unknown as to function. It had been tentatively marked as a fragment of retrovirus that did not code for protein; in other words, it had no known function in the body. It was exactly the right type of gene they were looking for, but was it the only one? Hannah had a moment's hesitation as she thought through whether to continue the entire analytical process for these two samples, or stop here and compare the others.

"Nyree, can we set the machine to stop at a particular gene

pair, rather than looking for differences?"

"Certainly." Nyree showed Hannah the commands to do that. Swiftly, Hannah pulled out the slide with Rebecca's sample, and replaced it with Ben's as the control now. Then, she randomly grabbed a slide from one of the deceased expedition members and placed it in the device. Again holding her breath, she gave the appropriate commands. A few minutes later, the screen resolved to show, side by side, the same section of DNA. It was identical. Hannah let her breath out in a whoosh. "There you are, you son of a bitch."

She needed to verify it. This time, she used a sample from the new patients, which had already tested positive for the CCR5 allele that Middle Easterners had in common. The same result came from the same section—none of the Middle Easterners had that particular section active. She had to get word out to the CDC that she'd found something, so they could start working on delivery of genetic therapy. She didn't have the sophisticated equipment here to cut out the defective section and replace it with something that would protect the patients. It was now up to someone else to unlock the cure that would save the world, but she, based on a tip from Rebecca, had just found the key.

~~~

"What is it?" Rebecca asked.

"I don't know, love. Hannah asked me to gather everyone as quickly as possible, and she especially wants you. She seemed excited."

"Could she possibly...I'll be right there."

JR went on to gather the others, as Rebecca finished taking the vital signs of the woman in the bed. "Your fever is down, Amina. That's good news. I must go to this meeting now, but I'll be back afterward to check on you again."

"Thank you, Doctor Rebecca."

310

Rebecca hurried down the hall to the conference room where JR had said they'd be gathered. He said Hannah was excited, that had to be good news, didn't it? She'd never seen the taciturn Hannah excited. It had to be big, whatever it was.

Because she'd tarried to finish her task, Rebecca was the last to arrive. When Hannah saw her, she began clapping her hands and smiling, nodding her head as others began to follow suit. Rebecca stopped, confused.

"What?"

"You, my friend, are a genius," Hannah said. "You did it. You remembered the key information, and we've found what's causing the difference in behavior of this virus. We now have the information we need for devising a gene therapy to cure it."

Rebecca's hand flew to her mouth as tears sprang to her eyes. "A cure?"

"Yes, without a doubt. Sit down and I'll explain it to everyone."

Rebecca sat, but could hardly stay still as Hannah went through a complex explanation of how some genes don't code for things like eye color, how tall you'll be or blood group. What Rebecca had read about was often called junk DNA, because it seemed to have no function. The dimly-remembered article mentioned that some of the sequences within this so-called junk DNA were retrovirus fragments that, when activated, were implicated in several complex diseases, cancer being one of them. The burning question was, how did they become activated? And the answer seemed to be by microbes, whether viral or bacterial.

Hannah went on to explain that the CCR5 gene that Ben and Rebecca had discovered to have two alleles, or forms, was particularly involved in the immune system, and that it had a dual role. One was to summon leukocytes, or white blood cells, and one was to code for proteins on the white blood cells that serve as magnets to the T cells. Here, she paused to explain the function of T cells.

"Think of T cells as genetic bullets," she said, unconsciously using a phrase that had been used with more sinister intent in the outside world recently. "There are thousands of diseases that can affect the human body. What we call immunities are actually the T cells that recognize each antigen and kills it. That's a simplification, but it will do for now. Just remember, each disease has a specific T cell to kill it when your immune system recognizes it."

"Now, what's happening with the H10N7 virus is that one allele of the CCR5 gene codes for a protein that activates a particular fragment of junk DNA. In this case, it's a fragment of H10N7. We've had that in our DNA all along, but it apparently lost its potency at some time in the distant past. If you have the allele that codes for the protein, it activates the fragment, so the T cells recognize it and fight it. Based on your experience here in Antarctica, I'd say that the process is so innocuous that you don't even know you've had an immune response.

"The kicker is, the majority of Middle Eastern people have the other allele only, and that one apparently doesn't code for the protein that activates the retrovirus fragment. The result is that the T cells to fight it aren't produced, and the virus that spreads from person to person is able to overwhelm the system, resulting in death as a side effect of a raging fever."

"What about the ones that have both alleles, like Ben?" Rebecca asked. She had followed the lecture perfectly, and was now focused on what she could do for her patients.

"My guess is that the standard allele codes for the protein, but in fewer numbers, so that the infection is being fought off for a while. However, because there aren't enough T cells developing, the patients eventually do become sick. You have a pretty good chance of saving them if you can keep the fever down and support the immune response. It isn't the virus per se that's killing them, it's the side effects of the fever. Keep them stable until their bodies have a chance to fight it off, and they'll recover."

"Thank God," breathed Rebecca. Then, "We have to get word to the CDC right away. And to the world."

"Way ahead of you," answered Hannah. "I called the CDC first. We don't have what we need here to get the gene therapy developed, but they'll put all the manpower on it that they can muster now. All you have to do is help these poor souls that they sent here to survive until we can get out of here."

The last phrase sobered everyone, most of whom had followed only with difficulty. They'd understood the part between Hannah and Rebecca well enough, though. A solution could be found. They'd be able to leave - someday.

Daniel was the first to voice the question on everyone's mind. "Do you think that means we can leave now?"

Hannah shrugged her shoulders. "That's up to the politicians, not me. It's going to take a while to get the gene therapy established, let alone distributed worldwide. Until then, we're still a danger to anyone without the antibodies to fight this thing off."

"I guess we're still stuck here, then. But at least we can count on going home someday." With that, Daniel excused himself to call Sarah and then the president with the good news.

Chapter 31 - That damned virus has mutated?

"But you can't come home now." It was a statement, not a question. Sarah only said it because Daniel didn't. She didn't know what to do with her anger. It was no one's fault, and of course Daniel had to go, as he'd insisted. Thank God she hadn't gone, too. Thinking about little Nick's first Christmas and first birthday without his daddy was hard, but if it had been both of them she didn't know how she would bear it. Even if Nicky would never remember. Of course, his grandma Emma and great-aunt Sally doted on him, as did Martha Simms. He would have been well cared-for, and if she were there, she would at least have Daniel's arms around her. For the millionth time since he'd left, Sarah felt as if something were tearing her in half.

His news was good, though. A possibility for a cure, she should be excited. Right now, she just felt tired. Daniel was chattering about something...oh, their plans to move into the cave any day now. How beautiful it was there, and how he wished she could see it for herself. Her head was buzzing, hard to hear what he was saying.

"Sarah? Sarah, what's wrong honey?"

Sarah had dropped her head onto her arms. So tired. Daniel's face in the screen took on a look of alarm. He tried once more.

"Sarah!"

Daniel switched to a different Skype user, leaving the call with Sarah connected. Relief flooded him when Luke answered his SMS call.

"Luke, I was talking to Sarah and I think she passed out! Can you go see about her?"

With barely a nod and a quick 'k' on the chat, Luke left the room at a run, skidding past Sarah's door before he could stop himself. He opened it and ran in, taking in his niece's white face and shallow breathing. Wasting no time, he grabbed the phone and dialed 911. In response to the operator's questions, which he impatiently waited for, knowing that it would save time in the long run, then answered them. Address, name and age of the patient and what had happened.

Luke went around to the computer monitor and bent over Sarah's slumped body.

"Daniel, are you still there?"

"Yeah. Is Sarah okay?"

"Don't know, she's unconscious. 911 wants to know what happened."

"I don't know. We were talking, and she started to look sleepy, and then she just put her head down and I couldn't get her to talk to me. Luke, what's going on?"

"I'll call you back when we know, Daniel."

Luke relayed the information, such as it was, to the 911 operator. With the land line tied up, he took out his cell phone and speed-dialed his wife.

"Sally, who has Nick, you or Emma?"

"I do. What's wrong?"

Luke spared a thought for the woman who could read him like a book, even from just a few words over the phone.

"Sarah's sick. Can you call Emma and have her meet me at the hospital?"

"Oh, my God, Luke, sick with what?"

"Don't know. Just get Emma down here, okay? The ambulance should be here any minute, and I'm going with her."

After Sally said she would, Luke looked around Sarah's desk. He wouldn't put it past some of the protesters to have sent her something harmful in the mail, but he didn't see anything that led him to believe she'd received a package or envelope from outside. Even a thorough search of her desk drawers revealed nothing more unusual than the bottom right drawer filled with little Nick's toys for when he visited mommy at the office. Luke ran his hand through his hair, standing it on end. What could possibly go wrong next?

Moments later, he was in the back of an ambulance, watching as the attendants took Sarah's vital signs, started oxygen and an IV and reported to the ER where they were taking her. It wasn't a long trip; Boulder wasn't a very big town. They arrived even faster than the ambulance had made it to the office, if Luke's sense of time wasn't off. Bursting through the doors with her stretcher, the attendants rapid-fired more information to a man in scrubs, maybe the ER doctor. He directed them into the partitioned room, Luke following. That's when Luke realized that the room was in chaos. Dozens of people wearing the same look he was sure he had were in the room, trying and failing to stay out of the way of the rushing medical personnel.

"What the hell?" He didn't realize he'd spoken out loud until the man directing Sarah's gurney answered.

"It looks like that damned virus has mutated."

Luke stopped cold. He knew without asking what virus the man meant. Though the attention of the world and even the bulk of the attention of the Rossler Foundation was on the toll in the Middle East, Luke was among the insiders who understood that almost two million Americans of Middle Eastern descent had been affected so far as well, not to mention hundreds of thousands more scattered across the globe. Even Israel had a few thousand cases, despite their draconian quarantine measures.

"Excuse me, are you a doctor?" he asked.

"Resident. Were you in the ambulance with this woman?"

"Yes, sir."

"Get this mask on right now. You're under quarantine. Are you related to her?"

"Her uncle."

"Contact her family. Tell them under no circumstances are they to come here. This place is on lock-down."

Another man might have buckled under the news, but Luke had a lifetime of dealing with crises behind him. He took note of the cubicle where they put Sarah's gurney, then loped out of the room to call Sally back.

Once he'd calmed Sally, told her to watch for symptoms in the baby and reached Emma to turn her away from the hospital, he Skyped Daniel. Luke tried to school his face, but Daniel saw there was bad news the moment he saw it, covered as it was by a mask.

"What, Luke? Tell me."

"Daniel, I'm so sorry, and I don't know whether they've confirmed it, but this place is swarming with flu patients. The ER doc told me it appears the virus has mutated."

"God help us," Daniel answered, when he was able to speak. "Are you there with her?"

"Yes, but the hospital's in lock-down. They told me to make sure Ryan and Emma didn't come. The baby's with Sally, and she's watching him, for, you know."

Daniel closed his eyes, sighed and opened them again to stare into Luke's.

"Make sure they keep her fever down. That's about all you can do for it, but she'll recover if they don't let her fever kill her. Tell them. And tell them, we've found the key. They'll have something to fight this with as soon as possible. I have to go tell our virologist about the mutation."

"I'll keep you posted, Daniel. And I'll let the doctors know about the fever."

His phone calls finished, Luke went back into the chaotic ER to find the resident he'd spoken to before. He needed to tell him how to save Sarah's life.

~~~

In spite of his deep worry about Sarah, Daniel knew where his duty lay. After informing Rebecca and Hannah, he made sure he understood Hannah's discovery and could recite the facts in a way that Harper could understand, and then called the White House.

Harper had just finished dinner when an aide whispered to him that his presence was urgently required in the Oval Office. Telling the First Lady he'd meet her in their private quarters as soon as possible, he followed the aide back to his office. As soon as he saw Daniel's face, he knew that something was about to change—he could only hope it was for the good.

In typical good news/bad news fashion, Daniel first brought his friend up to speed on the breakthrough that meant that if the researchers could work fast enough, they could halt the spread of the virus, not alleviate it but halt it. He attempted to explain, but the president could see that something was distressing him. Daniel's face didn't match the good news.

"What's troubling you, Daniel?" he said, abruptly, interrupting the lecture.

"There's more news."

"Spill it."

"The virus seems to have mutated there in the States. Sarah's a victim."

Harper uttered an expletive, then gave Daniel his condolences. "That's tough, my friend. I'm so sorry."

"The good news is that she and the others should be able to fight it off. Man, I wish I were there. She needs me, Nigel."

"I understand. Listen, we're going to get you home as soon as possible. Try not to worry. Are you comfortable with the care she's receiving?"

"I don't know. I don't have much information. One good thing is that Luke is there. They've detained him at the hospital under quarantine. I'm surprised I'm the first to tell you about this."

"Frankly, so am I. More heads may roll, yet. Esther and I will be praying for her, Daniel."

"Thank you, Nigel. I'll keep you posted."

With Daniel's report came a number of tasks for the President to perform, the first being to call the CDC and find out what the devil those clowns were doing now. He would have thought they would have solved their communications problems with him after what happened to their Director a few weeks ago.

Chapter 32 - Do I have the legal ability to order that?

The news that the H10N7 had started to affect people whose heritage had no known links to the Middle East was out via the grapevine before the news media picked it up. All over the world, people who assumed they were immune had gotten lax about their quarantine compliance. Into hospitals that were already overwhelmed with the initial wave poured more and more patients. Medical personnel who, hearing that their patients weren't Middle Eastern, failed to mask and glove before they were brought in were also exposed. Within twenty-four hours of Sarah's collapse, it was as if someone had shouted 'fire' in a crowded theater. Panic ensued.

Luke felt fortunate that the doctor he first talked to wasn't past his residency. He had a slightly better chance of having the man listen to him about Daniel's information than the stressed-out head of the ER. Doctor Hanson was his name, and he was interested to learn that his patient was the famous Sarah Rossler. As soon as he had made her as comfortable as possible, he had a chair pulled into the cubicle for Luke and sat down on the rolling stool himself.

"Tell me more about this," he said.

"I think I can do better than that. One of the CDC virologists who's down there where this thing started might be willing to talk to you, if she thinks you can sway others to begin the treatment that's been working there."

"Do you mean to tell me they have survivors?"

"One so far, out of six patients of mixed blood. The others are still being treated, and the doctor that's with them is cautiously optimistic. We can find out what's happening with them. But it was these patients that were the key to the virologist figuring it out."

"I'm all for it. Let me get someone to pay attention to your niece and make sure that fever stays down, and then let's go where there's less noise and make that call."

A few minutes later, Dr. Hanson led Luke into the doctor's lounge and offered him a soda from the mini-fridge.

"No thanks. I'll just give Daniel a call. He's going to want to know how Sarah is before he lets you talk to anyone else."

"That's fine."

Luke made the call, explained to Daniel who Hanson was, and then handed over his phone.

"Dr. Hanson, Luke tells me you're taking care of my Sarah."

"Yes, sir. Her uncle did the right thing to get her in right away. From what he's telling me, I'd say we have a good chance to pull her through. I have a nurse watching her vitals for the smallest rise in temperature, and we'll cool her off right away if we see that. Would it be possible for me to speak with your doctor and your virologist? If they can give me the scientific mumbo-jumbo that will explain this thing, I think I can get it used throughout the hospital. You'll save a lot of lives."

"Sure thing. Just make sure Sarah pulls through, Doc. I should be with her and instead I'm stuck here for the next six months." Luke heard the anguish in Daniel's voice, and even the doctor, who didn't know him, had a moment's empathy.

"We'll take good care of her, Mr. Rossler."

There was a slight delay while Daniel got Rebecca, then left her with the Skype call while he went for Hannah. By the time they got back, Rebecca had done a creditable job of explaining the mechanism of the virus and what they'd found out about CCR5.

321

She handed the phone over to Hannah.

"Good afternoon, Dr. Price. I'm Eric Hanson, an ER resident here at Boulder Community Hospital. Has Mr. Rossler informed you of what we're facing here?"

"Yes. I'm so sorry we didn't figure this thing out before it could mutate," she answered.

"Do you have anything to add to the retrovirus and T cell discussion I just had with Dr. Mendenhall?" he asked.

"Perhaps. I want to let you know what section of the DNA sequence is mediated by the CCR5 alleles, so you can determine whether the virus is still acting there, or somewhere else. I'll also tell you how we found what we did. Rebecca has told you how to treat your patients, yes?"

"Yes, ma'am."

"Very well." Hannah proceeded to give Hanson the ideas she had to curb the mutated virus before it accelerated the depopulation of the earth. When she informed Hanson of the rate of spread the original virus, he groaned, causing Luke to sit up in alarm. Hanson ignored him.

"All right," he said, when she finished. "I'll get the word out here as fast as I can, but you should probably call the CDC. I understand the hospitals are being overrun like a cookie crumb at a picnic in an anthill."

"Already did," she replied, her usual terse style making him wonder if he'd offended her.

"Okay, then, I've got my work cut out for me. Thanks for giving me the rundown."

Hanson handed Luke his phone back. "I owe you one. Say, what's your name?"

"Luke. Luke Clarke. Save Sarah and we're even."

322

"We're going to do our best. Why don't you go on back and sit with her while I consult with my boss?"

As a result, out of dozens of hospitals in the region that didn't get the word so quickly, Boulder Community had the best track record in pulling their patients through the crisis. When all was said and done, they would later learn that they had a 98% survival rate. Meanwhile, they ran out of beds and had to cooperate in a region-wide shuffle of patients, sending everyone who didn't have the flu to University of Colorado Hospital Anschutz Medical Center, while all flu patients filled up beds in every community and parochial hospital in the area between Colorado Springs and Ft. Collins. Other states were using similar triage methods to try to isolate the flu cases from the rest of the population, with little success. Most of them left the research to the CDC and simply treated their cases with ice baths and antiviral medications, letting the illness run its course.

Meanwhile, the CDC and every cooperating researcher worldwide were searching frantically for a vector with which to deliver the genetic therapy that would give the Middle Easterners a chance. So far, just keeping their fever down hadn't helped in the Middle East. With no antibodies specific to this antigen, as soon as cold therapy was stopped, the illness worsened. They weren't going to recover unless the gene therapy solution worked.

~~~

Some of the challenges that gene therapy as a science experienced at first, just after the Human Genome Project was completed and doctors started targeting the diseases known to be genetic in origin, had been solved within the past few years. The 10th Cycle Library medical section was responsible for some of the solutions, in fact. In the records, researchers had found a reference to an innocuous virus that could be used as a vector for in-body delivery of cells to specific body parts. For example, Parkinson's patients could now expect to be cured when perfect copies of the defective gene responsible for the illness were delivered in this way to a certain part of the brain.

Another discovery was a way to use stem cells from chimpanzees, to deliver in-vitro gene therapy. In this instance, ethical concerns about using human stem cells were sidestepped. Animal rights activists weren't happy about it, but so far the benefit to human beings had trumped their arguments. In-vitro gene therapy involved exposing the stem cells to the vector carrying the good genes in a laboratory setting. Once the culture had developed sufficiently, causing the stem cells to become differentiated as the type of T-cell required, they were introduced into the patient's bloodstream, where they continued to grow new, perfect cells.

Both methods had their good points and bad points. In the first, getting the new genes to go into the DNA sequence in exactly the right spot and then stay there was an issue. In the latter, the stem cells were a bone of contention. No sooner than the CDC began working on Hannah's discovery, scientists quickly became convinced that the first method was not going to do the Middle East any good. The illness was systemic, so introduction into the bloodstream was the better choice. Ironically, to be cured of this virus, the patients were going to have to be exposed to another virus.

On the other hand, though scientists thought it would be simple to do it in-vitro, the amount of therapeutic cells needed was overwhelming just because of the sheer numbers of patients. Consultation with their counterparts in the world's most advanced countries convinced the CDC that they and the others would have to get the authority to take over every lab in the West to make the therapeutic substance in such volume. The acting Director contacted the president's staff and asked for an audience.

"Mr. President, I'm here to tell you that we have found a

therapy that will cure this virus, if only we can produce enough of it."

Harper's joy at the words 'cure this virus' turned to concern when he heard the caveat.

"What do you need?"

"We need you to announce it, first, sir, if you will. Then we need the authority to force every capable lab to make it. It's going to interfere with research and commerce alike, but it won't be for long. Perhaps three weeks, then they can go back to business as usual, and we'll have it under control."

"You're kidding!" Harper said, though he was aware that more momentous words were required. Turning to his Chief of Staff, he asked, "Do I have the legal ability to order that?"

Then, thinking more of the positive outcome, he went on. "You know what? Forget legality. I'm doing it and we'll sort out the legalities later. We don't have time to waste on red tape."

"Sir, I'd suggest that you make the announcement, followed by your strong suggestion that they should voluntarily cooperate. If that doesn't get the response we want within hours, you can take the next step. That will give us time to investigate the question, but get some labs working on it right away."

"Schedule the announcement."

So it was that, at the last possible moment, with the Middle East on the brink of annihilation by disease, President Harper's face appeared on millions of TV screens, with a grin not seen since it all began.

"My fellow Americans, and friends across the globe. I am delighted to tell you that, due to the dedication of our brightest scientists, working without cease since this terrible epidemic began, a cure has been found. I will leave the details to the

Director of the CDC to explain. I'm just a politician, don't follow most of this science stuff too well, but they tell me that the illness is caused by the virus exploiting a vulnerable gene in some of us, and that they have a way to replace that one with a one that the virus can't interact with. If you or your loved ones are sick, know that we are working on this just as fast as we can.

"I want to particularly single out the dedicated scientists in Antarctica, who, despite being almost universally blamed for this accident of nature, have worked tirelessly to find a cure. Dr. Rebecca Mendenhall, Dr. Ben Epstein and Dr. Hannah Price all deserve credit for what may well be the salvation of the entire world. Dr. Epstein might have lost his life by contracting the virus if it hadn't been for the determination of Dr. Mendenhall to save him. Dr. Price, who found the key, did so because of a suggestion from Dr. Mendenhall. While they all deserve credit, I hail Dr. Mendenhall as a heroine; the most valuable player on the winning team."

Here, Harper had to pause while applause drowned out his next words. When the accolade had died down, he went on.

"To the laboratories and pharmaceutical companies within our country, I say, we need your help. Hundreds of millions of patients across the globe are doomed to die of this disease if we don't get this cure to them very, very quickly. The Director tells me that it will take the capacity of every lab in this country along with all others in the world that have the equipment to make the genetic medicine, to manufacture enough to save what's left of the Middle East. I urge you to do your patriotic duty, to our great country and our ill citizens, but not only to them. Do your duty as a human being to fight this with your expertise, your facilities and your immediate cooperation. When the CDC contacts you, you'll be given the formula for the gene therapy and the instructions for producing, packaging and transporting it. I am well aware that I have the ability to issue an executive order to that effect, but I believe it won't be necessary; I believe that Americans are still kindhearted people who have always done the right thing as they see it, and will do so again. I believe that our nation and its businesses will lead the way in cooperating in what is, after all, in everyone's best interest.

"And now, the Director of the CDC."

Harper stepped aside despite a sudden cacophony of questions from the assembled reporters. He lifted both hands and made a quelling gesture, then held out his right hand, palm up, in the direction of the microphone. The media would get most of their questions answered in the next few moments, and any they had remaining would be answered by the CDC or not at all. Harper's next move would be dictated by the response to his call for cooperation.

With no time to lose, every lab in the US and most other developed countries began producing the gene therapy as quickly as they could. One thing they needed to know was how much or how little would be effective. The smaller the dose that would save lives, the more lives they could save with the production of which they were capable. The ethical question was, who do we choose to treat with the first, smallest doses?

They had plenty of patients on hand to give it to, but if they waited to see the results, the wasted days would doom countless more. Primary researchers had a massive conference call, came to a consensus about the minimum effective dose, and stated the standard. It came down to a form of roulette. Millions of pre-loaded syringes were shipped as rapidly as possible to the countries most affected, and each doctor followed his or her own rules. Where there weren't enough doses for everyone, and that was in most places, some doctors gave them to their sickest patients, others to those just showing symptoms, and in the most backward countries, nurses simply dosed the patients whose beds were closest to their supply closets until the syringes were all used.

The second wave of medication that went out had a few more cubic centimeters in the syringes. Until the first batch of patients to be dosed showed improvement, each shipment would have slightly more in each dose. The CDC was acting as a clearinghouse for the information as well as imposing standards on the labs that were producing the medication, so that each batch was uniform in dosage, whether it came from the US, Great Britain or Germany—wherever labs were producing it.

As the results came in, it became apparent that those whose illness was in its second week of symptoms and who were near death lived a few days longer after receiving the therapy, but in the end it only prolonged their agony. This was seen by the radical elements as yet another attack by the West, and they urged the healthy family members of the ill to refuse this treatment.

When the World Health Organization became involved and urged governments to curb the ability of the family members to refuse it, it ratcheted up the political tension even more. Protests outside of hospitals all over the world hindered the ability of medical personnel to come and go, and several hospitals were severely damaged by suicide bombers whose avowed purpose was to stop the West from turning their people into science experiments.

The second batch was more effective. Now that it was known that the sickest patients couldn't be saved by it, instructions were to give it only to patients in the first week of symptoms, and most of those patients survived. It was decided that medical authorities would give the medication only to those who might, with its use, survive, leaving the patients who were sickest to die untreated. Again the radicals screamed that the genocide was continuing. Where before they had protested against the therapy, now they protested that it was being deliberately withheld.

Nevertheless, with breakthroughs on both gene therapy and cold therapy happening hourly, week seventeen of the crisis drew to a close with the numbers of deaths sharply decreased. For the first time, though new cases were still being reported at the same rate, the death toll fell well below its previous one-hundred percent, to about seventy-five percent.

A tough decision fell on WHO and CDC when they collaborated to forbid the use of the gene therapy on anyone who had passed the tenth day of symptoms. Those patients were considered unrecoverable. Instead, millions of family members who had shown no sign of illness but were exposed by their loved ones were given preventative doses. Within a few days, the rate of new cases dropped dramatically. Among those still falling ill were the thousands of followers of the Ayatollah Kazemi, who bought his propaganda that the medicine was intended to poison them.

Meanwhile, strict quarantine protocols limited the spread of the mutated form of the virus in the US, while most of those patients survived due to superior medical care. Sarah emerged from her syncope to learn that she was under treatment and that Luke was taking massive doses of antiviral meds to prevent becoming ill in the first place. Her first rational thought was of course for her baby, but when Luke assured her that he'd shown no symptoms in the past week, she relaxed and became a model patient. It was the fastest way she knew to get sprung from the hospital, assuming she wasn't now a carrier. That had yet to be established for the B form of the virus.

It was demoralizing to Sarah to learn that the foundation was running just fine with neither Daniel nor her at the helm, until Luke pointed out that it meant they could take a vacation now and then, with Sinclair and Nicholas running a tight ship in their absence. Even have another baby, if she wanted to. She began to enjoy her rest, especially after she was past the danger point and no longer had to freeze in the ice bath every couple of hours.

Both on a local level, between the Rossler Foundation and

the expedition, which had now moved completely into the valley, and a world-wide level, it began to look like things would eventually return to normal.

Chapter 33 – We're going home!

The fifty-four souls who for one reason or another were stranded at Purgatory Canyon reacted with joy when Daniel informed them that the President was allowing them to go home. Even though it was near the end of the travel season, transportation was arranged. Summers begged to be allowed to stay, but in the end understood that even he couldn't cope with six months of solitude, and got on the helicopter when it was his turn.

Even though they were overjoyed to be going home after all, the core group of scientists knew that there was a cost. President Harper had warned Daniel that there would be Congressional hearings. It was ironic that the people who had been applauding their effort to find the cure a few days ago were now asking whether they had known about it from the beginning. This, along with ugly assertions that it was certainly suspicious. A handful of scientists without sophisticated equipment were able to 'find' the key, when world-class laboratories had made no progress? Highly unlikely. The emphasis on *find* was always meant as a veiled hint that they had the knowledge because they developed the virus in the first place. The group was in for some uncomfortable times, but Daniel assured Harper that they would come through just fine, as they were blameless.

Chapter 34 - As if the microbes had been dumped from the air

Esther Harper was worried about her husband. He'd been through many crises in his six years as President of the United States, but the current one was by far the worst he'd had to face. First, all those poor Middle Easterners, dying like flies, countless numbers of them. You couldn't even begin to visualize those numbers—how was it possible there was anyone left? Nigel seemed to feel guilty about every single one of them, even as he staunchly defended the Rosslers as blameless, just the victims of a grisly time-bomb from the 9th Cycle. As she now understood it, the fault was in fact within the DNA of the people who had fallen ill, something that was introduced into their genetics thousands of years ago. It was no one's fault at all, really.

She didn't pretend to understand it, but she could see her husband aging in front of her eyes, like a time-lapse photograph. When he took office, Nigel was a hale and hearty man. He'd been tall, fit and trim, and his dark wavy hair was frequently cited by the silly gossip rags as the reason for him being the heartthrob candidate.

Now, he was stooped with the weight of millions of deaths, his eyes were always bloodshot, and the hair was now a beautiful shade of silver, not a single strand of dark brown left. Esther wasn't a shallow woman. She would love her husband and stand by him no matter what. She'd weathered the vicious rumors that he had affairs, because she knew better. She'd survived the grueling second campaign. And she would survive this; but she wasn't sure about Nigel.

Unaware of her concern, Harper dragged himself out of bed at five forty-five and took a quick shower, then dressed in readiness for his briefing on the morning of March 6th. He had a feeling of dread, which he didn't understand. For the past week, the new numbers of cases of the virus had dwindled, and even those who did report in were being given the gene therapy as soon as they reported. The death toll had dropped dramatically as well. Almost everyone who started showing symptoms since the second shipments of medication survived, except those who refused it. Surely God couldn't have yet another lightning bolt up His sleeve. And yet, Harper reflected twenty minutes later, he could be wrong.

He'd known that the mutated form of the virus had swept his nation as if the microbes had been dumped from the air. Everybody got sick at once. The CDC couldn't even determine an index case, because one day no one was sick, and the next hundreds of thousands had it. But, medical professionals had responded well, and so far it appeared this form of the flu was no worse than the garden variety that came in seasonally, took off a few elderly or immune-suppressed kids, and disappeared with the spring.

The fact that this thing had *started* in the spring was an unconscious fact in the back of his mind, unnoticed as yet. Still, a week later, people were already recovering, not going through that agonizing two-week decline. And quarantining was working, or appeared to be. He'd ask Rebecca Mendenhall what she thought the next time they spoke. She not only had a good head on her shoulders, but she was always able to help him understand without using all that medical jargon.

This morning's briefing, though, brought the news that the mad Ayatollah Kazemi had a theory about where it had come from. His accusation was that the United States, in particular, had devised this illness and set it loose among its own people to act as a distraction. He was now saying that, not only did America turn loose the original virus among Middle Easterners, but also this mutated form was set loose among Americans so that he and other Muslim leaders would think they'd been mistaken. As if now that there were non-Middle Eastern victims, he should just forget about the original crime. In his ranting, he named Harper personally as the mastermind behind this plot.

What was worse, there were plenty of gullible Americans who bought it. Responsible media was saying there should be an investigation, but those who had a grudge against Harper from before were proclaiming this idiocy as truth and calling for impeachment. Harper was speechless with rage that his character would be impugned in this way. He had his faults; what man didn't? But, how had it come to this?

"I want that lunatic silenced," he roared. His advisers wisely kept their mouths shut. Naturally, they couldn't carry that out as an order, Harper just needed to vent.

Then he had a more practical idea. "Get the Press Secretary in here right now. I'm going on national TV and tell them that this is such a crazy idea that it must be that crazy man who thought it up. Maybe *he* had this mutation designed and deploying it is an act of biological warfare. If I find out that's true, we're going to wipe Iran off the face of the earth once and for all. I'm tired of dealing with those assholes."

It may not have been the most politically correct statement to make, but most of the people in the room agreed with the sentiment, and those who didn't were smart enough to realize it was just a fit of temper, and that Harper would have a more reasoned approach to whatever they could find out about the origin of the mutation. After all, never in the history of the United States had a president been called upon to deal with so many crises not of his own making. A lesser man might not have been able to do it at all. A fit of temper now and then didn't make him a bad man, or a bad president.

~~~

After a week in the hospital, Sarah was released and Luke's quarantine was lifted because his blood showed no sign of the virus. When baby Nick saw her, he squirmed out of Sally's arms and made a beeline for Sarah on all fours, then pulled up on her legs and almost swarmed up her body like a monkey. Sarah reached down to pick him up and staggered with his weight.

"Can we call Daniel?" she said. "I want him to know I'm home."

Luke had been updating Daniel almost hourly, not only about Sarah, but also about the political shit-storm that was raging around them. But he knew Daniel would want to hear from Sarah anyway, so he went to their home office to get a laptop and set up a Skype video call.

Even while Sarah had been sick, she kept seeing in her mind's eye the numbers mounting in the spreadsheet, with that terrible caption on week nineteen: Total ME Wipeout. Raj had an interesting way of separating the end of his world from his work. After all, he and Sushma shared the genetics that left them vulnerable to the virus. That made her ask after them.

"Are Raj and Sushma okay?" she said to Luke, as he returned with the laptop.

"Oh, yeah. You know Raj took Sushma and went to what he called his safe house as soon as it became clear what this virus was doing. He's been working from home since right after you had him make that projection, and they're living on disaster supplies he laid in when he bought the place."

"Oh, that's right, I forgot," she said. "Where is he again?"

"Somewhere in the mountains around Lake Tahoe, I think. Not sure. Anyway, neither he nor Sushma has been out of the house in weeks, but we hear from him daily. They're fine."

"Thank heaven for his paranoia," Sarah said, smiling. "Where are Grandpa and Grandma, and Sinclair and Martha?"

"On their way. They didn't want to overwhelm you. They're

bringing dinner."

If only Daniel were home, all would be right in Sarah's world. She sighed contentedly. "Let's make that call."

"Hi, sweetheart," Daniel said, the look on his face saying more than any words could. For Sarah, the rest of the people in the room disappeared, all but little Nick on her lap. She held him tight and pointed at Daniel's face on the screen. "Look, Nick, its Daddy!"

"Mama," responded the baby.

"Looks like you need to get home ASAP, sweetheart," she laughed. For a few minutes, all the cares of the world disappeared as the pair realized how lucky they were, even if they were thousands of miles apart. Both had come through with their health intact, and Daniel would be home in a matter of days.

Chapter 35 - The homecoming

The helicopters would be outside to pick them up in a matter of hours, so everyone was busy wrapping up their packing and last minute errands.

Robert and JR arrived at the hospital site to make sure Summers was ready to go. They found that the fumarole had been enclosed within a waist-high barrier, and paused to look into it.

"Looks innocent enough," Robert remarked.

JR, who was still skittish about the lava plume below them, didn't think so. The thing was sinister, with its topping of sickly-looking green algae and the steam wisping off it from time to time.

"How do you reckon the virus got in there?" he asked, not really expecting an answer.

"Well, if someone fell in and was sick, it might migrate to the algae for self-preservation," Robert mused.

JR looked at him in horror. "Do you mean to tell me those bugs have will and volition?"

"That's more a question for Hannah, I think. But I can imagine a microbe switching hosts if the first one is no longer viable."

"Like, all his blood boiled away?" JR said, with a touch of the macabre.

"Exactly," said Robert. JR shuddered and strode off, forcing Robert to jog a little to catch up.

~~~

The homecoming was subdued, not because the expedition members weren't ecstatic to be home, but because the mutated strain of flu was still keeping the population of the US in limited contact with each other. Before they could leave a quarantined

337

area of the airport, they each had to submit to a blood test to determine that they weren't carrying it. Now that the original H10N7 was in retreat, their antibodies to that strain didn't pose a problem.

Robert had come to the US with them this time, having accepted a permanent position on the Rossler Foundation staff, much to Cyndi's delight. He would make himself available for the coming Congressional investigation, and then return to Australia to wrap things up there and pack the rest of his belongings for the move. Rebecca had also been invited to do so, but hadn't yet made a decision, as much of her planning depended on what JR intended to do from now on. The military personnel had been met at the plane by other military personnel and spirited off without so much as a goodbye to their erstwhile detainees, and the recovered flu patients were similarly grabbed and taken to nearby research facilities. Daniel was concerned about them, but could not prevent their being taken into custody.

Naturally, the support workers made a beeline for their own homes, so it was just the core group that was met by a chartered 15-passenger van and taken to Daniel's home for a private celebration of their return. Sarah, still a little weak, but radiant, threw herself into Daniel's arms as soon as he stepped in the door.

"My love, I'm so happy you're home," she whispered. In answer, Daniel gave her an enthusiastic kiss, and an apologetic look.

"I hope you were expecting guests, Baby. I seem to have brought a few." With that, he threw the door further open and in streamed the happy expedition members, sure of their welcome. Sarah hugged JR next, and then Rebecca, followed by each of the others, even Hannah and Ben, whom she'd never met. Ryan, Emma, Luke, Sally, Nick, Bess, Daniel and JR's parents, and even Sinclair and Martha followed suit. Raj and Sushma only were missing from what the Rosslers considered the family group, as Raj had yet to be talked into leaving their safe haven for any reason whatsoever.

The celebration went far into the night, but at last the guests all went either home or to a hotel where the out-of-town guests had been booked because there were too many to stay with the locals. Daniel and Sarah stepped quietly into Nick's room to take a look at their sleeping child, who had warmed up to Daniel as if he'd never been gone. After kissing him gently on the forehead, they went arm in arm to their room, where they clung to each other emotionally. Assuring each other that they never wanted to be separated for so long again, they sealed their promises with that physical connection that transcends all words, and afterward went to sleep in each other's arms.

~~~

There were still numerous cases of flu to contend with in the Middle East, even though new cases had diminished dramatically with the gene therapy. However, the US had turned its attention to the cases at home. Doses of the gene therapy were still being manufactured as rapidly as possible and shipped to the Middle East, where the only people who were still dying from the virus were those who were under the spell of Kazemi or his ilk. It wasn't so much that the citizens of the US were heartless—after all, there was plenty of medicine to go around, and they'd pay for it with their taxes for many years to come. They just had notoriously short attention spans.

Fortunately, as Sarah's case had shown, they proved to have much milder symptoms, little more than the seasonal flu that usually swept the country in the fall. A course of antiviral medication, the usual precautions to get plenty of water and rest, and to stay home until all symptoms were gone, were all it took for most people to recover without complications. Early detection, compliance with quarantines and the radical response that medical authorities took with the first wave of cases stopped it from becoming the disaster that everyone feared it could have been.

The usual percentage of immune-compromised individuals died before a vaccine was developed, with the help of Sarah and others who'd come down with it initially. Afterwards, it receded into the public's usual case of apathy for an old news story.

Abroad, however, and in Harper's daily security briefing, the threat represented by the radical Muslim religious leaders, continued to be of concern.

Chapter 36 - Let us strike on their sacred holiday

Despite the fact that the virus was winding down in the rest of the Middle East, Kazemi, still claiming to be the al-Mahdi, continued to rail against Western bio-warfare. His points were heeded by many, even among the former patients, now recovered thanks to Western gene therapy. They didn't understand and couldn't appreciate what had been given to them—a repaired gene that would immunize them against this strain of flu for the rest of their lives, at a staggering cost.

It was fortunate that the 10th Cycle library had helped with the development of a relatively simple procedure. Had an in-body method been required, the cost of saving even one life would have approached one million dollars. As it was, the average cost of manufacturing, shipping and administering the gene therapy was less than a quarter of that per dose. Nevertheless, when considered in terms of nearly a billion patients, saving them was more costly than waging war against them.

None of that mattered to Kazemi. He couldn't comprehend that anyone, even infidels - and who knew what they would do? - would bankrupt their treasury to save a lukewarm ally, much less a bitter enemy. He therefore believed that there was a hidden agenda, and that it would come out in more violence against his people. It was his intention to strike first.

Accordingly, he called his lieutenants together to make plans for another coordinated strike. Even if he no longer had the will to use what few nuclear weapons he had left to command, he did have a horde of suicide bombers and they could cause havoc if deployed correctly.

"Ahmad, how many martyrs are ready to die for our cause?" Kazemi asked, when all were together.

"A little less than eight thousand, Your Honor. More than half of the original twenty thousand who volunteered are now dead of the infidel flu," he added, by way of explanation. He wisely left out his following thought; that many of them might have been saved if it hadn't been for Kazemi's ill-informed ban on his people using the gene therapy.

"They shall receive the same reward in paradise," intoned Kazemi. "They are still martyrs in our cause." Ahmad had the impious thought that he'd rather go out shooting back, or even as a suicide bomber, than sick and burning up with fever or his kidneys exploding. Kazemi was still talking.

"They will not expect us to hit the same targets again. See that we do. Also, this time take out the embassies of the United States wherever they are. I want the US to have no capability left for diplomatic relations. Take out all foreign embassies in Washington. Let the countries blame the US for not protecting their diplomats."

"Ya al-Mahdi, when do you want this to happen?" Ahmad asked, knowing that such an ambitious plan could take months.

"Let us strike on their sacred holiday," said Kazemi. "July fourth. Many will think the explosions are just fireworks. By the time they know differently, it will be impossible to save the buildings. Lay waste to Washington D.C., as the infidels did to our kinsmen in Baghdad."

Three months, thought Ahmad. Could he pull it off? He could only try.

Chapter 37 - We'll figure it out when we get back

It was a small wedding in mid-June, the bride and groom wanting to keep it low profile while the world was still in mourning for more than a billion dead. In respect and honor of the dead, they asked that nothing be submitted to the media, and that the ceremony remain private; closed especially to journalists. The bride's and groom's families were there of course, as well as Sarah's extended family and special friends from the Foundation, those who'd been with the Rosslers from the beginning and a few good friends made along the way. President Harper and the First Lady slipped out of Washington for the day. JR and Rebecca were humbled that the couple would honor them in this way, but Daniel wasn't surprised. President and Mrs. Harper were among the most down-to-earth people he'd met in the upper reaches of world leadership, and he'd met quite a few.

The bride and groom made a striking pair, Rebecca taller than average and her bridegroom towering over her. When the officiant said, "You may kiss the bride," JR made sure that everyone observing understood Rebecca had been well and thoroughly kissed. Applause broke out, and the couple ran back down the aisle to the strains of "Home" by Phillip Phillips.

During the reception, Rebecca tossed the bouquet over her shoulder and it landed in the hands of both Angela Brown and Cyndi Self, who, rather than fight over it, handed it to Rebecca's mom to be preserved for a keepsake. Neither woman was certain she even wanted to be the next to be married, but both secretly thought about their prospects. Robert grinned ear to ear when he saw that Cyndi had started out with the lion's share of it. His mother would like her, he thought. Maybe she'd be willing to have a holiday and come with him to Aussie to help him pack up.

Then it was time to leave for a wedding night in downtown Denver at the Four Seasons, a gift from JR's parents and grandparents. The following morning, the couple boarded a Delta flight direct to Athens. They would enjoy two weeks there before returning on July 4th, racing the sun to be home for fireworks that night

On the long flight east, Rebecca asked JR what he intended to do about his advanced studies. Without a degree, he couldn't expect to achieve academic acclaim, but as she suspected, JR wasn't sure that was what he wanted anyway.

"I've had a taste of the field, Becca," he told her, entwining his long fingers with hers and admiring her wedding ring as he spoke. "I think I'd be happier just exploring. There are so many mysteries of *this* cycle, and we're just the ones to unravel them, don't you think?"

"Will Daniel support your proposals?"

"I think so. We didn't get much of a chance to discuss it. I know your research will keep you close to home a lot of the time, but you could come on some of the expeditions with me, couldn't you?"

"My darling, I wouldn't miss any of them for the world. We'll figure it out when we get back. I've agreed to join the Foundation staff, as you know, but the terms haven't been set."

Since they were on honeymoon, wanting to forget the cares of daily life, neither paid any attention to the news media until the morning they were to leave for home. Then there was no choice.

Chapter 38 - Anything that could go wrong

Ahmad was just about done with the Ayatollah Kazemi. First, the man had given him an almost impossible mission, to coordinate a simultaneous strike against, not just the seats of government of every country in the West, but also against the embassies of the United States wherever they were to be found. Not satisfied with that, he also wanted every foreign embassy in Washington destroyed at the same time. There had been three months to pull it off when Kazemi ordered it. He seemed to have no idea what planning must go into even a small coordinated strike.

To make sure no one fulfilled their mission early and thereby warned other targets, the men, and a few women, who were to carry out the suicide bombings were drilled, over and over again, on contingency plans, backups and communications. Elaborate plans to get the personnel into the countries where they were assigned to carry out their missions, and even more elaborate plans to acquire or transport the raw materials to manufacture the explosives, prepare the vehicles that would carry the resulting bombs, and make certain that no last-minute mistakes would abort the missions, were laid, analyzed, scrapped and re-built.

Even as he carried out his orders, Ahmad couldn't help but believe that Kazemi had, as the infidels would say, gone off the deep end. At times, he even seemed to be ready to reveal the plans for the strike. Kazemi's speeches had become more and more delusional, as he alternately called down the wrath of Allah on the infidels who had caused this deadly disease, and shook his fist, both metaphorically and physically, while spewing hate-filled threats about what he would do when he came into the full power of his incarnation as the Twelfth Imam.

It was unfortunate for the faithful, Ahmad thought, that they took literally Kazemi's instructions not to trust in Western medicine, but instead in the faith of Islam. Because they did so, thousands who didn't need to die did, cursing the name of the greatest infidel of all, the collective population of the United States of America. It made Ahmad's task doubly difficult that his trained bombers kept succumbing to the virus as well, until he decreed that they would enter quarantine as soon as their training began, so as not to lose any more once they began training.

By the weekend of the 28th of June, all was in readiness, except for the last few anointed to be slipped into the US and one or two other Western countries. Kazemi had especially enjoyed the irony of sending the operatives into the US across the Mexican border. Their vaunted security was so tight, except for the long border with Mexico that was riddled with tunnels, miles of unattended desert and several border crossings where partygoers streamed across and back with only a largely futile token security check. It was such a joke, in fact, that American comedies were made about it all the time, and the government didn't even attempt to suppress them.

Naturally, such a strategy meant that they were then exposed during the drive to Washington, but it was surprisingly easy to evade discovery. Americans were so afraid of being politically incorrect or being accused of profiling that they bent over backward to welcome even the most type-cast mujahedeen. If the mission hadn't been so serious, Ahmad would have had a good laugh with al-Mahdi at the foolish Americans. It made him think of the great Persian king of old, Cyrus the Great, who conquered Babylon while its careless inhabitants were carousing and drunk.

All that remained now was to prepare the vehicles. Scores of explosives experts were in place to see to that, while the drivers prepared themselves spiritually for this, their great sacrifice in the cause of jihad.

~~~

On the morning of July 4th, more than a hundred suicide bombers made their prayers, though some would wait until a new day had nearly dawned before it was time for their mission. The strike was planned for eight p.m. in the Eastern time zone of the U.S., just as fireworks displays were about to begin. Suicide bombers would hit all street approaches to the White House at that precise moment. Elsewhere in the city, nearly two hundred embassies would also be attacked at the same moment. Cars filled with explosives would be driven through gates and barricades, while individuals carrying explosives under their robes would walk into crowds wherever they could find them and push the buttons.

At the same moment in every country in Europe and the Americas, so as to create the most confusion possible, both the seats of government and the American embassies would be hit. As the Americans once described the first shots in their war of independence from Great Britain, it would be the 'shot heard 'round the world.' Kazemi would have liked it if his enemies in Africa and Asia had also been included in the planning, but it was too risky. Even Israel would be spared this time, because if the Mossad were to catch wind of the plans, it would all fall apart. Ahmad had no one he could trust to successfully infiltrate Israel for such a delicate mission. It was too bad that the worst enemy of all would be spared this time, and that the strike would put them on even higher alert.

Because he was who he was, the son of his father and a proud man, Ahmad had done his best to carry out his orders with every hope of success. Because he was very intelligent, though, he had no doubt that the strike would be only partially successful, if that. There were too many places where something could go wrong. Casualties among the infidel would be heavy, but this was not the way to destroy them. And besides, everywhere a human being was involved, there was room for error. What did the Americans call it—Murphy's Law? Anything that *could* go wrong probably would, and at the worst possible moment. These thoughts, however, he hid from Kazemi and from those who reported to himself. When the worst happened, and it would, he had a plan.

~~~

JR and Rebecca had had a wonderful two weeks, electing to tour the ruins on their own so that they could spend as much or as little time as they wanted at each major site. They promised themselves that they would come back some day when they had more time to explore the more modern of the many tourist attractions.

Their plane took off right on time, and they settled in for the fifteen-hour flight to Denver. They would arrive at about six and be in Boulder by seven, just in time for a family barbecue at Daniel and Sarah's house followed by fireworks beginning at dusk, around eight p.m.

Chapter 39 - What the hell's going on, Daniel?

JR and Rebecca wouldn't make it to that family barbecue, however. At precisely six p.m. Denver time, with their flight still waiting for a runway for landing, Washington, D.C. went up in the smoke of more than two hundred suicide bombs, all coordinated to go off at once. The immediate effect was that all planes were ordered down and the airports closed--with anyone who happened to be inside at the time confined where they were until they could be cleared by TSA.

Inside their plane, chaos broke out as the pilot announced that there had been an attack of some sort on Washington, and that they would be making an emergency landing within moments. The mainly Greek-speaking occupants were confused about the emergency part of that announcement, since they had expected to land within moments anyway. The English speakers focused on the 'attack on Washington' part. What could that be about? It wasn't until they were down and could see monitors all over the waiting rooms that they discovered Washington wasn't the only one.

London, Paris, Berlin, Athens--*Athens*! The list went on and on. As news commentators filled the airwaves with speculation and drivel, it became clear that the attack had centered on Washington, DC, since it was the wee hours of the morning in the European capitals. For that reason, not much carnage had resulted in Europe, though there was plenty of damage. A few attempts had been foiled because alert police in some countries had stopped suspicious-looking cars en route to their destinations on streets otherwise empty due to the hour. The Americas hadn't fared so well. Mexico City had suffered terrible human casualties because the bomber had struck just as the downtown dinner hour was commencing. Other capitals in South America suffered similar fates. That it was a Friday night made it particularly devastating, since more people were out and about on a Friday.

As soon as they reached an area where their cell phones would get a signal, both JR and Rebecca made calls to their families. JR reached Daniel first.

"What the hell's going on, Daniel?"

"It isn't clear, we're just getting the news. I can't get through to Harper, so I don't know if he and the First Lady are okay. When can you get home?"

"I don't have a clue. They've evidently decided that anyone who was in an airplane at the time is a suspect. We have to be cleared by TSA before we can leave."

"Sit tight, I'll see if I can grease the wheels. Are you two okay?"

"Yeah, fine, just shaken up by the news. I'd like to get Rebecca home to her family. She's talking to her mom right now, and it sounds like her mom is hysterical."

"Okay, I'm calling Luke."

"Hurry, bro."

JR sat with his arm protectively circling Rebecca as tears streamed down her face. He couldn't formulate the question he had without risking an emotional storm, so he simply held her until she was ready to talk. It took a long time.

"Honey, all those people!"

"I know, Babe. I know you wish you were there helping, but I'm thankful that you're here with me. I just wish we could get home."

"Yeah, my mom is freaking out that we were still in the air when it happened. I guess she thought we'd fall out of the sky with such a disaster going on."

"Daniel's trying to get us out of here. You'll be home to reassure her before you know it."

"What does this mean, JR? Why has this happened?"

"Unless I miss my guess, it's retaliation for the virus. It may just be the first salvo, but I don't see them attacking Boulder."

"What if they do? They have to know we're there. What if they nuke Boulder just to get us? We should get far away, so if they want us, they don't have to kill three hundred thousand people to get us."

"Babe, you're thinking crazy. That's not going to happen."

"But, what if it does?"

"Okay, in the first place, I don't think they have any nukes left. If they do, I doubt they'd reach us here. Let's just sit here quietly until we're cleared and then go home and see what Daniel knows."

Rebecca recognized the practical value of the suggestion and stopped peppering JR with 'what-if' questions, but her nimble mind couldn't help but try to unravel the reason behind the attacks. What good would they do, from the perspective of the Middle East? The only thing she could come up with was revenge. And in that, she wasn't far wrong.

Chapter 40 - I'm terrified

By the time for Fajr in Tehran, the Ayatollah Kazemi knew he had failed. Much damage had been done, but far less than he had imagined, and some of the martyrs had not reached their destinations at all. Only in America was the damage sufficiently satisfying, but even that was a hollow victory. Ahmad had brought him the news that the hated President Harper was unharmed and on American television saying that a few bombs and dead Arabs wouldn't deter the US from following its course. Congress would meet the next day to decide whether to declare war. Ahmad had offered his resignation, and Kazemi had accepted. This was not their way; Kazemi suspected that the West had corrupted the boy. But he let it go. Ahmad had done the best he could.

Kazemi was weary. After prayer, he would take his rest and consider what to do next to defeat the infidel.

~~~

Harper felt he should be *doing* something. Four hours after the city was rocked with explosives, he was still restless, unable to comprehend how this could have happened, and on such a massive scale. He'd been with the National Security Council all evening, but there had been nothing but finger-pointing from those who should have been advising him. At eleven-thirty, he dismissed them, with instructions to be back the next morning at seven a.m.

Now he paced in the White House bedroom he shared with the First Lady. "Esther, should I have seen this coming?"

"You aren't a prophet, Nigel. You're only as good as your advisers. If anyone failed, it was they," she said, as reasonably as she could. "Come to bed, darling. You can save the world tomorrow."

Harper looked at his wife, seeing the worn face that had

replaced the beauty he married. Had his presidency done this to her? Would he be able to look back in a few years, and say, 'I did a good job; I'm proud of it'?" At the moment, he couldn't answer that question. Hundreds of DC cops, FBI and representatives from the other security agency were losing sleep tonight, investigating, and determining how this had happened. How could he sleep when that was going on?

"My love," he confessed, "I'm terrified."

"Why, darling, I've never known you to be afraid of physical danger!"

"No, that's not it. I'm afraid of what's coming tomorrow and the next day and the next. We thought when we stopped the virus that the brinksmanship would be over. It isn't over, and I don't know what the world will look like when it is."

Chapter 41 - May Allah let me …

The Erfan Grand Hospital, Abad, Tehran, the best private hospital in all of Iran.

A 45 year old man covered in a biohazard suit from head to toe walks in the door to reception. Inside everyone else is dressed the same as he, and he is taken to a room to be sterilized again. The otherwise well-organized hospital is chaos. People looking alien in biohazard suits; people sitting or standing everywhere, crying and in despair.

There are sick people everywhere, on the floors, under the beds as well as on them, a few in the chairs of the waiting rooms meant for family members of patients. The nursing staff is clearly overwhelmed, trying to cope with the sick and their families. The only thing to distinguish this place from a frontline battlefield aid station is that there is no blood on the floors or the hands and clothes of the staff. Instead, this is one of the few hospitals in the region that have not barred their doors to new patients.

The man is taken to a small ward, where he looks through a glass partition at a 34 year old woman and two young children, aged 4 and 8 to his certain knowledge, all lying in one bed. An old man and woman are lying next to each other on a mattress on the floor. His family—father, mother, his wife and his two children. There is a nurse tending to them, but none of them are moving. If only his wife would look up, so that he could say goodbye with the love in his eyes. They don't even see him. He stands there looking at them, seeing their shallow breathing and the sweat on their bodies. He is not allowed to go in to them.

He can trace his roots back to the great Persian kings: Cyrus the Great and Darius. His father's name is Dariush, after one of the great kings of Persia. His forebears are even mentioned in the book of Daniel in the infidels' Bible. They are a proud people with a long and rich history. The dream has been for generations, and the man has been brought up to always work and strive for it—the restoration of the great Persian Empire which once stretched as far as Athens, modern day Bulgaria, Egypt, and Libya.

One by one, their ragged breathing stills as they all die in front of his eyes, while the tears stream down his face. He tries to scream to Allah but no sound comes out of his throat. He stands witness to the destruction of his family for two hours before it is over. Finally, before he turns to leave, he whispers softly "May Allah let me die a death a thousand times worse than this if I do not avenge the death of my loved ones on the evil one who did this."

Slowly he walks away, making his way through and over the sick and dying, with the moans and crying burning into his mind to haunt him for the rest of his life – a broken and lonely man. Blindly, he makes his way to the sterilizing room, where he is again sterilized, given a new protection suit and taken out to a waiting car to be returned to his office.

<<<<>>>>

Remember Your Free Gift

As a way of saying thanks for your purchase, I'm offering you a free eBook which you can download from my website at www.jcryanbooks.com

MYSTERIES FROM THE ANCIENTS

10 THOUGHT PROVOKING UNSOLVED ARCHAEOLOGICAL MYSTERIES

This book is exclusive to my readers. You will not find this book anywhere else.

We spend a lot of time researching and documenting our past, yet 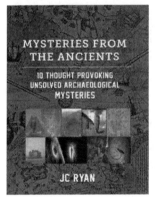 there are still many questions left unanswered. Our ancestors left a lot of traces for us, and it seems that not all of them were ever meant to be understood. Despite our best efforts, they remain mysteries to this day.

Inside you will find some of the most fascinating and thought-provoking facts about archaeological discoveries which still have no clear explanation.

Read all about The Great Pyramid at Giza, The Piri Reis Map, Doomsday, Giant Geoglyphs, The Great Flood, Ancient Science and Mathematics, Human Flight, Pyramids, Fertility Stones and the Tower of Babel, Mysterious Tunnels and The Mystery of The Anasazi

Don't miss this opportunity to get this free eBook now.

Visit www.jcryanbooks.com to download it now.

Thank You

Thank you for taking the time to read my book. Please keep in touch with me at www.jcryanbooks.com and also sign up for special offers and pre-release notifications of upcoming books.

Please Review

If you enjoyed this story, please let others know by leaving an honest review on Amazon. Your review will help to inform others about this book and the series.

Thank you so much for your support, I appreciate it very much.

JC Ryan

More Books In The Rossler Foundation Mysteries

THE TENTH CYCLE

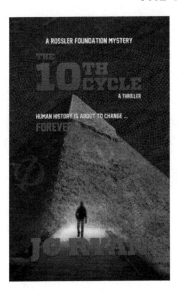

A CONSPIRACY THRILLER

THE TRUTH ABOUT HUMAN HISTORY IS ABOUT TO BE REVEALED

WILL WE BE ALLOWED TO KNOW THE TRUTH?

The First Book in the Rossler Foundation Mysteries "THE TENTH CYCLE" is a full-length novel, a provocative techno thriller about human history, conspiracies and an ancient society with power and money that will stop at nothing to reach their sinister goals.

Amazon USA Link -
http://amzn.com/B00JMV358M

Amazon UK Link -
http://amzn.co.uk/dp/B00JMV358M

NINTH CYCLE ANTARCTICA

WAS THERE A HUMAN CIVILIZATION IN ANTARCTICA IN THE PAST?

WILL WE EVER KNOW?

IS THERE AN ANCIENT CITY UNDER THE ICE OF ANTARCTICA?

The Second Book "NINTH CYCLE ANTARCTICA" is a full-length novel, a stimulating thriller about an attempt at uncovering true human history in the face of adversity and is a follow on from **The Tenth Cycle.**

Amazon USA Link -
http://amzn.com/B00K8LRTLE

Amazon UK Link -
http://amzn.co.uk/dp/B00K8LRTLE

GENETIC BULLETS

A CATASTROPHE OF BIBLICAL PROPORTIONS 35,000 YEARS IN THE MAKING.

THE WORLD WE KNOW IS ON THE VERGE OF DESTRUCTION ...

THERE IS NO ESCAPE. OR IS THERE?

The third book **GENETIC BULLETS** is a full-length novel, a stimulating medical thriller about genetic engineering human persistence and resolution in the face of destruction.

Amazon USA Link –
http://amzn.com/B00M0DQGXU

Amazon UK Link -
http://amzn.co.uk/dp/B00M0DQGXU

THE SWORD OF CYRUS

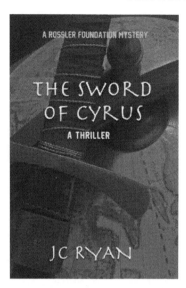

200 MILLION SOULS ARE SCREAMING FOR REVENGE.

THE SWORD OF CYRUS WILL EXACT THAT REVENGE

THIS TIME THERE IS NO ESCAPE.

The fourth book THE SWORD OF CYRUS is Book 4 in the Rossler Foundation Series, a full-length novel, a stimulating techno thriller about the danger of nanotechnology to human existence. This book is a follow up of **Genetic Bullets**.

Coming in October 2014   www.jcryanbooks.com